THE PATRIOT

JENNIFER MILLIKIN

JNM, LLC

ISBN: 978-1-7326587-8-3
www.jennifermillikinwrites.com
Cover by Okay Creations
Editing by My Brother's Editor

ALSO BY JENNIFER MILLIKIN

Other titles in the Hayden Family series (Interconnected standalone)

The Maverick

The Outlaw

The Calamity

Standalone

Pre-order Here For The Cake - releases May 2nd, 2024

The Least Amount Of Awful

Better Than Most

Return To You

One Good Thing

Beyond The Pale

Good On Paper

The Day He Went Away

Full of Fire

The Time Series (Standalone)

Our Finest Hour

Magic Minutes

The Lifetime of A Second

WAR HERO RETURNS HOME

ALISON STEIN FOR THE SIERRA GRANDE GAZETTE

What was that sound you heard this morning? It was the town of Sierra Grande breathing a collective sigh of relief. Beloved hometown hero, Wesley Hayden, returned home yesterday, this time for good. After twelve years serving in the United States Army, Hayden has returned to settle into place as his father's right hand man of the Hayden Cattle Company.

Hayden's twelve years of heroic service included three tours in the Middle East, where he served on the Explosive Ordinance Device Squad.

Hayden was unavailable for comment at the time of publication, but we're anxiously awaiting his first appearance in town. A hero's welcome is in order.

1

DAKOTA

*F*IVE YEARS AGO

The second he walks into the lake house, I notice him. Not because he is a sight to behold, with his short hair the color of mesquite and angular jaw that could've been carved from marble, although I admit those traits are enjoyable. No, my attention has been captured by my response to him: the lurch of my stomach, the erratic beating of my heart, the goose bumps covering every inch of my flesh. Is this what magic feels like?

He doesn't see me. I'm standing off to the side in the living room, hidden from easy view by Emily and Paige's backs. We've formed a little circle, drinking from our red plastic cups and surveying the scene before diving in. We don't know anybody here, aside from Jason, the homeowner, and even then we've only known him for about five hours. We'd gone on a walk around the lake after lunch and he was outside cleaning up his yard. One well-muscled attractive guy and three females walking past? Didn't seem like too much of a stretch when he asked us to come to the party he was throwing tonight. I think he likes Emily. He only had eyes for her when he opened his front door and saw the three of us standing there. He was polite, getting us drinks and chatting, but he needed to be a good host and greet some others who'd shown up. We shuffled away, but he kept looking over, checking to make certain Emily was still around.

Right now, her lips are moving, but I don't hear what she says. Paige must hear her, because she laughs, and I smile automatically, my brain understanding this is an appropriate response even though I am paying zero mind to her. How can I when every cell inside me has been called to attention?

My eyes, *my entire body*, remains locked on the newcomer. He strides through the house, his presence commanding. He walks up to Jason, and they greet each other with a half-hug accompanied by a solid back slap, but it's the look they share that makes me curious. The look is bloated with meaning, heavy under an unseen weight.

Jason leads the new guy out of the house and into the backyard. The adrenaline doesn't leave my body just because he has left the room.

When our cups are empty, we make our way outside, too. Music blares from a speaker set up on a cheap plastic chair. The backyard gently slopes down until the bright green grass turns into dark blue water. A small aluminum boat drifts at the end of a long dock, but it's tied up so it can't float away. It's a stunning view, but wasted on me. I might appear to be absorbing my surroundings, but really I'm looking for *him*.

Panic ricochets through me. I don't see him.

I search in what I hope is a covert manner, but he isn't to be found in any of the groups of people standing around or in the line for the keg. How does someone whose presence filled a room so completely, disappear?

"Let's dance!" Emily shakes her shoulders, her fingers wrapping around my wrist and pulling me closer. It's a country-rock song, something very danceable, and we make the most of it. There isn't a whole lot I like to do more than dance.

The song switches and we keep going. After two more, I pause and stick out my tongue and fan my face. "I need a drink," I shout above the music, shimmying out of her grasp.

I'm on my way to the keg when it happens. The shuffling of bodies, just enough to create a chasm in the crowd, and our eyes meet. He's sitting on a picnic table, his feet propped on the bench below him. His gaze is sharp and swift like an arrow, piercing my chest, anchoring me to this moment.

He doesn't smile. His eyes don't light up. Nothing about his posture invites me over, but I can see the words he's thinking as if his thoughts are available for public consumption. And then, floating out from between those perfect lips, are the words I knew he'd been thinking.

Come here.

I'm not one to follow orders, but this feels less like a command and more like a plea. I put one foot in front of the other, and then it hits me.

I never had a choice. Not from the moment he walked into the house. This was always going to happen.

His intense gaze stays on me as I walk to him, plucking a bottle of liquor from an empty table as I go. I don't know what kind it is and I don't know who it belongs to, but I do know he finds this amusing. A small upward movement of the corner of his mouth is all that breaks through his stoic veneer, but it's enough.

I slow down as I approach, like a Mack truck putting on its brakes far ahead of a red light. The insane amount of attraction I feel for this person needs a good bit of road in which to slow itself. My goose bumps have returned.

I'm three feet away from him when I stop and take a sip, trying like hell not to grimace at the burn of liquor. "Did you come to a party just to hide out in the back all by your lonesome?"

Something flickers in his dark eyes. "All by my lonesome?" His voice is deep and rough. His Adam's apple bobs as he speaks and I feel the urge to run my tongue along it.

"That's what I said." My eyebrows lift, offering a small challenge.

The corner of his mouth crooks up higher. He sticks an open palm into the air between us. I don't know if he's reaching for me or the bottle, but I go with the bottle. Just because I have the desire to throw myself in his arms doesn't mean he shouldn't work a little harder for it.

He takes a sip of what I think is probably whiskey, doesn't appear to fight any sort of grimace, and sets it on the table beside him. The message is clear, *If you want it, come over here and get it.*

"My grandma used to say that," he explains. "All by your lonesome."

"I'm sorry."

"Why are you sorry?"

"You said *used to*. Past tense."

He nods once. "Right. She passed a couple years ago."

"I'm sorry."

"You said that already."

Now I'm the one fighting a smile.

His gaze lowers to my T-shirt. "Kappa Kappa Gamma?"

At first I'm confused, and then I remember I borrowed

Emily's little sister's shirt. I was never a sorority girl, not by a long shot.

I shake my head. "Not mine. I borrowed it. I'm a few years past that stage in life."

His chin lifts, his nod slow and measured. "Are you a friend of Jason's?"

A smile tugs on the corner of my mouth. "I've known him for less than half a day. I'm guessing you've known him for longer than that?"

"Military," he answers, and then nothing more.

I'm quiet, waiting for him to make the next move. And he does.

He holds out his hand again, and this time I know it's for me. My hand sinks into his, and when our skin touches the goose bumps covering me turn into tiny fires. But these flames? They feel so very good.

His eyes widen just the tiniest amount. His lower lip peels away from his upper, leaving a thin space between them. A flash of fear darts across his face.

"Wes," he grits, as if his name can barely make it past other words stuck in his throat.

"Dakota." My voice trembles, which is fitting, because at this moment it feels as if there's an earthquake shaking me from the inside out.

He tugs gently, bringing me closer.

It's inevitable.

This. *Us.*

I step into his arms, and it doesn't feel new. It feels like the place where I belong, and am only late arriving to.

2

WES

Present day

"Which one of you fuck faces didn't count the herd yesterday?" Harsh and angry, my voice slams through Cowboy House and into the ears of the sleeping cowboys.

Josh scrambles from bed, reaching for his boots without a thought to the pajamas he's still wearing. Denny, Bryce, and Markham (who everyone calls Ham, instead of Mark), are slower to sit up, but even they are moving, pushing up from bed and rubbing at their eyes. It's Troy who's still in bed, and I'd bet my last shiny penny he's the asshole who left a heifer in the field. How the wolves didn't get to her, God only knows.

With narrowed eyes locked in on Troy's sleeping form, I stride forward. The wary gazes of the other men bounce off my blue and yellow flannel shirt. Here in Cowboy House, I'm the wolf.

Troy's closely cropped blond head is all that's visible. The rest of his body lies nestled beneath the standard-issue Hayden Cattle Company navy blue blanket, as if his mother came and tucked him in. *Snug as a bug in a fucking rug.*

I flick his ear with my middle finger, the same way my dad did to me and my brothers when we were younger. Difference is, we learned to stop being idiots. I don't know that Troy ever will.

Troy yelps and his eyes fly open. He takes me in, and I watch the understanding dawn in those ridiculous blue eyes of his.

"Get up," I growl at him.

Even this he does slowly, and my irritation soars. When I wake up at five every morning, I get out of bed like a man, not this pussified joke stretching out his arms in front of me right now.

"Were you the one to count heads yesterday?"

I see him swallow, his fingertips on his right hand nervously tapping against his bare thigh like he's playing the goddamn piano. The guy sleeps in his underwear, and for a quick second I make a mental note to add a T-shirt to my choice of sleepwear so I no longer have anything in common with him.

He nods reluctantly, but I see the lift of his chin, however slight it may be. Instead of angering me, I find his quiet defiance a relief. Weakness on the ranch has consequences. Empires have fallen for less.

"You left one out in the pasture. I came across her this morning."

He runs his hand through his hair, his shoulders dropping an inch. "At least it wasn't a bull."

Behind me, one of the cowboys sighs, knowing Troy's mistake immediately.

I step closer, but it's awkward because Troy is still seated on his bed, not standing on his own two feet like a man should, which makes his face just about dick-height to me. To remedy that, I grab his shoulders and haul him up.

"Every head in that herd matters. Got it?" My voice is low, but my words carry meaning.

Troy nods once, stiff and sharp, the defiance gone. He knows what a loss it is to lose even one cow.

Now that I've made my point, I pat his upper arm roughly and step back. "Let me know if you need a calculator. I'm sure the Merc carries one."

I turn back to the collection of cowboys in their various sleep clothes. "About time to get to work."

They go in separate directions, and I head out of the low, long building that houses them.

I'm striding up the yard toward the homestead, morning dew leaving behind beads of moisture on my boots, when I hear an old, wrinkled voice say, "What time did the sun rise this morning?"

A smile breaks onto my face. The owner of that voice never fails to cut through my layers of bullshit and reach the person underneath, the person I was before I spent two tours in Iraq and one in Afghanistan.

"Coffee on the porch this morning, old man?" I climb the stone-lined steps of my parents' house and settle in a chair beside my grandpa.

"Brought extra for you," he responds, his wrinkled hand gesturing to the tall, scratched, green-speckled thermos and empty cup.

"Is this thing older than me?" I ask, gripping the thermos and lifting it off the table between us.

"That thermos is like me—old and ugly, but it's still got some use."

"Nah"—I shake my head—"you're pretty as a picture."

He cackles and slaps his thigh.

I twist off the top and pour the steaming hot, black

liquid into my mug. It's almost to my lips when I catch sight of the front of the cup. *Kiss me, I'm the ranch wife.*

I chuckle to myself. Gramps either didn't realize which mug he'd grabbed or did it on purpose. Knowing him, it's the latter. I sip the nearly scalding coffee, wincing not at the temperature but at the strength of the brew.

Gramps must know what I'm reacting to, because he murmurs, "One guess who made it."

"Warner?" My younger brother never measures and always over-pours the grounds. Funny though, I don't mind his lack of precision when he's making us a drink in the evening.

"Damn straight." He looks out at the green lawn, the wrinkles around his eyes deepening as he smiles mischievously and lifts his cup. "This jet fuel just might have me doing a cartwheel."

I laugh as I lift my mug for another drink, the air streaming from my nose pushing away the rising steam. "Please don't. You know it's a half-hour to the hospital."

Gramps grows quiet, then says, "You didn't answer my question."

I hold in my sigh. When he asked me what time the sun rose this morning, he wasn't actually seeking the information. It was his way of ascertaining if I'd been up earlier than usual, if my sleep had once again been plagued by nightmares.

"Early, Gramps. The sun came up early. And it's a damn good thing I was out too, because a jackass cowboy missed one and she was out there by herself all night." As I say it, I look out in the direction of the field where I found her, though I can't see it from here. My family's land is too vast.

"Troy?" Gramps asks, immediately knowing the culprit.

"Yeah."

"What did Troy do now?" My brother, Warner, steps from the house. He's tall like me, and just about as broad-shouldered. I'm two years older, and as I constantly remind him, far more handsome. Once upon a time, Warner was deliriously in love with his high school sweetheart Anna. They were married before they could legally buy alcohol. A few years later they had a kid, and a few years after that they had another. One day not too long ago, Anna decided she needed space to find herself, and she left Warner and their two kids, now nine and twelve, behind. Apparently to find herself, she needed to lose everything else. She settled a couple hours away in Phoenix and still hasn't served Warner with divorce papers, and he's too hung up on her to initiate the proceedings himself. He tries to stay upbeat for Peyton and Charlie's sake, but I can tell he's hurting badly inside.

In my book, Anna and Troy are about on the same level. Two people whose collective common sense doesn't add up to a whole lot.

"He left a heifer out overnight," I answer Warner, my gaze sweeping away from him.

"Shit," Warner mutters. "Wolves get her?"

"No."

He breathes an audible sigh of relief. "What did you do?"

I stretch my right leg out and lean back, wincing slightly at the strain. I'm only thirty-seven, but this body has been put through hell. "Went to Cowboy House and woke him up. Told him he's about as useful as a flaccid dick in a whorehouse."

Gramps howls with laughter as his coffee sloshes over the rim, little brown specks seeping into the porch's wood floor. "The military sure taught you a few things," he says, grinning, "not the least of which was a foul mouth."

I shrug as Warner walks closer, coming to a stop at the porch railing. "Some habits are hard to break," I explain.

"Like waking up and riding around before the sun comes up?" Warner asks, his gaze fixed on me.

"How would you know unless you're up too?" I counter.

"You're not the only early riser in this place. Most of your family gets up just after you. We've all seen you riding out, a lone cowboy on his horse. The exception is Wyatt, obviously."

Of course. Wyatt, the youngest of us three boys, is always sleeping off the night before, if he's come home at all. I'm not sure how much longer our dad's planning to put up with it. I'm surprised he hasn't kicked his ass out yet. On a ranch, everyone contributes.

The front door opens loudly and Jessie leans out, one hand planted on her hip and a sharp look on her face. She's the youngest of the four Hayden siblings by nearly twenty years (from me, the oldest), and she's always up to something. We started calling her 'Calamity Jessie' before she was coordinated enough to run, for two reasons. One, she was walking chaos, always into something. And two, she swore like a sailor and had a wildness about her, just like Calamity Jane. She's seventeen now, and she's tucked away a lot of her personality, but I bet it'll return when she's older and more comfortable in her own skin. In a few months she'll pack up her car and move two hours south to Phoenix to attend Arizona State University. I don't even want to begin to think about the mischief she'll cause there.

Jessie directs her glare at Warner. "I told you to come tell these two breakfast is ready."

Warner lifts his palms in front of his chest. "I got distracted. Wes was using military phrases again."

I shake my head and stand. "Shut up, Warner." I reach out a hand to help Gramps, but he bats it away.

"The day I can't stand up on my own is the day you can lay me in the ground next to Janice." He gives us all a hard look and uses the chair's armrests to help him rise. He looks at us three, defiant and proud. "I miss your grandmother, but I'm not ready to go yet, as you can see."

Warner and Gramps file into the house. I toss the remaining coffee from the two mugs over the railing and grab the thermos. Jessie stands in the door, keeping it open for me, and as I pass through she says, "Dad told me he wants to see you in his office after you're done eating. He's in a mood, so good luck." She flips her head and the ponytail on the top of her head flies around.

I acknowledge the message with a nod and walk through the house to the kitchen.

If I was a wolf in Cowboy House this morning, then my dad is a grizzly bear.

"DAD?" My knuckles rap twice on the door, and although the door is ajar it doesn't budge. This entire house was built with solid wood and stone. It does wonders for soundproofing but isn't so kind on fingers getting slammed in doors, and that's something we've all learned the hard way once or twice.

"Come in," my dad calls. His voice is craggy, like a rake scraping through loose gravel. When I was a kid I thought he was making it sound that way on purpose, in a bid to emulate the cowboys we watched in western movies. Now I know it's from years of yelling, of early mornings and late nights around a campfire, and cigarettes he snuck when he thought we weren't looking.

Pushing open the heavy door, I step into my dad's office. It's large, more rectangle than square. Bookshelves line one wall, and there is nothing on those shelves but books. No framed family pictures, no plants, not even a set of deer antlers. Opposite that wall is a stuffed mountain lion perched on a set of large rocks. This is the mountain lion that terrorized our land for a good bit of time eight years ago when I was still overseas. Warner and my dad went out one day and set up camp with two cowboys, Josh and someone who doesn't work for us anymore. They hunted all weekend and on Sunday afternoon, just when they were getting ready to head back to camp and call it a failure, Dad spotted the lion in a tree. He took aim, but the lion was on the move by then and Dad only grazed him. It was enough to injure the big cat, and when Dad and the others found him, the lion was mad as hell and before my dad could shoot him again the lion raked his claws over my dad's chest. It was Warner who fired the kill shot.

At the time, on the other end of a phone in a desert in the Middle East, I'd told them they were lying. Warner insisted they weren't, and the next time I came home, Dad showed me the scars to prove it.

I've fought insurgents, disabled explosive devices, and had my fair share of drunken and testosterone-fueled bar fights, and there's only one thing in the world that makes me shrink, and he happens to be sitting in front of me. Beau Hayden is an intimidating man, both physically and mentally, and his reputation bursts at the seams with more fact than fiction. He's the owner of Hayden Cattle Company, and hand to God I swear the term *tougher than nails* was invented just to describe him. I've seen the man slam his thumb with a sledgehammer and, aside from uttering the work *fuck*, not let on it ever happened. His skin resembles a light-tan leather, and the wrinkles around his eyes deepen by the day, but his full head of hair evens out the years ranching has added to his exterior.

Instead of taking a seat, I pause behind one of the two chairs in front of his desk and grip the fabric at the top. "Jessie said you wanted to see me."

His eyes soften at the mention of Jessie. Miracle child that she is, we all soften when we think of Jessie. Four miscarriages after Wyatt, they had given up and stopped trying. Years later the pregnancy came as a shock, and I think finding out it was a girl was one of the happiest moments of my mom's life. They named her Jessamyn, after my grandma Janice's mother, but I don't know that there's been a day in her life that we called her anything but Jessie. Well, aside from calling her Calamity.

My dad folds his hands in his lap and leans back, looking out the large window on his right. I wonder what he thinks when he sees the land that has delivered him his greatest joys and staunchest hardships.

His eyes sweep back to me. "I'm selling off some land—"

My mouth opens to argue, but his stiff upraised palm stops me.

"Don't say it," he instructs. "Whatever it is, I've already thought it."

My lips stay pursed in a tight line. He watches me, his eyes growing smaller the longer his gaze stays on mine. "When the place is yours, you can make your own choices. But right now, this place belongs to me, and I'm making the decisions I need to make to keep this place on top. Property taxes have been going nowhere but up, and that's land we don't use. We'll make money on the sale and decrease our tax burden."

"It'll make us look like we're having financial trouble," I spit out, despite his earlier command.

"Hard choices are hard for a reason, Wes."

It's his way of telling me he has already decided.

He lowers his palm back to his desk. "I reached out to a realtor. She's putting in some calls to development companies I would prefer to sell to. Places with standards and a backbone. I don't want some pansy-ass people who'll use the land to bring in big box stores and ruin Sierra Grande."

I smirk. "Is that what you told the realtor to write in the listing?"

The corner of his mouth quirks, and it's as much of a smile as I'll get out of him while discussing this.

If my mother is my father's first love, and the ranch his second, then Sierra Grande is a close third. Like many of the people still living in the town, Dad was born and raised here. The Hayden Cattle Company is as much a fixture as the Bar N, the local watering hole located in a poorly revamped barn.

"I want you to take point on this project. I'll go to the first meetings with you from prospective buyers, but after that, it's your responsibility." He gets up from his chair and walks to the window while I busy myself picking my jaw up from wherever it rolled to when it hit the ground. Aside from the time I spent in the military, I've been working the ranch my whole life and I've never been given responsibility in the running of it. It should make me happy, but mostly it worries me. My dad is getting older, and he's pulling back.

When I recover, I say, "This is a pretty big project for you not to handle on your own, Dad, or at least have a big hand in."

He turns, his dark eyes piercing me like arrows. "Are you not up for it?"

"Of course I am," I assure him.

"I thought you might want to be part of what will ultimately edge our property. After all, this place will be yours one day." He doesn't look away, doesn't mention the fact that right now, the way things are, the Hayden Cattle Company cannot be mine.

Four generations of Hayden cattlemen run through my blood, and I want to sit at the helm of this family ranch more than I want food or air. It twists me up inside knowing I may never get what I've spent my whole life dreaming of.

It will go to Warner, though he doesn't want it like I do. If he passes it up, it will go to Wyatt, and who the hell knows what will happen then?

Without me, the Hayden Cattle Company may not have a future. The worst part? I could rectify my situation, but it seems an impossible task.

My dad shakes my hand and tells me he'll direct the calls from the realtor my way. On my way out of the office, I bump into my mom. She's walking with Peyton, the older of Warner's two kids.

She kisses my cheek and squeezes my hand. "Are you taking on the project?"

I nod. She smiles faintly, her eyes creased in concern. "It will be good for you. Good for the ranch. Your dad's getting old. He needs to slow down."

"Right," I agree. Sometimes I think he's evergreen, and other times I see his age. "What are you two ladies up to this morning?"

"Milking goats," Peyton answers. She has her mother's blond hair and dimpled left cheek. "Grandma's going to show me how she makes goat cheese."

"No school today?" I ask.

Peyton shakes her head. "Nope," she answers, popping the 'p'. "We have the day off school. Teacher in-service."

I don't know what that is, and I'm not curious enough to ask. "Well, have fun with the goats."

I peel away from them and head outside, get on my horse, and go join the cowboys mending fences.

Today will be the kind of day where I add a new callus to my hands.

3

DAKOTA

No. Please, no. Someone tell me that did not just happen.

It's my last pair of high heels. My favorite pair, the black ones with the gold-studded heel. And now one of them is no longer a *heel.* It's a *flat,* courtesy of the curb and my misstep.

I pause on the sidewalk beside a skinny Aspen tree. A long, deep breath draws in slowly through my nose, my chest expanding, and I hold it until my throat burns.

"So screwed," I mutter on the exhale. *I am so screwed.* This is my last pair of work-appropriate shoes. What am I supposed to wear tomorrow? Hiking boots? Converse? I can't think about that now. I need to figure out how I'm going to hobble my way into the office.

Looking around, I see the streets of downtown Colorado Springs are as crowded as they're probably ever going to get, which is to say *not much.* The inhabitants of this town are smart; they can be found on one of the gazillion hiking trails, not pounding the pavement in one high heel and one flat like me.

I nod at an older man who passes, waiting patiently for

him to get far enough away, and then I remove my intact shoe and crouch down. It pains me to do this, like an actual twist in my gut, but what choice do I have? I bring the heel down against the curb until the second shoe matches the first, then slide it onto my foot and stow the broken heels in my purse. They're officially the weirdest thing I've ever carried in my bag. I square my shoulders, look up at the small glass and concrete building in front of me, and march into the front door like wearing flats with the hem of my black dress pants dragging on the ground is something I've done on purpose.

My family's office is one of many in this building. The lobby smells like the cucumber melon scented lotion I used in high school, and a small dark green velvet love seat and matching couch sit near the elevator bank. I've never seen anybody using them, so at this point, I'm certain they're just for decoration.

I keep going past the ornamental couches and walk to the second to last door on the left. Wright Design + Build is written in dark gray lettering on the frosted glass door. My dad started this firm before I was born, and we joke that it's his third baby. I've been working here for six months. *Learning the ropes*, he says in a hopeful tone. He has always hoped to pass down his business to me or my sister, Abby. The problem is that Abby isn't interested, and I'm, well... me. I'm more creative than analytical, more right brain than left. I couldn't possibly run this large of a business. The only reason I'm working here now is because I was fired (let go, downsized, *whatever)* from my event planning job. I was hesitant to take my dad up on his offer, but I needed money. To eat, to live, and to do that other thing I do with my money that I haven't told anybody about.

Sheila is the first person I see when I walk into the

small reception area. She's been with the company as long as I can remember, and her personality is what some would call prickly. When I was a little girl, I was frightened of her, but that stopped after a company picnic when she cussed out some boys who were picking on me. After that, we became thick as thieves. Or at least as thick as you can be with your father's administrative assistant who you see sporadically until you work for the company and become her kind-of boss who probably doesn't deserve to be.

Sheila's seated but bent over in her chair, digging through her over-sized purse. "Good morning," I say to her poof of feathered hair. Sheila never got the memo on discontinuing the use of a small round brush and Aqua Net. Either that, or she got the memo and wrote expletives on it and marked it return to sender.

"Hello to you, Dakota. How are you doing?" She says all this while still moving aside the contents of her purse and does not once look up at me.

Briefly I contemplate telling her about my shoe debacle, but then she'll ask why it's a big deal when I have so many other shoes, and then I'll have to tell her I don't have more shoes, then she'll ask what happened to my once-impressive collection, and then I'll have to lie because there's no way I'm telling her I had to sell them on an app for way less than I paid for them.

"Great," I lie, plastering a smile on my face. When Sheila doesn't look my way, I drop the smile.

"Your dad's in conference room B." She finally straightens and looks at me, blowing hair from her pink-lipsticked mouth. "He said to tell you to go see him when you arrived."

I tap my knuckles on the top of her desk and nod.

"Thanks, Sheila." I start for the conference room when Sheila's voice stops me.

"Oh, Dakota? You have lipstick on your teeth."

My fingers fly to my teeth a few seconds before I remember I don't even wear lipstick. "I do not."

Sheila laughs. "Gets everybody. Even men."

I shoot her a playful dirty look and keep going down the hall. Offices line either side, and on the walls between the doors are framed pictures of our finished projects.

The conference room is just up ahead, and through the glass walls I see my dad sitting at the head of the table. I push open the door and step in, and my dad smiles at my approach as I walk the length of the long oak table and take a seat beside him.

"Hi, Dad."

"Hey, Junior."

The affectionate nickname brings a smile to my face and a punch to my gut. Growing up, I wanted to be just like my dad, and I stuck closer to him than his own shadow. That was until I turned into a fourteen-year-old rebellious monster who did what she could to drive her parents to the brink of insanity.

"What's up? Sheila said you wanted to see me." I lean back in the chair and cross my ankles, startling when it's not my heels that bump the ground but the backs of the shoes. The conference room door opens, and Brandt and Jon step in. They are both architects who've been at the firm for years.

"You wanted to see us?" Brandt asks, taking a seat opposite me and nodding at me in this clipped way that communicates his dislike for me. It doesn't bother me. The feeling is mutual.

My dad brings his palms to touch and rubs them back

and forth, his eyes shining. This is what he does when he smells a new deal brewing. By the looks of his obvious excitement, it's a good one.

"I got a call from a realtor in Arizona this morning. The Hayden Cattle Company is looking to sell some acreage."

"Are you looking to develop land in Arizona?" Brandt asked, surprised.

I don't know why he looks like he's been caught off guard. We've worked out of state before.

Dad shrugs. "I might be, if the price is right."

"That's great, Dad." He's been searching for a new project since we finished the retail center in Denver.

He leans forward, propping his elbows on the desk and steepling his hands under his chin. "This is better than great, Dakota. This is unheard of. Beau Hayden is a hard-ass and he's never sold any of his land, and not because people haven't offered to purchase it. Remember Rich Calloway from Brandywine Developers?"

I nod even though I don't remember him.

"He thought he was going to get in good with Beau by showing up on the ranch and making him an unsolicited offer. The way he tells it, Beau met him on the front porch with a shotgun and told him he had ten seconds to get back in his truck, then began counting." He laughs, and I can tell how much he respects this old-school frontier way of doing business.

"That's pretty severe," I respond.

"Could be to some, I suppose. But to men like Beau, men who've been pouring their blood, sweat, and tears into their ranch, and watched their ancestors do the same, it's an effective form of communication." Dad places his palms on the desk and pushes to stand. He leans on his hands and looks at us. "This one is going to be a little different though. I, as an individual, am going to be the buyer. Then I'll hire Wright Design + Build to do the development."

I blanch. "Can you do that?"

He nods. "Most definitely. I've been looking for something to invest in for quite some time, and this feels like the right opportunity."

We're quiet around the table. I don't know what there is for any of us to say.

Dad directs his gaze at me. "We are flying out this afternoon and meeting with Beau and the realtor tomorrow morning."

My eyebrows cinch. "We?"

He points to his chest. "Me." His finger rotates my way. "And you. I want you to design it."

Brandt makes a choking noise. He tries to cover it up with a fisted hand at his mouth and a fake-sounding cough.

"Dad, I don't think—"

"You're ready for this, Dakota. Really. You grew up around this business and you've been in the office learning everything you need to know. Also, you have a real knack for it."

It's his stare, the belief in his gaze, the certainty in his voice, that suspends the argument hovering in my throat. Well, that and the fact we have an audience.

I want so badly to be worthy of his unyielding confidence in me. But the truth is, I'm not sure I'll ever make up for the pain I've caused him.

"I'll go home and pack a few things," I tell him, and his face splits into a grin.

"Sheila will email you the flight information," he says, sitting back down and pulling his laptop closer. "Meet me back here at one." His shoulders are lifted, pulled higher by the possibility of winning a big deal. It's a lovely thing to see;

for so long his shoulders drooped as if the weight of the world was using him for push-ups, and it was largely my fault.

"See you soon," I say. "Don't eat, I'll bring us lunch." I wave half-heartedly at Brandt and Jon.

My dad focuses on the computer, and I step away from the conference room with a stomach that feels as if fireflies are buzzing around inside it.

I wonder what my mother would say if she were here? Would she believe in me, the prodigal child, the way my dad does?

Maybe.

Or maybe not.

I spent the longest time thinking it was my fault she was dead. And there's a small part of me that still does.

"Abby, are you home?"

I called my sister as soon as I sat down in my car. The phone is on speaker, resting in my car's cupholder, as I tap my chipped cherry red nail polish on my steering wheel.

"No, I took the girls to the Children's Museum." She sounds distracted. She's probably watching them climb the monstrous treehouse in the middle of the museum. "What's up?"

"Dad asked me to fly with him to Phoenix to look at a prospective property. He's going to buy it himself and hire the company. He wants me to design it and—"

"That's wonderful!" Her shriek fills the cabin of my small SUV. "Seriously, Dakota, you totally deserve it. Like, for real."

My lips curve into a smile. My big sister morphs into

Valley girl language when she's excited. I love that about her, because the rest of the time she's a grammar nazi. It's both a welcome break and a reminder that she's human.

"Thanks, Abby. It'll just be for a couple days. Long enough to take a meeting with the seller and see the land." Though now that I think about it, I don't know when we're flying back. I haven't looked at the itinerary Sheila sent, and my dad never said. A couple days is probably a safe bet.

"No worries," Abby assures me. "But I am going to miss watching The Bachelorette with you tonight. Who will eat popcorn with me and laugh at the catfights?"

"Armando?"

She snorts. Abby's husband would never watch that show with her, and we both know it.

I pull into the driveway of Abby's house and cut the engine. "I just got to your house. Please—"

"You just got home," Abby corrects. "It's your home, too."

"Right," I say, because I'm not interested in having that discussion again. Despite the fact that I live with Abby and her family, it is not my home. *Home* isn't something I have at the moment, but I am grateful I have a place to live. "Give Taylor and Emerson kisses and hugs from me."

"Will do," Abby says cheerfully. "Enjoy Arizona," she adds, then hangs up.

I climb from my car and glance up at the monstrous house. It's Abby's dream home, and this is Abby's dream life. Stay-at-home mom, husband who adores her, successful-ish healthy cooking blog. She'd never say it, but I'm the smudgy fingerprint on her recently Windex'd mirror of life. Little sister who lives with her, who can never seem to really get her shit together? I'm a square peg that doesn't fit in her round holes. Which, now that I'm thinking about it, sounds pornographic.

Abby decorated the house herself, but it looks like a professional designer came in and had their way with the place. The vibe is casual but elegant, filled with deceptively expensive furniture and artwork that is just quirky enough to escape being labeled pretentious.

When I get to my room, I pull my suitcase from the top of my closet and toss it on my bed, where it falls open. Peeling off the black slacks I'm wearing, I fold them and place them inside for tomorrow's meeting. I throw in pajamas, a blouse, underwear, and an extra set of clothes for an *in case* situation. Once I've gathered my toiletries, I pull on a pair of jeans and trade my work blouse in for something better for travel. I pull on my boots because I can't stand wearing jeans with anything but heels or boots, and I'm currently out of heels. Speaking of...

I leave the room and walk up one flight of stairs, past six doors, and into my sister's room. Her closet is massive, and even though I'm in there for black heels, I grab a really cute sundress too. She won't miss it. She has a hundred others.

I deposit the heels and dress into my suitcase and zip it up. I turn around, casting one last glance around the room, and spot two pieces of mail on my dresser. I grab them and stuff them in my purse without a second glance. I know what they are. Late notices don't vary in size or shape. I would know, because I'm painfully familiar with them. I dream of a day when every month isn't a juggling act, when I can buy a friend lunch and not experience the sheer terror of thinking the server is going to tell me my credit card was declined.

It's what I get for being involved with a married man. Does not knowing Barrett was married make me any less culpable?

Speaking of... I peek at the date on my phone, to be sure.

I always call on the twenty-seventh. I pull up the number in my contacts and hit the button.

"Colorado Springs Women's Shelter. Debra speaking."

"Debra, hi. It's Dakota Wright."

"Hey, hon. I've been on the lookout for your call today."

"You know me too well."

"What'll it be, Dakota? Same as usual?"

"Yes, please. Same card."

Debra's quiet for a little bit, then announces, "All good, dear. It went through. I know I say it to you every month, but I mean it. We appreciate your donation and how far it goes toward helping these women."

"Happy to do it," I tell her. We say goodbye and I hang up. We'll have the same conversation one month from today.

I've heard helping people makes everyone feel good, both the giver and the receiver. And that first month I donated, it did. I felt lighter when I placed the call. I'd been racked with guilt when I found out my boyfriend was another woman's husband. The fact that I'd ended the relationship immediately didn't lessen the heavy burden, and then the guilt doubled when *she* found out about *me,* and tried to end her life. Standing on my welcome mat with a box of his things in his arms, Barrett admitted he'd found her lying beside a bottle of pills. He cried as he spoke. I volleyed between suffocating guilt and blinding rage.

I wanted to atone somehow for the role I played in what happened, no matter how blind I was. Sometimes though, mostly late at night when I'm kept awake by the sounds of my sister and Armando's lovemaking in the bedroom above me, I mull over my relationship with Barrett. No lipstick on the collar, perfume on his skin, or tan line on his ring finger, but there must have been something I missed. He couldn't have been *that* skilled of a liar. A part of me wonders if I didn't let myself see it, didn't want to lose the comfort Barrett brought to me. I'd met him shortly after my mom died. He'd inserted light into a very dark time for me, and perhaps I was too afraid to look any deeper. We only see what we want to. Until I actually saw him with his wife. Game over. And all the guilt I felt about my mom doubled down, smothering me. I needed a way to release it, like the valve of a pressure cooker. And then it came to me. A women's shelter. Barrett wasn't abusive, but the emotional toll of his double-life left me bruised. It drove his wife to near death. Who better to receive my donation than women who'd been hurt at the hands of their beloved?

Donating to the shelter removed a chunk of my guilt... for a while. Six months later, it serves only to sadden me. Just another penance I pay for bad choices made in the past. The second penance is removed automatically from my bank account each month, and it's been happening for a lot longer than the women's shelter. Such is life. It never goes the way you think it will.

I look around my room one more time to make certain I haven't forgotten anything, then haul my suitcase off the bed and leave. I stop in the kitchen on the way through the house and grab one of the ridiculously delicious oat bars my sister makes. She uses superfoods (Goji berries! Cinnamon and turmeric!) and they're addictive. Abby has a natural talent in the kitchen.

With an oat bar wedged between my teeth, I leave the house and lock it behind me. I slide my suitcase into the back of my car, toss my purse onto the passenger seat, and call my dad's favorite deli to place an order for take-out. When I waltz back into conference room B at five minutes to one, my dad is sitting in the same spot. It's quite possible he hasn't gotten up other than to refill his coffee.

"Lunch," I announce, setting his paper-wrapped sandwich in front of him.

"Good call on the boots," Dad comments, pointing at my feet and then unwrapping his Italian sandwich with extra meat. "Beau needs to see we're not city folk."

"Folk?"

He shrugs, taking a bite. "Trying it out."

I shake my head, my expression deadpan, and he laughs.

"Did you see Emerson or Taylor?" he asks hopefully. He's a huge softie when it comes to his grandbabies.

"Abby took them to the Children's Museum."

"Do you think I'm still the favorite?"

I take a bite and brush a piece of shredded lettuce from my lip. "I'm sure you are, Dad." Emerson, the younger of the two, has a different 'favorite person' every week. Whoever it is, she lavishes with attention.

While we eat, he shows me aerial images of Hayden Ranch. Its sheer size is almost incomprehensible. "Biggest ranch in the state," he tells me.

I want to ask him why he's chosen me to lead the charge on this one, but I'm not sure I want to know the answer. Maybe he pities the mess I got myself into with Barrett. Or maybe he really believes in me. Either way, I don't want to hear it.

"Let's head to the airport," he says when we've finished. He gathers the paper trash from our lunch and stuffs it into the bag. On our way out of the conference room, I glance back at him.

"Hey, Dad? You have lipstick on your teeth."

His hand goes to his mouth before it falters and he laughs. "Damn you, Sheila."

4

DAKOTA

"HON?" MY DAD CALLS THROUGH MY HOTEL ROOM DOOR. "YOU ready for dinner?"

I look down at myself and consider a change of clothes, but when I remember the name of the restaurant in the lobby of our hotel, I think better of it. My jeans and boots will be just fine at a place called The Corral.

After the relatively short flight to Phoenix, we had an almost two-hour drive to Sierra Grande. We didn't stop to eat, because my dad just wanted to get here. In short, I'm starving.

I answer the door and we walk down the stairs to the lobby. The Sierra is a nice hotel, cute and very western, with mahogany wood-planked walls and large framed pictures of famous cowboys and cowgirls.

"Two for dinner, please," my dad says to the young hostess when we enter the restaurant. She shows us to our table and leaves two leather-backed menus plus a drink menu on the table. I take a seat and look around. The restaurant has continued the western theme. The chandeliers are made of wagon wheels, and the tables are covered in red and white tablecloths. A galvanized steel tray in the center of the tables holds ketchup, mustard, and hot sauce called *Kick Yo' Ass* with a donkey on the label.

Our server approaches, a smiling girl who's probably only a few years older than the hostess. Her pink-tipped long blonde hair is gathered into a ponytail that hangs over her shoulder. She wears large turquoise earrings and the friendliest grin I've ever seen, and in each hand is a large glass of water with a lemon wheel perched on the rim.

"Hiya," she warbles, the word soft and pretty like a dove's coo. She sets down the drinks.

"Hi… Josephine." I read the little rectangle pinned to her maroon polo and return her grin.

"Welcome to The Corral. Have you two been here before?" Her head tips to the side and she taps a teal blue fingernail against the edge of the table.

We shake our heads. She bounces her shoulders in a half-shimmy, and says, "I had a feeling you weren't from here."

"Colorado Springs," I answer.

"I've been there, it's beautiful. What are you doing in Sierra Grande?" She looks between me and my dad, then her eyes widen, and she adds, "If you don't mind me asking."

"No, no, it's fine," my dad assures her. "We have a meeting with a rancher."

"Ah." She nods knowingly. "Beau Hayden."

It's not a question, and I find that amusing. He must be the only rancher in this area.

"Do you know him well?" I ask, leaning forward and tucking my hands between my knees. Any inside information we can glean about the man will help us in our meeting tomorrow morning.

"Not Beau, no. I don't know any of them *well*. I went to school with the youngest of the three Hayden brothers." A look passes through her eyes, like something has brought her internal happiness down to a simmer. It doesn't take a psychologist to figure out it has something to do with the youngest brother.

"Anyway, enough chatting. I'm sure you're hungry." Josephine takes our order and doesn't say much when she comes back to drop off my wine and my dad's beer.

"Thanks, Josephine," I say as she slides the wine across the table to me.

"You can call me Jo. Everyone does." She smiles again, but it's not as bright as it was when she first approached our table. *Before* the youngest Hayden brother was brought into the conversation, however briefly. Maybe it's my imagination running wild, but whatever happened between them, it was enough to upset her.

Dad and I spend dinner strategizing about the meeting. Beau Hayden shoots from the hip (I hope not literally, but then again Rich Calloway learned that lesson the hard way), so we know not to show up at the ranch talking about anything fluffy. He needs numbers without fuss or preamble.

When Jo clears our plates, I sneak my hands under my flowy top and unbutton the top button of my jeans. I definitely overate.

My dad asks, "Jo, can you point me to a store where I can buy a few toiletries? I forgot a couple things."

"The Merc is just around the corner." She thumbs behind her shoulder. When she sees our confused expressions, she adds, "It's short for mercantile. Sorry." She laughs. "I already forgot you're not from here. Dessert?"

"No, thank you," I groan, and she laughs again.

We pay the check, and I feel this weird desire to hug Jo goodbye. She is sunny and warm, and I want a little of that feeling. I don't though, because I'm not interested in frightening her, and instead give her a look I hope conveys how much I want to hug her. Like an eye-hug. Is that a thing?

Jo waves goodbye to us and we walk back through the small lobby to the staircase. It's wide, with an ornate wooden rail, and I'm glad we opted to take the stairs instead of use the elevator. Out of three floors, our rooms are on the second, so it's not like I'm burning off even a bite of steak, but I *feel* like I am and that's what counts.

"'Night, Dad." I lean in and kiss his cheek at his door.

"'Night, Junior."

The pang hits me the way it always does, and I hide it just like I always do.

I go to my room, take a shower, and watch Netflix on my phone until I fall asleep.

"I DON'T KNOW what I was picturing, but this wasn't it." My shoulder presses against the window of our rental car as I strain to take in the landscape.

The town of Sierra Grande is in a valley, and it's flat with scrubby large bushes. I was picturing the Hayden Ranch as a cabin-type home on the same landscape, but I couldn't have been more wrong.

We drove north out of Sierra Grande and the bushes gave way to pine trees and cottonwoods. I hadn't been expecting the vegetation, or the purple, orange, and pink wildflowers dotting the landscape.

"We just crossed over into Hayden Ranch territory," my

father says, his flattened palm running the length of an imaginary horizontal line.

"How could you possibly know that?" I ask, certain he's about to make a joke.

"I studied a map of Beau Hayden's property last night before I fell asleep."

"Me too. The town, I mean. I researched the town. I learned a lot about what I think Sierra Grande is missing in terms of retail space."

My dad glances over. He's impressed. "You should tell Beau in the meeting."

I nod, and nerves turn over in my stomach.

We continue to climb in elevation, and soon we're running parallel to the town. The roads look like a grid, and a large street which I've learned is called High Street, runs through what is obviously the center of town where all the shops and stores are, and eventually gives way to homes. It has a decent-size population, but the way Jo automatically knew about the Hayden family makes me think it's a place where everyone knows everyone else. Or, at least, everyone knows the Haydens.

"And here we are," Dad announces, slowing as we approach a large metal sign held up by two wooden posts. The sign reads Hayden Cattle Company. He turns, the car tumbling off the paved road and onto a long dirt driveway, where maybe a half-mile away a house sits. Despite my dad's slowed speed, dust kicks up on either side of the car, and it hits me that this is a convenient way to force visitors to announce their presence.

Or maybe it's just an unpaved road, Dakota. Jo's reaction coupled with the Rich Calloway story has me building a fantasy of the Haydens in my head, and it mainly centers around some hillbillies stepping out of the massive house at the end of the long driveway chewing on a piece of wheat and pointing shotguns at us.

I remind myself it was Beau Hayden who agreed to this meeting, and my overactive imagination needs to take a Valium.

"Well," is the only word I can think to say as we get closer to the house. It's really not a house. It's a compound. The home is a two-story and sprawling. Richly-colored dark brown logs and stone in varying shades of gray make up the exterior. A huge porch makes the front of the house look inviting, and plants flank the walkway leading to the front door. It's rustic and western and unexpectedly elegant.

We come to a stop thirty yards from the home's entrance, the dust settling around the car.

"We've got this, Junior." My dad holds out a fist and I bump it.

I climb from the car and am met with the smell of horses and dirt, grass and pine. It's earthy and comforting. Together we walk toward the oversized front door, and I'm no longer entertaining the thought that hillbillies are going to walk out. Now I'm seeing a blonde woman, hair in an elegant bun, wearing a cream silk blouse tucked into Wranglers and embroidered cowgirl boots. Obviously these are details I've picked up from movies, because where the hell am I getting these ideas?

We climb the steps and pause at the door, sharing a look. Dad knocks on the door, and while we wait I look around. A set of chairs and a table sits off to the side of the long porch. It looks like the perfect place to relax and drink coffee in the morning, the steam rising up from your cup while you listen to the horses whinny, or watch a bunny scamper around the flowers in the beds on either side of the porch steps.

The door opens and my attention snaps to it like a

rubber band. Standing in the opening is a young girl with hair the color of honey. It's piled on top of her head. She wears too much eyeliner and hot pink sparkly eyeshadow.

"Hi," she says cheerfully. Her ready grin reminds me of Jo from last night.

"Hello," my father says. "We have a meeting with Beau Hayden."

"Yep." She nods. "He asked me to get the door when you knocked. He and my brother had to check on one of the foals. They'll be right back." She steps away from the door and sweeps her arm out. "Come on in."

If I was impressed by the outside, I'm a thousand times more in awe of the inside.

The walls are made of the same wood, and the vaulted ceilings have beams running the length and then meeting at the apex. A fireplace sits in the middle of the room, two-sided and made of the same stone as the exterior, and it reaches all the way to the ceiling.

"Your home is lovely," I remark, taking in the leather couches and cow-print rug near the fireplace.

"Thank you," a different voice responds.

Turning, I watch a woman enter the foyer. She's not wearing a cream silk blouse, but she is wearing Wranglers and boots (not embroidered). Her hair, the same color as the young girl who answered the door, brushes her collarbone.

"Juliette Hayden," she says, hand extended as she walks closer.

"Dakota Wright." I step into her handshake. Her grip is firm, and just from this single, quick interaction, I get the feeling she is no-nonsense. "This is my dad—"

"Mitch Wright, Mrs. Hayden," my dad interjects, introducing himself. "It's nice to meet you."

"Likewise, Mr. Wright." Her tone is clipped, but not in a

rude way. She has a restless energy, like maybe she was doing something when we showed up and needs to get back to it.

"You and Miss Wright can wait in my husband's office, if you'd like. He'll be along any moment, along with the realtor." She offers a tight smile. "Seems like everyone is running a bit behind today."

"Mom, I can show them the way."

My shoulders jump a little at the young girl's voice behind me. I'd forgotten she was there.

"Thank you, Jessie." With a nod at my dad and me, the Hayden matriarch strides away.

"This way, guys," Jessie says, stepping around me.

If Mrs. Hayden hadn't said Jessie's name, I wouldn't know it. Not that it's the young girl's fault. I'm guessing she's about seventeen, and I can say with one hundred percent certainty that when I was seventeen, I wasn't answering doors politely and showing people to my father's office. Getting high, getting drunk, and cutting class were my three biggest hobbies, until my parents threatened to kick me out. After that, I took care of the problem for them, by moving out the day I turned eighteen.

Jessie leads us through the living room and down a long hallway, then into a room. "The table is set up for the meeting." She motions at a round table near a window. A silver tray with water bottles sits in the center of the table.

"Thank you, Jessie." I walk to the table and pull out a seat. My dad chooses the seat beside me, and Jessie disappears from the room.

"Nice pile of bricks," my dad elbows me as he says it.

I laugh. "You mean wood and stone?"

"Something like that, yeah." Just as I finish my sentence I hear it... the unmistakable sound of boots on the floor, getting closer and closer. My fingers curl into fists at my sides, and for a quick second, I feel like retching. My first meeting with my dad, and a high-stakes one at that.

What if I fall on my face? What if I say *um* too much? What if I say something idiotic or struggle to find the correct word? What if—

Beau Hayden strides through the open door. He's a big man. His shoulders barely fit through the doorframe, and he's tall too. Wrinkles etch his forehead and his eyes. He's an intimidating man.

Dad and I stand to greet him, and behind Beau, a second person walks into the room. He's as tall and broad-shouldered as Beau, and dark hair peeks out from under the ball cap he wears. He steps out from behind Beau, and my grip on reality ripples.

It can't be.

My legs turn to vapor and I grab the edge of the table to stay upright. My vision swims, my throat constricts. Dad looks back at me just as he reaches Beau and the man who has turned all my senses upside down, and the look on his face is clear—*what the hell is wrong with you*?

If only I could tell him. I'd tell myself, but even I wouldn't believe me.

"My daughter, Dakota," I hear my dad say. I focus my gaze on Beau. My face stretches into a smile, small and polite, and I refuse to look anywhere but at him. Certainly not to the other man in the room.

The man I spent one night with five years ago.

"This is my son, Wes," Beau says, introducing him to my dad, then to me. I nod politely, training my eyes on the wall behind Wes so I don't actually have to look at him.

My dad, Beau, and Wes come to the table and sit down. Mechanically, I do the same. How the hell am I going to get through this meeting? I can barely grasp on to a coherent thought, let alone speak one.

I force my gaze up.

Up from the pattern of wood grain in the table.

Past his gray button-up covered chest.

Landing on his angular jawline, his cheeks pulled taut, his brown eyes that still hold secrets and pain.

And absolutely zero recognition of me.

5

WES

DAKOTA.

Dakota *Wright.* Five years later and I'm finally learning her last name.

How the fuck am I supposed to concentrate with her sitting across from me? After that night in Colorado, I never thought I'd see her again. How is it even possible that she works with the development company looking to buy the land we put up for sale? How, on God's green earth, can this seriously be happening right now?

I've done everything I can to forget about that night. Not because of her. Because of *me.*

I cried in front of her. Fucking cried. It was my first night back in the states after I was discharged from the Army. I'd stopped in Denver on my way home to Arizona and visited a buddy who'd gotten out the year before me. He was having a party at his lakeside place and wanted me to stay with him.

I'd been so ready to let loose, to start life as a civilian. Until I went home and eventually took the rightful title of owner of HCC, I was a free man. And I took advantage of my freedom that night. I stayed on the edge of the party, watching the girl in the middle of it all wearing the sorority shirt. It was cropped and showed her tan, flat stomach. She danced around under the white lights strung from the trees, laughing with her friends. Then she walked away from them, her gaze found mine, and everything happening around us was put on pause. She came toward me, hips swaying and a look on her face that told me she felt as knocked off her axis as me. On her walk over, she snatched a bottle of whiskey off a nearby table and took a swig. She stopped just out of my reach, and it nearly killed me because I wanted her in my arms with a ferocity I'd never felt, and haven't since.

After that, there wasn't a person at that party who thought we weren't going home together. Anybody looking at us would've called us soul mates. And we made the most of the hours we spent together. But then I went and cried. I motherfucking cried in front of the most beautiful, fun-loving, smartest woman I'd ever met. All she did was ask me what the Middle East was like, but it brought tears out of me when all I wanted was to shove down everything that happened and lock it up tight. Who could blame me for getting the fuck out of there after she fell asleep?

Or for acting like I don't recognize her right now?

She knew who I was right away, and it took everything in me not to bypass her dad and her vise-grip on the edge of the table and gather her into my arms.

Now I'm averting my gaze and I can feel hers burning holes into me. I don't blame her. I'd throat-punch any dick-head who did to my sister what I did to Dakota.

"Hi, I'm so sorry I'm late," someone at the door says, and I turn around to see who's come in.

"It's okay, Jericho, please join us." My dad gestures to the empty seat between me and Mr. Wright.

I'd completely forgotten the realtor my dad hired was coming today. When he'd said Jericho Barnett, I'd pictured an old man with more hair in his ears than on his head, but this is definitely not a man. This is an attractive forty-something woman wearing a tight shirt and an even tighter skirt. She shakes hands with everyone but my father, whom she apparently already knows, though I don't understand how.

My dad starts speaking, and Jericho sits back. In my attempt to keep my eyes off Dakota, I make the mistake of looking at Jericho. A sly smile turns up one side of her mouth, and I snap my eyes back to the water bottles in the center of the table. I recognize that look from women, and I'd be lying if I said I haven't been a willing recipient in the past. But not today. Seeing Dakota has officially fucked me up for a while, I already know it.

In an effort to focus on what my father is saying, I squeeze my knee under the table until it's borderline painful. It does nothing to help me keep my attention on my dad, and now my knee hurts.

Dakota's dad is talking, and in order to look at him, my eyes have to pass over Dakota. It's only a second that I see her, but it's enough for me to catch the angry set of her jaw.

"...We were shocked and excited to hear about your listing, Beau. Dakota and I have spent time learning about your land and thinking of how we can use it." He looks to Dakota, silently encouraging her to speak for the first time since my dad and I walked into the room.

This also forces me to look at her or risk being unnecessarily rude, which later my dad would kick my ass for even though I'm a grown man.

I drag my eyes to her. *God, she is gorgeous.* Every bit as beautiful as the day she shimmied around in that T-shirt and short jean skirt. The blue blouse she's wearing today has fallen open just slightly, revealing to me the tiny mole on the underside of her collarbone. I also happen to know she has a matching one next to her belly button. But as much as she resembles the woman from before, she looks different, too. There's something about her eyes now, a dullness that snuffed out her spark. I wonder what tamed her wild nature. In all fairness, I'm not the same guy she met that day. In the years that have passed, the trauma has had time to simmer, the way a stew is always better the day after it's cooked. The flavor of grief has evolved into crushing regret, the kind that eats you from the inside.

With fire in her eyes, Dakota squares her shoulders and glares at me, her gaze softening just slightly when she looks at my dad. "I've given a lot of thought to how we would develop your land should you choose to sell to us. The Hayden Ranch has only belonged to Hayden men since the ranch's inception, and I imagine that's a great source of pride for you. As it should be," she adds, her eyes flitting to me for the shortest second and landing back on my dad. I wonder if this is her way of telling me she's not interested in addressing me?

She continues. "My guess, Mr. Hayden, is that you would rather be eaten by one of the bears roaming these mountains than watch a big box store do business on land that was previously in your family for generations."

"Sounds about right," my dad says, a chuckle in his response. I nearly choke from shock. My dad rarely laughs, even with us kids, and the fact that a complete stranger (to him, not me) has made him have that response is something I can hardly believe.

Dakota nods smoothly. "I'm glad to hear I'm on the right track."

"So what do you plan to develop if not some strip mall?" my dad asks.

Dakota hesitates. "I have some ideas, but I'd like to spend a little more time looking at the land in-person, and also in town learning what the people of Sierra Grande could use. Would you mind giving me a day to figure that out? I won't have to take up any more of your time, I can email you the ideas." She emphasizes the word *you*. What she's really saying is, *I won't be emailing you, Wes, you crybaby who's pretending not to recognize me.*

"Don't you worry about taking up anybody's time, Miss Wright—"

"You can call me Dakota, Mr. Hayden."

"And you can call me Beau, Dakota."

You both can call me shocked. What the hell? Since when does my dad like anybody this much? I glance at Mr. Wright. He's looking at his daughter with unfettered pride.

"So, Dakota, I was saying you don't need to worry about taking up my time." Dad clamps a hand on my shoulder. "It'll be Wes's time you're taking up, and I'm certain he won't mind giving you a tour of the property or the town tomorrow."

I think there was a small part of me that knew he was going to say that, so at this point, I'm not even surprised.

"Sure," I say tightly. *Sounds fun*. Dakota will be imagining the ways she'd like to kill me, and I'll be trying to forget I cried in front of her while simultaneously fighting off the erection that always happens when I think about all the other things that happened that night.

Like when she pulled me into the trees after the sun went down...

And unabashedly stripped off her clothes while I watched, and then walked into the lake...

Shit. Why didn't I wear a looser pair of jeans today?

"I'd love to be with you on that tour, if you don't mind," Jericho pipes up for the first time since her late entrance.

I don't even know why she's here. She didn't add anything valuable to the meeting, and she won't add anything valuable to tomorrow's tour either. She's good for making the transaction official, I suppose, and as far as I can tell that's about it. She can't tell Dakota anything about the land that I don't already know.

And I'd be lying if I said there isn't a small part of me that wants Dakota to myself.

Dad looks at me. "I'll leave you to work that out. I need to get back."

Everyone takes the hint. Chairs scrape the floor, Dakota grabs a water bottle and twists off the cap. She turns so she's facing the window and drinks deeply, as if she's parched. A fraction of her profile is visible, and her delicate throat undulates as she swallows, the same way it did when she tipped the whiskey bottle to those full pink lips.

"Wes?" Jericho interrupts my blatant staring.

Annoyance flares. I look at her expectantly, waiting for whatever it is she needs to say. My jaw flexes as she stares up at me, eyes widening slightly. Her lips part an inch, and I wonder if this is a game women play... the game of, *this is what I'd look like if I was on my knees in front of you*.

A throat clears. Dakota's. I turn just in time to catch the angry look on her face before she pivots and walks around the table, passing by me without a second glance. Her father follows, but he nods at me as he goes.

"Did you need something, Jericho?"

"Tomorrow?" she asks, adjusting the stupid face she was making. "What time?"

I look down at my boots and cross my arms, thinking

about what a shit show this has the potential to turn into.

"Eight a.m. Meet me at the property."

She balks at the early time, but doesn't complain.

I follow Dakota and her dad out front, and Jericho walks beside me. It irritates me. She's making it look like we know each other better than we do, as if I haven't known her the same amount of time I've known Dakota's dad.

Jericho goes to her car, a fancy black two-seater, and Dakota and her dad walk to a white sedan. I let Jericho go with a terse wave, and walk closer to Dakota.

"Eight tomorrow morning," I call out to her back. She whips around. Her expression is one of polite, cool interest, but it looks crafted. Like she painted it and set it on her face like a mask to conceal what she really feels underneath. If it weren't for the hand fisted at her side, I'd be inclined to believe the façade.

"Great," she says, nodding. "I'll be here."

I turn around and go back to the house, but I don't go inside. I stand in the shadow from the stone pillar and watch that little sedan bump its way over the dirt road, kicking up dust.

The night I met Dakota, her face had imprinted on my heart and soul, even though I hadn't wanted it to. We'd met at two in the afternoon on a hot summer day, and by three a.m. I thought I'd memorized most of her expressions. I saw flirty, silly, funny, happy. As we laid in the bed Jason told me was mine for the night, she talked about her parents and what a naïve young girl she'd been to leave home so early, and I saw sadness.

Which is how I know that beneath the anger I saw flashing in those brown eyes just now, I glimpsed her sadness.

And I'm the asshole who put it there.

6

DAKOTA

I'VE DONE EVERYTHING I CAN TO CALM MYSELF DOWN. DEEP breathing, meditating, punching the shit out of a pillow. Turns out, none of those things work when what you really need to do is confront the person who either doesn't remember you or is pretending not to. And, oh, by the way, he's also a potential seller of heretofore exclusive property and you're the hungry buyer.

Wes Hayden.

Wes *fucking* Hayden.

He looks like a slightly aged version of the man I met one hot summer afternoon five years ago, which is to say he's unfairly gorgeous. No man should have eyelashes that dark and long, or lips that full and nibble-worthy. And if that shirt he wore rolled up over his forearms gave anything away, it was that he's still covered in ropy, thick muscles.

Just thinking about him makes my body come alive. My hand brushes over my stomach, the pads of my fingers tracing the path his fingers traveled when they touched me.

There isn't a single thing I don't remember about that night. He was quiet, hiding somewhere inside himself, a soldier released from duty for the first time in over ten years. I wiggled my way into his arms and his mind, and he opened up.

We'd had an incredible afternoon, and when the sun went down the night got hotter. Skinny-dipping in the lake was the first of our shenanigans. It was followed by sneaking past the party in our dry clothes and soaking wet hair, and finding a shower in the house. We made use of the shower, the bathroom counter, the floor, the bed.

Wes towered over me, and his hands were huge. He lifted me as if I were made of nothing but feathers, and all I could think was *here's a real man.*

I'd never been with anybody in such a primitive way, in a way that was raw and needy, and lacked civility. We took what we wanted from each other.

We never went back to the party. We stayed in the room, and we alternated between talking and sex, a pattern that kept us up until the sun was close to rising. Eventually, exhaustion won and we fell asleep. When I woke up, Wes was gone.

I'd gone to the party with two friends, one of whom lived on the other side of the lake, so I walked back to her house in flip-flops and my borrowed sorority shirt. I was too embarrassed to admit to her that I cared about Wes ghosting me, so I told her it was something we'd agreed on before we'd hooked up. "No strings attached," I'd said. For what it's worth, I don't think she believed me. I may have been a wild child, but there was something about sex that was sacred to me.

But apparently not to Wes. He doesn't even remember me.

Rolling over, I give the second pillow on the hotel bed one more good punch, then a second for good measure, and stand up. I can't lie in here wallowing anymore. I've already left a Dakota-sized dent in the mattress.

I run a brush through my hair, swipe under my eyes for mascara that ran during my breathing and punching, and pluck my purse from the chair in the corner. On my way down the stairs, I fish my phone from my pocket and video call Abby.

"Hi, what's up?" she answers, something long and red sticking out of one side of her mouth.

I squint at the screen. "Is that a red bell pepper?"

She nods, pulling it from her mouth and chewing on the bite. "I'm making a snack plate for the girls."

Of course she is. Because she's my sister and she's perfect. Sometimes Abby has cookies waiting for Taylor and Emerson when they get home, but most of the time it's a fruit and veggie platter with pretzels thrown in for good measure. Usually there is a homemade dip like tzatziki or chocolate hummus. To my knowledge, this snack plate has been her most pinned image and highest viewed recipe on her website, ranking only slightly above Instant Pot coq au vin.

"How are the girls?" I ask, clearing the last step on the staircase and making a sharp right into the lobby. I don't really know where I'm going, but I've got to go somewhere. I don't need to wait for Wes and that sexed-up realtor to explore Sierra Grande. I have two feet and two eyeballs and I can put them to use just fine.

"Girls are good. Emerson found a turtle today. Don't ask me how, I have no idea. She wants to keep it." Abby takes another bite of bell pepper. "I asked her where it would sleep and she said your bed."

I narrow my eyes at my sister's laughing face. "Very funny."

"Thanks, I try."

I exit the hotel and pause on the sidewalk, looking right and then left. After a second's consideration, I go left.

"I need to put you down, hang on," Abby says, and I find myself looking at the kitchen ceiling while I listen to the sound of her sharp chef's knife slicing away on her butcher block cutting board. "Are you coming home tonight?"

"No," I answer, pushing off the brick wall I'd been leaning on and looking around. The hotel is on a busier street, and storefronts line both sides. Shading my eyes from the sun, I try to read the names in the nearby windows. "I have some more work to do here. Learn the town and get a feel for the property and what the townspeople want to see developed. You have to go slow in a place like this. They won't take kindly to us marching in and throwing in a strip mall."

Abby finally picks up the phone so I'm no longer talking to the ceiling. "Don't you ever tell me you're not good at anything. Listen to you, thinking of what people want instead of acting like some corporate raider and shoving your agenda down their throats."

I look away, pretending I didn't hear the compliment. After all the hell I put my parents through, I have a hard time accepting that I could possibly be doing something *good*.

"Anyway, Dad and I won't be coming home until tomorrow evening, probably. Maybe Saturday morning. We don't have a return flight booked yet."

Abby smiles into the phone. She looks like our mother, with fair skin and blonde hair made blonder by highlights. "Proud of you, Little D."

I frown playfully at the nickname, and Abby laughs.

We say goodbye, and I put the phone back in my pocket.

At the end of the street is a sign with a huge white arrow and the words *Bar N*. A quick glance at my watch tells me it's not quite an acceptable time to have a drink.

But what the hell? Dad's taking a nap, and it's not like I have anywhere to be right now.

Now I get it. The reason for the name Bar N is that the place actually is a barn.

From the outside it looks like a regular barn. If it weren't for the trucks parked haphazardly in the grass around the place, I'd think it was a place where horses should be. Oh, wait, that's a stable. What animal goes in a barn?

This one, apparently, I think as I walk in. A makeshift bar runs half the length of the left wall, and folding tables dot the floor in such a way that it leaves a big open space in the middle. I'm assuming this is a dance floor, but without any dancers, it looks a bit depressing.

I go to the bar and order a vodka soda. I almost ask what choices I have for vodka, but think better and hold my tongue at the risk of earning myself a dirty look from the female bartender with the partially shaved head.

"Thanks," I tell her, throwing down some cash and taking my drink to an unoccupied table. There are plenty to choose from.

I've been sitting for no fewer than three minutes when an older, crackling voice speaks up behind me.

"Aren't you a pretty thing?"

I take a deep, slow breath and turn around, ready to flip the middle finger to an asshole who needs to be reminded this isn't fifty years ago and I haven't placed my life's hopes and dreams on being complimented by him.

Something about him makes me stow my trigger-happy middle finger. He's an old man, probably somewhere around eighty, but his eyes are bright with life.

"Haven't seen you around here before." He points a wrinkled, age-spotted finger at me. "And no, that was not a pick-up line, even if it sounded like one."

Laughter bubbles up. I lean back in my chair and extend a hand. "I'm Dakota Wright. Here on business."

"Waylon Guthrie. Here since I learned to walk."

This is perfect. This man must know everything about Sierra Grande. "Would you like to join me?" I ask, gesturing to my empty table.

It's painful watching Waylon get up, grab his drink, and gather his lightweight tan jacket, but I don't offer to help. He strikes me as a man who wouldn't appreciate the insinuation that he needs it.

I clear my purse off the tabletop and make room for Waylon's things.

"Well," he says, huffing out a breath as he settles beside me. "Took long enough."

I hold up my drink. "To new friends."

"To new friends," he echoes, tapping his bottle to my glass. He takes a drink of his beer, wipes the back of his hand across his upper lip, and says, "What kind of business brings you here, Dakota?"

"I'm looking at purchasing some land."

He whistles. "Rich lady, huh?"

I cough on my drink, picturing the depressingly low number of my bank account and the late notices that are still in my purse. "Uh, no. I'll be developing said land."

"You going to put in a Starbucks?" His lip curls as he speaks.

"Do you want me to?"

He slams down his beer. It's less than half-full, so the liquid doesn't make it over the rim. "Hell no."

"I didn't think so."

"What are your plans then?"

"That"—I reach over to poke his upper arm—"is where you come in."

He gives me a disbelieving look. "How's that?"

"You've been in Sierra Grande since you learned to walk. Tell me, what does the town need?"

"Nothin', if you ask me." He makes a face. "If you asked my daughter and granddaughter, they'd tell you something different, probably."

"Maybe I can do that. Ask your daughter and granddaughter, I mean."

Waylon reaches behind himself, fishing his wallet from his pocket. He opens the billfold and retrieves a rectangular white card and hands it to me. "That's my daughter's nail salon. They might do more than nails, hell I don't know." He waves a hand in the air. "Pay her a visit. Get your nails done." When he says this, he waggles his fingers. "She'll tell you what this town needs."

I tuck the card into my wallet. "Let me get you a refill, Waylon."

And that is how, on my second night in Sierra Grande, I end up very buzzed with the old man I nearly flipped off.

7

WES

SHE'S LATE.

Dakota was supposed to be here fifteen minutes ago and I feel like a dumbass for being so keenly aware of that. Watching the clock like a whipped schoolboy. Pathetic.

I walk away from the window that faces the road, and go to the kitchen to rinse out my coffee cup and set it on the drying rack. Somewhere in the distance, a car door slams shut.

Before I open the front door, I'm careful to rearrange my features. Cool indifference is what I'm going for, maybe with a side of *I forgot you and everything about that night.*

I pull open the door just in time to watch Dakota falter on the second step. She regains her footing and keeps going. When she notices me standing in the open door, she stops short, her eyes wide, and she sucks her bottom lip between her teeth.

Jesus... this girl. How am I going to spend a morning with her in my truck? From three feet away I can smell her sweet, mouthwatering scent, the same one I couldn't define that night at the lake and don't have a prayer of defining now.

Her jeans are so tight she might as well have them painted on, and they're tucked into cowboy boots. I draw in a shaky breath, but it doesn't quite fill my lungs.

"You're late," I say, and it sounds angry even though I don't mean it to be. I don't like the way she puts me off-kilter.

"My apologies," she says tartly, in a way that conveys she isn't sorry in the least.

A throat clears and we both follow the noise with our eyes. Gramps sits in a chair, watching us. I must not have noticed him when I was looking out the window. I was too busy watching for Dakota.

He stares at me, waiting for me to introduce him. "Dakota, this is Leroy Hayden, my grandpa. Gramps, this is Dakota."

Dakota walks over and shakes his hand. "It's nice to meet you," she tells him, smiling down at him.

I can already tell he is dazzled by her. "You can just call me Gramps. Are you a friend of Wes's?" The excitement in his voice at me possibly having a *friend* is mortifying.

"Uh, no." Dakota shakes her head. "I'm here on business."

Gramps turns a confused look to me. "We need to get going, Gramps, but Dad is inside. He can explain the business that Dakota is here for." To Dakota, I say, "Ready?"

"It was nice to meet you, Gramps." She winks at him and turns, going back down the steps.

For a moment I'm frozen, struck dumb by the sway of her hips and remembering the night she was swinging them on the dance floor.

I hurry after her. "This way," I tell her, chucking my chin sideways toward the side of the house where I park my truck.

She keeps three feet between us as we walk, and I can feel her silent questions coming at me through the separation.

Why did you disappear that morning?

Do you remember me?

"The black one." I point ahead to my truck with the light gray HCC insignia on the driver and passenger doors. "Hop in. I have to tell the guys something."

Dakota listens but doesn't say a word. I veer right and stride to Cowboy House. It's only thirty feet away. Most of the cowboys are out working, but Josh is sitting out front under the awning, sipping black coffee. He hurt his wrist two days ago while we were working on the fences and is babying it while it heals. In the old days, when my grandpa and great-grandpa ran this place, there'd be no nursing an injury. These days, we're more interested in keeping the cowboys healthy than toughing something out. Still, there's plenty of pain in life that only grit will get you through.

Josh's eyes are on me as I approach, but as I get closer to Cowboy House, I realize Josh isn't looking *at* me but *through* me.

I don't have to turn around to know who he's looking at.

"Hey," I growl, "you want to keep your eyeballs?"

Josh's attention snaps back to mine. "Yes, sir."

I come to a stop in front of him. "That's Dakota Wright. She's here on business. You got that?" My meaning is loud and clear—she's off-limits.

He nods once.

Now that that's out of the way, I can say what I came over here to say. "I'm going to be out this morning. You're in charge of the cowboys." Truth is, Josh is just about the only cowboy I trust to take care of the rest of them. He's responsible, level-headed, and not afraid to smoke someone for stepping out of line.

"How's that wrist?" I ask, looking at the bandage wrapped around his right forearm.

"Should be fine by tomorrow."

I doubt that. Three days doesn't seem like enough, but I'm not going to question him. The man can make that choice for himself.

With a duck of my chin, I turn around and head back to Dakota. She's standing beside my truck, her shoulder resting against the passenger door. Her arms are folded and she has one ankle crossed over the other with the toe of her boot pressing into the ground.

"It's locked," she calls as I get closer. "What's there to be afraid of up here? The big, bad wolf?" She uncrosses her arms and gestures around. "Someone would have to be crazy to mess with this place. I bet every one of you sleeps with a gun nearby."

One corner of my lip turns up into a half-smirk. Dakota is both right and wrong. Right in that we sleep with guns nearby. How else do we protect our home and our legacy? We're miles from help, should we need it.

She's wrong in that there's nothing to be afraid of up here.

I stride up to her, reaching across her body for the door handle. I'm close enough to hear her sharp intake of breath and smell whatever goddamn smell it is that intoxicated me so long ago. My stomach tightens and my chest constricts. The woman is a snake charmer, a siren, capable of destroying a man. Specifically, me. Or, she would have before, anyway. I don't think there's any heart left in me to destroy.

"I don't need you to get my door," she spits out, then

seems to remember this meeting is professional, not personal, and softens her tone. "But thank you."

I don't stick around to assist her in climbing up. She's wearing boots and jeans, not a dress, and besides, my truck has running boards. She can manage the climb, but I'm not sure I can manage watching her.

I round the front of my truck, looking away from the windshield on purpose, and think about my family decree that's kept me from being declared future owner of this place.

The successor of HCC must be married.

But what woman could love someone as fucked-up in the head as me?

"THIS IS IT."

I press the brake gently, letting the truck roll to a stop and cutting the engine. "Pretty much everything you see right here is what's for sale."

I glance at Dakota, reading her profile. She hitches forward and rests her forearms on the dash. "Got it."

"Do you want to walk it?"

She turns sharply, her dark gaze falling over me. The question seems to have taken her by surprise. "Aren't we waiting for Jericho?"

I shake my head. "I called her when you were running late and told her to give us an hour. She'll be along after a while." I wish she weren't coming at all. There's so much tension between me and Dakota I could slice through it like softened butter. Adding Jericho to the equation is bound to make it worse.

"Well, then." Dakota opens the door and hops out. She

turns back to look at me, ass still planted in my seat. "Are you leaving me to do this alone?"

My eyes narrow. I get the feeling she's jabbing at me about leaving her to wake up alone. If only she knew how I haven't forgotten even the tiniest curve of her body.

I hold her challenging gaze for a moment too long, then jump from my truck and walk around it to where she stands, clad in those tight jeans and white V-neck tee. Her hair is twisted up on her head, her slender, delicate neck in juxtaposition with the fire blazing in her eyes.

"Come on," I say, gruffer than I intend to, and start walking.

Dakota puts three feet between us, just like she did before. She's about one pace ahead of me, and I watch her walk. She touches the top of the dried grass where it's overgrown, pokes at a puffy bush.

"What is this called?" she asks, pointing to a light green plant. "They're everywhere."

"Mormon Tea."

"And that one?" She points behind me. "With the white flowers?"

I don't need to look to know what she's pointing to. There's only one plant that produces white flowers out here. "Cliffrose."

She nods quietly and keeps walking. "Can you please tell me when I'm in the middle of what's for sale?"

"Sure."

We keep going, and neither of us says anything. The silence is far from companionable. It's thick, heavy, and I swear to God it's giving me heartburn.

I stop walking and watch her go another twenty yards. "You're there," I call out, and she stops.

She turns toward Sierra Grande. The town is visible

from here. The property we're selling sits right up against the town limits. Dakota shades her eyes with one hand and keeps looking out, turning her head right and left a little at a time, taking it all in.

She's beautiful, standing with her strawberry blonde hair against the mountainous desert backdrop. She's not from a ranching family, but between those boots and the feisty attitude, she appears to be cut from the right cloth.

"What are you looking at?" I ask, coming closer to her. I stop five feet from her. It feels like a safe distance.

"I want to know what people will see when they come out here to use whatever it is I'm going to put here."

My head cocks to the side. "Is that right?"

"Yes." She looks me square in my eyes as she says it, daring me to tell her otherwise.

My feet move me a step forward, and I'm honestly not certain it's a step I consciously took. "I have three more meetings with other buyers, but I guess I'll just call them and cancel. I didn't realize you'd won the property."

She steps one foot closer to me. "I didn't realize I hadn't."

What happens next isn't my fault. She's the one wearing that V-neck, showing that damn tiny mole. My gaze drops down to her collarbone, to the little fleck of brown, and lower, to her belly button, where I know its twin is. Her gaze follows mine, and when I drag my stare back up her body to meet her eyes, I see pure rage.

"I knew it," she seethes, her words dripping from between clenched teeth. "I knew you hadn't forgotten me."

I don't know what to say. I have no clue how to make myself verbalize all the things I'm thinking, everything I'm feeling. If this were a movie or a romance novel, I'd pull her to me roughly and kiss her until our lips felt bruised.

Reflexively, I reach out. My fingers barely brush her arm,

and she lets me touch her for the most excruciatingly short second before she yanks her arm away as if my touch were acid.

"Don't you dare," she hisses.

"Dakota, I—"

"Wes?" Jericho's voice breaks through layers of tension and resentment, anger and humiliation.

I turn and watch her teetering across the dirt in high heels. Did she not understand where she was meeting us?

"Wow," she says, laughing lightly. "I called your name five times. You two must've been deep in conversation."

Neither Dakota or I respond. What's there to say?

"Anyway..." Jericho's gaze flits between me and Dakota, trying to glean something from our collective silence. "What do you think, Dakota? About the property?"

Dakota's posture relaxes, her shoulders softening, and she looks back out at Sierra Grande. "I love it. I think I could do something really special here. I need to meet a few more people and get some ideas, but I already have a couple."

"More people?" Jericho asks, catching on to the word Dakota used.

Dakota glances at her, her eyes moving down to the heels, and her mouth moves like she's trying to hide her laughter. "I met a man last night at the Bar N. He had some thoughts about who I could talk to."

"Who?" I ask.

Dakota regards me with frosty eyes, and I think it might be worse than when they're on fire. "Waylon Guthrie."

"Doesn't ring a bell."

She smirks. "Don't worry, he knew plenty about you. And your family."

I ignore the little dagger she just threw my way and look out over the valley where Sierra Grande sits. Up above the scrubby desert, where the landscape turns to pine, that's where the Hayden Ranch sits. It's commanding in its place, like a castle watching over the town. Some people appreciate the position, feel safe because of it. Others resent it. That's the thing about being on top. Everyone thinks they know you, and what they think they know is almost always far from the truth.

"Whoever buys this property, they're going to have to get a crane out here to remove all those pecan trees," Jericho says, one corner of her top lip curled up in disgust. I follow her gaze out to a grove of sad-looking pecan trees. They don't grow naturally here, and nobody ever knew how they came to be. Gramps says someone passing through tossed some seeds on the ground, and that was all it took.

Dakota levels me with a steely stare, but she speaks to Jericho. "Wright Design + Build wants the property, Jericho. I understand you have other interested buyers, but let me be the first to throw my hat in the ring." She strides back through the desert, headed for my truck, not waiting for anybody to follow.

Jericho says, probably to me but I'm too busy watching Dakota's retreating form to look her way, "I can't tell if I like her."

No worries, Jericho. I'm afraid I like her enough for the both of us.

I start for my truck too, but I'm careful to walk at Dakota's pace to maintain our distance. It seems best that way.

8

DAKOTA

I KNEW IT.

The asshole remembers me. I almost feel like calling Paige, one of the friends I went to the party with that night, except I haven't talked to her since the morning after my night with Wes, when I showed up at her lake house. I don't even have her number anymore.

Our falling out was my fault. I was sad about Wes, and somehow what he did brought into question for me all the decisions that I had been making. That's when I decided that I'd worn out my welcome in that phase of my life. It was finally time to go home. Too chicken shit to call first, I'd showed up on my parents' doorstep only to learn that my mom had suffered an aneurysm two days prior.

Two days.

Two fucking days.

What had I been doing on that day? Nothing. I should have been with my mother. I should've never left my parents' house. I shouldn't have been so headstrong and wild, acting like I had the market cornered on being a teenager and wanting freedom, as if my parents had never felt such feelings before.

After I came home, I read up on everything I could find about aneurysms. I kept seeing the word *stress*. And hadn't I caused my mother enough stress over the years? In my grief, I saw this correlation as causation.

"Did that make you feel better to stomp away?" Wes asks as he climbs into the truck. He looks at me expectantly, as if the question isn't rhetorical.

"Did it make you feel better to pretend not to remember me?" I ask, but I don't look at him. I'm too busy watching Jericho step gingerly in those dumb high heels. To be fair, they're super cute. Right now, I might think any high heels are cute, seeing as how my only pair broke a few days ago.

"For the record, no, it did not," Wes answers. He starts the truck and turns it around, driving it back to where we turned off the main road.

"You can take me back to my car at your house," I tell him.

He looks at me, bewildered. "Why? Don't you want to go to town and talk to people?"

My answering laugh is empty. "I learned last night that I'd be better off doing that by myself. Waylon told me—"

Wes waves his hand dismissively. "Fuck that guy. He doesn't know what he's talking about."

I glare at him. "He knows you, your daddy, and your granddaddy. His words, not mine. And he told me you rarely come to town. So, no, I don't need you to show me around town. Maybe it's *me* who should be showing *you* around town. Seems I already know more people than you."

He lets out an irritated sigh and shakes his head. The truck reaches the main road and he goes left toward town, not right toward his house and my waiting car.

"Stubborn ass," I murmur.

I think he's going to give me one of his signature hard looks, but he shocks the hell out of me and almost chuckles. An almost chuckle from the world's most impenetrable man. Imagine that.

I don't say anything else on our way into Sierra Grande. In my side mirror, I spot Jericho's little black car. I don't know what her deal is, but I know what I saw when she walked into Beau's office yesterday. Her eyes slid over Wes like they were her hands taking off his clothes.

I don't blame the woman. He's gorgeous, has a nice body, and he's rugged and manly. I could tell her that he ghosted me and then pretended not to know me, but it probably wouldn't even make a difference. The heart wants what it wants, or some horseshit like that.

Well, not this heart. This heart is closed off. I learned the hard way that men are more trouble than they're worth. I believed Barrett was a good man, and then eventually ended up following him home from the farmer's market to a two-story cookie-cutter house, parking down the street and watching him hug a little boy and play basketball with an older child. That same night he'd shown up, fresh from his 'business trip.' Confronting him didn't even make me feel better. I'd packed my apartment, paid thousands to break the lease, and then right after that, I lost my job. I was lucky to have my sister and a place to go, but I also had a hefty dose of guilt. Then the guilt doubled when Barrett came for his things on move-out day and told me about his wife. And that's when I made my next choice, one that I thought was good but now feels more like falling on a sword.

Wes circles around looking for a parking spot big enough for his truck. He finally finds one and we park and hop out. It might be my imagination, but I feel eyes on him. When I look at people's faces for confirmation, I see nothing but polite nods.

Jericho meets us in front of Waylon's daughter's nail salon.

"Getting your nails done?" she asks me, but it's in this patronizing voice that tells me how badly she thinks I need the service.

Nope, I just bite the cuticles off myself and spit them on the ground. I'm dying to say it just so I can see the look of disgust in her eyes and the poor attempt to cover up a shudder.

"This is the first place Waylon directed me to. His daughter and granddaughter work here, and he thinks they'll have some good ideas as to what the people of Sierra Grande would like developed in their town."

Jericho nods tightly, looking down at her own fresh hot pink manicure. "I think I'll just slip into the coffee shop and wait for you to do your research." She looks hopefully at Wes. "Care to join me? I'm sure nail salons aren't really your thing."

Wes opens his mouth to respond but I answer first. "Great idea, Jericho. I won't be long."

I don't intend to glance at Wes, but my eyes are drawn to him. His lips are pulled into a thin line, his posture stiff.

I turn away and open the door of the nail salon, a little bell ringing above my head.

The place is half-full, and a blonde woman looks up from where she sits with another woman's hand in hers. She pauses her filing and asks, "What can I do for you, honey?"

"I'm looking for Stacia Guthrie?"

"That would be me," the woman says, not exactly cheerfully but not rudely either. More like she's curious and a tad reluctant. I don't blame her.

I walk closer to her workstation. The woman having her nails done gives me a look that lets me know I'm interrupting her.

"Pardon my interruption," I apologize, smiling at her glare. "That's a lovely shade of purple."

"Thank you," the woman says, mellowing.

"Did you need something?" Stacia asks, resuming her filing.

"I met your dad last night at the Bar N, and—"

Stacia blows out a hard breath and it moves the long side sweep of bangs that touch her chin. "What did he do now?"

I laugh. "I can see why you'd ask that. He's a bit of a firecracker." I pull out the business card I tucked in my back pocket when I got dressed this morning. "I'm Dakota Wright. I work for a development company looking to buy some property on the edge of town."

A guarded look creeps into her eyes, but I'm expecting it. In some places, people get excited at the idea of development, even call it *progress*. In other places, development represents change, and that's a bad thing.

"I've been put in charge of coming up with how the land can be used. And I'm not interested in coming into Sierra Grande and acting like I know what should be built based on what it looks like you all are missing." Waylon's Starbucks comment comes to mind. "I'd like to hear from people who live here about what they'd like to see added to their town. Hopefully, my interests and the town's interests align."

I don't want to over-promise and under-deliver, so I add that last part for insurance. I can't agree to build a one-room schoolhouse that teaches underwater basket weaving, even if it's voted on unanimously by the entire town of Sierra Grande.

Stacia glances at the woman whose nails she's doing. They have a short conversation with their eyes. When she looks back to me, her gaze is a little less guarded. "This is Ashley," she motions toward the woman with her head. "She's hosting a book club tonight. It would probably be a good place for you to come and get some ideas."

My hands clap together in my enthusiasm. Maybe it's not very professional, but I'm genuinely excited to add something beneficial to this town. "Yes, perfect. Thank you."

I take out my phone and type in Ashley's address, then tell them both that I'll be there at seven.

With a wave at Stacia, I go back through the door and over to the coffee shop to find Jericho and Wes. Maybe Jericho has entranced him already with her spiked heels and tight skirt. Honestly, it might be better for me if she has. I can't afford to let down my guard with him. I need to have a professional relationship with Wes, not a personal one.

The sight that greets me in the coffee shop causes a tickle of laughter in my throat, but I cover it up with a cough. Jericho sits with her legs crossed at the ankles, elbows bent and perched on the table, and she's leaning forward. A hundred bucks says her stance is making her blouse fall open just enough, and it's by design. Wes leans back against his chair, one booted foot crossed over his other leg in a figure four. There's a cup of coffee in front of him, probably black because I can't imagine him ordering something with milk or syrup.

I walk toward them, doing my damnedest to ignore the flutter of relief in my stomach. Jericho and Wes could excuse themselves for some alone time in the bathroom, for all I care.

Right?

Yes, totally. I wouldn't care at all.

"Hi," I chirp, dragging over a chair from the empty table beside theirs.

Jericho straightens her body and her shirt. "How did that go?"

"It went well. I got an invite to a book club meeting tonight. Hopefully it will give me enough ideas to roll with."

"Look at you, making friends all over this place." He sounds sarcastic, and maybe even a smidge jealous.

"What can I say, I'm a friendly gal."

"I'm aware." Wes's gaze drills into me. Those two words are like the tip of an iceberg, the tiny amount that shows above the water's surface. When it comes to me, Wes is aware of so much more. Not just my body, either, though he became intimately acquainted with that, too. No, in the darkest hours of that night, I told Wes how I'd been wanting to go home, how I'd hurt my parents by leaving. That's when he opened the door into his heart just a crack and showed me the pain that lives inside him.

Pain I can see is still residing in his eyes, though his face doesn't look haunted, the way it did that day when I spotted him sitting by himself. That was back when everything was fresh and new, the wound not yet scabbed over. Maybe now, all he has left are scars.

And I know a thing or two about scars on a heart.

I rip my gaze away from his. "You two all set? I need to get my car, Wes. I have work to do before tonight."

Wes and Jericho stand, and when we get out front into the sunshine, Jericho tells me she'll let me know if our bid gets chosen among the others. She says it in this annoying way, like Wright Design + Build doesn't have a shot in hell. I know she's fielding other buyers, and I wonder who they are and what they're offering.

"When are you meeting the other buyers?" I ask Wes when we're in his truck.

He glances at me. "Next week. Nobody flew out here so quickly to see us the way you and your dad did."

"I'm the only one-night stand popping up from the woodwork to buy your property?" I can't help the jab. I'm feeling prickly after Jericho insinuated she doesn't think I'll win the bid.

Wes gives me a hard look. It's the first time either of us has openly said what happened. "No," he murmurs, his tone incongruent to the expression on his face.

My eyebrows lift. "No? I'm not the only one? There are more?" A stab of jealousy slices through me.

"I wouldn't call you a one-night stand." He says it like he's angry.

My arms fold in front of my chest. "What else would you call it?"

He looks like he's about to say something, but then he shuts down, as if someone somewhere flipped a switch. The truck shifts into drive and he takes us out of town, and as we pass the point where the scrubby bushes kiss the pines, it hits me.

Wes is a cowboy prince, tucked away up here in his log and stone castle. What is it he's hiding from?

9

WES

She's only a few feet away, sitting in the passenger seat of my truck, but she may as well have a force field around her. Untouchable. Unreachable.

And yet, against every cell in my brain issuing caution, I want to reach out. Hold her. Touch her. Kiss her the way I did that evening in the lake, with an urgency that propelled us to seek a bedroom.

We're winding our way around the mountain, and pretty soon we'll be back at the homestead, and I'm dying to say something. I can feel the hurt and fury coming off her in waves, two emotions she has every right to feel.

I need to make her feel better, I can't stand knowing she's sitting over there hurt because of my inability to handle my shit. I take a deep breath and start.

"You wore a short jean skirt. Your legs were tanned and looked like they could've been carved from sandstone. You danced with your friends and laughed. You were the most beautiful thing I'd ever seen, and it hit me that you were the reason I re-upped each time my four years were over. So people like you could keep living, keep fucking up, keep being human." My stomach turns over as I talk, the sensation of releasing these thoughts so foreign it feels like they should belong to someone else. "You weren't just a one-night stand, Dakota."

You were so much more, and you terrified me. I can't bring myself to say it out loud. She's smart enough to put it all together, to take what I said and fill in the cracks with the words I cannot say.

"Thank you." Her voice is soft and supple, and it brings out in me an ache for her I buried a long time ago. I thought of her constantly after that night, and eventually I knew I had to tuck away my memories of her.

I grunt my response like a caveman, because I don't know what else to say and I feel too bare and I don't particularly care for the feeling. Add to it the fact that—

"What the fuck?" I shout, my eyes trained on the building a couple hundred yards away from the homestead. A beat-up late-model truck is parked at an angle in front of Cowboy House, and the person who it belongs to has no business on my ranch. I step on the gas and send dirt and dust flying.

"What's wrong?" Dakota asks. She leans forward, peering out the windshield, trying to spot an obvious problem, but there isn't one. Not to her, anyway. There certainly is to me.

I drive up to Cowboy House and slam on the brakes, locking my arm across Dakota so she doesn't go flying into the dashboard.

"Stay here," I instruct, throwing it in park and getting out.

I'm livid. My fury-laced blood boils under my skin.

The hinges protest as I yank open the door to Cowboy House. "Dixon," I bark. "Get out of here, you motherfucker."

I cross the kitchen and round the corner to the sleeping area. Dixon slouches in a chair beside Troy's bed. I'm too late. Troy is already fucked-up.

Dixon's eyes are small and beady, and I'd like to carve them from his head. "Don't answer to no one," he says slowly, his chin tipping up insolently. "Especially not a rich prick like you."

Inside I'm shaking, but on the surface I'm steady. It's what the military ingrained in me, something I don't think will ever wane.

"You talk stupid, but I happen to know you're pretty fuckin' smart. So why is it you're coming around here for customers?"

"Your boy sought me out."

"Get the fuck out."

Dixon glances down to Troy, a satisfied smile etching his face. He stands up, and even at his full height, he's nearly a head shorter than me.

I hate everything about the guy.

I hate the way he slouches when he walks, how he has no pride, no honor, no positive contribution to society. He's a predator who preys only on the weak, and in my book, that makes him scum.

He slinks past me, pushing his shoulder into my arm as he goes. He's like a ball of fluff, hardly moving me. I walk behind him, my steps loud and heavy, making certain he knows I'm on his heels.

He opens the front door and Dakota literally falls into him, as if she were reaching for the door handle when the door opened and her forward momentum carried her into the open space.

"Fuck yeah, baby," he crows, holding on to her upper arms. "You're making it easy for me."

She presses away from him, face scrunched in revulsion and fear, but he keeps his grip on her arms.

If I thought seeing Troy drugged up on his bed made me mad, it's nothing compared to watching Dixon put his hands on Dakota.

My first punch lands against his lower back. Dakota goes stumbling against the wall as he releases her, making a heavy breath sound as she hits the wood. I spin Dixon around and bury my second punch in his stomach.

"Oof," he grunts, doubling over.

I'm not done. Dixon needs the point driven home. I push him outside and follow him through the open door. In my peripheral vision, I see Dakota, pressed against the wall with her eyes shut tight. She's terrified, but I can't help her now. There's a drug dealer on my property trying to make customers out of my employees.

Dixon is on his feet, but he's bent over, hands on his knees, catching his breath. He stands when I walk up to him. He looks at me with contempt, sniffles, and takes a swing.

Behind me, Dakota screams. She must've followed me out.

I duck out of the line of Dixon's hand and follow up with a fist straight to his nose. Blood pours from him instantly, like water from a faucet.

Suddenly there are more people than just me, Dakota, and Dixon. Josh, Denny, Bryce, Ham, and Warner. Even Wyatt is here, and he's probably still half in the bag. Josh grabs Dixon's arms, pinning them behind his back, without a question to me about why we're fighting or a thought about his own injured wrist.

"You stay off my property," I seethe, my voice low and

menacing. "You don't talk to my cowboys. And you never, ever look at her again. You got that?"

Dixon spits blood into the dirt between us. "This is a free country, Hayden. You of all people should know that."

"Not for you." I tip my head closer. "Don't test me, Dixon."

Josh drags him back and Denny jumps in, helping him walk a struggling Dixon to his truck. I turn my back on the scene and look at Dakota.

"Are you okay?" I ask, at the same time Warner and Wyatt walk up to me.

"What the fuck happened?" Warner demands.

"Found Dixon in Cowboy House with Troy," I growl, remembering the contemptuous and lazy look on his pinched face.

"Did he—?" Wyatt asks.

I cut him off with a terse nod.

"Fuck," he groans.

Behind us a truck starts up and tires screech, sending dust billowing toward us. Dakota blinks against it, and I can taste its chalkiness.

"Boss?" Josh asks, coming closer, the other cowboys around him. "What's going on?"

The name surprises me, taking hold of something in me. At the rate I'm going, I'll never be the cowboys' boss, even if it's the thing I want most in the world.

I rub a hand over my face. I'm suddenly really tired, and Dakota is still staring at me like she can't process what just happened.

"Get in there," I say to Josh, inclining my head to Cowboy House. "Sit with Troy. That fucker got a needle in him. Make sure he's okay." The guys sidestep me, Warner, and Wyatt. Every one of them tries damned hard not to look at Dakota as they pass her.

"Josh," I call out, and he turns back to me. "Call me when Troy comes out of it."

I'm not looking forward to that conversation.

Dakota walks closer. Her boots are dirty, and her hair has fallen out of her bun, cascading over her shoulders in soft, messy waves.

She comes to a stop in front of me, her eyes searching. I wish I knew what she was thinking.

"Dakota, these are my brothers, Warner and Wyatt."

Warner steps forward first, shaking her hand, and then Wyatt.

"Dakota is the land developer Dad and I are working with," I explain.

"Is that all?" Wyatt eyes me meaningfully. "You sure didn't like when Dixon looked at her."

"Shut up, Wyatt. He touched her too, for the record."

Wyatt shakes his head, his eyes full of regret. I understand. Wyatt was friends with Dixon when they were little kids, back when Dixon's dad was an HCC cowboy. That was before my dad caught him stealing and fired him. I didn't keep tabs on what happened to the family after that, but from what I've picked up over the years it sounds like one bad choice led to another, until it was too much to come back from. Still, a tough upbringing doesn't excuse the choice to peddle drugs around town. Funny thing is, as tough as my dad may be, he believes in second chances. Dixon's dad refused to apologize or take ownership of what he'd done, but if he had he would've probably saved his family all the heartache.

Wyatt and Warner say goodbye and walk back to the

house, leaving me and Dakota and the world's most awkward silence.

"So, uh... I'll come by tomorrow morning and show you my plans, if that's okay?" Dakota asks. "I'm certain tonight will yield plenty of ideas." She sidesteps me and goes toward her car.

"Sounds good. See you in the morning," I say, watching her walk away.

She gets in her car and drives off, the cloud of dust marking her progress until she reaches the paved road.

Pulling my phone from the pocket of my jeans, I pull up Jericho's number and hit the send button.

"Sell the land to Dakota Wright," I instruct when Jericho answers.

"Two other firms have offered more than your asking price, Wes, sight unseen," Jericho informs me smugly, like she's been hiding an ace in one of those stupid high heels she wears and couldn't wait to wield it against Dakota.

"You heard me," I nearly bark. "And I'll be the one to tell her," I add, then hang up. I don't have time for Jericho's jealous behavior toward Dakota.

This has already been the most tiring fucking day in a long time and it's only halfway over. The cowboys are watching Troy, my family's busy doing the hundreds of things owning a ranch necessitates they do, and even though I should go inside and help out, I'm too keyed up.

I know what I need. I turn on my heel and head for the stable. My horse, Ranger, whinnies when he sees me. He's a chestnut-colored purebred Appaloosa stallion, and I got him the day I came back to this ranch after the Army. My first horse, Shogun, died while I was overseas.

"Let's go for a ride, boy," I tell him, taking my saddle down from the rack and fitting it over him. I run my hand over his white starburst facial marking and he nods his approval.

We set off, no destination in mind. Ranger always helps me think. The rhythm of the ride, whether it's a cantor or a trot, makes life seem a little clearer. It takes the big things and makes them small again. It reaches into the center of my chest where sometimes it's hard to breathe and makes space.

It helps me forget my final deployment, and the two people I couldn't save.

10

DAKOTA

"Hey Junior," Dad says when I walk into his hotel room. I'm fresh from a much-needed nap and shower. After drinking with Waylon last night and getting up early to meet Wes, not to mention the sheer emotional exhaustion of being around Wes, I deserved that two-hour nap.

He sets down the book he's reading and looks up at me. "How'd it go?"

"Well, I'd say. The land is beautiful, Dad. It's just high up enough to get amazing views of Sierra Grande, and there are these pecan trees that would be gorgeous if given the right care. I talked with someone today and got an invite to a book club meeting. I'm hoping to talk to some ladies and get ideas."

My dad lets out a low, appreciative whistle. "I knew you'd be good in this role, Dakota, but you're really knocking it out of the park. Is something about this town special to you? You seem to care more than the average project manager I've worked with."

I swallow. "No. I just don't want to be the kind of

company who comes in and does as they please without regard. Like wearing muddy boots on white carpet."

The pride on his face is unadulterated, the kind of pride that's so shiny and pure only a parent can feel it for their child.

I duck my head so I don't have to see it anymore. I don't deserve it.

"Have you talked to Abby recently?" I ask to change the subject.

"About an hour ago. Emerson answered." The proud grandpa look he often wears overtakes his face. "She told me about the turtle."

Oh God. The turtle. I forgot about it.

My dad cocks his head to the side. "I remember when you girls were young and I traveled a lot for work. It was hell on me. I used to bring home a postcard for each of you from whatever city I'd been in, even if I'd been there before and you already had one."

I smile. "I remember that. We loved racing to see who could get to you first when you walked in the door."

He chuckles. "Those days go by quickly. Your mom used to tell me that the days are long but the years are short."

A burning sensation pricks my nose and I turn away. I run my finger along the back of a chair and will the sensation to fade. "Do you want to get an early dinner? I saw a diner I want to try. Small-town diners are the best, right?"

Dad gives me a long look before he says, "Sure, Dakota. Small-town diner it is."

"For the record, I was right," I tell him, slapping down my plastic-covered menu on the chipped but clean Formica countertop.

"Oh yeah?" Dad asks, drinking his strawberry milkshake.

I tuck my freezing cold hands between my knees and lower my head to the straw of my peanut butter chocolate malt. "This is the best."

"I agree." He pushes his shake away like he's trying to keep himself from having too much of it.

"Everything good here?" The waitress stops and looks at us. Her name is Cherilyn, and she has a pillowy bosom and generous arms, and she looks like she gives the best hugs.

"Best we've ever had," I answer.

She hoots. "That might be true if you were from around here, but my gut is telling me you aren't."

Geez, what is it with the people in Sierra Grande? Do they have specialized brains groomed for the detection of outsiders? It's not as if I'm inappropriately dressed for the landscape like Jericho with her heels in the desert terrain. I'm wearing cowgirl boots, for God's sake. I look the part.

"I know who you are," comes a man's voice nearby.

I jump, turning to look at the owner, seated two seats down the counter. He's probably as old as Waylon, and he wears a short-sleeved plaid shirt that has seen better days.

He raises an overgrown eyebrow. "I saw you in town this morning with the oldest Hayden boy. I haven't seen him in a coon's age."

Coon's age? Where the hell am I? Sierra Grande might be a small town, but backwoods it is not.

Cherilyn rolls her eyes and points at the plate of chicken fried steak sitting in front of the man. "Hank, eat your dinner. You get wild when you're hungry."

"Hmph," Hank says, pushing out his lips like a child. "You'd look twice if you saw a Hayden in town, too."

"I see the youngest one often enough," Cherilyn retorts, turning around to the kitchen window when the cook smacks the little silver bell. She lifts two plates and spins, placing them in front of me and my dad.

"Here you are." She smiles. "Don't let Hank scare you away from Sierra Grande with talk of the Hayden family. Their ranch was the reason this town was built and people around here would do well to remember that." She glares pointedly at Hank before walking off, plastic water pitcher in hand.

"You know," Hank says, leaning over to look at my dad. "This is your daughter, right?"

My dad nods, his eyes wary.

"For a second there when I saw them together this morning, I thought maybe the Hayden boy was finally going to get to take over his parents' ranch after all."

My eyebrows pull together as I cut into my chicken. "What do you mean?"

"It's this old Hayden rule. The ranch can't be handed down to an unmarried son. Beau's getting up there in age, only a few years younger than myself. He might've handed it over to the oldest boy by now, but the guy's not married. Maybe he's a ho-mo-sexual."

I cough on my chicken, both because of the way Hank pronounced the word and the fact that I happen to have intimate knowledge of Wes's sexual preference.

"What?" Hank asks. "Wasn't okay when I was young, but it's okay now. I gotta grandson who's gay. Has a boyfriend, too. Lovely couple. Sent me a Christmas card last year. Anyway..." Hank turns back to his dinner.

I send a wide-eyed look to my dad, who gives me the same look and shrugs. We eat our meal with a handful more distractions from our chatty seatmate, but he's moved on from the Haydens.

I, however, have not.

Why hasn't Wes married? Given what's on the line for him, wouldn't he try harder to find a woman?

It's not a question I can spend time pondering, because I'm due at the book club. We pay our bill, and Dad whispers to Cherilyn to put Hank's dinner on our tab. We say goodbye to Hank, and Dad winks conspiratorially at Cherilyn as she refills Hank's iced tea.

I drop my dad at the hotel and type Ashley's address into the GPS. It's fifteen minutes away, so I turn on the radio and try to listen to the local country station, but I can't stop thinking about Wes.

You wore a short jean skirt... you were the most beautiful thing I'd ever seen.

Earlier today in his truck, he was *trying*. Trying to do what, though? Make me feel better about letting me wake up alone after we slept together? About being nowhere to be found in his friend's house as I crept down the stairs and through the kitchen, praying nobody would witness my walk of shame?

All I know is that today in the truck I saw a glimpse of the guy I met that carefree afternoon on the lake, the very last of all my carefree afternoons, and then he morphed into whoever that was who stomped into the place where the cowboys live and beat the snot out of some guy.

Not some guy, though. A drug dealer, from what I could tell. Someone who'd already given drugs to one of Wes's cowboys.

Wes is protective of his crew. And of me, apparently. I think he might've let Dixon go without it getting violent, but then I didn't listen when Wes told me to stay in the truck.

To be fair, why would I listen? I'm not a child. I don't need to follow directions just because I've been told to.

I went to investigate, to make sure Wes was okay. The way he acted when he saw the old truck parked outside the low, long building told me there was a problem.

And then I fell into Dixon's pockmarked arms. He smelled foul, like body odor and chew. He grabbed me, and that's when Wes lost it.

The violence frightened me, but his command of the situation was undeniably attractive. Wes feels... *safe*. But there's no denying there's something inside of him, something raw and untamed.

My mind is still turning over the conundrum that is Wes when I pull up to Ashley's house.

It's a low-slung house with a gigantic, mature tree in the center of the front yard. It's old, but well-maintained. Trimmed hedges line the front, and a porch swing dangles from two hooks in the ceiling.

I check my reflection in the rearview mirror and get out of the car. Ashley answers almost right away.

"Hi there." She grins, pulling me inside by my forearm.

Her demeanor is much nicer than it was when I interrupted her manicure. She leads me into the living room, and when I spot the folding table covered in bottles of wine and booze with mixers, I understand why she's more welcoming to me.

"Everyone, this is Dakota," Ashley trills, pointing at me. "Dakota, this is everyone."

I look into the nine or ten faces of women seated on couches and mismatched chairs that have probably been hauled in from other parts of the house. Waving at them, I say, "Thanks for having me tonight."

"Dakota is here for some research," Ashley tells the group as she refills a glass of white wine. "She's building property on the edge of town and wants to know what we'd like to see built."

"I'm one of a few companies looking to buy property that's for sale," I clarify. "It's not a for sure thing, but I've told the seller I'll bring them some ideas for what I'd put on the land. They don't want to see it made into a strip mall filled with chain stores, and I agree with their opinion." I look out at the woman and spot Stacia among them. With a small smile and a nod in her direction, I ask, "So please feel free to share with me your thoughts on how you'd like to see the land developed."

They all start talking at once. There are suddenly so many voices filling the small room, it's like taking the lid off a stockpot of boiling water.

One woman wants to see an equestrian center.

Another would love a nature conservatory.

Someone else mentions tourism, which gets me thinking. Tourism brings money and creates jobs. The weather in the Verde Valley, where Sierra Grande sits around other small towns, is fairly consistent all year long. I know because the dear old internet told me so.

Suggestions fly at me at warp speed, and I write them all down on the small notebook I pulled from my purse, but my mind is stuck on the tourism idea.

Book club begins, and it's not a book I've read, which isn't a problem because I'm busy mentally sifting through ideas.

When the book has been discussed, and the ladies are all two or three drinks deep, the gossip begins. And the first topic is, shockingly, *me*.

"So." One woman, Sarah, turns and casts a curious look at me. "A little birdie told me Wes Hayden was in town with a beautiful young woman today. Any chance that woman was you?"

I give her a teasing look. "Are you calling me beautiful?"

She snorts with laughter. "I suppose. So? Was it you? Is someone finally going to tame that wild stallion?"

"It's Hayden land that's for sale, Sarah," a woman across the circle speaks up. "My husband told me so."

They all look to me and I nod my confirmation. "He was showing me the land this morning, and we came into town so I could meet Stacia and ultimately end up here tonight with all of you."

"Sounds to me like a romance novel," another woman crows, and two other ladies laugh. "Next you'll be knocking boots."

We already have.

I keep the thought to myself and laugh along with them. "You have very active imaginations."

"My daughter went to high school with him," the woman besides Stacia says. "She says he was crazy and fun back then, the life of the party. She tried to reconnect with him when he got home from the Army, but he was different. She said the light in his eyes was gone."

The room grows quiet, and then the woman who made the comment about the romance novel says cheerfully, "Maybe Dakota can turn the light back on."

I smile and laugh at her suggestion, and the chatter resumes. It moves away from me and Wes, thank God, and on to some other poor soul.

I use the break to follow Ashley into the kitchen where she's removing plastic wrap from a plate of cookies.

"Thank you for having me tonight. I'm going to take off. I have a lot of work to do ahead of my meeting with the Haydens in the morning."

She lifts the tray and turns to me. "I hope you got what you came for."

I nod vigorously. There are so many ideas bouncing around in my head right now, it's hard to think straight. "I did."

Ashley dips her chin at the tray she's holding. "Take a cookie. Marjorie makes them herself."

I remove a toffee cookie and take a bite. "Oh my God," I mumble, brushing crumbs from my lips. "Those are incredible."

"Yep," she agrees, leading the way back into the living room. "And they're about to disappear. Marjorie has been trying to think of a way to sell them and make some money, but she hasn't figured it out yet. Right, Marjorie?" Ashley looks at the woman on the other side of Stacia as she slides the platter onto the coffee table.

"That's right. For now, it's the book club who gets the fruits of my labor."

"Well, thank you, Marjorie, for the delicious cookie." I hold up the toffee cookie in my hand. "And thank you, everyone, for having me tonight. Thanks to all your suggestions, I have a lot of work to do now." I wave at them all and let myself out. Once I'm in my car, I gobble the cookie like I didn't just eat dinner a couple hours ago. It's that damn good.

When I get back to the hotel, I grab myself a glass of wine from the restaurant bar, go upstairs, and hunker down for a long night of work. By the time I go to bed at one a.m., I'm armed with a solid plan to present to Beau and Wes in the morning.

11

DAKOTA

"BEAU. WES." I NOD MY HEAD IN TURN AT EACH MAN. "GOOD morning."

Beau says hello and shakes my dad's offered hand. Wes does the same, but even as I turn my back to him and walk to the burnt red leather couch in the living room, I can feel his gaze searing me.

Dad and I walked into the house expecting to be taken back to Beau's office. Instead, Beau asked us to join them for coffee in the living room.

It's the room I stared at the first and only other time I've been in this house, just a few days ago when Wes's little sister Jessie answered the door. The double-sided floor to ceiling stone fireplace is remarkable. On the mantle sits a coat of arms, with a man on a horse reared on its hind legs, and the words *Legacy, Loyalty, Honor* emblazoned on the bottom center.

I can't help but think of Wes and what this means to him, how legacy, loyalty, and honor have been ground into him since the day he was born. It seems a heavy load to carry, even for the strongest of arms.

I take a seat beside my dad on the couch opposite Beau and Wes. Seeing them together, separated only by a mere twelve inches, is like looking into the future. This is what Wes will look like in thirty-odd years.

"Dakota," Beau says, leaning forward to grab his coffee cup off the table between us. "What have you got for us?"

I reach for my bag and remove the plans I worked so hard on last night.

I prop the artist's notebook on my thighs and open it to where I made my rudimentary drawings. "I'm no artist, as you can see." I grin at Beau, and try damn hard not to look at Wes. "But these are a few ideas I came up with after visiting with some ladies in town last night."

"Tourism would benefit this town, and here's how I'm thinking we could create a place people in Sierra Grande would use, and create a tourist attraction at the same time. This," I point at the first drawing, "is the main attraction. An upscale version of the Bar N. No offense to the operator, of course, because an establishment like the Bar N has its place."

Deep, rich laughter breaks through my spiel. Beau holds a forearm over his stomach and chortles like Santa Claus. Beside him, Wes smirks in this obnoxiously sexy way.

"Did I say something wrong?" I ask tentatively.

"Establishment," Beau says around his laughter. "You called that shithole of a bar an *establishment*."

Relief turns up the corners of my mouth. Thank God I didn't offend him.

"Just be honest, Dakota, and call the place what it is," Beau instructs.

"Fine," I respond, laughter bubbling in my throat. "It's a shithole."

Wes's smirk turns into a deep, rumbling chuckle. Beside me, I feel my dad laugh.

Beau nods, waving his hand in my direction. "Okay, now that we've called a spade a spade, please continue."

I look back down to my sketch. "This," I point at the paper, "would be a courtyard in the middle of two restaurants. Maybe one is more casual, and the other a little fancier. It can stock local wine and beer. I did some research and found there's a fairly robust wine country out here, and it would play well to use local products. The entire place could be rented out for weddings, and that's a second revenue stream aside from tourism. Additionally, the property can host a farmer's market and open it up to vendors of the entire Verde Valley."

I pause to catch my breath. In just a few days time, the project has gone from just a piece of property my dad wants to buy to something weirdly personal. I care about these ideas, and the people they would benefit. "Also," I add, "I'm planning on calling it The Orchard. There is a small grove of pecan trees near the back portion of the property, and though they don't look healthy now, I've been learning about how to properly care for them, and I'm confident they just need a little TLC. They're unique to the area, and I want to incorporate them."

Beau captures his chin with his thumb and forefinger and nods slowly. The look on Wes's face is unreadable, and it makes me wonder if he's placed a neutral mask on his face on purpose. Whatever he's feeling, he's hiding it.

Beau's gaze leaves my paper and raises to my dad. "You've got yourself one hell of a daughter."

"Don't I know it," my dad replies, his voice brimming with love and pride.

My shoulders curve forward, as if I can shrink away from

the undeserved praise. Wes frowns, and despite the negative look, I welcome the break in his stoicism.

"Wes?" Beau says, looking at his son.

Wes looks at us. "Mitch." He nods at my dad. "Dakota." His gaze falls over me, and there's something about it that makes my stomach coil in anticipation. "We'd like to sell the property to you."

A giant smile breaks out on my face, and if I'm supposed to be handling this win in a more professional manner, I'm failing miserably.

"We like your plans, Dakota, and the care that you're showing to Sierra Grande and the Verde Valley as a whole." Respect comes through in Beau's gaze, and it's the first time I feel like maybe, just maybe, I've earned it. Coming from a man like Beau, someone who doesn't seem like he doles out respect haphazardly, makes me believe that maybe, just maybe, I've earned it.

"Thank you," I answer. "I appreciate it. And I'll make sure the person we assign to come out here and oversee the day-to-day operations understands the level of care expected of them."

Surprise slams onto Wes's face like a tsunami on a deserted beach. "You're not going to be the project manager?"

"Um, no. We'll send someone with a lot of experience who will carry out all my plans, and I already have someone specific in mind," I assure Wes, and then Beau. I don't actually have anybody in mind, but whoever takes over will be fine. My dad doesn't hire half-wits.

"I want you, Dakota." Wes clears his throat and looks at his dad. Beau's eyebrows are raised in Wes's direction. "We, I mean," Wes amends. "We want you."

Beau doesn't say anything, but he knows just like the rest

of us that once this deal goes through, the Haydens have no say-so in how anything goes with the property. This request is based purely on something else. Something that altogether confuses me.

"Dakota," my dad says my name, a pleading edge hidden beneath his tone. I hear what he's not saying. *Nobody has signed on the dotted line, so don't do anything to fuck this up in the final hour.* "What do you think about staying out here to manage the project?"

First I feel panic, but I rein it in by reminding myself that as soon as the sale goes through the property will be owned by my father, and there will essentially be no reason for me to have contact with Wes.

When I don't respond right away, my dad says, "Dakota?"

"I'll consider it," I say quickly, looking at my watch and fighting back the panic. "Gentlemen, we have a flight to catch. And a long drive to the airport. I'll be in touch, but rest assured Sierra Grande will be in great hands no matter who stays here full-time, because I will make certain of that."

I stand, and so does everyone else. My dad shakes Beau's hand across the coffee table, then Wes's. "Usually my firm celebrates by taking the seller out to dinner," my dad tells them. "Once the deal goes through, we'll be back out here to hire a general contractor. Can I take you out to dinner then?"

Both Beau and Wes nod their agreement, then Beau and my dad start for the front door. I replace the notebook in my tote bag and wind my arm through the straps. As I turn to step around the side of the couch, there's a tug on my elbow.

"You're leaving?" Wes asks under his breath, something that sounds a lot like disappointment running through his voice. "Just like that?"

"Yes. The choice should be one you're familiar with." I give him a hard look. He's made it clear he doesn't see me as a one-night stand, but that doesn't completely erase how it felt to wake up alone.

He ignores the remark. "Am I going to see you again?" His voice is low and urgent, and it reaches into that part of me I buried after Barrett.

"Dinner, remember? But, seriously, you let the last five years pass without seeing me, I'm sure you could manage."

It's as if my last two sentences have rolled right off him. He completely ignores my indignation and instead looks at me with eyes loaded with feelings he seems unable to express.

My boiling blood decreases in temperature, and I find myself softening. "I'm considering coming out here full-time, but I'm not sure yet." I don't want to let my dad down, and I really care about what we're going to create in Sierra Grande. I think I'd miss being here to see the small moments as the project progresses, even when I'm keeping tabs on it from afar.

"What's there to think about?" Wes asks. Understanding dawns on his face. "You have a boyfriend, don't you?"

The air changes, becomes thick and charged with electricity, and I think if I licked the air I could taste his jealousy.

"Retract your claws, tiger." I stare into those dark eyes, and the buzzing feeling in the air slips over my skin, covering me until I'm submerged in its current. Like the moment I met him, my decision feels inevitable. "I'll take the role."

"Thank you," Wes murmurs, his face relieved. His hand leaves my elbow and comes to rest on my hip. The pad of his thumb moves up and down, skimming across the fabric of my top.

"Dakota?" my dad calls from the open front door. "We better get going if we want to make our flight."

I glance up into Wes's eyes, then turn to face the two men at the door. My movement forces Wes's thumb to fall away from me, and immediately I miss his touch. "I've decided to stay here," I say to Beau. "I'd like to make sure the building comes to life the way I've told you it will. Once the deal is complete, I'll be back."

Beau looks pleased. "My lawyer will draft the papers and we'll make it a done deal." He switches his gaze to me. "Dakota, every May our family hosts a cookout for the cowboys, and you're certainly welcome to join us since you'll be in town. We can get you the specifics at our dinner."

I shoot Wes a quick glance, tell Beau I'd love to attend, and walk out the door.

Then my dad and I drive to Phoenix, return our rental car, and travel home to Colorado Springs.

WE FIGURED out the logistics on the drive from the airport to my sister's house. This entire next week I will be at home, preparing to live in Sierra Grande for the foreseeable future. As nerve-wracking as it all is, I'm excited. I love living with Abby, but I need my own space. I need to stand on my own two feet, and she doesn't need the added stress of taking care of her wayward little sister anymore.

I'm digging through my purse for house keys when I see the late notices I'd stuffed in there before we left a few days ago. It's a sad fact of life that most problems follow you no matter where you go.

Dad drops me off and I walk into the house, finding Abby in the kitchen, also known as her happy place.

"Hi." She has her back to me and she's sliding a tray of brownies out of the oven. "For me?" I ask over her shoulder. "You shouldn't have."

She blocks me with her side and shakes her head. "They need to cool. Welcome back, by the way." She slides the pan onto the top of the stove. "I got a call for you yesterday," she says, turning around and laying her big sister look on me. "A bill collector."

Which one? I keep the question to myself. She doesn't know how I spend my money. I'm sure she's confused about what I'm doing with what I earn. Certainly not using it to pay her rent.

"I'll take care of it," I answer in what I hope is a nonchalant way. "Probably something of Barrett's that lists me as a contact."

The answer works. She drops it and asks, "How was Sierra Grande?"

I take a seat at the kitchen island and fold my feet underneath me. "Good." I picture Wes's face. "And weird. By the way, Dad says he wants to come over to visit tomorrow."

Abby nods and sticks a finger in the glass bowl with the brownie batter stuck to the sides. "Weird how?" She puts her finger in her mouth and passes the bowl to me.

I do the same as her and lick my finger clean. "Is that healthy?" I ask, pointing at the mostly-empty bowl.

"I'm not telling," she singsongs.

I peer around her at the counter and spot a can of black beans. "For real?"

"Shush. You'd never know it unless you know it." She turns on the water in the sink and rinses her hands. "Now, tell me why Sierra Grande was weird."

"It wasn't the town that was weird so much as the client Dad and I met with."

"Six fingers on one hand?" she guesses.

"No." I laugh.

"Warts on his lips?"

"Ew." I make a face. "Stop guessing, you're terrible at it."

She shrugs. "Continue."

"I had a one-night stand with him a long time ago." According to Wes, it was not a one-night stand, but I beg to differ.

Abby's eyes become the size of dinner plates and her arms flap at her sides. "Lake Guy?"

She's the only person who knows about Wes. And after I told her, I tried to forget about it myself.

"Yeah," I say, the word drawn out. "So, we're buying the land and Dad wants me to oversee the development."

Abby turns serious. "From here, you mean?"

I shake my head. "I'm going to move there temporarily to work."

"Why don't you sound excited? Is it Lake Guy?"

When she calls him Lake Guy, it makes me think of a merman emerging from the water with seaweed dangling from his body. "Wes. His name is Wes."

She nods slowly, as if she approves of the name. "Okay, is it Wes? Are you still attracted to him?"

I nod. It's amazing how that one small motion can confirm something that feels like it could swallow me whole.

"Are you going to start something?"

My head shakes. "He's guarded. It seems like he keeps everyone away. Besides, you know how I feel about men."

She makes a face. Barrett lives in her recent memory just as he does mine.

I tap the center of my bottom lip, thinking. "There's something else about him, though. Like there's a current running underneath everything. Like he's a string pulled taut."

"Wes is a military veteran, right?"

I blink, surprised she remembered that detail. "Yeah."

"Have you considered that he might have PTSD?"

I think back to the night I spent with him, how he opened up just the tiniest amount and his emotions came rushing out. I wonder how much he keeps inside, stuffed to capacity, making it so he cannot take on anything else.

Abby's suggestion rolls around in my mind. "Maybe..."

"When you're around him, do you get a feeling? A sense?"

I get plenty of *feelings* when I'm around Wes, and none of them have anything to do with PTSD. When I'm around Wes, my entire body feels like it's been shocked with electrical voltage.

"Honestly, the only thing I can sense is how much he loves his land and his ranch and his cowboys." I wiggle my eyebrows. "And he can wear a pair of jeans like nobody's business."

Abby cackles and hoots. "I think I might have to get some tight cowboy jeans for Armando."

I crack up thinking of khaki slacks wearing Armando in tight jeans. Abby shoots me a dirty look and pulls over the brownie pan. She presses a finger to the top to see if they're cool enough to slice. They must be, because she cuts them into nine squares and places one on a plate, then slides it to me.

She circles the island and puts an arm around me. "We'll miss you, but I have a feeling you're about to embark on quite the adventure. A hot, tortured cowboy?" She fans herself with her hand.

I roll my eyes, but my stomach flips at the thought of Wes. "Stop."

"I will not," she answers in her big sister voice. She squeezes my shoulders with the arm she has wrapped around me and then releases me. My teeth sink into the brownie at the same time she reaches the back door and opens it, leaning out and yelling, "Brownies, girls."

Emerson and Taylor run in. Taylor gives me a hug, but Emerson hangs back. "You aren't my favorite person this week," she explains.

"Got it," I tell her, winking. She hides her smile behind a cupped hand.

Abby sets two plates with brownies down on the table, then whips around as if a thought has just occurred to her. "Who's going to try my food before I put it on the blog?"

A second bite of the surprisingly delicious brownie is in my mouth, so I cover it with a hand and say, "I'm sure it won't be too hard to convince your husband."

Abby makes a face, then looks around like someone might overhear us, and says, "I like you better."

I laugh, a big belly laugh, and then it nearly devolves into tears, because under my excitement is fear to take on a project so large.

And to think, four days ago my biggest problems were debt and a broken high heel.

For the record, I still have both those problems.

12

WES

THE TRUCK BUMPS ALONG THE WINDING ROAD DOWN FROM THE mountain and into town. At the same time, my fingers on my right hand stamp out a rhythm on my thigh. It's been two weeks since Dakota was here. We signed the purchase agreement and our attorney took care of the rest. The dinner meeting we're headed to now is just icing on the proverbial cake.

"You alright, Wes?" Dad glances over at me from behind the wheel. He's wearing his nice shirt, the one with the pearlescent buttons, and his tan suede cowboy hat. He'd asked my mom to join us, but she was too busy with Warner's kids. Something about 'grandma time.' The woman was tougher than rawhide when we were growing up, but she melts like ice cream in the sun when it comes to her grandbabies.

My hand stills. "I'm fine, Dad."

After a moment, Dad says, "Dakota seems like a good woman. Smart, strong, takes pride in her work."

I prop my elbow on the passenger door and look out the

window. "Are you going somewhere with your commentary?"

"You can be an ass when you want to, you know that?"

I sigh. Of course I know that. I just don't know how to not be one, not when I feel like I'm being pushed. It hasn't escaped my attention, or anybody else who has functioning eyeballs, that Dakota is the whole package. A smug grin fights to break onto my face as I think of the things I know about her that all those other people don't.

Like how impatient she becomes when fingers trail up the inside of her thigh.

I cough and act like I'm adjusting my belt buckle, but what I'm really doing is making more room in the front of my jeans. It's one of many reactions I have to thoughts of Dakota, including the uncomfortable thing my chest does when I think of her. It tightens and loosens at the same time, like it's trying to hold on to the feeling but also relax enough to enjoy it.

"I can't change the stipulations of HCC ownership, Son. Do you ever think about that? About who this place is going to go to if you don't get married?" Stress seeps into his tone.

Fuck, I hate that rule. It's archaic and outdated.

But goddammit, I want the ranch. The dynasty. My birthright. I fell in love with ranching the moment I was old enough to swing my leg over a horse.

The old rule makes me feel controlled, like someone is putting their arms around me from behind and squeezing. One of the things I hate most in this world is being controlled, but in this instance, I don't see a way around it.

"Unless you want the HCC to go to Warner or Wyatt, you'd better get your head in the game and get the fuck over whatever happened to you in the Middle East." His voice is stony, the tanned skin of his face stretched over hard planes.

Is this his idea of tough love?

The thing is, I know he's right. The only thing holding me back is *me*. I'm stunting myself in some form of reparation for *them*. The woman and child I didn't save. The bomb I couldn't deactivate. They haunt me, they live inside me, their terrified expressions slipping out from the cracks in that locked box I keep in my chest. Their blood is on my hands, and I will never forgive myself.

"I'm working on it, Dad." It's all I can say, and it's true. If I can feel for Dakota, maybe I can also feel something inside me besides crushing guilt. She gives me hope. Hope that maybe I won't always have to be a man followed by ghosts.

We're almost to the restaurant, and he doesn't say anything more. Maybe he knows he's pushed me far enough.

He parks, and when I get out I use the privacy I have on my side of the truck to wipe the sweat from my palms. Dakota unnerves me.

I'm rounding the back of the truck when I see Dad reach into his pocket and pull a small medicine bottle from his jeans pocket. He shakes four little white pills into his palm and tosses them in his mouth. I'd be more impressed with his waterless swallow if it didn't worry me. He's had arthritis in his hip for a while, and it seems the longer it goes on the more anti-inflammatories he's popping.

"I don't want to hear it," he growls when he sees me watching him.

"I don't have a damn thing to say," I inform him. Shame gnaws at me. He wouldn't spend so much time in the saddle if I would just fucking get over my shit and get married.

As we walk into the restaurant I have the strangest desire to hug my dad. I can't even think of the last time that happened.

Dad tells the hostess who we're meeting and she leads us to a table where Mitch and Dakota are already seated. They both stand when we approach. She wears a pale purple dress, something that falls to just above her knees and goes up to her collarbone and shows nothing except her arms. I want to laugh at the disappointed feeling inside me, like I'm a child who has been denied a treat.

Dad and Mitch greet each other like the friends they're becoming. Me and Dakota? Not so much. Our hello is awkward. I go in for a half-hug thing and she extends a hand at the same time, so it ends up bumping against my sternum. She apologizes quickly and takes her seat.

I choose the seat next to her and try not to be too obvious when I inhale her delicious scent. Between her perfume and the natural smell of her skin, the mixture is mind-blowing. Over the past two weeks, I picked up my phone to call her a hundred times, but could never quite make myself go through with it. I'm thirty-seven years old and I've done three tours with the Army in the Middle East, but I can't quite pull up the courage to call this woman.

My palms are sweaty again and I surreptitiously wipe them on my cloth napkin underneath the table. "How have you been, Dakota?" I look her directly in the eye for the first time. Her hair is pulled back away from her face and she wears little gold studs that bring out the strawberry color of her hair.

"Good," she answers. "I've been here for a few days, just getting some meetings set up with contractors. My dad flew in this morning so he can help me choose the right contractor for the job. We met with a few different possibilities this afternoon." She glances at her dad. He's already deep in conversation with my dad, and from the snippets of conversation I'm hearing, it sounds like they're talking about elk hunting.

Her posture changes when she sees she's only talking to me, not her dad or my dad. Her shoulders drop away from her ears and she twists the delicate gold band she wears on her pointer finger. "How have you been?" she asks me, looking up into my gaze.

I love how she just softened for me. How she trusts me enough to relax, to be herself.

"I missed you," I tell her, my tone gruff, the words coming out on the louder side of a whisper. What the hell made me say that? I don't know, but I can't take it back. And maybe I don't want to.

Dakota's lips fall open, the tip of her tongue peeking out and pressing against the center of her upper lip. She regards me that way for a second, then says, "These past two weeks? Or the past five years?"

"Hi everyone, thank you for coming into Sierra Steak tonight!" A loud, falsely cheerful voice hacks directly into the center of the moment Dakota and I were sharing. Before it's totally over, I hold up five fingers on one hand. *The past five years*. It's as much a surprise to her as it is to me.

Dakota rips her heated gaze from mine and reluctantly shifts it up to the smiling server. I follow suit, frowning at my ruined opportunity.

Mitch orders a bottle of wine for the table. After that, there are no more opportunities for me and Dakota to have a private conversation. Dakota tells us she is back at the Sierra, but staying in a bigger room at the end of the same floor, and that they're almost certain they've chosen a contractor. Dad tells them about our ranch, not the details anybody could find by conducting an internet search, but the stuff nobody hears about. The struggles with the price of beef, the price of hay, the hunters who trespass (some knowingly and some unknowingly). Mitch talks about how he and his wife built his firm. At the mention of his wife, Rosemary, Dakota shifts in her seat and looks away from the table and out at the restaurant. I'd bet a hundred dollars surveying the landscape is the last thing she's doing right now. There's something else charging through that smart mind of hers, and it doesn't look enjoyable.

"You should bring your wife out with you the next time you come out," my dad suggests, buttering a piece of bread from the basket in the center of the table. "I bet she and Juliette would get along."

Dakota's eyes flash to her dad, and they share a look. "Actually, my wife passed a couple years ago. A brain aneurysm in the middle of the night. It was the second of two. Dakota took care of her after the first one left her in need of help."

"I'm sorry to hear that," my dad says, but to me, his voice is only background noise. I'm watching Dakota.

She blinks, long and heavy, her eyelashes pressing against her skin, and twists the napkin in her lap. When she opens her eyes, she takes her wine glass and drinks twice. Her gaze dances to me, and then away, but it was long enough for me to see the pain inside them. Maybe this is why I'm drawn to her once again. Maybe she carries pain around inside her, too.

The atmosphere is awkward for a few moments, but Mitch steers the conversation back on course. It's obvious he's practiced in this situation. Dakota, however, remains quiet.

Dinner finishes up. My dad reminds Dakota of the barbecue we're hosting next weekend. Mitch orders a round of whiskey neat for the table. Dakota declines. Over her head, Mitch smiles at something near the entrance.

"Hon, I've got a little surprise for you." He grins indulgently at his daughter and looks across the room again.

Confusion cinches together Dakota's eyebrows. She turns to see where he's looking, and her eyes widen.

Following her gaze, the only thing I see are two little girls walking hand in hand with a woman and a man trailing behind them. One of the little girls, the one with long blonde hair, looks directly at our table and her eyes light up.

She runs straight at us and flings herself at Dakota. "You're my favorite person!" she exclaims, her voice high-pitched and sweet.

Dakota laughs and presses a kiss to her temple.

My stomach drops. Does Dakota have a daughter?

Thoughts slam through my brain, ping-ponging around incoherently. My lips remain shut tight except for when I'm introduced to Dakota's sister and her family. I suffer through playing nice with them, when the only person I'm really interested in is the little girl in Dakota's arms.

"And this is Emerson," Mitch says, pointing at the child who has not yet let go of Dakota.

Rage mounts inside me. I sip my whiskey, trying my damnedest to calm down.

Maybe it's not what it looks like. Maybe I'm assuming, letting my imagination run wild.

The little girl, Emerson, turns in Dakota's arms and levels a full stare right at me.

All the muscles in my stomach tighten and my entire world flips upside down.

Or, maybe, the situation is exactly what it looks like.

13

DAKOTA

"My God, Dakota," Abby whisper-hisses as we walk Taylor and Emerson to the hotel room they booked for tonight and tomorrow night. Her lips are so close I can feel the whoosh of her breath against my skin.

"What?" I whisper back. I don't know why we're whispering, but a whispered comment necessitates a whispered response.

"Wes," she mouths, raising her eyebrows and making a face that conveys her appreciation for him. Or, at least, for his physical appearance.

I giggle. I can't help it.

"You're right," she continues to whisper, casting a quick glance behind us to make sure the girls are still skipping together a few feet away. "He is not just a Lake Guy. He's a Wow Guy."

"A Wow Guy?"

She nods solemnly.

"I'm surprised you got that from tonight. He was being even more reserved after you guys showed up." Truthfully, he was borderline rude.

"Nah." Abby waves her hand. "He seemed overwhelmed. And he kept looking at Emerson." She gasps and grabs my forearm. "What if he thinks Emerson is your daughter? She was all over you, and Dad only introduced her by name, not as my daughter specifically." She gasps. "What if he thinks she's his? The age fits."

My amusement fades as I picture his face when Emerson buried her head in my chest. Maybe I mistook shock for rudeness.

"Aw, crap. I'm going to have to call him and explain." I can't imagine what he's feeling right now.

The hand dangling at my side is tugged. I look down and see Emerson staring up at me. "Auntie Dakota, can I sleep with you tonight?"

I look at Abby with alarm. I need to call Wes, and I can't do that with Emerson in my room.

Abby bends down so she's on eye level with Emerson. "Aunt Dakota has a little work to do tonight."

Emerson crosses her arms and stomps her foot in the most classic display of resistance. I purse my lips to keep from laughing.

"How about," I offer, bending down beside my sister, "you fall asleep in your mom's room, and then when I'm done working I'll come get you and put you in my bed? That way," I pause to poke the tip of her nose, "we can wake up together."

"Me too!" Taylor shouts from behind me. I rotate and gather her into my arms.

"Yes, you too, Taylor."

Abby and I stand, and she mouths the words *Thank you* above the girls' heads. We get to her room and Abby opens the door. The girls run in, but she leans on the doorknob and eyes me.

"What?" I ask, weirded out by the look on her face.

"You're... different. He makes you uneasy."

"You say that like it's a good thing."

Her head tips sideways. "I think it might be."

I frown.

"You're stuck, Dakota. You ended a long, unhealthy relationship six months ago, and you think Mom's death is your fault even though it isn't, and I don't know what's going on with your financial situation but collectors are calling looking for you."

My cheeks warm. "I hope your goal isn't to make me feel good about myself, because you really suck at it."

She grins. "All I'm saying is that I think you should give Wes a chance. I don't see what you have to lose."

Abby's probably right, but I don't want to think about it right now.

I say goodnight to Emerson and Taylor, and tell them I'll come get them after they're asleep. "Make sure you and Armando take advantage of a kid-free room tonight," I whisper-hiss.

She rolls her eyes. "Right, after he stayed to have another drink with Dad? Sex is off the table for sure."

I wish her good luck and tell her to text me when the girls are asleep. On my way to my room, I take a detour. I need a drink before I call Wes.

"Whiskey, neat," I tell the bartender. I'm making up for the drink I declined earlier. The first time I tried whiskey was the day I met Wes. Since then, I've developed a taste for it.

He hands me the rocks glass and I take a sip. The liquid burns so good on the way down.

Wes's face plows into my mind. The man confuses the hell out of me. One minute he's reciting for me the details of the day we met, and the next he's withdrawn and growling his words.

I finish my whiskey and release my hair from the low ponytail I'd gathered it in for the meeting. Someone touches my elbow, and my heart leaps into my throat. *Wes.*

I twist in my seat and look into the eyes of a blond, blue-eyed man with wavy hair. Either he has a baby-face, or he's barely twenty-two.

"Can I help you?" I ask, stifling a grin. He's a tad wobbly on his feet.

"I was just wondering if the lady needs a refill?"

"No, I'm okay, but thank you." I actually wouldn't mind another drink, but I prefer to buy it myself. I might be broke, but I know better than to let any guy think him buying me a drink makes me indebted to him.

"Aw, come on," the guy croons, leaning an elbow on the empty bar top beside me. "Just lemme buy you a drink."

"Nope, I'm good." This time I shake my head for emphasis, in case his hearing has been rendered useless by alcohol.

He frowns. "Bitch." He bobs his head as he uses the word, and his eyes are half-lidded.

"Is there a problem here?"

The voice comes from nowhere and everywhere at the same time. It slips over me, shielding me from drunken stupidity.

Wes stands beside me, inserting himself between me and the guy. He smells like man, and body wash, and heaven.

"Don't bother buying her a drink." Dudebro waves his hand around. "She'll tell you no. She's a bitch."

Before I can register what exactly has just happened, Wes has his hand pressed to the side of the guy's head and his head pressed against the bar. "What did you say?" he whispers into his ear.

"Nuh… nothing." The guy squirms.

Wes hauls him up by the back of his shirt. "In Sierra Grande, we treat women like ladies. Apologize to her."

The guy won't look me in the eyes. "Sorry," he stammers.

Wes tosses him off to the side as if he is no more than a used dishrag. The guy stumbles back to his friends, who are all watching with wide eyes. Wes stares them down until they turn away.

"Pricks," Wes mutters. "Who doesn't stand up for their friend?" He motions to the bartender to bring two more, pointing to the empty glass in front of me, the very same empty glass that started that whole mess.

The bartender busies himself pouring our drinks, and Wes pins his gaze to mine. "We need to talk, Dakota."

My adrenaline is still racing from the whole scene, and I can't form a sentence, so I nod.

Wes tosses cash on the bar and picks up the drinks the bartender has set down. He leads us to an empty booth in the corner.

"So," he starts, wrapping his fingers around his glass. "Is Emerson mine?"

I press the pads of my fingers into my eyes and give my pulse a few seconds to slow down.

"No," I answer. "And she's not mine, either. She's my niece."

"I thought…" He trails off, rubbing a palm over his face. He looks at me, and I think I see relief in his eyes, but there's something else in there too, and it stuns me. *Disappointment?* "I had a whole speech planned."

I sip my drink. "You can still give it, if you want."

He smirks. "No, I'm good."

I pout. "Shame. Would've been interesting. Maybe I'd get treated to more hot and cold signals from you. Surely it would have been the source of a little fun."

My words hit home. I both hear and see his sharp intake of breath. Emotion rolls over his face, reminding me of booming thunder and driving rain. Stormy is the perfect way to describe this man. He sets his forearms on the table, and his whole body leans forward with them. The intensity draws me in, the same way a person walks closer to a fire just to feel the heat and watch the lick of flames.

"What do you think I was going to say?" His voice is thick, husky.

"Oh, I don't know. Something like, '*If Emerson is mine, then I want custody.*'"

He shakes his head. "Wrong. I was going to ask you to marry me."

It's a good thing there isn't anything in my mouth right now, because I'd be choking on it. "What?" I sputter.

"I'd want a child of mine to grow up with two parents, the way I did. The way you did."

"Well"—I clear my throat—"Emerson isn't either of ours, so crisis averted."

He nods slowly, sipping his drink. His gaze grows even more intense, and I find myself squirming under it.

"I have a proposition," he murmurs, running the pad of his thumb over his lower lip. "Just hear me out. It's going to sound crazy."

Crazy enough to need a caution? "What?" Trepidation colors my tone.

His head is cocked to the side and he sizes me up, like he's determining if I'm ready to hear what he has to say. "The Hayden Ranch can't be passed down to someone unmarried—"

"I already know that."

He gives me a questioning look.

"I've made friends in this town, remember? And the Haydens are a hot topic."

It's obvious that irritates him.

"Right," he says. "Anyway, I'm thirty-seven and I'm not getting any younger. What if—"

"Are you kidding me right now?"

"Are you going to let me finish a sentence?"

"Not when your sentences are borderline insane."

He has the decency to look at least a little embarrassed. "No, I'm not kidding. My dad is getting older and as of right now he doesn't have someone to pass the HCC on to. I don't know what else to do, and you and I appear to be pretty damn compatible—"

"Ah, yes, the foundation of every good marriage. The appearance of being compatible."

"Five years ago we had something instantly—"

"That you walked away from. Or did you sneak?" I hunch my shoulders and pretend to creep.

"I goddamned cried in front of you." His voice drops low.

"*That* was your reason for ditching me?"

He pinches the bridge of his nose. "Yes."

I throw my hands in the air. "Oh, well, this ought to be fun! Marry a guy who runs at the first hint of vulnerability? Sign me up."

"This arrangement would benefit you, too."

My arms cross in front of me. "How's that?"

"I'll pay off your debt."

The air leaves my lungs. My fingers curl into fists on the tabletop. Anger and mortification fight for primary emotion.

Wes's face takes on a pleading expression. "First off, I'm sorry. I shouldn't have pried into your business. But for a hot second, I thought Emerson may have been mine, and I panicked. I have an Army buddy whose job is to monitor bank accounts for suspicious activity, and I asked him if he could find out anything about you."

An indignant noise slips from my mouth. "So you were gathering intel? This isn't the military, Wes. I'm not your opponent."

He looks at me with apology. "Life is different in families like mine. I have a hundred and fifty years of legacy to protect. If we don't come at every situation on the defense, there wouldn't be a ranch left to fight for."

The corners of my mouth turn down. "That's depressing."

He shrugs. "It's life."

"Are you going to ask me why I'm in that much debt?" My gaze dives to the table. I can't look him in the eyes.

"Wasn't planning on it."

His answer makes me look up. "Why? You think you've invaded my privacy enough for one night?"

"I shouldn't have pried into your business."

"You said that already."

"Well, I meant it."

"Well, I'm not going to marry you."

He finishes his drink and pushes it across the table toward the back of the booth. I watch, dumbfounded, as his hand slides across the table and grazes the inside of my arm. His touch is rough and callused, the hands of a man who spends his days working under an Arizona sky. "Think about it, Dakota. It's mutually beneficial. And it's not like we hate each other."

"Now that you've brought it up, what do we feel for each other? Are confusion tactics another delightful lesson you learned in the military? You send signals most people would understand as attraction, then you take what is supposed to be a sacred institution and make it a business proposal. I can't figure you out."

His face is impassive, and his eyes harden as if guarding a secret. "You don't want a man like me, Dakota."

"That's not for you to decide, Wes."

"I'm a special brand of fucked-up." He speaks with detached certainty, like he's a book that has already been written and the writer has thrown away their pen.

I laugh once, a mirthless sound. "Aren't we all?"

I look into his eyes, and what I see there breaks my heart. He doesn't believe he's worthy of love. It's as simple as that.

Suddenly, I'm exhausted. Maybe it's the whiskey. Or maybe it's Wes. Either way, I'm done. "I need to go back to my room. I have to move two sleeping children into my bed so they can wake up beside me."

One side of Wes's mouth tugs up into a sad smile. "That sounds like a good way to wake up."

I squint at him, willing him to hear what he has just said. That very sentence is exactly what I mean about confusion tactics.

I don't have the energy for more discussion. Instead, I slide from the booth. Wes follows me out to the lobby.

"Will you at least consider my offer?" He looks hopeful, and it strikes me just how much he wants me to say yes.

Seeing this makes me... well, pissed. His mixed signals would make any woman angry.

I reach up, cupping his cheek, my fingers scraping over his coarse five o'clock shadow. His head moves the tiniest degree, leaning into my touch.

"No," I answer, my voice sweet. "And also? Go fuck yourself."

14

WES

"The fuck's wrong with you?" Warner strides across the backyard toward me, his eyebrows pinched together as he studies me.

"Nothing," I grit out, continuing my work of cleaning the grill because the last person who used it was apparently too busy to clean it. I highly doubt the people who come to our annual barbecue want to eat charred bits of who knows what.

"Did the grill hurt your feelings?" Warner asks, grinning as he gets in my face.

I shoulder him away and keep scrubbing. "Unless you want our guests to eat whatever was last cooked on here, shut up and let me clean it."

"I think it's clean, Wes."

He's right. It's clean. But damn, the physical exertion feels good. My nerves are snare-drum tight.

"When was the last time you got laid, Wes?" Warner sinks down into a seat and leans back, his legs stretched out and his hands cradling the back of his head. "By something other than your own hand?"

"Fuck off," I mutter, replacing the lid on the grill.

He shrugs. "Who the hell knows, maybe I will get the fuck off… I hear the gorgeous Dakota is making an appearance today. She can give me a hand."

My head snaps to attention. "I'll use pliers to slowly pull out your fingernails if you go near her."

Warner slaps his thigh and howls with laughter. "I knew it. Wes has a crush."

I stare at him for a second, watching him enjoy this moment too much, then decide against giving him an open palm on the side of the head. Leaving behind his waning laughter, I walk into the house. My mom's standing in the kitchen, mixing up a giant bowl of her famous potato salad.

"Hi, Mom." I pull a beer from the fridge and twist off the cap, bringing it to my lips and drinking deeply.

"What's got your panties in a twist?"

My eyes roll up toward the ceiling and I take one more drink of my beer before lowering my chin. "Why do you think I'm mad?"

She eyes me knowingly. "The way you stomped in here and angrily drank that beer."

"You can't angrily drink a beer," I argue.

She snorts. "Oh yes you can. And you just did."

"I'm fine, Ma."

She passes by me and swats my arm. "If you say so."

I stand at the sink and finish the beer while I look out the large window that faces the backyard, and beyond that, hundreds of acres of Hayden property. I want that land almost as much as I want to see Dakota, which is to say I want it a fucking lot. If she thinks my behavior is confusing, she should be thankful she doesn't have to live inside my body. These days, every thought I have seems to contradict the previous.

My breath sticks in my throat as images of Dakota roll through my mind. That strawberry blonde hair, the fair skin, the way her nose crinkles when she really smiles. I've been in plenty of scary situations in my life, but Dakota strikes a fear deep inside me I've never felt before.

She reaches into a part of me I keep locked away, and for good reason. She makes me lose control, and losing control means *feeling*. I don't want to remember. I don't want to feel. I don't want to experience my last mission. I want to keep it all locked up tight. Dakota is a threat to that desire, and yet I can't force myself to push her away like I should. No, instead I asked her to marry me in the most unromantic and unceremonious way possible. What an asshole.

I finish my beer, toss it in the trash, and leave the kitchen. I stop in the living room and peek out, just to see if Dakota's here yet. She told my dad she'd come, but after last weekend at the bar, I'm not so sure. All week long I wanted to call her, but I've been too chickenshit.

A swing of blonde hair catches my eye. Jessie's out on the front porch, sitting in a chair with her knees pulled up to her chest.

She looks up when I step outside. "Hey, Wes."

Her unlined skin, her scattering of freckles and pimples, remind me of how young she is. When I was seventeen, I was getting shit-faced at desert parties and leading girls to my truck bed for make-out sessions where I would go as far as they would let me. Is that what she's doing? Lying down in some horny teenager's truck when we think she's at her friends' house?

The big brother in me shifts into protective mode. It was okay for me to do that with girls, but it's not okay for my baby sister to be the girl doing that. Because it's just... *not*. Pushing aside that thought, and the realization that many of those girls who laid in my truck bed likely had a protective brother too, I settle down next to Jessie.

"What are you doing out here by yourself?" I ask her.

She gathers her long hair over one shoulder and starts braiding. Instead of answering, she shrugs.

"Right." I nod. "The shrug. A universal teenage response. I believe I was a grunter." I make the sound, deep and low in my throat, and am rewarded with a half-smile from her. "Anything you want to talk about?" I'm hopeful now that I got fifty-percent of a smile. And knowing Calamity Jessie, it could be anything.

She gives me a look of horror, like she can't believe I'd dare to ask her to talk. Her cheeks turn pink, and she shakes her head.

Well, shit. And I thought I was making progress.

In the distance, a car catches my eye. *Dakota*.

It rained during the night and tamped down the dirt, so there's not much dust from the approaching car. I lean forward, watching the car get closer, my heartbeats picking up the pace.

"And here I thought you came out here to talk to me," Jessie says, a smirk the size of our property in her voice.

"I did," I respond, my eyes on Dakota's SUV.

"Keep telling yourself that," Jessie counters, moving her chin back and forth in that sassy way only a teenager can accomplish. I'd probably tweak my neck if I tried that.

The vehicle rolls to a stop. My heart that had been beating so furiously also comes to a stop, like my whole body is holding its breath.

Dakota gets out of the car, her eyes zeroing in on me. She bites down on the side of her lower lip, her chest rising and falling with a deep breath. She stands there, staring at me, and the whole world melts away. It's only me and her and the electricity crackling between us.

Dakota's eyes stay locked on me. I get up from my chair, my eyes falling to the ground for just a moment's reprieve from the intensity.

"She looks gorgeous," Jessie comments wistfully. Somewhere in my brain, I realize I should tell Jessie she is beautiful too, but I have the confusing feeling that I'm underwater. Somehow, in the landlocked state of Arizona, I'm drowning in an ocean.

"I'll be right back," I murmur, walking across the porch and down the stairs.

"Hey," I call out, meeting Dakota halfway between her car and the front steps. She's wearing a dress, something that stops mid-thigh and swishes around her legs when she walks. I swallow hard, trying to get rid of the lump of embarrassment in my throat. She had every right to tell me to go fuck myself.

"Nice to see you again." My tone is too rigid. The words are almost laughable, because they barely skim the surface of how I feel about her.

"You too, Wes."

My chest swells when she says my name. I've never liked the sound of it more than when it slips from between her lips. *Dangerous. So incredibly dangerous.*

I can't help my smirk. "Is it? I believe your last words to me were something along the lines of *go fuck yourself.*"

She shakes her head. "It wasn't 'along those lines'. Those were my exact words." She gives me a sweet but challenging look. "I've had some time to calm down."

"Hi, Dakota!" Jessie's voice breaks through, sailing like a harpoon through the water I'm drowning in.

Dakota waves and smiles. She starts for the porch where

Jessie's leaning a forearm on the railing and trying to rein in her excitement. I fall in step beside her.

"I love your dress," Jessie says as we're climbing the steps.

"Thank you." Dakota runs a hand across her torso. "I stole it from my sister's closet. She'll never miss it." She winks, and Jessie laughs.

"I wish I had a sister." Jessie glances guiltily at me. "Not that having three brothers a million years older than me isn't great, but..."

Dakota places a hand on her shoulder. "I get it. Sisters are something special. Mine came to visit last weekend and I miss her already."

I step forward, opening the front door for Dakota and Jessie. They walk in, and Jessie starts telling Dakota all about school, and the 4H club, and a guy she thinks is cute. She's talking at a lightning-fast pace and saying more to Dakota than she has to me in the past four months.

My mom walks into the living room and says hello. She and Dakota spend two minutes making small talk, but my mom isn't one for trivial exchanges. It's probably why she and my dad have been married for forty years.

Mom motions out to the backyard. "Everyone's out there, Wes. Why don't you take Dakota out back and let your brothers scare her away from Sierra Grande?"

Dakota's worried gaze slides over to me. I chuckle. "Don't worry. What my mom means is that Warner likes to tease, and Wyatt... Well, Wyatt is a bit of an enigma right now. He's still finding his footing in life."

"Needs to find it pretty damn soon," my mom mutters. "Before he finds his ass on the sidewalk with a suitcase beside him."

"She says that once a week," I whisper, leaning in closer

to Dakota. Immediately, I straighten back up. She smells too good for me to be that close to her.

Out back, Warner and Wyatt halt their game of cornhole when they spot Dakota by my side.

"How'd this guy talk you into coming back here?" Warner asks, slinging an arm around me. I fight the urge to push him off.

Dakota smirks. "Your dad invited me."

"Is that your way of saying you're here because my dad asked, not Wes?"

Dakota pins him with a shrewd gaze. She knows he's trying to lure her into saying something about me. Her eyes drop down to his hand and she points. "I haven't met your wife yet. I'm assuming you're married?" Her subject change isn't at all subtle, and I know it's on purpose.

He flinches, just barely, the question as painful as the answer. Not that he'll show it. He lets me go and steps over to Dakota, throwing the same arm that was around my shoulders over hers. "Only by a technicality. You interested?" He points from himself to Dakota with one finger and looks at me. "We look good together, yeah?"

I stare him dead in the eyes, and he laughs. "Can you believe this guy?" he asks Dakota. "So serious all the time."

Her lips purse together and her shoulders shake with suppressed laughter.

My eyebrows lift. "Don't you have a game to play, Warner?"

"Yeah, Warner," Wyatt calls, annoyed. "I need to finish kicking your ass."

Warner makes a face, but Wyatt's threat is enough to get Warner to unwind his arm from around Dakota and stalk away.

"I'm sorry about him," I tell her in a low voice. "He's an ass."

"He means well," Dakota says, shrugging. She watches Warner and Wyatt gather the bean bags from the ground.

With my brothers out of earshot, now's as good a time as any to apologize to her. "About last weekend after dinner—"

"It's fine, Wes. Really. I get it."

Does she though? Does she get that it's not that I think so little of marriage, but that I think so little of myself as a partner? When I was younger, I had big plans to spend four years in the military and then get out and live a normal life. A normal life included marriage and kids. Running this ranch. I could see it all in front of me as if I were following a map. One deviation from the path was all it took to change everything. I didn't want to leave behind men I'd fought with, the friends I made who began to feel more like brothers. I re-upped, and after I'd done it once, it was easy to do again.

It changed me. It took away the man who thought he'd put in his time serving his country and then fade into the civilian world, living the good life of being a husband, a father, and a rancher. It made me what I am now—a man with a beating heart who is capable of feeling love but incapable of letting love penetrate.

Dakota is here, right here in front of me, so close I can run my fingers over her collarbone and kiss her pink lips, a woman who filled my entire world the first time I saw her. I tried to get over the feeling in my chest, the one that told my brain I could never give her what she deserves. I attempted to let her in, to talk about what happened. The result? Tears. Total inability to get past them. I couldn't do it.

The only way I could survive my feelings was to turn away from her, return to the ranch, and work tirelessly. It was an imperfect solution, and that was never clearer to me than it is now.

I know that to solve my problem, I'm going to have to face the even bigger problem I deal with every day. But who would want to? Who would want to go back there? It's bad enough I have to relive it in my nightmares.

As my grandma would've said, I'm stuck between a rock and a hard place.

15

WES

I'M SITTING ON THE OUTDOOR COUCH WITH WARNER AND Wyatt watching the cowboys play horseshoes. My mom, Jessie, and Dakota sit on the opposite couch, talking about something I'm not paying attention to. Judging by the glances Dakota keeps throwing my way, she's not paying attention either. Gramps went inside to take a nap, and Warner's kids play tag in the yard.

"Who wants to be the grill master today?" Dad asks, walking out to the group. In each hand, he carries a tray piled with hotdogs, hamburgers, steak, and chicken. It looks like a lot of food, but the cowboys eat like teenagers.

"Me." I jump up.

"Wasn't aware the couch had an ejector seat," Warner taunts.

I take a tray from my dad. "Feel free to help," I say to Warner. "You too, asshole," I tell Wyatt, pushing against his leg as I go by him. They each get up and follow.

"Language," my mother warns, but it doesn't matter. The kids are at the far end of the yard, screaming and dodging each other.

Wyatt and Warner stand beside me at the grill. Warner gets started on the steak and chicken while I heat the second grill for the hot dogs and hamburgers.

"You know," Warner muses as he places the last chicken breast on the grill. "For someone with a crush the size of a bull, you sure aren't acting like it."

"Wait, what? Who is Wes crushing on?" Wyatt asks.

Warner gives him an irritated look. "Open your whiskey-soaked eyes."

"Fuck you, I'm not drunk," Wyatt responds, obviously hurt. It makes me think maybe his drinking goes deeper than partying. Maybe he's running from something, too. I hide behind the ranch, but maybe Wyatt uses the bottle. Maybe we're not so different.

"You mean you're not drunk *yet*," Warner responds, and I watch anger and shame fall over Wyatt's face like a curtain. Anger wins out, and Wyatt shoves Warner hard in the back. Warner flies forward a couple feet before I catch him. He circles around to go after Wyatt but I get between them. "Not now," I say to Warner, holding my hands against his chest. I turn around to face Wyatt, but I'm addressing both of them. Under my breath, I say, "This is a family fucking picnic you dipshit. There are children here. Knock your shit off before I take you in the barn and beat both of your asses."

Wyatt glares at both of us and stalks away. Warner turns back to the grill like nothing happened.

After a long, quiet minute, he says, "He has a problem, Wes."

"Don't we all," I mutter, adding the hamburgers and hot dogs to the hot grill.

"Fuck, Wes," Warner says in a voice so frustrated it gets my attention. He runs a hand through his hair and takes a deep breath. "You're so damn secretive. Dakota is hot and your chemistry with her is off the charts, but you won't say a damn word about her. You won't talk about what the hell happened to you in the Army, but you get up early every morning and ride Ranger like you're running from something." Warner gives me a hard look, but the bruised feelings are floating right there beneath the frustration. "You came back a different person. Nobody faults you for it, but it would be really damn nice if you trusted someone enough to at least talk about it. And maybe you wouldn't be such an asshole all the time, too."

I don't know what to say to him. He's right, but who the fuck am I supposed to talk to? To understand, you had to have been there. Seen action. Taken fire and feared for your life. I could tell Warner about it until my face turns blue, but he would never really get it.

"Maybe sometime we'll talk, okay? Just not now." It's an olive branch, words that might be empty but are meant to make him feel better. Our eyes meet and I see the brother who used to be my best friend, the one who shared my bedroom until I was twelve and wanted my own space.

He nods and reaches down to open the beer fridge built into the barbecue station. He removes two, twists off the tops, and hands me one. It's a silent acceptance of my olive branch.

My mom has set up three picnic tables on the grass so they are in one long row. Places are set for each person, and each table has bowls of potato salad, chips, baked beans, and all the sauces and fixings a person could want to put on their hot dog and hamburger.

"Dakota," Wyatt calls from across the table. "How's the project going?"

"Well," she answers. "We're breaking ground tomorrow. I

hired a general contractor last week and he moves quickly. The skid steer arrives at six a.m. and we'll start grading out the land." A smile spreads across her face as she talks, and I wonder if she knows it's there.

Wyatt takes a bite of his hamburger. "Are you planning on staying in Sierra Grande to oversee things?"

It hits me that we haven't talked to Wyatt about any of this. These are questions he wouldn't have if we'd discussed stuff with him. To be fair, he's usually drunk, sleeping off the night, or working with the horses. He doesn't have his hand in the day-to-day running of the ranch, nor does he seem to want to.

"As of right now I plan to be here for the summer," she answers, but there's uncertainty in her voice. Her gaze flickers over to me and then back to Wyatt.

"Is that how long you think the project will take?" he asks.

"It will definitely take longer than that. But the bulk of my work will be in the beginning, while we're finding contractors and getting it all started."

"Right." Warner nods, interjecting himself into the conversation. "And when are you and Wes going to admit your feelings for each other?"

Everyone around us freezes except for Jessie. She laughs loudly. I give Warner a dirty look and the mischievous look in his eyes disappears. He thought he was helping me out, as if the problem was that I was shy and needed a nudge to ask out the pretty girl I'm sweet on.

Dakota saves the day, laughing melodically and calling Warner a troublemaker. Conversations resume, but they're stilted. When we're done eating, Warner's kids beg to ride horses. I offer to take them. It's a great excuse to get the hell away from the table.

"Let's go get the horses," I tell Peyton and Charlie, standing up from the table and tossing my napkin on my plate.

We walk to the stable and they talk nonstop about their mom's new house in Phoenix. "It has a pool in the backyard," Peyton boasts.

"With a water slide built into rocks," Charlie adds, his chest puffing out proudly.

"Sounds fun." *And not at all like your mother is trying to buy your love to appease her guilt about blowing up your family.* When they're older, they'll see that. Right now, she's just a cool mom.

I pass Ranger as the three of us walk through the stable and give his face a quick rub on my way by. He's a great horse, but he's not kid-friendly. I need our oldest mares for my niece and nephew.

After I get them ready, I lead Pumpkin and Priscilla out to the round pen. Charlie needs help getting up, but Peyton has no problem fitting her boot into the stirrup and getting her leg over.

I stand back, watching the gentle mares walk the round pen. Despite my annoyance at Warner's comment earlier, I'm feeling happy enough to tip my eyes to the sky and appreciate the beginning of a sunset.

"Are you seeing anything good up there?"

My lips curl involuntarily into a smile at the sound of Dakota's voice, but I tuck it back. She stands a few feet away, a flattened palm over her eyes to shield them from the sun. She comes to stand beside me, propping a foot up on the fence and resting a bent elbow on the top rung. Her chin nestles into her hand and she watches the kids ride. The breeze lifts her hair off her shoulders and swirls it around her face. She laughs at something Peyton says, tipping her head back while her shoulders shake.

I think about the picture we make standing here, limbs propped on the pen. Probably a pretty good one.

Dakota looks over to me. "It's fun to see you with your family. For years whenever I thought of you, I could only picture you at the lake house. Seeing you here paints a better picture of who you are."

My thumb runs the length of my jaw. "You thought of me?"

She shoots me a withering look and gently smacks my arm. "Are you telling me you never thought of me?"

"I—"

"Uncle Wes, I'm bored," Charlie calls.

"Remind me not to take him on a trail ride," I mutter, hoisting myself over the fence and leading Priscilla to the gate. Charlie hops down with my help. I grab hold of the reins and offer them to Dakota. She shakes her head.

"You scared of horses?" I ask, eyebrows raised. It would be nice to find something that ruffles her feathers. She seems so calm and in control all the time. The opposite of me.

"I'm wearing a dress." She pinches the fabric above her belly button and pulls it out from her body.

"Right." I nod. She releases the dress and it floats back to her body.

"You can ride sidesaddle."

She makes a face and shakes her head. "I think I'll skip this time."

Peyton's horse stops a few feet from me and she dismounts. "I'm done, Uncle Wes." She keeps a tight grip on the reins and waits for me to give her instructions.

"Here." I reach for the halter. "I'll put the horses away. You can go on up to the house."

"Your grandpa said he was setting up a projector and movie screen in the backyard," Dakota tells Peyton, pointing over her shoulder toward the house.

"That means ice cream and popcorn." Peyton smiles at Dakota. To me, she says, "Thanks for putting the horses away."

I nod and she turns, heading for the house.

"I'll take one," Dakota offers, stepping into the round pen and taking Priscilla's reins. She leads the horse out and stops, waiting for me.

"I take it you're not scared." Pumpkin and I walk out of the round pen and I stop to close it before continuing on to the stable.

"Of horses? No."

"What are you scared of?" I glance at her from the corner of my eye as we walk.

"Not being a good person."

That's not what I was expecting her to say, especially because she's the best person I know. "I think you're a pretty good person."

"Was he fun like that when you were a kid?"

I blink, confused by the abrupt subject change. "Who?"

"Your dad. Did he set up projectors for outdoor movies and serve ice cream and popcorn?"

I make a grunting sound in the back of my throat. "Hardly. He worked us. We were up doing chores before school, and our summers weren't spent traveling, that's for damn sure."

"That's what dads do, you know? Turn soft when they become grandparents."

"Is that right?" We reach the stable and I walk in ahead

of Dakota. I lead Pumpkin into her stall and do the same with Priscilla.

"My dad was really strict when my sister and I were growing up." Dakota grabs a brush from the tack hanger on the wall and steps into Priscilla's stall. She holds the brush in the air and looks at me. "May I?"

I nod, remembering the night we spent together and the few things she'd revealed to me about feeling guilty for being away from her parents. She brushes the horse using slow, rhythmic strokes. I'm about to tell her I get the feeling she has spent time around horses when she starts talking again.

"My dad was so strict that I left home at eighteen." Her gaze flickers over me. "I still went to college, but I lived with friends. I loved my parents, but I just couldn't handle how tightly he tried to hold on to me. The more I wanted freedom, the less inclined he was to give it. It broke my mom's heart when I left, but they were a package deal, and I just wanted *out*. I did my own thing for a long time, only seeing them every so often. The longer I was gone, the harder it was to return." She meets my eyes, then resumes grooming. "Eventually I met you, and a few days later, I went home. I decided it was time to get my shit together and be a real daughter." Tears shine in her eyes. "But I never got to, not really. I showed up to find my mom had suffered an aneurysm two days prior, and she was never the same again. I cut all ties to the life I was living, and moved back home to take care of her. As much as I could, anyway. I wanted so badly to make up for what I did to her." She looks up at me. "Did you know stress can contribute to aneurysms?" She shakes her head sadly. "Well, I managed to give her plenty of stress."

"It's not your fault that happened to her." I can see the regret assailing her, and I wish I could take it away.

She gives me a sad look. "You don't know that."

"I'm about as certain you didn't cause it as you are that you did."

She frowns at me, but I see gratefulness in her eyes. "How about you, Wes?"

"What about me?"

She replaces the brush on the tack hanger and steps from the stall, closing it behind her. "What's in here"—she taps lightly on the center of my chest—"that's giving you so much trouble?"

My mouth goes dry. My weight shifts. "Nothing," I say, my voice like sandpaper.

Her eyes fall.

I have the overwhelming urge to tell her, to split open my chest and release all the painful memories. "Dakota, I—"

"Wes!" Wyatt runs in. His eyes are terrified. "It's Dad. He... he just..." He shakes his head, lowering his hands to his knees and sucking in a deep breath. "He was playing catch with the kids and he said he wasn't feeling well. He sat down on the couch and then he fell over. Wes, he fucking fell over."

Fear grips me instantly, but I make it a point to remain calm as I walk over to Wyatt. An emergency situation is hindered by hysteria. Placing my hands on his shoulders, I lift him until he's standing upright. His eyes are wide and his skin is flushed. It reminds me of when he was six and terrified of how quiet the ranch was at night. Mom had to put a sound machine in his room to soothe him.

"Has anybody called 911?" I ask.

"Warner did. Mom was still on the phone with the operator when I left to run over here." Wyatt looks at me with pleading eyes. He needs me to be the big brother, to assure him Dad will be fine.

And that's exactly what I do. "Dad is too ornery to die, Wyatt, okay? So don't go worrying about that. It might even be extreme heartburn. That can sometimes mimic the signs of a heart attack." My own chest is tightening up right now, just thinking of a life without my dad. But I won't allow myself to think that way.

Wyatt nods, more composed now. "Okay, yeah."

I turn my brother around. "Let's go." I start off in a steady jog toward the homestead. I look over my shoulder when I get closer and only see Wyatt behind me. I glance left and catch sight of Dakota's figure in the diminishing light. She's going toward her car.

I yell her name and she looks at me. "I'll be here," she yells back, pointing at her car.

I nod my understanding and turn back to the house. I take the steps two at a time and rush through the front door. My gaze locks in on my dad, leaning back on the living room sofa, his gaze fixed on the ceiling. He's not clutching his chest or moaning in pain, not the way you see on TV. My mom sits beside him, body turned so she's facing him, a phone balanced on her thigh. The screen is lit up with an active call, but the line is quiet.

"Mom," I hurry over.

She swings her fearful gaze up to me. "Wes," she whispers.

"It's okay, Mom. Dad, I'm here."

His eyes flicker my direction but his head remains upturned. "I know, Wes." His voice is choppy. "I can still hear."

I chuckle and look at Wyatt. "See what I mean? Too ornery to die."

For a brief moment, my comment brings a small smile to my mom's face, but it quickly disappears. I open my mouth to say something but I stop, halted by a distant, rhythmic chuffing sound of helicopter blades. I know it's not a Blackhawk, but for the briefest moment, that's what I think of. The sound is unforgettable.

The dispatcher's voice fills the air. "Ma'am, the helicopter is four minutes out. Did you give him the aspirin?"

"Yes. Thank you," my mom says, stress outlining her words.

A lot of being in the military is waiting. *Hurry up and wait*, we liked to say. But none of the waiting I've done before compares to these four minutes. Every second is an hour.

"Where's Gramps?" I ask, looking around.

"He took Jessie out back. Or maybe Jessie took him." Mom pinches the bridge of her nose. "Your father didn't want either of them here."

I frown. We're family, and no matter how scary something is, family sticks together. I'm sure in the moment when everything was first happening, everybody bent over backward to keep my dad's stress as low as possible.

"Warner with the kids then?"

Mom nods. I glance at Wyatt. He's sitting in the chair across from my parents, his head in his hands. The whirring of the blades is close now.

"I'm going outside," I announce as I head out of the living room.

The helicopter is white with the red medical symbol on the body. It looms large in the sky, getting bigger and bigger as it drops lower and lower.

Dakota leans against her car, her long hair whipping around and her hand tented above her eyes, watching the chopper land. Our eyes meet, and I have the sudden urge to rush to her, to pull her body against mine and hold her close. To let her hold me. I'm much more scared than I'm letting on.

The bird sets down, and two flight paramedics hop out. One carries an aid bag, and they both turn back around to haul out a stretcher. We all start into a jog, and I meet them halfway.

I speak first. "Male, sixty-seven, possible myocardial infarction. Awake and responsive." Pertinent information, no greeting. I spent enough time around medics to know the basics. One of them glances at me briefly, surprised, but all she says is, "Where is he?"

I lead them to my dad, then grab my mom's hand and pull her back so the paramedics can do their job. One takes his pulse while the other starts oxygen. They position the stretcher, then ask me and Wyatt for help to get him on. We follow their directions, lifting carefully, and Dad doesn't even fight the help, which tells me he's in more pain than he's admitting. The four of us position ourselves at each corner and carry him out front. We pause when we've cleared the steps, and one paramedic releases the wheels. She and her partner take over then, rolling my dad forward in a hurry and yelling back to us, "He's headed to Sedona General."

"Go tell Mom," I instruct Wyatt. He runs inside. I watch the bird lift into the sky, clear the tree line, and turn. Before long, it's out of sight.

Dakota stands beside her car, in the same exact spot, as if she's glued down. When our eyes meet, she pushes off and comes to me.

"Is there anything I can do, Wes?"

That feeling I had before, where I wanted to hold her and be held by her? I give in to it now. Her surprised gasp fills the air as I pull her in. Her body is tense for a second and then she melts. Her arms wrap around my back and she hugs me tightly.

It's not until this moment that I remember Dakota has been through this. She has felt this fear. She understands. She doesn't tell me it will be okay, because she knows it might not be.

"Wes?" My mom's voice comes from the front door. Dakota and I break apart and I look at my mom. She's standing with a small bag looped over one shoulder, and her purse in her other hand. "Will you drive me to Sedona?"

I can't remember a time when my mom has asked me to drive her anywhere. It's general knowledge on the ranch that if you're driving with my mom, you're the passenger.

"Of course, Mom." I dig into the front pocket of my jeans and come away with my keys. "Let's go."

Dakota backs away to her car. "Keep me updated?" she asks, pausing in the open door. I nod at her. She drives off, taillights shining.

Mom climbs in the front of my truck, Warner, Wyatt, and Jessie in the back. Gramps is staying behind with Warner's kids.

It's an hour drive from here to the hospital, and we're quiet the entire way.

If I had to guess, I'd say every one of us is busy having a conversation with God.

16

DAKOTA

I've checked my phone no fewer than two dozen times since I woke up this morning. I haven't heard from Wes. I've been reminding myself that no news is good news, but the prolonged silence makes me nervous.

I made it to the jobsite first. Scott, the general contractor I hired, pulled in ten minutes after me. We went over the projected timeline and drank our store-bought, extra-large coffees.

Thanks to the mostly flat landscape, the site preparation should be relatively easy. It has allowed us to rely on a skid steer to prepare the site and avoid using an excavator.

The skid steer operator was late but Scott advised me not to say anything because not everyone can operate the machine and since we'd only need him for this narrow window on a month-long job, it was best not to look at my watch anymore.

So instead of looking at my watch, I checked my phone for news on Beau. Of course, looking at the phone also informed me of the time, but I ignored it. The operator eventually arrived. He's been working for a few hours, and making progress. So much of the land is already clear of desert debris.

A few hours later, I'm talking with Scott when my phone rings. I hold up a finger, telling him to hang on a moment, and answer. It's an unknown number, but I'm hoping it's Wes. He could be calling from the hospital or someone else's phone.

"Hello?" I answer with restless anticipation.

"May I please speak with Dakota Wright?"

The air whooshes out of me. Avoiding Scott's gaze, I reply, "You are."

"This is a representative from a collection agency. I'm calling on behalf of City Urgent Care. Multiple attempts to collect a debt have failed, and—"

"Sorry," I blurt. "I think you have the wrong number." I end the call and shrug at Scott.

Scott has a knowing look on his face. "Someone named Tim must've had my number before me because I get calls for him constantly."

I chuckle. "And of course it happens when I'm waiting for an important call. Anyway, what were you asking me?" I halfway listen to Scott, and the other half of my thoughts are busy with the collector's call. Near the end of my relationship with Barrett, a quadruple sinus infection sent me to urgent care. Barrett had said he was going to pay the bill, but that pesky little situation where I found out he was married put the kibosh on that. And urgent care without insurance? Turns out it's expensive. I got paid last Friday, so I can pay the bill, but it will leave me with so little in my account after the charity payments go through. And that's where using my credit cards to live on comes into the depressing equation.

The rest of the afternoon passes without a word from Wes. On the bright side, the future home of The Orchard now looks like it can house more than dried desert grass and scrubby brush.

The crew knocks off for the day, and I decide not to risk my barely passable credit score by ignoring the urgent care bill any longer. I sit in my car and pay the bill on my phone, watching the crew drive out as the payment processes. It feels freeing to cross it off my mental list of bills to pay, but when I think of how long that list is, nothing but depression fills me. Hacking away at my debt is going to be like using a pointed nail file to chip away at a boulder. I know what I have to do, but doing it feels next to impossible.

Tossing my phone in my purse, I start up my car and head off the jobsite. I pause at the turn-off. I can go left to town, or right toward the Hayden Ranch.

My car swings right, as if it made the choice for me. It won't hurt to stop by and just see if Wes's truck is out front. If it's not, it's safe to assume he's still at the hospital. I won't knock on the door and bother anybody. If he's not there, I'll call him.

I pause near the dirt turn-off for the Hayden Ranch, my car idling parallel to the metal arch with the HCC insignia. Tenting my hand over my eyes, I look for a truck parked out front. I see three, but it's hard to know if one of them is Wes's because they're all the same. Probably HCC issued. I'm going to have to drive up.

I take the half-mile drive at a slow pace, my eyes peeled for Wes. Nobody is out, and it's eerie, as if what happened to Beau has thrown a wrench into moving parts.

I'm about to turn around when I see him. Shadowed by a stone pillar, Wes leans against the porch railing, his eyes on my car. In his hand is a tumbler. Based on the amber color of the liquid, I'm guessing it's whiskey. Our eyes meet and he does a cowboy nod. The expression on his face is fathomless. He chucks his chin to the side, an invitation.

I throw my car in park and climb out. I stop a few feet shy of him. "How's your dad?"

His jaw tenses and he sips from his glass. "I just got home a few minutes ago and I was about to call you. He had a bypass this morning. You wouldn't know it, though. He came out of surgery and told me to get my ass back to the ranch." His thumb strokes the side of his glass. "He said somebody needs to be here running this place."

The lost look on Wes's face makes me want to wrap my arms around him. "I'm glad he's going to be okay."

He grunts. "I think we have different versions of okay. He's not going to be able to run the ranch after this. The surgeon said he needs to stop." A hand rakes through his already messy hair. Something tells me it's been a well-traveled path over the past eighteen hours. "And then his cardiologist, who I didn't even know he had, showed up and said he'd advised him to stop running it two years ago. Apparently he had a stent put in back then and the only person who knew was my mom." Wes finishes his whiskey and retreats to a set of chairs.

I follow, sitting in the chair next to him. "What happens now?"

Wes's head moves slowly back and forth, eyes downcast. "I don't know."

The invisible armor Wes usually wears is absent. On his face I see the brokenness that exists inside him and it rips my heart to shreds. I want to run my hands over his skin, spreading them over him like a magic elixir, bringing healing to his deepest wounds.

"Wes," I say his name softly.

"Dakota." My name on his lips is rough, callused like his hands.

"I've been doing some thinking." A deep breath fills my lungs, and I let it out noisily. All night I turned Wes's suggestion over and over in my head until I nearly made myself sick. Round and round I went, and I kept coming back to the same conclusion. Here goes... "If your offer still stands, I'd like to take you up on it."

His head snaps up. He's quiet. Each second that passes feels like a minute. "You mean, marriage?"

"Yes." This single word weighs much more than I thought it would now that I'm here and saying it out loud to Wes. As it is, I still can't believe I've changed my mind. As soon as he left the hotel bar that night I began to turn the idea over in my brain. The more the surprise of his offer wore off, the more I could see just how mutually beneficial it could be.

He gets the ranch.

I get a clean slate. I can start from zero.

"You don't have to do that, Dakota."

"I know I don't *have* to. But I see the practicality of it. We both get what we want."

The side of his steepled hands press against his lips. "True," he says slowly. "So, that's it then? We're going to get married?"

I feel a small stab in my heart. As a child, I didn't spend a lot of time dreaming of my happily ever after. That was more Abby. So why is it that I'm feeling more than just a twinge of regret in my chest? I push it away and tip up my chin. "I suppose so, but we should discuss the parameters."

"Parameters?"

"Yeah. The rules. How long are we supposed to be married? What happens if one of us develops feelings for the other? How do we take care of our more…" I pause to search for the right words. "*Primal* needs?"

"I hadn't thought of any of that before I brought it up."

"Seriously?"

He scowls. "The criteria of a marriage of convenience hasn't been sitting around in my brain, just waiting to be pulled up for use."

"No? Weird."

He gives me a dirty look, but even his dirty look is more brooding and sexier than what is really necessary, and I'm entirely positive he doesn't even know it. "We need to hammer out details, Wes. Otherwise, this won't work."

"I don't know, Dakota." The stress rolls off him. "I guess I didn't really think it through. I thought marriage would solve my problem, and you had a problem I could help with, too—"

"I'm still not happy you violated my privacy."

"And I'm still sorry I did it." He holds up his hands in a request for forgiveness.

I blow out a breath. "Whatever. It's over. Let's move on to how the hell this is all supposed to work out."

Wes rubs his eyes. "As for how long we're supposed to be married, I guess I just assumed marriage is a forever kind of thing."

I twirl the small pendant on my necklace as his words sink in. He would sign up for forever with me? "Marriage might be a 'forever kind of thing' for those who go the normal route. You know, falling in love, getting engaged, then taking a trip down the aisle. But what about us? You want to be married to someone you don't love for the rest of your life?"

He gives me a side-eye. "Dakota, the relationship progression you're describing isn't in the cards for me."

"What about being married to someone you don't love? That doesn't bother you?"

"Yes. No. Shit, maybe." He sighs. "Look, Dakota, I don't know. I can't tell you what the future holds, but I know that I wouldn't have asked you to do this with me if I thought you were a bad partner. We had something once, and if there's anybody I'd marry, even if it's in this crazy way, it'd be you."

There was a time when I'd laugh at a conversation like this, but that was before I learned harsh truths. People take vows and mean them, and then cheat. People take vows and mean them, and then marriage itself is the cheater. My dad signed up for a lifetime with my mom. He got thirty-two years and even though he puts on a brave face, I see sadness in his eyes every single day. From what I can tell, you can go into marriage with all the good intentions in the world and still wind up screwed one way or the other.

I might be disenchanted with marriage, but I can't give it away altogether. "One year, Wes. I'll give you one year."

A terse nod is his response. He looks like he can't take any more of this. He offers his hand across the small table separating our chairs. His dark brown eyes locked on mine, he asks, "Do we have a deal?"

"A handshake?" I ask, looking disbelievingly at his outstretched palm. "Shouldn't we have something a little more official, like a contract?"

"In my world, there isn't anything more binding than a handshake. A man's word is his honor."

I look into his determined eyes and, for a second, I consider bounding away like a frightened deer. But then I think of the insufficient funds notices clogging up my email. My warm palm presses against his. The buzzing starts up, and I push it away. We're officially business partners.

I drop his hand. "How is this all going to go?"

"Well." Wes captures his lower lip between two fingers and pinches while he thinks. "We should let everyone think we're dating for a short time. Make them think we're hot and heavy, whirlwind courtship, soul mates, all that."

"I feel like I should tell you that I'm not the greatest actress."

"Me neither, but we'll figure it out." His lips quirk up. "In two weeks we'll announce we're getting married."

Whoa. Apparently to Wes, a 'short time' is two weeks. "Don't make it sound so romantic. I might swoon." My voice is flat and dry. "You don't think your family will have a problem with our 'whirlwind courtship'?" I make air quotes.

"They'll be shocked, but they'll get over it."

"Okay." I cross my arms in front of myself in an attempt to dispel the discomfort I'm feeling at how apathetically we're discussing something that is supposed to be special. I might be disenchanted with the institution, but a small part of me must still believe in it.

Wes stares at me, and I stare back.

I need to steer us into safer territory, pronto. "When does your dad get to come home?"

"Maybe a week? I'm not sure." He yawns as he speaks.

He probably didn't get any sleep last night. I need to leave anyway. I have my own dinner to eat and an email to send my dad about our progress today. But I am most definitely not telling him about my deal with Wes. Not yet, anyway.

I stand up, and Wes does too. Movement in the front window catches my eye. Jessie waves. I wave back and spot Warner and Wyatt sitting in the living room.

"We have interested eyes," I murmur, and he chuckles.

"So we do. No time like the present, I guess." Wes palms my lower back as he walks me out. Warmth spreads through me. It feels like his hand was always meant to be there, which is really annoying because it's only there for the benefit of people who are almost definitely peeking out of the window watching us.

I look up and my breath sticks in my throat. The sun set while we were talking and now stars blanket the dark sky, shimmering like the sunlight on the lake the day we met.

"I know," he murmurs. "Stunning, isn't it? Light pollution doesn't exist out here."

We reach my car and I stop, turning back to look at him. "For the record, I can see why you love this ranch. I understand why you're willing to marry for it."

His face is partially illuminated by the light shining through the large front windows. "It's easy to be fooled by the beauty of a night sky, or the sunrise behind the steam curling up from your morning coffee. Loving the ranch doesn't come from those experiences. Loving the ranch comes from the hardships she puts you through. The dust, the mud, the blistered hands, the aching back from spending a day in the saddle. Never knowing what she's going to put you through next. She's beautiful and unpredictable. She'll knock you flat on your ass and make you fall in love with her on the way down."

A strand of hair blows across my lips and he tucks it back, leaving his fingertips against the space just below my ear. My breath hitches, but it only serves to madden me. His touch is a ruse, and I need to start remembering that.

"That's a lot of human traits for an inanimate object," I say, my voice stilted.

He smirks. "She's not inanimate. Just look." He turns me around suddenly and steps into me, catching me with his body and giving me a place to steady myself. He keeps one hand on my hip and his face over my shoulder. Pointing, he says, "Look at her move. Blades of grass swaying in the breeze. Cottonwood leaves shifting." In the stable, a horse whinnies.

My eyes close and I feel the breeze, and the man pressed against me. Just this once, and then I'll stop. But, wait… all this touching me gently and pressing against me, is just an act. And since I'm supposed to be selling our new relationship…

"Wes?"

"Hmmm," he rumbles, and I feel it everywhere.

I spin around, and I'm still in his arms. "We're going to have to start hanging out immediately."

He tenses, then relaxes. "Right."

"As in, tomorrow night. And every night, if you want it to be believable."

"I can come by after work and get you. We'll go somewhere to eat."

It's the most depressing planning for a first date in the history of first dates. But I mean, really, how exciting do I expect it to be?

The curtain moves again. Wes's back is to the house, and he's so big he covers me completely. I let my arms run up his back and into his hair and press my lips to the space right beside his mouth. Whoever is watching will think we're kissing. When Wes walks back in there, he'll be answering some questions.

"Dakota?" His voice is low, asking for me to explain why I'm mauling him this way.

"We have an audience," I explain.

He clears his throat. "Right."

I end our fake embrace and open my car door. I'm lifting one foot into the car when his hand encircles my wrist and pulls me into him.

He doesn't say a word, but he doesn't have to. His lips brush over mine, and though they are barely touching the electrical current is there. I drag my lips away to suck in a much-needed breath.

"We might as well give them something good to ask me about when I walk back in there." He lets me go as suddenly as he seized me.

I climb into the car, feeling frazzled. Frankly, I feel like I was just grabbed and kissed. Oh wait, I was.

Before I close the door, he says, "I'll see you tomorrow."

My body flares with excitement, but I'm careful not to show it.

When I've driven far enough away from the house, I let out a wild yell to release some of the adrenaline, then I laugh like a howling, deranged coyote.

I'm in bed in my hotel room when I get a text from Wes.

It worked. My brothers and sister were all over me.

I grab my phone and type out a response. ***Excellent. We should come up with a name for our plan. Operation...???***

The typing dots appear. The typing dots disappear. Appear. Finally his message comes through. ***Do we have to?***

It took all that time for him to decide on those four words? ***Too military?*** I ask.

And that's the end of our conversation. I fall asleep to the thought of what my family is going to say when I tell them.

17

DAKOTA

Here's what I thought would happen: I tell Abby I'm soon-to-be-engaged to the Lake Guy aka the Wow Guy and then she vomits whatever sneakily healthy recipe she's working on while simultaneously trying to keep her bulging eyeballs in her head.

But, no.

I've just called Abby to tell her I'm going to marry Wes and she's silent. The silence stretches on for so long that I grab my phone from where it sits in my center console and steal a glance while I drive, just to make certain she's still on the line.

"Uh, Ab?"

"Processing," she answers.

I deposit the phone back into the cupholder and wait, my lips pursed. Finally, she exhales slowly.

"You're going to get engaged to Wes after you speed date for two weeks?"

"Yes."

"Please help me understand."

I blow out a noisy breath. Something warm spreads

through my chest cavity. A pinch of embarrassment, a dash of shame, maybe a couple shakes of reluctance. "He needs to take over the ranch because his dad just had a heart attack, but he can't do it without a wife. I—"

"Why does he need a wife?" I can tell just by her tone that her face is scrunched in judgy disbelief.

"Archaic family rule. Outdated or not, a rule is still a rule."

"And this is where you come in?"

"Yes."

"What are you getting out of this? Because I know it's not a happily ever after."

I bristle. "Not everyone pins their future on the idea of a happily ever after."

"Is this because of Barrett?" She's using her exasperated big sister voice. "Just because he broke your heart and disrespected his own marriage doesn't mean the institution is worthless."

I don't blame her for the question, even if it does irritate me. I haven't spent a single second thinking about Barrett since I arrived in Sierra Grande. "I'm getting something out of it, too."

"And what would that be?"

"I'm in debt and Wes is going to pay it off."

Silence again. I pull into the parking lot of the meeting I have this morning. I'm pretty excited to pick out tiles for the restaurant. I'm a few minutes early, though, so I can keep talking.

"Clearly you're shocked," I say, flipping open the visor and checking my makeup in the mirror.

"Actually, no. I'm the one who hands you your mail and fields phone calls from collectors. It wasn't hard to put two and two together. I think what would shock me is hearing how it happened, because I don't see you running around wearing Cartier and Louis Vuitton."

I don't want to tell her. I'm embarrassed. But she's my sister, and she's worried. "I donate most of my income to two charities, and before you say anything, I know it's foolish. I know I need to stop."

"Oh, Dakota. Are you serious?" Abby's voice is softened with pity, and I don't like the sound of it. "What charities?"

"A local women's shelter and The Aneurysm Foundation."

Abby sighs. Loudly. "And does it make you feel any better? Going into debt so that you can give to these causes?"

I look out the window at the pavement and say, "No."

"Does Dad know?"

"Of course not."

"Why don't you tell him? I'm sure he'd help you out."

"I don't want to need Dad's help."

"Whether you *want* to or not, you do."

"I've found a way out of it on my own."

"Right. By marrying someone you don't love."

"Marriage wasn't about love until the mid-nineteenth century, Abby. The Greeks saw lovesickness as a type of insanity and modern-day Tibetan Ma women raise children without active fathers. Also—"

"Stop, stop. I know what you're doing. And as much as I hate it, I'm really curious about how you know all that."

"I took a class on it at a community college when I was nineteen."

"Of course you did. So." I picture her placing her phone in the stand she keeps in her kitchen and leaning her forearms on the countertop. "You're going to marry Wow Guy?"

I blink out at the red brick warehouse. "Better than marrying Underwhelming Guy."

Abby snorts. "I suppose so."

I look at my watch. Nine fifty-seven. My meeting starts at ten. "I have to get going, Ab."

"Just tell me you'll rethink the donations? If you're unwilling to cancel them, maybe decrease their amount?"

"I will." I'll have to, unless I want to find myself in this situation again somewhere down the line.

We say goodbye, and just as I'm reaching for my phone to end the call, Abby says my name softly.

"Yeah?"

"Do you know what you're doing, Dakota?"

"I'll be fine, Abby. Promise."

We hang up and I head toward the front entrance, my mind stuck on Abby's final question.

Does anybody ever really know what they're doing? From what I can tell, whether people admit it or not, most everybody is just winging it. Life, love, parenting, careers, happiness… we're all just doing the best we can.

I push my impending marriage sham out of my mind and pull open the glass front door, offering my winningest smile to the receptionist. She's older, her chestnut hair streaked through with gray, and she wears dangly feather earrings.

"Hi, I'm Dakota Wright. I have a meeting with Daryl."

"He's expecting you, honey. Come on, I'll take you back." She stands up from her desk, and I see what can only be the names of all her grandkids on the front of her light blue T-shirt. Without being a weirdo and staring at her chest to count, I'd guess there are seven or eight names. She steps in front of me to lead me down a small hall. The back of her shirt reads *#1 Grandma*.

I follow her into the warehouse. It smells industrial, but I can't make out any specific scent.

She stops short and shouts, "Daryl, Dakota's here for your meeting."

A man probably about the same age as her steps from an open door off to the side of the space. The receptionist disappears, and Daryl and I introduce ourselves. We talk at length about the project and tile. The entire time we're discussing size and color, Wes lurks on the periphery of my thoughts.

I choose a large herringbone tile in a muted medium green. The aesthetic is modern farmhouse. I haven't picked out lighting yet, but I'm picturing something black and copper.

Daryl shakes my hand after he sends the square footage calculations to his assistant. She'll handle the billing. "I've heard a lot about the new building out there in Sierra Grande. My wife Jean said it's going to be a wedding venue/wine bar/restaurant/picnic area/farmer's market. That's a whole lot of things wrapped into one."

I smile. "I guess so. The chapel is an open-air concept, and can be rented out for weddings, large parties, what have you. The wine bar and restaurant will be open the rest of the time, and there will be space between the two buildings for fun lawn games and lots of outdoor dining. The farmer's market idea is still being worked out, but I'm hoping for one Sunday a month. I want it to be a place for the locals, but also for people from neighboring towns." I shrug, embarrassed but pleased. I love talking about the project and I can get carried away.

"I think that's great." Daryl nods his head excitedly. "To date, the only thing Sierra Grande has been known for is the Hayden Cattle Company. And the oldest Hayden boy was in the paper awhile back, when he returned home from the military. I don't remember specifics, but it was about his service and return home. My wife would remember. She loves personal interest stories." He shakes his head and waves his hand. "Anyway, listen to me rambling. Come on," he touches my elbow as he shows me out of the warehouse and up through to the front.

He goes to stand beside the receptionist seated behind the desk. "We'll be in touch about a more specific timeframe for delivery." As he speaks, he lays a hand on her shoulder, and I notice the nameplate on her desk. *Jean*.

This is exactly why I love this project. Supporting local companies means something to me. I want to support Daryl and Jean and the children who made them grandparents seven or more times.

We say goodbye, and as I round the building, I get a glimpse of Daryl and Jean. She's laughing at something he said, and he brushes a knuckle over her cheek.

An odd feeling starts somewhere in my body, sharp like a prick then turning dull like an ache.

It's not that I want a T-shirt with my grandkids' names on it. But it's not like I don't want it either.

18

WES

As soon as the morning chores are finished, I hop in my truck and drive to Sedona General.

My dad's heart attack shook me more than I've let on. I sat in the waiting room all night long and during his surgery, wide awake, memories of my childhood clipping by. He was tough, but he was loving. He's the reason I can throw a baseball, ride a horse, and deliver a mean uppercut. When someone seems larger than life, being confronted by their mortality is like being struck in the face with a two by four.

Dad's asleep when I get there, but my arrival rouses him. Mom's sitting on the bench seat near his bed, a book open on her lap. I have the urge to rush to my dad, but I don't. The display would embarrass him.

Instead, I touch his shoulder and say, "Got some chores for you when you're ready, old man."

He eyes his IV in disgust. "Please tell me you're here to break me out of this joint."

Mom points a finger at him. "Don't even think about it." To me, she says, "He tried to remove the IV about an hour ago. An alarm went off."

Dad releases a string of expletives. Mom smirks. Her arms cross and she gazes at me with the look that tells me she already knows the answer to what she's about to ask me.

"Jessie called. Got anything you want to tell me?"

I'm a grown-ass man, but right now I'm feeling more like that time in high school when I tried to hide a beer bong in my closet. Dishonesty has never been my strong suit, and I'm about to tell a whopper.

"Dakota and I are dating." *And also soon we're going to get engaged, only to be married soon after that. But you'll learn that in due time.*

Mom's eyes narrow farther. "And?"

"Nothing. I just wanted you guys to know Dakota and I are dating."

"Jessie said you were putting on quite the display in front of the house last night." Her gaze is intense, and I feel myself shrinking. I have to remind myself I'm an adult. For a short woman, her presence is formidable.

Dad makes a face and grumbles, "Your dating life isn't worth this damn drama."

"No, it's not," Mom says slowly, working through it in her mind. "PDA and my son don't go together. So why make certain to be so public?"

"Warner, Wyatt, and Jessie are the public now?"

"Everyone is the public to you," she counters, taking a shot at my tendency to keep everything locked up tight.

Fuck. Why did I think I could pull this off? "I guess we just can't keep our hands to ourselves."

"You two have palpable chemistry, I'll give you that." Mom's head turns back and forth deliberately. "But, that's not it. Why don't you try telling us the truth?"

Dad's head tips to the side and he sighs. "Fucking Christ," he mutters.

I almost laugh, but my mother's stern expression stops me. I have every intention of telling her once again that I'm dating Dakota, but what comes out of my mouth is the truth, because lying to my parents has always been my weak spot.

"I'm going to marry her."

My mom's eyes bulge like the world's strongest man has squeezed around her middle. My dad's face turns serious. He's no longer irritated at being involved in a discussion about my dating life.

"You're planning to marry her, Son?"

I nod.

Mom points a stiff finger near his face. "This is because of you. If it wasn't for that dumbass rule, he wouldn't be trying to marry someone he doesn't love or know—"

"I know her," I interrupt.

Her eyes flash to me. "A few weeks doesn't count."

I shake my head. "Wrong. I met her five years ago in Colorado."

"What?"

"And we—"

I stop at my mom's upraised palm. "I don't want to hear it."

"I was going to say we connected."

She huffs. "Wes, you can't marry someone you *barely* know and don't love just because you want the ranch."

"He's going to have to marry someone sometime, Juliette." Dad's voice is quiet, but strong.

Mom sputters. "I want him to love his wife, Beau. He deserves to be in love."

"Even if he loves the woman he marries, it doesn't guarantee a ride into the sunset. Life is tough, and that includes love."

Mom looks down at the floor, her eyes closed. I've never known them to have marital issues, so I don't think my dad's speaking from experience, but I'm uncomfortable nonetheless.

"I know what I'm doing, guys. I promise."

Mom's head lifts. "What does she get out of it?"

I bristle at her hard tone. "She has a name."

"What does *Dakota* get out of it?"

There's no way I'm sharing Dakota's private financial information, so I shake my head and say, "She wants to help me. And it's not like we don't like each other. I told you—"

"Yes, yes. You connected." She makes air quotes when she says 'connected'.

I go silent. So does my mom. Her arms are crossed and she stares me down. "I'm not happy with this, Wes."

I shrug. "I love you, Mom, but I'm not asking for permission. This is my choice, and I'm making it."

Dad must think we're done here, because he announces that he's going to sleep.

"I need to get back to work," I say to both of them, even though my dad has his eyes closed. "I don't know what your plans are, Mom, but I won't be home for dinner. I'm seeing Dakota."

"What's the point?" Mom asks. "Go to the courthouse now."

"Everyone else thinks we're dating."

"Who cares? Call off the charade."

It's hard to explain, but I don't want my siblings to know. I don't want them to look down on what I'm doing with Dakota, or, worse, be constantly waiting for her to leave like Anna. I want them to believe in us. I want them to see me as the big brother who finally came to his senses and got married.

"No, Mom, and I'd appreciate it if you wouldn't say anything."

She sighs. "Fine." She pretends to lock her lips and toss out the key.

"Thanks." I nod at her. "Do you want a ride back home?"

Mom glances at Dad. "I'm going to stay here tonight, but I'd love fresh clothes and a shower."

She grabs her purse, tucks her book inside, and kisses my dad's forehead. He's either already sleeping or a damn good faker.

On the way out, my mom stops to chat with a nurse. While I wait I pull out my phone and send a text to Dakota telling her my parents know everything.

She's not thrilled, which is understandable. In fact, her exact response is: ***I wish you were kidding.***

Are you having second thoughts? I ask, but she doesn't respond for a few hours.

Wyatt and I are working in the round pen with a horse when her answer comes through.

No. I'll see you tonight?

I type out my confirmation, and Wyatt says, "Quit texting your girlfriend. We have shit to do."

I slip my phone into my back pocket. "Fuck off."

"I'm happy for you, Wes. For real."

I stop in my tracks and look at him. He sounds genuine.

"Thanks, man."

He nods and gets back to what he was doing.

19

DAKOTA

DESPITE WES'S PARENTS KNOWING THE TRUTH, HE WANTS TO keep it from his siblings, and Wes and I agreed to continue on with our two-week whirlwind courtship. So far, it looks like this:

DAY ONE: Wes picks me up at the hotel. We eat dinner at a place just outside of town. I have a burger. Wes has a steak (shocker!). Conversation is weak and I can't figure out why. Wes acts like he didn't just kiss me the night before. I get that it was for the sake of our scheme, but you'd think it would put us smack in the middle of friendly familiarity. Apparently not. He drops me off at the hotel. A minute later he texts me and apologizes for his weird behavior, blaming it on not sleeping well. I tell him to put down his phone and focus on driving.

DAY TWO: We see a movie. No chance for conversation.

. . .

Day Three: Conversation shows real improvement, which might not be saying much because the bar was set pretty low. There was nowhere to go but up. We go to a bar for a drink and Wes tells me funny stories about growing up with two brothers, and says that Jessie was a shock to everybody, especially his parents who miscarried four babies after Wyatt. I feel uncomfortable knowing this personal information about Juliette and Beau, and also my heart hurts for them. When Wes drops me at my hotel, he high-fives me. I feel annoyed. Once upon a time, he was inside me and so the bro-ish behavior feels beneath me.

Day Four: Happening right now.

Wes knocks on my hotel room door and I answer. He's wearing sweats and a T-shirt, and the first thing I think is that it's incredibly unfair how good he looks when he's not even trying.

I step back and he walks in, bringing with him the smell of body wash. A paperback book is tucked under his arm. He settles at the small table in the corner. Behind me, the heavy hotel door closes loudly.

I climb on top of the made bed and sit cross-legged. I'm wearing sweats too, and my hair is piled on top of my head.

"I like what you've done with the place," Wes says, his gaze focused on the wall beside the bed.

I follow his stare to where I've tacked up a map of Sierra Grande and a copy I made of Brandt's blueprints for The Orchard. I've drawn on the blueprint in bright colors, mostly landscaping ideas and games, and a book drop in the shape of a large birdcage. “I took the liberty of appropriating the wall space for my use. I’m sure the hotel won’t mind as long as I put their picture back on the wall when I’m done.” I glance down at the generic picture that used to hang on the wall but now leans against it.

“You did your research,” he says, nodding to a sheet of paper taped to the bottom of the Sierra Grande map.

My chest swells at the pride in his voice, eating up his praise like a kitten lapping milk. I climb off the bed and go to the paper, running my hands over the block letters written in black Sharpie. “I was brainstorming ideas for what to name the project. In my research about Arizona I kept seeing the five C’s of Arizona.” I bounce a fingertip off each C: cotton, copper, cattle, citrus, and climate. “But I couldn’t get the pecan trees out of my head, so I went with The Orchard.”

“The sad-looking pecan trees took precedence over what makes Arizona’s economy?” He asks the question with a smirk, but his tone holds wonder.

“I already told you, those pecan trees are special and I’m not afraid to give them what they need to help them flourish. You see some derelict trees, but I see potential.” I shrug and sit back down on the bed. I’m three minutes late for The Bachelorette, so I grab the remote and turn on the TV.

Wes spends a nanosecond looking at the screen, then rolls his eyes and opens his book.

“Don’t act like you’re too good for this show,” I tell him.

He doesn’t respond, but he does smile. I peek at his book. Grisham. I was expecting Louis L’Amour, which makes me giggle and Wes glances at me. I shake my head at him, indicating *it’s nothing*, and turn my attention back to the TV.

Fifteen minutes in, I catch him watching. "Ohhhh," I tease. "Someone likes the show they acted too good for?"

He frowns like I need my eyes checked and goes back to his book. The next time I catch him watching, I keep the teasing to myself.

We order a pizza, and Wes runs down to the front desk when it arrives. We eat the entire thing. The Bachelorette ends and we move on to Wheel of Fortune. I'm good at the game, but Wes is expert-level. He guesses the word long before any of the contestants.

I throw my last piece of crust in the open pizza box. "So far tonight I've learned you read novels, and should be a contestant on Wheel of Fortune. I feel our relationship is really progressing. We'll be married in no time."

Wes grabs my crust and takes a bite. "Roping and riding aren't my only talents."

"Don't I know it," I say, then realize how sexual that sounded. "I mean... well, I didn't mean to make it sound like..."

Wes laughs at my awkwardness. "I know what you meant."

The show ends and Wes stands, glancing at the digital clock on my nightstand. "It's late enough to go home now."

There's a tug on my heart, like I don't want him to go. I push it away. "Right." I get off the bed and bend over, brushing crumbs from the bedspread.

"Thanks for having me over." He's swiping at the bed too, brushing off crumbs I'm not sure are really there.

I straighten and find he's only a foot away from me. It's the closest he's been to me all night other than when he walked in, and I'm once again hit with the mouthwatering smell coming off him.

"No prob." I dart around him, my voice at least two

octaves higher than it should be. "So, what's the plan for tomorrow?"

"Are you asking me out on a date?"

I huff a sound of playful exasperation. "I suppose so. There's a concert in Desert Oasis park. The one downtown," I add, in case he needs me to explain.

"I know of Desert Oasis Park," he responds with a twinge of agitation in his tone, but he's pretty much saying *I grew up here, remember*?

"Great. Spares me the chore of having to send you directions." I flip him a sassy smile. "Anyway, I've heard it's a big deal. I'll be there, and I'd like you to join me."

He nods once, in that slow cowboy way. "Then I'll be there." The words are as slow as his nod, and a flush warms the back of my neck.

"Great," I say brightly, attempting to cover up his effect on me. "I'll be the one in the red dress."

Wes heads for the door. I follow him.

He pauses in the open doorway. Looks back at me. Brushes a kiss on my cheek. The heat on my neck burns hotter. I feel branded, like one of his cattle. "Thanks for tonight. You're the best almost-fiancée a guy could ask for."

"No prob," I say in my best unaffected voice, but to my ears, it sounds like I'm choking on something.

He leaves, going right instead of left toward the elevator and main staircase. Curious, I watch him disappear through the stairwell door. I've only been that way once, because I didn't want to chat with the front desk person and those stairs empty out to a side door with very little foot traffic.

I close my door and hurry to my bed, grab a pillow, and scream into it. The agreement seemed like a good idea at the time, but five days into it and I'm wondering if I was wrong. I think I might have real feelings for Wes, and that's going to make all this far more complicated.

I contemplate calling my sister, but I don't want to have that conversation. I promised her I'm fine.

Instead, I pull out my phone and start looking for local clothing stores. I need to buy a red dress.

20

WES

I DON'T PARTICULARLY CARE FOR HOW I'M FEELING RIGHT NOW.

Dry mouth.

Tightness in my chest.

Stomach that may or may not send my lunch back into the world.

Nerves.

A feeling that was beat out of me in the military. Nerves were a problem. Nerves could derail my job. Nerves could be the difference between safely deactivating a bomb or being blown into a puzzle nobody could ever put back together.

I'm not supposed to worry about that anymore though. Passing through the military exit door and into civilian life should just take it all away, right? As if changing your surroundings should magically erase years of experience.

I have to drive through town four times before I find a parking spot, and it's nowhere near the park. I walk through town, and the closer I get, the thicker the crowd becomes. Dakota wasn't exaggerating.

The park is packed. Blankets transform the grass into a

sea of color, chairs cover the sidewalks. Parked food trucks line the street, each one with lines ten or more deep. There must be people from other towns here. It's like the whole Verde Valley has gathered in Sierra Grande.

I stand back along the periphery and scan the crowd for Dakota, trying not to meet any curious gazes. It's difficult. I can feel people looking at me, just like I did the day I drove Dakota into town to talk to the nail salon owner. My chin lifts, but on the inside, I'm fighting the urge to hop back into my truck and drive home. I know what the people of Sierra Grande think of me, and I don't want their pity.

On my third sweep, I spot her. Or, actually, it's she who spots me. Her waving arms call my attention and I start for her, stepping around the maze of blankets.

She also wasn't lying about wearing red. The closer I get, the better I can see her dress. It's strapless, and the color makes her hair look more strawberry than blonde. When I'm a few blankets away she climbs to her feet and smiles. It disarms me, and I barely catch myself from stumbling over the corner of a blanket.

She greets me with a quick hug, and the second her body is pressed to mine a small fraction of my nerves melts away.

"How was your day?" I ask, trying to settle onto her blue and white blanket. It's awkward, fitting my frame onto this small blanket, like a bear settling into a twin bed for a long winter's nap. Finally, I figure out that I can sit upright with my knees bent and my feet on the grass.

"Good." She sinks down beside me and reaches for her water bottle, her hair brushing my forearm. "Great, actually. The order for the tile went through today. I'm thrilled with how fast it's moving already. I mean, I know problems will arise. They always do." She gestures with an outstretched palm. "Lumber will be backordered because the warehouse had a beetle infestation." Her other palm lifts, like each one contains a potential setback. "Another project in a neighboring town will have ordered all the concrete on the week I need it. And on and on and on," she offers me a grin. "It's keeping me on my toes."

"I stopped by it this morning. It's coming along."

She gives me a look. "You stopped by? It's not exactly easy to get there from that road."

I almost blush. Un-fucking-believable. I gave myself away. "I was curious."

"Hmmm." She taps her chin. "Curious... or, perhaps, you missed me and were too chicken to call me, so you went to a place that reminds you of me."

I stare at her and try like hell not to have a reaction. I think I'm successful, but her smirk tells me I'm wrong.

"That's what I thought," she singsongs.

"You don't know," I argue, but it's weak sounding.

She turns the full force of her gaze on me and I tighten the hands I have wrapped around my knees to keep them in place. "Oh, Wes, yes I do know."

She's right. She has my number. Former soldier, cowboy, rancher, tough guy I like to think I am, she can pin me to the wall with that brain of hers.

A small smile curves the corners of her mouth upward. She breaks the spell by looking toward the stage where the band is setting up. When I don't think she can see me, I suck in a deep breath. She fucking knocks it out of me on a regular basis.

And she does it again when she says, "We need to discuss some logistics of our arrangement."

She looks at me, and I nod at her to continue. Her gaze sweeps the people sitting nearby. In a lower voice, she says,

"I tried to talk to you about this last week, but your dad was in the hospital and I didn't want to push you emotionally." Her hand rests on my arm and she leans closer. I should get a medal for resisting the temptation to bury my face in her hair. "Have you thought about this past the part where we both get what we want?"

"Not really," I start, the wheels in my brain beginning to turn. "I guess I just thought we'd be married, whatever that means."

Dakota lifts one eyebrow. "*Whatever that means* doesn't work for me. I need specifics. Am I supposed to move in with you? Do we sleep with other people? Because I don't know about you, but I"—she pats her chest— "cannot be celibate. I'll make the Wicked Witch of the West look like Florence Nightingale."

The mention of us sleeping with other people makes my stomach turn over. She has a valid point, but still...

Clearly, I am the worst at this marriage of convenience bullshit. I know nothing of how to structure a deal of this magnitude. I feel like an idiot for proposing an idea when I didn't have any planned parameters. "Do we have to hammer it out now? Can we just let it flow for a little while?"

Dakota lifts a solitary finger into the air. "On one condition."

My eyebrows lift, silently asking her what she wants.

"I need a beer. Badly. This talk has made me thirsty."

My entire body sighs in relief. Behind Dakota, I spy a beer stand. "That I can do."

While I stand in line for beers, my mind runs through everything Dakota said. But instead of thinking of her exact words, what really sticks out to me is the ease I feel when I'm around her. Most of the time when I'm around people I have the desire to move, to be in motion, like I'm going to come out of my skin. Dakota makes me want to settle, to let go. I turn around, seeking her out in the crowd. She's leaning back on her arms, her face upturned to the waning sun, her eyes closed. For a brief second, I let my mind wander into forbidden territory… a place where I'm allowed to be happy. It's a place where Dakota looks at me like she couldn't possibly love me more. We're married because we want to be. We have kids. Our hearts belong to the ranch, to the soil we ride on, to the grass where our children play.

It's a pipe dream, but I can't help it. What if I'm drowning, and Dakota is my life preserver? How long am I supposed to keep refusing to grab hold?

On my walk back to Dakota, with a beer in each hand, my expression looks exactly like it did on my walk to the beer stand. But inside? I feel lighter. Like even the concept of grabbing on to the life preserver was enough to give me life.

I settle back down beside Dakota and hand over her beer. "You weren't kidding about this being a popular event," I comment, my eyes sweeping the crowd. I'm noting the best exit points. We shouldn't need them, but nobody ever died from being too prepared.

"I got here an hour ago to get a spot," Dakota says as she sips her beer.

"And you were still this far back? Guess you should camp out next time."

An uncomfortable look passes over her face. "Right." She laughs, but I can tell it's forced.

Then it hits me. An image of Dakota setting up her blanket near the back corner of the park, passing up the closer open spots on purpose.

Because of me.

Because she wanted to make sure I didn't feel trapped.

Because she knows I have PTSD, even though I haven't told her.

Because I'm the fucked-up guy who needs special attention.

"Wes?" Dakota's voice is soft.

"Yeah?"

"Look at me." Her words are accompanied by a gentle cupping of my cheek and the slightest pressure, urging me to comply.

I do. And when I look into her eyes, I hate what I see.

Pity.

The band starts up and Dakota startles.

I yank my chin back to the front.

I finish my beer and go for another, looking out over the crowd while I wait. Thirty feet away from Dakota, I see Dixon's blond hair. He's leaning against a tree, looking out. When he meets my stare, he smirks.

"Sir?" The voice belongs to the girl at the line of taps.

By the time I order and pay, Dixon is gone. Hopefully he's crawled into whatever hole he came from.

I sit back down and sneak a glance at Dakota. Her shoulders are lifted, and her chin tips up determinedly.

She looks like she's about to throw me yet another life preserver.

One guess as to what I'll do with it.

21

DAKOTA

WES IS DRUNK.

He's not hammered in a *take off all your clothes but your shirt and pass out* way. But definitely in a way that he has no business operating a vehicle.

To be fair, I'm not sober either. After the awkwardness where Wes realized I'd chosen the back corner of the park on purpose, what else was there to do to fill the silence between us? Yeah, the band was playing and so it wasn't actually quiet, but there was nothing but dead air between him and I. Multiple drinks it was.

Now the consequence of that choice is staring us right in the face. The concert is over and I don't know what to do from here. I finish folding the blanket and tuck it under my arm.

"So..." Wes says, looking around at the people passing us.

I answer by tucking my top lip into my bottom lip and raising my eyebrows at him.

Wes digs into the pockets of his jeans and produces his keys. "Can I see you tomorrow?"

"We'd better." I frown, watching his keys spin around the keyring on his finger. "Believable whirlwind romance and all." I reach for his keys, but he pushes them back into his pocket. Even in his buzzed state, he is surprisingly agile.

My arms cross in front of my chest. "You cannot drive right now."

"I'm aware."

I hold my tongue until a group of four people passes us. "So you were going to... what? Walk around by yourself until you sobered up?"

"Sit in my truck, actually. Read the news on my phone."

I make a disbelieving face. "I think you can still get a DUI for being behind the wheel, even if your car isn't actually in motion." I only know that because I looked it up on the internet after I got drunk with Waylon and was curious about the law in Arizona.

"Then I'll walk around for a while," Wes says.

Why is he acting like he can't wait to be away from me? Was my choosing that spot in the park that bad? I thought I was being considerate.

I shrug like I don't care. "Suit yourself. I'm going to get some pie." I start to turn around but his voice stops me.

"Pie?"

"Yes, have you ever heard of it?"

He almost smiles. Considering it's the most he's smiled in the past two hours, I'll take it. He walks beside me, his hands shoved in his pockets.

"Here we are," I announce, holding out my arm to the windowed storefront with the words *$9.99 Dinner Special* painted on the glass in bright pink and orange.

Wes doesn't look convinced but he opens the door for me. We settle into a booth and he peeks at me from over the top of his menu. "Is this like that show? Where they find dives that serve great food?"

I laugh. "Nope."

Wes's mouth falls open. "Seriously? It's not a hidden treasure or something like that?"

"No. It's your run-of-the-mill diner with varying shades of brown food and most of it is fried." I pick at a chip in the Formica tabletop. "Have you never been here? It looks pretty old. It must've been around when you were in your heyday."

He looks like he wants to comment on my use of the word *heyday* but decides against it and instead glances around, studying the place. "It does look familiar," he says haltingly, as if trying to understand why.

The server from the time I was here with my dad steps up to the table. "Hi there. What can I get you?" She takes another second to look at me and her eyes light up in recognition. "It's you! The out-of-towner. Still in town, I see." She glances at Wes. "And if it isn't the oldest Hayden boy. I haven't seen you in a very long time."

Wes shifts in his seat. He picks up the menu only to drop it with a plastic-y *thwack* on the table. "Yeah, uh..."

"Don't worry"—she bats at the air—"I don't expect you to remember me. I worked here when this place was a pizza joint. You used to come in here after Friday night football games with all your friends. You all made a hell of a mess and you were loud, but you tipped well." She chuckles at the memory.

Recognition lights up Wes's eyes, and the effect it has on his entire face is captivating. It erases ten years of stress from him in an instant. He snaps his fingers and points at her. "Cherilyn."

My eyes fly to her chest, searching for the name tag she wore last time. It's not there.

She grins broadly. "Bingo. Now tell me, are you two in here for the peach or the cherry pie? Because I have one slice left of each."

"We'll take them both," Wes answers. "À la mode, please." He winks at me.

I'm too stunned to say anything. Where is the brooding man from the concert? Did one connection from someone in town turn his frown upside down? Remind me to introduce him to Waylon and every woman at the book club. Maybe he'll perform an Irish jig.

Cherilyn is back two minutes later with the pies. She sets both plates in the middle of the table along with two forks.

"Cherry or peach?" Wes asks, fork poised.

"Both," I tell him, loading up my fork with a bite from each and waggling my eyebrows.

"I thought you'd say that."

"Oh, so you think you know me?" I don't even attempt to hide the flirtatiousness in my voice. Sitting beside him on that blanket in the park, but feeling as if he might as well be back on the ranch, was excruciating. Now that Wes is back from his quiet place, I'd like to keep him here with me.

He sinks his fork into the peach pie and takes a bite. "I like to think I know you pretty well."

I'm almost positive he's going to take his comment somewhere sexual, but he shocks me when he says, "I know you're more ambitious than you admit. You get uncomfortable when your dad compliments you. You have great ideas, but you're the only one who doesn't seem to know it. Also, you have a big heart. If you didn't, you wouldn't be intent on using local suppliers to build a business that will create jobs and offer a place for people to showcase their goods."

My stomach flips and tears sting behind my eyes, but I

keep eating just so I have something to do with my hands. I've never felt so stripped bare by a person's words.

Wes's fingers reach under my chin and force me to look at him. "Even right now, you can't accept what I'm saying."

"That's not true," I argue, even though I know he is one hundred percent correct.

I've been looking at the deal we struck as a rouse meant to fool everyone else, but our next words make me wonder if we're really only fooling ourselves.

"If only you could see what I see when I look at you." These tender words are in sharp contrast to the rough man speaking them. Something gentle lies beneath his jagged exterior.

I look into his eyes, and with as much meaning as I can muster, tell him, "That makes two of us."

He blinks twice, and in a shocking turn of events that my brain can hardly comprehend, I think he might actually be *trying*. Trying to let me in, to open up, to allow goodness to shine its warm light on him.

We finish the pie and pay. Wes promises Cherilyn he won't be a stranger. My hotel room isn't far, and although I'm more than capable of walking back alone, he insists on accompanying me. The food coma and post alcohol exhaustion sets in almost as soon as we step foot from the diner. By the time we both reach the front door of the hotel, we're taking turns yawning.

I linger at the entrance, trying to choose my words carefully. "I'd rather you not drive on those dark winding roads when you're this tired."

"I'll be fine," he insists, his voice husky. "But it's nice to know you care."

"Well, you are my soon-to-be fiancé. What is it, nine more days and you'll announce our engagement?"

A short stream of air huffs from his nose. "Something like that." He turns his head and yawns again.

"Wes, just sleep here. I have a couch in my room. I mean..." I fumble over my words and blush. "It's not like we haven't stayed in the same room together before." Though, admittedly, what happened before will not be happening tonight.

He eyes me for a long moment. "Is me driving home really going to worry you that much?"

"I'm not usually a huge worrier, but exhaustion while navigating dark winding roads sounds like a recipe for a car accident. So just stay. If anything, it'll get the town talking, which we need to do anyway." Nothing about our behavior during the concert tonight would have tongues wagging. If anything, we looked like two people forced to share a blanket.

"On one condition."

My eyes narrow. "What?"

"Don't even think about taking advantage of me."

I laugh and tuck my hands into my chest. "I'll keep my paws to myself."

He grabs one of my hands and pulls me into the hotel. We walk up the stairs and into my room. I have no idea who sees us because I refuse to look anywhere but in front of me, but I have no doubt there will be talk tomorrow. There may even be phones ringing right now.

We get inside the room and I go straight for the bathroom. When I come out, my face is scrubbed free of makeup and I'm wearing my pajama shorts and tank top. Wes sits on the couch wearing boxer briefs and an undershirt, and I fight with the strength of a prizefighter not to allow my gaze to travel south. On my way to bed, I see his jeans and shirt are folded in a very precise way and rest on his boots. He's also found the extra blanket the hotel placed in the top of the closet, and swiped one of the pillows from my bed.

I climb into the bed and watch him lay out on the couch. It's almost comical, watching him try to fit his frame on the too-small couch. There's no way he won't wake up with a sore neck tomorrow.

"You don't have to sleep on the couch," I tell him, sitting up and pulling the sheet around my waist.

He swings his legs around and stands up quickly, as though someone poked his ass with a pin. "Wasn't planning on it," he says, striding over. He pulls back the sheet and climbs in beside me.

"You were going to wait for me to fall asleep and then get in, weren't you?"

He smirks. "I guess now you'll never know."

I laugh and shake my head.

It feels impossible to settle down with Wes lying eighteen inches away. His nearness creates electricity, and it results in a low, buzzing hum that covers my entire body.

"Goodnight," I whisper, turning on my side and facing away from him.

"Goodnight," he says, his voice thick and sleepy.

I'm not sure how long I lay there, but it feels like forever. Wes's breathing evens out, and the steady rhythm lulls me to sleep.

I sleep peacefully, dreamlessly, until Wes begins to thrash and scream.

22

DAKOTA

THERE'S A BAKERY ON THE CORNER, ACROSS THE STREET FROM the hotel. It's a stretch to call it a bakery, because it also serves savory breakfast food. Nonetheless, it's called The Bakery. The people in Sierra Grande seem to prefer names that don't leave any room for interpretation—see, Bar N.

The Bakery is where I'm headed now, in the red sundress I picked up off the floor and draped over myself without making a peep. Wes was sleeping hard, heavy breaths coming from between parted lips. Is it possible for sleep to be grateful? Because that's how his serene face appeared to be—so damn thankful to be in a state that was not disrupted by a nightmare.

Oh, Wes...

The light changes and I cross the street, but all I can think about is waking up to Wes's flailing limbs, and his pained, incoherent yelling. Whatever plagues him during waking hours comes out to torture him when he's asleep.

His yelling and thrashing lasted fewer than ten seconds. It didn't wake him, but it kept me from sleeping for nearly an hour. Something tells me I'll be drinking more coffee than usual today.

The smell of salty breakfast meat and warm pastry at The Bakery wakes me up a little. The aroma is already familiar. It's the third time this week I've come here. It's possible I'm addicted, but there are far worse things to be addicted to, so I'm not too worried.

"Hey, Greta." I smile at the red-haired woman behind the counter. Unlike my strawberry blonde locks, Greta's hair is more of a rust color, and wound into a poofy bun at the back of her head.

"Dakota, how ya' doin' today?" Greta rests her generous forearms on top of the glass display case. On one wrist she wears a delicate gold watch. On the other, a Native American beaded bracelet.

"I'm great," I answer, lying right through my teeth. Actually, I'm exhausted, and I'm in a fake relationship. The only thing going 'great' for me right now is The Orchard. Which is arguably a pretty big thing to have going well.

"Good to hear." Greta nods, and I'm supremely thankful she isn't better at reading people because even I can hear the falseness of my tone. Seriously, what hope do I have of convincing anybody Wes and I are so desperately in love that we're sprinting to the altar?

I'm just about to ask Greta how her morning is going when her eyes widen and she turns around faster than I would've thought was possible. "I almost forgot," she says when she turns back around, holding a small box. "You're new to town, so you don't know, but we get these delivered once a week." She sets the box down where her forearms had just been and pushes it to me. As I reach for the box, she says, "Those are from a bakery about ninety minutes away. They're a big hit, and they don't last long. I saved a couple for you, but I have to warn you, next week you're on your own."

I open the box. Blueberry muffins, and just the sight and smell instantly have my salivary glands doing their job. "Thank you." I grin excitedly at Greta. "How did you know I love blueberry muffins?"

"Because people who don't like blueberry muffins are fools, and you are no fool."

"I like you, Greta."

"Likewise, dear. Now, what else can I get for you?"

One finger taps the center of my lower lip as I consider the menu. What does Wes like? I've seen him eat steak. And a hamburger. He likes meat. I mean, obviously. He's a cattle rancher. Can there be such a thing as a vegetarian cattle rancher? Talk about a conflict of interest.

"I'll take two breakfast burritos with bacon, make one spicy please, and a side of homestyle potatoes. Add an avocado toast on whole wheat." I pause to consider, knowing it's unlikely Wes is an avocado toast guy, but keep it anyway. I like avocado toast. "And two tall coffees."

Greta eyes me knowingly. "That's an awful lot of food for a little thing like you."

I shrug and go for my best innocent look. Greta wiggles her eyebrows and laughs knowingly. Everyone loves a lover. No matter that it's one of the fake variety.

She gathers my order and loads it into a paper bag. I hand her my credit card and she swipes it. "Good for you," she says when she hands the card back to me. "No sense in you being lonely while you're here."

"I agree." I wink at her and slip the small box with the muffins on top of my bag.

"Any chance you want to divulge who kept your bed warm last night?" she asks, her tone cajoling.

I shake my head immediately, then remember it would benefit us for people to start talking. "Well." I draw out the word. "Let's just say his name rhymes with Jess Braydon."

Greta pouts playfully. "Oh, honey, don't expect me to work out your word quiz. I opened the store this morning." She glances at a customer who's just walked in. "See you soon, Dakota."

I say goodbye and retrace my steps back to the hotel. With the bag balanced in one hand, I slide my key card into the slot and open the door as quietly as I can in case Wes is still sleeping.

Creeping in, I gently place the bag on the small table and look at the bed. No Wes.

My fists curl into tight balls of anger. How could he ghost me again? How could—

The faucet in the bathroom turns on. A breath I didn't know I was holding rushes out of me. Wes steps from the bathroom. His hair glistens as if he's just run wet hands through it. He wears only jeans and his smile is an unlikely combination of sexy and bashful. I can't even begin to discuss the abs that go on for days and days. I will not think about dragging my lips across the plateaus of muscle, or sliding my tongue through the valleys.

When I drag my lust-filled gaze up his body to finally look him in the eyes, I find he's wearing a smug smirk.

I'm on the verge of telling him to stow that obnoxious grin, but my growling stomach intervenes. "I brought breakfast," I say, nodding my head at the bag on the table.

Wes nods. "I'm starving." He removes everything from the bag and spreads it out on the table.

I sit down across from him and swipe the burrito that isn't labeled 'spicy'. "I thought you ghosted me again."

"I know," he responds, unwrapping the foil from the remaining burrito. "Your face shows your thoughts."

"I wish you suffered from the same affliction," I gripe, taking a bite. "You can be difficult to read. And when I say difficult, I mean impenetrable."

Wes sits back. He is stoic, not saying a word, and proving my point about being difficult. He removes the lid from the coffee and pauses for a fraction of a second to smell the black liquid before taking a sip.

Either he's particular about his coffee or he takes pleasure in the moment before the first sip, the one where the steam curls over your nose and the scent informs your brain of what's coming a millisecond before your taste buds do the job. It's definitely not the former, because that's not Wes's style. Which means I've just discovered something insanely cute about him, and it makes me want to get out my shovel and pickaxe and start mining for more quirky gems.

I wait until his mouth is loaded up with a huge bite, then ask him what his nightmare was about. I do this on purpose to give him an excuse to not answer right away. I thought it was the considerate thing to do. In hindsight, I shouldn't have said a damn word about the nightmare. Silent, brooding Wes from last night at the concert is back, only he took steroids during the absence and now he's adding twitching jaw muscles to his foul mood.

"You don't have to tell me anything, obviously. But seeing as how I was the person you woke up—"

His eyes fly to me. "I woke you up?" It's a question, but it doesn't come out like one. It sounds more like a horrified realization.

"Yes." I'll leave out the part where he kicked and hit me. It wasn't like it was *that* hard. More like half-hearted blows from a person who has just been sedated but isn't fully under yet.

He palms his forehead, leaning the weight of his head into his hand.

"Wes," I reach out and brush my fingers over his arm. "Everything is okay."

He gives me a derisive look, and it cuts me to the quick. "Everything is not okay, Dakota. You heard me having a nightmare."

"So? People have nightmares all the time, Wes."

He laughs once, the sound scornful. "Not the same as the ones I have."

"What was yours about?" My voice is soft and calm, coaxing. Maybe if he talks about it, he'll feel better.

He shakes his head. "There is no way I'd ever tell you."

"Understandable." I ball up the tinfoil from my burrito and toss it in the empty paper bag. "But maybe you should talk to somebody."

Wes looks at the ceiling, his chest puffing up with a deep breath, and he slowly lets it go. "I'll pass."

I stand. I don't know what my plans are for today but I'm not going to sit here and beg Wes to get help he doesn't want. I'd have better luck showing my vacation pictures to a brick wall.

"I need to get ready for the day." I reach for my jeans and remind myself how badly I need to do laundry. I looked online yesterday and found a laundromat nearby. As much as it's going to suck, I'm going to have to spend a few hours there.

Wes stuffs the trash from our breakfast into the wastebasket. He looks down at the remaining food, pointing in disgust at the avocado toast.

"What is that?"

I'm so relieved that he seems to be taking a step toward an improved mood that I choose not to tease him for being the last millennial on the planet who doesn't know about avocado toast. When I tell him what it is, he informs me avocados belong in guacamole.

I give him a look that conveys just how hopeless I believe him to be. "Now that that's been cleared up..." I pull out a shirt and start for the bathroom. "I'm going to take a shower."

Wes grabs his perfectly folded shirt from its spot on top of his boots. I avert my gaze as he pulls it over his head because I refuse to be caught checking him out. Again.

"I'm late, and I'm going to get shit for it. I told my dad I'd move the herd today." Wes pulls his phone from his back pocket and looks at it. "Warner called. Twice."

I pause in the open bathroom door, my hand resting on the doorframe. "That's good though, right? Not the part where you're late, but the inference that you're late because you slept over? Kinda ratchets up the rapid falling in love rigamarole."

He smirks. "Rigamarole?"

"It's a word."

"I know. But I've never heard anyone use it besides my elderly grandfather."

"Well, now you have."

"The first time we met, you told me I was sitting all by my lonesome."

My head tips to the side. "I don't recall." Lies. I remember it like it happened twenty seconds ago. I'd never felt more alive in my whole life than the moment I approached Wes.

He stares me down. I can't tell if he knows I'm lying because his face goes stoic again. "Right," he says tightly. He pulls on his boots and heads for the door, pausing after he turns the handle. "What are we doing tonight?"

"Laundry."

"Okay."

I blink in surprise. I thought for sure he'd object to that. "I'm just kidding. I'll do laundry tomorrow. As for tonight, there's a place I'd like to take you, but I can't tell you where."

He turns around, regarding me with that cool look of his. "You can't tell me?"

I shake my head, and he huffs out a short laugh. He looks at me for a long moment, thinking about it, then says, "I'm in."

"Yes." My fist pump amuses him and he actually laughs. "Can you meet me out front of the hotel at five?"

He nods. "I'll be there."

It's awkward, him standing at the door looking at me. It almost feels like we should say goodbye with a hug or a kiss. Something a little more intimate than *see ya later, pal.*

But we don't.

He waves at me, a single stiff swipe through the air. I wave back, then step in the shower, reminding myself why I agreed to this plan in the first place.

A fresh start. Clean slate. A chance to press the delete key.

And I can't take my baggage into my new, unsullied landscape.

The knowledge hurts, a real physical ache, dull and in the center of my chest. I set up the charity payments in an attempt at reparation, but also as a way to bring myself comfort. But I can't move forward into the land of debt-free living while maintaining the status quo.

As much as it pains me, I'm going to need to stop the

payments. Tomorrow is the twenty-seventh. Debra is expecting my call.

I get out of the shower and towel off, then grab my phone. Stopping the donation to The Aneurysm Foundation is the easy one. A few swipes and it's over.

The next one? Not so simple.

I dial the women's shelter, fingers trembling. It rings and rings, and just when I think I'll have to leave a message, Debra picks up.

"Hi, Debra, it's Dakota Wright."

"You're a day early," Debra answers, her tone cheerful. "Same amount, same card?"

The words I have to speak tear at my insides, but I muster the courage. "I need to pause the payments, Debra. I just... can't anymore. I feel bad, and I hope you know I still think this is a cause so deserving of donations, but—"

"Honey, take a breath. It's okay. You don't need to explain yourself to me."

I exhale. "Thank you."

"You've been more than generous, Dakota. I'd love to meet you sometime if you ever want to stop in."

"That would be lovely, Debra. Thank you for understanding."

"Sure thing. I've got to go, but you take care."

We say goodbye and hang up. And that's it. The chains I wrapped around myself are lifted.

I feel jumpy and weird, full of excess energy.

I'm combing my wet hair when an idea strikes. I got paid yesterday. With my recurring charity donation currently paused, that means I have money. I can buy myself a good pair of hiking shoes and explore one of the local trails.

In less than an hour's time I'm wearing new shorts, a long-sleeve shirt designed for being in the sun, and hiking shoes. A new hat fits securely on my head. A water bottle holder is clipped to my waist.

I'm following a trail that is said to be moderately strenuous, and crosses over the Verde River in one mile. It's almost silent, and soon, even my thoughts are quiet.

It's exactly what I need to relieve the chaos I feel swirling inside me when I'm with Wes.

23

WES

This is what I love.

Muscles working to the point of screaming exhaustion. Sweat-soaked shirts dried by the sun, dust coating the leather of my boots.

Ranger keeps me beside the herd, guiding them. Warner rides twenty feet behind me, doing his part. Josh, Bryce, Troy, Denny, and Ham make up the remainder of the perimeter. Together, we direct the herd to a new pasture for grazing.

Grass-fed meat is what the people want these days, and fuck if the HCC won't be the ones to give them the very best pasture-raised, pasture-finished beef.

The cattle make it to the new grass without any trouble. I hop off Ranger and slip his lead around a post. My muscles complain as I stretch, arching my back and rolling my head in a slow circle. The saddle will fuck up your bones, that's for damn sure.

My eyes are on the herd, but my mind is on Dakota. Sweet, feisty, determined Dakota.

This morning I woke up in her hotel bed. She was gone,

but her scent lingered on her pillow, on the sheets, on my clothes. Her red dress was missing from the back of the chair, and her pajamas were in a pile on the ground. Right away I knew she'd gone for breakfast. I sat up in her bed, rubbed my eyes, and thought about what would happen if I kissed her. Blame it on being surrounded by her scent.

I almost did it too, when she returned with breakfast and stared at me without a shirt on. Our agreement nearly sprouted wings and flew out the window. Then she told me I had a nightmare and the wings disintegrated and the agreement crashed back down to earth.

Dakota witnessed the very thing I'd only have revealed if my life depended on it. I've had the same dream over and over ever since it happened. That's the kind of shit I keep locked up tight, but lately, it's been getting worse. More vivid. It seems to me the further I get from it, the more it should be getting hazy around the edges. I wish that were the case.

And now Dakota knows. It's like my heart and my mind are in a disagreement, and while I was sleeping my heart went behind my brain's back and exposed my worst moment. Like some traitorous part of me *wanted* her to know.

"Where the fuck are you, Wes?" Warner steps into my vision and waves a hand in my face.

I smack it away. "Get your eyes checked, asshat. I'm right here."

Warner wipes sweat from his upper lip with the side of his hand. "Ten bucks says your mind is wherever it was you stayed last night."

Technically, he's right. Just not in the way he thinks.

"Can't fool you." I clap a hand on his shoulder.

"How's Dakota this morning?" He grins, proud of

himself because he knows he's accurately assumed where I was. "Good? Bet she wakes up pretty with all that just-been-fucked hair."

The hand I still have on his shoulder tightens. He tries to shrink away but my fingers dig in, holding him in place. In a low voice, I say, "You only talk about Dakota in a way that is one hundred percent respectful from now on." Trying to get a rise out of me is his second favorite hobby (the first being playing with his kids), and normally I don't bite because I know what he's doing, but when it comes to Dakota, I can't seem to take the ribbing.

I release him, but he doesn't move away. He grins in this goofy way, his playful nature keeping him from getting his feelings hurt. If I'd done that to Wyatt, he'd stalk away sensitive and injured.

As good-natured as Warner is, he's also really damn insistent. Right now, he's eyeing me meaningfully.

"What?" I demand, annoyed at his persistence.

"Why do you make it so damn hard?"

My eyes widen in annoyance and my chin makes tiny side-to-side motions. "What the fuck are you talking about?"

"You've never been late for work, Wes. Not a day in your whole damn life, and aside from the time you were in the military, I've worked by your side every day. Just allow yourself to talk about Dakota. Admit how much you like her."

Technically, this is exactly how all this is supposed to be going. My family, or at least Warner, took notice of my absence immediately. It's the first step toward the Wes and Dakota Fast and Furious relationship. I didn't think for a second I'd be hurting my brother's feelings.

But I have. I hear the hurt in his voice. He's doing that thing again, the one where he wants me to confide in him. I grab my water bottle, take a long drink, and glance at him.

Here goes nothing. “You’re correct. I stayed with Dakota last night.”

His eyes light up, but to his credit, he controls his excitement and keeps his mouth shut. *Shit*. I feel bad. Warner loves, well...love. He’s a romantic at heart. And he wants to see me happy. Just like he used to be with Anna.

“But it wasn’t the first time we’ve stayed together. Do you remember when I got out of the Army and I stopped at my buddy Jason’s place in Colorado on my way home? I met Dakota that night.”

Warner’s not able to stay quiet after my revelation, not that I can blame him. “You knew Dakota before she came here with her dad? Fuck...” His head shakes slowly, but his eyes are glossy with hope. “This is some fate shit, Wes. Seriously.”

Fate? I don’t believe in it, not after what I’ve seen. And I’m surprised to hear Warner does, considering what Anna did to him.

“Fate doesn’t exist, Warner.”

He starts to argue, so I ask him if he believes in fairies and unicorns, too.

“Sure, why not?” He shrugs. “Anything is possible. Not to you, of course, because you’re a macho ex-soldier cattle rancher whose hide is made from steel, and the jury is still out on whether or not your heart is capable of feeling.”

My lips turn down. Warner jostles me with his elbow. “I’m just fucking with you, man. I know you’re capable of feeling. I’ve seen the way you look at Dakota.”

“Yeah.” I nearly cough on the word. How do I look at Dakota?

“It’s okay to have feelings, Wes.”

“I know.”

“Do you?” Warner stands strong under my glare.

"Yes, I do."

He shrugs again. "Could've fooled me."

"Knock that shit off, Warner." I'm starting to lose my temper, but it's really just because I feel bad for keeping him at arm's length. "You know I love you. You're my brother." I shift, uncomfortable, which causes a flare of irritation to rise in my chest. Not at Warner, though. At myself. Why does it make me feel so damn uneasy to talk about how I feel?

"Aw, Wes, you love me?" Warner's joking tone doesn't completely cover up the happiness I hear in his voice, and it damn sure doesn't hide the satisfaction on his face. "Now you're making me blush."

A few feet away, Bryce and Ham snicker. I didn't see them there, but it's very possible they heard everything we just talked about, with the exception of Dakota. I spoke under my breath about her.

Warner grins at me, and for a brief moment, I feel jealous. What would it be like to live like him? No pressure about the ranch, no nightmares, no cares except being a good dad and finding a woman to hold at night. No guilt about failing people in their darkest, neediest hour.

I climb back onto Ranger even though I have no plans to actually ride anywhere. I feel restless and I just want to move my body. I relax into the saddle and tip my chin to the blue sky streaked with puffy white clouds. When I was younger, I would lie in the grass and look up at the sky on a cloudless day, pretending it was the ocean, stretching on and on into oblivion.

I attempt to do the same now, but instead of seeing blue, I see hazel. Hazel eyes framed by strawberry blonde hair, and a gaze so perceptive it sometimes feels intrusive. Dakota has seen me cry. Dakota has heard me having a nightmare.

Why isn't she running away? Why can't she see how

royally fucked-up I am? Doesn't she have any sense of self-preservation? But, of course, I know the answer. Her debt. Our arrangement. She wants to be rid of that debt so badly that she agreed to marry me.

A niggling thought burrows into my brain, and as much as I push it away, it slips through the cracks and presents itself.

Is it possible that, despite the warning signs plastered on my body, Dakota might actually have feelings for me?

"WES?" My mom pokes her head out of the kitchen, and I can see the top half of her favorite T-shirt, the one with the picture of three Shetland ponies on the front. She steps out when she sees it's me coming down the hall. "Come in here and help me. There's a leak under the sink and I'm trying to switch out the cracked section of pipe but the wrench is being a twit."

I chuckle at the word 'twit', but there's also a pang in my heart. My grandma used that word. Which makes me think of Dakota and her habit of using outdated words.

Following her into the kitchen, I head for the open cabinet under the sink and bend down to get a look. All the cleaning supplies and odds and ends that were under the sink are now in a pile in front of the oven. "Why didn't you ask Gramps for help?" I'm joking, and she knows it.

She nudges my arm. "I'm stronger than him."

I adjust my position so I'm sitting and turn myself around, scooting my shoulders and head under the sink. "I'd like to be there when you tell him that."

She laughs and hands me the wrench. "Just do the job I brought you here to do."

I fit the mouth of the wrench over the slip nut and twist. It doesn't budge. I do it again, this time with more force. Still no movement. I try again, grunting with effort.

"See," my mom says with unconcealed satisfaction, "it's not easy."

"My arms are tired. I've been working outside all day, Mom."

"No you have not." Her response is automatic and just a little too certain.

I lift my head to look at her and bump my forehead on the plastic pipe. "Mom, we moved the cows to the north pasture for fresh grass today."

She levels me with a look. "I'm aware. But you weren't doing that *all day*."

My neck is starting to yell at me for keeping it in that position, so I lower it and give the bracket another go. This time, it moves. "Whatever you say, Ma." I finish loosening the part and hand it to her. "Where's the new piece of pipe?" She places it in my held out hand like we're in surgery or at the dentist. It takes all of ten seconds to fit the pipe and tighten it into place.

She steps back as I wiggle out from under the sink and wipe my hands on a kitchen towel. They aren't actually dirty, but it feels like something I should do.

"You're not sick, are you Wes?"

Bewildered, I cock my head to the side. "No, Mom."

"So you overslept today for the first time since you were sixteen?"

I understand where she's going with this, and it rankles me. I'm a grown-ass man.

"Skip the coy questions and say what you want to say, Mom."

"Wesley Matthew, I am still your mother and I will get out the switch if you disrespect me."

"You never used a switch on us."

"Don't make me start now."

I hide my smile. Something tells me it wouldn't go over well for her to know I find her threats amusing. Leaning against the edge of the countertop, I cross my arms and wait for her to say what it is she really wants to say. My mom is usually a direct person, so her roundabout questions unnerve me.

She watches me for a moment, and I'm convinced she does it for theatrical effect, like she's hoping to make me squirm.

Whatever my mom's thinking, she decides to keep it to herself. She pats my arm and steps around me toward the fridge. "I hope you know what you're doing, Wes."

I nearly laugh, but in the way that shows just how unfunny something is. Of course I don't know what I'm doing. In fact, I'm doing the only thing I can think to do.

She gives up when I don't respond, opening the fridge and pulling out items that look like they could come together to make a meal.

"Don't count on me for dinner, Mom. Dakota asked me to meet her in town at five."

"No problem." My mom smiles, but there's something false in it. "Have fun tonight. And if your father asks, I fixed the sink myself."

I say goodbye and leave the house. I need to go back to my place and shower before I meet Dakota. I'm ten feet away from the homestead when my dad calls my name.

"Hey, Dad," I respond, walking closer to the round pen where he's standing. Wyatt's in the ring, working with a horse. Of everyone on this ranch, Wyatt is the best with the horses, especially the temperamental ones. "Are you supposed to be out here so soon after surgery?"

The look on his face clearly says *I'll kick your ass right this second.* He ignores my question and asks one of his own. "You going to see Dakota soon?"

"Tonight. Why?"

"I went to the feed store today. Saw Dakota coming out of the hardware store with that shit-for-brains Dixon." His expression is grim. "You'd better warn her to stay away from him."

"She knows, Dad." I think back to the day Dixon was in Cowboy House, the way he touched Dakota. "She knows what he's about."

He makes a *hmph* sound in his throat. "Make sure she knows, Wes. The guy is a hair's breadth away from jail on any given day. The sheriff's son is in rehab because of him and people have been talking about some petty crimes happening around town, and I'd bet my last stud it's him."

Wyatt walks up, holding on to the mollified horse's reins. "Dixon's cooking up there somewhere." He motions generally out to the mountains.

Dad pins him with an ice cold glare. "And you would know this how?"

Wyatt lifts a hand in silent protest of his innocence. "Rumors, Dad."

Wyatt might be right. Dixon has to be getting his drugs from somewhere, and maybe that somewhere is from his own two hands. It's entirely possible he's in charge of it all. He's smart enough, which is what makes him dangerous.

"Just tell Dakota what I said," Dad instructs, his voice harsh.

"Will do, Dad." I turn to leave but remember what my mom said about the sink. "By the way, Mom fixed the sink."

A small smile turns up one of his wrinkled, tanned cheeks. "Guess I owe her twenty bucks."

Chuckling, I turn away and head for my cabin. My mom and dad aren't perfect, but man, do they have a good marriage. And then my smile dies because I'm setting myself up for an empty proposal to Dakota so I can get the one thing I've wanted my entire life.

My parents have led with a good example, but I'm obviously not following it.

24

DAKOTA

"What do you think, Boss? Are you happy with the progress we're making out here?" Scott's gloved hand grips the wooden shaft of his shovel, his steel-toed boot resting on the flat edge of the blade. As contractors go, my dad said Scott's the best he has ever met. Despite my limited experience, I'm inclined to agree. I can't imagine a contractor working alongside his crews the way Scott does. And the fact that he calls me boss helps me think of him favorably, too. We're probably around the same age and he doesn't appear to have any asinine male pride about me being the one in charge. Unlike Brandt. One of the unexpected positives of working in Sierra Grande is that I don't have to see that guy every day.

I look around at the site. "Things are going well. I'm happy with the progress. I think we may even be ahead of schedule."

Scott makes a face. "It's bad luck to say that. Now something is bound to go wrong."

"I don't believe in luck, Scott."

He nods. "Well, whatever it is you believe in, do what's needed to keep it happy."

"Noted." I glance at my watch. "Scott, feel free to tell the guys they can finish up a couple hours early today, since we're, you know, *not* ahead of schedule."

He raises an eyebrow. "No can do, Boss. We need to finish framing today." He points to where three guys are hammering nails into boards. "Can't leave the structure partially finished. It needs the support of all the beams to stay upright."

"Right, of course," I say hastily, embarrassment heating the back of my neck. I knew that. I mean, I think I knew that. Scott doesn't know this is my first project on my own, and though I wasn't planning on telling him, the holes in my knowledge might do the job for me. "I need to get going. I'll see you tomorrow?"

"Bright and early," he answers, giving me a two-finger salute and walking to his truck, where he tosses the shovel in the bed.

I climb in my car and hurry to the hotel. I don't have much time to get showered and dressed before Wes arrives, but I make it with fewer than three minutes to spare.

On my way through the lobby, I cross paths with Jo, the server from the first night I arrived in Sierra Grande with my dad. I've seen her two other times, each from afar, as she was working in the restaurant. She smiles at me blandly, then recognition lights up her eyes and a genuine smile takes over her face.

"Hi..." she says, searching for my name.

"Dakota." I point to myself. "Jo, right?"

She nods. "Good memory. I take it your meeting with the Haydens went well that day? Seeing as how you're still here."

My gaze flits to the front door where I'm sure Wes will be any second. "Yes, it did. My family's company is building at the edge of town."

"How exciting!"

She seems genuinely happy for me, and her reaction makes me miss having a girlfriend to talk to.

"Well, listen, I have to get in there for my shift." She motions with her thumb at the restaurant, and I notice she's clutching an apron in her hand. "But it was nice seeing you again."

We say goodbye and part ways. I find Wes out front, standing beside the trunk of a mature cottonwood tree. He wears jeans, a ball cap, and the softest looking gray T-shirt I've ever seen.

"Hi." My eyes lock with his and my stomach muscles coil.

"Hey." His gaze is deep and dark, and his deep voice drifts across the twelve inches that separate us, curling into my airway like smoke.

People walk by, and cars pass.

Every second I spend with Wes makes me feel like we're balanced on a tightrope, and we've yet to determine our rhythm. We need to get our routine figured out, before someone falls.

"This way," I tell him, tugging lightly on his hand. He walks beside me and doesn't let go of my hand. He's quiet.

"You're good at this, you know?" I squeeze his hand to let him know what I'm talking about.

He looks at me with amusement. "Holding hands? It's not very advanced as romantic gestures go."

My head shakes. "That's where you're wrong. It could be a lazy hold." My hand goes limp to show him what I mean. "Or it could be a death grip." I tighten my hold.

"You see? Wide margin for error. You have to get it just right."

"And I got it just right?"

I nod. "You sure did."

A smile lifts one corner of his mouth. It's a little *aw shucks* mixed with *thank you kindly, ma'am*.

"So, where are we headed?"

I hold up two fingers on my free hand. "Two places. And the first one is right there." We walk two more stores up and duck into an Italian restaurant.

Wes looks a bit bewildered as I give the hostess my name and tell her I'm here for the to-go order I placed. She hands it over and I march out of the place.

Looking back at Wes, I say, "The second place we're going is a little different, but I think it will be good. I went for a walk last week after work and stumbled upon it."

We walk another block, then make a right into a residential neighborhood. I pointedly ignore Wes's quizzical look and keep going. Up ahead, a handful of people gather in a front yard.

"Is that where we're going?" he asks.

"This is a couple who host a happy hour in their front yard every Friday night. They saw me walking last week and invited me over. Apparently the invite is open to everyone in town. What a cool way to foster community, right?"

Wes nods slowly. He looks wary but not upset. We get closer, and the couple who live here spot us right away. But instead of saying hi to me, they are open-mouth staring at Wes, and then they're hustling over.

"Wes Hayden, you have got to be goddamn kidding me." The husband, Derrick, nearly falls over himself in his astonishment.

"Oh my gosh, Wes." The wife, Andrea, throws her arms

around him. She lets him go and stands back, shaking her head like she's trying to get ahold of her thoughts. She looks at me, pointing from me to Wes. "Wait, are you two together?" She doesn't wait for a response before she says, "This is the best thing ever. Wes, you're here. You're actually here!" She hugs Wes again, and Derrick peels her off him.

"Andrea always did have a soft spot for you, Hayden." Derrick claps Wes on the shoulder.

Wes looks dazed, like he's been staring at the sun, but he's coming to. His head bobs and he laughs. "It's been a long time, guys."

"Uh, yeah." Andrea's fisted hands go to her hips. "Seven years, Wes. You were here on R&R, then you went back to finish up. We were so happy when we heard you were home, but..." She trails off, shrugging.

Instinctively I reach over, placing my hand on Wes's forearm. He looks at me and smiles.

Andrea claps her hands together. "Please, please, please tell me how you met. And let's get a drink." Her hands wave around excitedly.

I hand over the antipasto platter and reach into my big purse, pulling out a bottle of wine.

Andrea cackles. "Wine in a purse? You're my kind of gal. Come on." She pulls me and I go along after her, glancing back at Wes. He winks at me before turning his attention to Derrick.

"So," Andrea says, grabbing two pint-sized glass mason jars. She takes the wine from my arm and twists off the top, pouring generously into each jar and handing me both. The remaining wine stays on the table. The rule at this happy hour is that you have to bring something, and you have to share what you bring. Last Thursday I mooched off Andrea's white wine supply, so this week I made sure to bring the same bottle.

"Spill, Dakota. How did you meet the most reclusive and handsome Hayden brother?" She taps her finger against her chin, reconsidering. "Well, maybe not the most handsome. They're all kind of dreamy, aren't they?"

I picture Warner with his playful smile and Wyatt with his defined cheekbones and mysterious nature. "Beau and Juliette know how to make them, that's for sure." I look over at Wes. His hands are tucked into his front pockets, but he's grinning at something Derrick is saying. "But I'm partial to one in particular."

Andrea grins. "And what a stallion that one is. Or was."

I tense at the word 'stallion'. Did Andrea have a relationship with Wes? Did she mean the word sexually?

Andrea keeps talking. "He was wild in high school. Desert parties, taking his dad's truck mudding, cliff diving at the lake." Nostalgia brings a soft-focus glaze to her face. "We had a blast. And then Wes decided to join the military. He came home and visited from time to time, but he wasn't so crazy anymore. Still fun, though. And then..." Andrea watches him talk to Derrick. "It was like a switch was flipped to the off position and taped down. Derrick drove out to the Hayden Ranch when he heard Wes was home for good, but Wes made it clear he didn't want anything to do with anybody. We saw Warner in town a little while after that happened, and he told us Wes would hardly talk to him either. Or anybody in their family for that matter." She cocks her head, studying him. "He's got that haunted look in his eyes, doesn't he?"

I see what Andrea sees, and so much more. Haunted is an accurate description. To that, I'd add anxious and easily provoked. But also loyal, confident, protective, heroic, generous, and loving. And there's a whole lot of vulnerability hiding behind a brick wall.

"He's working through some things," I tell her.

"Oh, I'm sure, I'm sure," she's quick to say, in a way that lets me know she's not trying to stick her nose where it doesn't belong. "How'd you meet?"

Wes catches my eye and nods me over. Andrea sees this and pours herself a glass from the bottle I brought, then we start over to where Wes and Derrick stand.

"Remember last week when I told you I'm in charge of the new buildings going up on the far edge of town?" I glance at Andrea as we walk. She nods her head, her silver hoop earrings swinging. "It's being built on land that used to belong to the Haydens. My family bought the land and we met at the initial purchase meeting." Of course, this isn't totally true.

Omitting the night we spent together five years ago hardly even qualifies as a white lie, though. Maybe one day, if Andrea becomes a real friend, I'll tell her the full story. For now, this one works.

"Aw, it was love at first sight." Andrea smiles at the romantic thought.

"Something like that." We reach Wes and Derrick, and I hand Wes his drink. He takes it from me, wraps his arm around my waist and pulls me in, pressing a kiss to my temple. My heart swells, but then I remember the gesture is for show, and the feeling recedes.

Andrea leans into Derrick and looks at Wes. "Dakota was just telling me you met at the meeting about her family buying your land."

Wes looks down at me, amusement in his eyes. "That's right," he says slowly, his fingers tracing the bottom edge of my shirt across my back. I swallow hard and block out the caress. “She came in talking about how she wanted to build something that would benefit the town and showcase local businesses, and I was sold. On the idea, and on her.”

If I didn’t know better, his words would melt me, cause my heart to liquefy and drip down into a puddle at his feet.

Andrea sighs. She’s clearly a fairy tale, hearts and flowers kind of girl. Good for her.

We stay another hour. Other people show up. Some know Wes, some don’t. They’re all older, mostly neighbors. For now, Derrick and Andrea are the only blasts from Wes’s past.

Before we leave, Derrick makes sure he has Wes’s number, and they make plans to grab a beer soon. I don’t know that it will actually happen, but I’m thrilled to see him at least trying. Andrea takes me by surprise by hugging me. “I’m a hugger,” she says with a shrug after she lets me go.

On the walk home, Wes glances at the purse slung over my shoulder. “I bet that purse is a lot lighter now.”

“It was kind of a workout,” I admit, using my free hand to rub my neck. “How are you feeling?”

Wes glances at me. I can tell he’s about to say *fine* or its equivalent, but he pauses, mulling something over. “Weird.”

I perk up at the idea of him actually admitting how he’s feeling, but try to dampen the response so I don’t spook him. “Weird how?” I press, keeping my tone light.

His head tips side to side as he considers his response. “Seeing them was a shock. But after it wore off, it was kind of… good.” His eyebrows scrunch together. “And that’s what is weird. Something feeling good is, well, weird.” He glances at me. “Am I using the word ‘weird’ too much?”

My head shakes. “You can use whatever word you want to describe how you feel.”

We reach the end of the houses and start on the sidewalk that puts us back into the main part of town. "How's your dad?" I ask.

"Stubborn as a mule. He and Wyatt were out working with a horse today." Wes glances at me, eyebrows drawn. "Actually, he mentioned he saw you coming out of the hardware store with Dixon earlier today."

Wes pauses, waiting for me to explain. I groan. "It was nothing, I promise. I went there on my way to the jobsite because Scott needed a tool, and Dixon was in there. We left at the same time, and he walked out behind me. He tried to talk to me, and I was as polite as I needed to be to get on my way." That's mostly the truth. He also asked me out, and I declined. Politely. I don't think Wes needs to hear that part of it. He already despises him, no need to stoke the fire.

Wes nods. "I told my dad you knew the deal with Dixon."

"All good," I respond. I hope we're done talking about Dixon. I'm more interested in the beginning of the sunset, the way the vivid pinks and oranges slip through the street, bouncing off buildings. Restaurants and bars are waking up. Music spills from a place on the corner.

Wes hesitates when we reach the hotel. He looks as if he's weighing his words. "Still planning on doing laundry tomorrow?"

The question confuses me. He looked like he was thinking of something a little more serious than laundry. "Yep. Should be tons of fun."

"My cabin has a washer and dryer. You could use mine. Sitting at a laundromat doesn't sound like a good way to spend your Sunday."

Actually, it would be nice to see Wes's place. "What time do you want me to come over tomorrow?"

"You could come over right now? It's still early." He

glances up at the sky, using it to tell time instead of his watch.

"Yeah, sure," I say, acting nonchalant, when it's the opposite of how I feel. Someone please hand me a pillow that I can scream into.

Wes gives me directions, telling me how to get to the cabin he lives in on his parents' property.

I tell him I'm going upstairs to gather my things and I'll meet him at his place. I'm so startled by his suggestion that I almost forget the black pants that are the most in need of washing. I throw those into the suitcase with nearly every article of clothing I brought here and zip it up.

The elevator is busy and I'm anxious to go to Wes's cabin, so I use the stairwell, my suitcase bumping down each step. The door opens up on the side of the hotel, and I have to walk all the way around the building to get to where my car is parked. My impatience has cost me time, but maybe that's a good thing. I need to take a deep breath and slow my racing pulse.

I load the hefty suitcase into the back of my car and head to Wes's, my fingers tapping the wheel the entire way. So much for calming down.

I don't think this invite to Wes's place is him wanting to be considerate of my weekend time.

Maybe...just maybe...he didn't want our night to end.

25

WES

I PICKED UP DAKOTA'S FAVORITE WINE ON MY WAY HOME. JUST in case she wants a glass while she waits for her clothes to go through the washer and dryer.

I also noticed Dakota didn't eat any of that appetizer she took to the happy hour, and neither did I, so I picked up a few ingredients to make dinner. It might just be an evening of laundry, but I can't have her over and not have anything to eat or drink.

I know my place is clean, because I keep it that way, but even so I take a walk around to make sure. It doesn't take long. My cabin is cozy, which is to say that it's small. My parents built three cabins, one for each son, when I was overseas. Two bedrooms, one bath, a living room, laundry room, and a kitchen. The size is perfect for me, but Warner needed more when he and the kids moved back to the ranch after Anna left, so they added on to his. Maybe someday soon, they'll need to build one for Jessie.

In less than a minute, I've determined the place is ready for Dakota. But am I?

I've never had a woman here. And I can't believe it, but

I'm nervous. Standing in the kitchen, I look out across the island and into the living room, trying to see my home through new eyes. Dakota's eyes.

So much of it is basic and forgettable. The couch, the bookshelf, the TV, the area rug my mom picked out. Dakota's sharp eyes will zero in on the framed pictures on the shelves. For a guy who keeps the military locked up tight in his chest, there are still parts of it I can't put away, and that group shot of my platoon is one of them. The other is the shadow box with my medals. It's confusing how much pride you can have in something that taught invaluable lessons when it's also responsible for ruining parts of you. Maybe that's not just the military though. Maybe that's the case with anything truly momentous.

A car drives into the clearing. From the front window, I watch Dakota park and get out. By the time I get to her, she's already at the back of her car, struggling to lift a massive suitcase from the trunk.

"Let me," I say, not waiting for her response. My hand bumps hers as my fingers wrap around the handle.

"I can do it," she grunts her argument, still trying.

I stand back and watch her struggle. "You can be really stubborn."

She tries again, then backs away with a huff. "Tenacious," she clarifies. "It has a better ring to it than stubborn."

To her credit, the suitcase is surprisingly heavy. It hits the ground with a dull thud. "Are you washing cement blocks? I should warn you, my washing machine doesn't do well with those."

Dakota follows me to the cabin, pausing on the first of three steps leading up to the front porch and looking it over. "It's a smaller version of your parents' house." She runs a hand along the wooden railing. "I already like it."

I look down at her from the porch. "You might want to reserve your judgment for the inside. Maybe it's atrocious."

She hops up the remaining two steps. "Given how great the outside is, I'm going to make a bet that the inside is just as good." She side-eyes me meaningfully and sails past me into the cabin. I remain outside for a moment to get my bearings. Maybe she was only talking about the cabin, but I don't think she was.

Like I thought, she focuses on the Army picture immediately. I set the suitcase just inside the small laundry room door and stand back, watching her look at the photo. Her hand rises, hovering an inch away from the glass, as she tries to pick me out of the crowd.

I give her ten seconds, then offer help. Between the fact that we're all wearing the same clothes and my hair was buzz cut, I look different. She doesn't look at me when she says, "I found you right away. Most handsome guy in the group." She looks back at me with a wink. "Call it a gift."

I come closer. I've looked at the photo so many times I have it memorized, but I want to see what she sees. I'm on the left, sandwiched between Shepherd and Bensimmon. Some of us smile, others are straight-faced.

I hear Dakota's sharp intake of breath when I reach over her shoulder and brush my fingertips over the glass. I'm so close I can feel the heat rising from her bare shoulder. "This was taken pretty soon after basic training. A bunch of boys trying to be men. We thought we were invincible." A sharp pain flits through my chest. I point at Shepherd. "He didn't make it home."

Dakota gasps, her hand lifting to cover her mouth. "Wes, I'm so sorry."

I nod. "It was awful. Especially"—I point at another guy—"for him. Hunter. Everyone was close, but some people just click and become brothers. Those two were brothers." I lost touch with Hunter after he exited, but heard from Jason that he moved to Phoenix. I've made it a point not to keep in touch with Army buddies, but maybe it's time. Maybe I can talk to them without it setting me back mentally and emotionally. Maybe I'll give Hunter a call one of these days.

Dakota sniffles. I take my hand from the picture and touch her jaw, gently turning her head so I can see her. Her eyes are wet with tears, and one escapes, traveling down her cheek. Her capacity to feel anguish for a person she never met astonishes me, and something in my chest constricts.

My fingers are still touching her jaw, and my voice comes out husky. "I didn't mean to make you sad."

She shrugs. "Too late. I'm really sorry about your friend."

I take a step back so she can turn all the way around. "He knew the dangers when he signed up. We all did."

"It doesn't make it any less sad." Her face crumples and the unshed tears fall.

I can't take it. I pull Dakota into my arms, hold her against my chest, and try like hell not to drown in her overwhelmingly sweet scent.

Her tears don't last long. Soon she's pulling away from my chest and wiping under her eyes. "Sorry about that," she laughs softly and her cheeks bloom light pink. "I was just thinking about your friend, about what you've been through, and the next thing I knew I was crying."

"Follow me." I incline my head. She follows me to the kitchen. "I have just the thing for that," I tell her, pulling the chilled wine from the fridge.

I hand her a glass and pop the top off a beer using a metal opener screwed to the wall. "Cheers." I hold out the bottle and she clinks her glass against it.

"Alright," she says. "I guess I'd better start what I came here to do." She makes a face and walks over to her suitcase, bending down and unzipping it.

"I'll make some dinner while you're doing that." I start the oven and open the fridge again, removing ingredients and setting them on the counter.

"You cook?" Dakota asks, stepping over the open suitcase and into the tiny laundry room off the kitchen. It's just big enough for a side-by-side washer and dryer and sink. There's also a door that leads to the back deck, and it's nice to have when it rains and my boots turn into a muddy disaster.

"I cook a few dishes well, and a lot of other dishes poorly." I grab a knife and begin dicing an onion.

Dakota's laugh trickles out from where she's bent over shoving clothes into the machine. "Are we having one of the dishes you cook well, or one you cook poorly?"

"Shit, I hope it's the former, but I've been cooking for one for so long I may be wrong about it."

Dakota adds a scoop of detergent from the box on top of the washer and closes the door. She regards the dials and then chooses a setting and hits the start button. She steps back into the kitchen. "Are you telling me you've never brought a woman here and cooked for her?"

"Never." I scrape the diced onion from my cutting board into the cast iron pan. It sizzles in the butter, and my stomach turns over with a growl. Dakota drags in a breath. "Oh my God, that smells good. I definitely miss cooking. I'm like you. A few good dishes, many others not so well." She peers into the pan, waving her hand over the steam to bring more of the smell to her. "Why haven't you cooked for a woman? It's quite the skill, you know. Assuming you prepare one of the dishes you cook well, any woman would be putty in your hands."

I crack two eggs into a bowl and look at her. "Including you?" My heartbeat falters, my breath slams into my throat. Where did that come from?

Dakota handles it like a champ. She barks a laugh with her wine glass poised at her lips. "I guess I walked right into that one."

I laugh with her, but it feels false. "You said it, not me." But... what would happen if she was putty in my hands? How would that go? Pushing away those thoughts, I focus on my task. I add the ground beef and wash my hands, then add the bread crumbs, cheese and seasonings.

Dakota leans against the counter, watching. "Meatloaf?" she asks, and I hear her trepidation.

I look at her from the bowl where I'm combining the mixture. "You've never had my meatloaf. Trust me."

"I have no choice but to. All my clothes are here."

"Good point." I form the mixture into a loaf and slide the pan into the oven.

Dakota makes a face at my messy hands. I have a teenage moment where I lunge at her with upraised, slimy hands and she shrinks away, laughing. "Gross," she moans. "Wash your hands twice."

We sit on the front porch while dinner cooks and the first load of laundry is going through. The sun has officially set, but its memory lingers in the sky, a steady fade. It will be a little while longer until the stars stamp it out with their brightness.

"It's beautiful here, Wes." Dakota looks out at the trees. "It feels like nothing bad could happen. Like you're tucked away from the world."

"Crime can happen anywhere."

Dakota scoffs. "Out here? Someone would have to be out of their mind."

"It would be unwise, that's for certain. They'd encounter people hellbent on defending themselves."

"Has anything like that happened?"

"Not really. We've had some nasty fistfights between the cowboys. One pretty angry cowboy who tried to steal an HCC truck after my dad fired him."

Dakota's eyes widen. "And? What happened?"

"My dad shot out a tire, then pulled the guy from the truck and held him down until the police showed up."

Her head moves slowly back and forth. "Your dad is a badass."

I smile. "Yeah, he is. That was twenty years ago though. He's getting older."

"Right," Dakota says softly, and between the single word and her tone, I'm reminded of our agreement. Somehow, I haven't thought of it once since I showed up at her hotel earlier. I've been too busy enjoying my time with her.

I glance at her profile. Her perfect, straight nose, her plump lips, her thick eyelashes. The way her chin tips up just slightly, perpetually defiant. She looks at me, smiles, but it's a little sad.

"What?" I ask.

She finishes her wine and places the empty glass on the small table between us. "You let down your guard with me. You brought me here and let me see that photo." She breathes deeply and angles her body so she's addressing me directly. "Every month I donate to two different charities. The Aneurysm Foundation, and a battered women's shelter. That's why I'm in so much debt. For a long time I donated more than I could afford, and used my credit cards to pay for everything else. It was a way for me to atone."

I recognize the openness on her face, the vulnerability, but I'm not able to give it the attention it deserves just yet. The word she used, *atone*, has captured me.

"I understand your connection to aneurysm, but battered women? Were you hurt, Dakota?" My blood begins to warm.

"No," she says quickly. "I was in a long relationship with a man who was married, though I didn't know it. I felt so guilty when I found out, and I kept going over and over our time together, wondering if there were signs and I just ignored them. The women's shelter was the best place I could think of aside from sending restitution directly to his wife." She huffs out a mirthless laugh. "And before you ask, I know I could ask my dad for help. I was a difficult teenager and a rebellious young adult and I can't tell him about the debt. He believes in me, thinks I've climbed back up from my fall from grace. The prodigal daughter. That has more value than my debt." She rubs her palms on her shorts. "I canceled the payments recently. Getting on the right track. I just thought I'd share that with you, since you told me about Shepherd." She sends a weak smile across the eighteen inches separating our chairs. "You don't own the rights to letting guilt fuck you up."

I swallow. Her words run back through my mind. There's so much she has just said, and I don't know where to start. So instead of saying anything that won't be good enough for the vulnerability she has just shown, I thank her for trusting me.

"Same to you," she says. "Thank you for trusting me enough to invite me over and let me see your place."

I nod at her. How had it escaped my attention that offering my home to do her laundry was a show of vulnerability? And it's not like it was done with reluctance, either. I wanted her here. Wanted to share this part of me with her.

The washer dings. Dakota gets up and walks inside.

The oven timer goes off. I follow her in.

Dakota switches clothes and starts a new load. I throw together a quick salad and serve dinner at the kitchen table. Dakota sits while I grab another beer and refill her wine.

Dakota moans when she takes her first bite of meatloaf. I chuckle, and she places a palm over her heart. "Please don't ever stop making this for me."

"Never," I promise, then freeze. "Or at least, I'll make it for a year."

We meet eyes briefly, then look away.

We don't talk much after that. I think we're talked out.

After dinner, we play spades. Dakota has way more laundry than she realized, and the clock creeps later and later. It's midnight by the time her laundry is finished. For the same reason she asked me to stay with her last night, I'm asking her to stay with me tonight.

"The second bedroom has a bed. My mom made it up like a guest room. We'll put fresh sheets on, because I have no idea when those were last washed since nobody has ever slept on them."

Dakota rifles through her clean clothes and pulls out a T-shirt and soft-looking shorts. "Lead the way," she says, yawning and pointing down the hall.

We change the linens together. I brush my teeth and give Dakota the unused toothbrush from my last visit to the dentist. She stands beside me at the sink, and we sneak looks at each other in the mirror, except we're not really sneaking because we're being obvious about it. We brush, spit, rinse. Dakota puts her hand on my forearm and pushes me out into the hallway. “Sorry, but I have to pee, and that isn’t something I’m doing with you in the room.”

I step into my bedroom and remove my shirt, then exchange my jeans for pajama pants. She calls my name when she comes out of the bathroom. I step into the hall. She has this soft look on her face, and I see the same girl from five years ago, the one who split my world in two. “Yeah?” I swallow back the memories.

“Thank you. For being a listener, and a chef, and a laundromat. And also, for giving up so much of your life to protect our country. You’re a hero, Wes. Really.” She comes to where I stand in my open bedroom door, rises up on her toes, and brushes a kiss on my cheek. She turns and walks back to the guest room, closing the door gently behind her.

And I stand there, glued to the spot, the feel of her lips still on my cheek.

26

WES

Sweat burns my eyes. The child whimpers. The woman is silent, but her terrified eyes scream louder than if she were to open her mouth. I'm on one knee in the middle of the street. The town is free from civilians, except for the unlucky ones the insurgents kept to use as martyrs. My guys stand around me, taking fire, while I work on disarming the bomb strapped to this woman and child.

"Not much time, Hayden," Milicevic yells.

I don't answer. All my energy is going toward the explosive. Thirty seconds and counting.

A whizzing crack fills the air, someone beside me slumps to the ground. My eyes stay trained on the woman and child, but the sorrow fills me anyway. I don't need to see who it was. They are all my brothers.

"Hayden, fall back," Milicevic commands.

I grunt my answer. No. My fingers work faster, seeking out wires, trying to understand a bomb that is homemade and also high tech, something that was carefully crafted to confuse the opposition—me.

"Now, Hayden. This is an order," he barks in my face.

He doesn't wait for me to obey. Arms wrap around my chest from behind and he drags me back.

The child's tears create paths in the dust caking his cheeks, like a river with muddy banks.

The woman never opens her mouth.

So I scream for her.

"WES? WES, WAKE UP."

My eyes blink open. The muscles in my legs and arms are coiled tight, as if they've been in motion. My heart races, blood and adrenaline tearing through me.

My vision adjusts to the darkness and I see the outline of a woman. "Dakota." My voice is hoarse, with a pleading, almost desperate, edge.

"You were having a nightmare," she whispers, leaning over my bed. Tentatively she reaches for me, her hand splaying out on my chest. Her fingers curl and uncurl, and I see what she's doing. She's not just soothing me. She's soothing my *heart.*

I wait for the embarrassment to warm my neck and face, but it never comes. Instead I feel... relief? How can that be? I shouldn't be turning toward her like this, shouldn't be closing my eyes and allowing her sweetness to melt into my damaged parts.

"Wes?" My name is a question, and I know what she's asking.

"No," I say quickly, even though part of me wants to say *yes* and tell her about my dream.

Tell her and be free of some of it. Would the wound begin to heal? Is it even okay if it does? Do I deserve to heal? The more time I spend around Dakota, the more I begin to think that maybe I can have a sliver of the happiness I once wanted for myself.

Dakota climbs onto the bed and sits back on her heels. The outside edge of her bent leg presses against my side. She leans down, lips grazing my cheek, sliding over to the corner of my mouth. “I can take your mind off it,” she whispers, her breath warm on my skin.

It’s not even an offer that needs consideration. The answer is *yes, absolutely, of course, I’ve been waiting five years to be with you again.*

Desire rushes through me, hot and intense. I need her now. If I am the wound, Dakota is the salve.

I roll her over without warning and she gasps. I cover her body with the length of mine, prop myself up on a forearm, and turn on the nightstand lamp. The yellow light casts a soft glow.

“I need to see you,” I explain, staring down into the depths of the hazel eyes I’ve never forgotten.

“Same,” she chokes out, cupping my cheek.

My head dips low and I skim the tip of my nose over the pink flush on her cheeks. Her fingernails rake through my hair and down my neck, sending a shudder through me.

My mouth moves over hers, and she meets me with the hunger I remember from before. Her back arches, breasts pushing into me, hips urging me on. Going slow is not in the cards for us right now.

I sit up and help her take off her shirt, then grip the waistband of her shorts. She lifts her hips, the cotton fabric clearing her legs and landing somewhere in the room. At a time like this, pausing is required even in the midst of frenzy. I need to appreciate what’s in front of me. Dakota with her soft, creamy skin, her curves, her feminine shoulders. I don’t think I’ve ever appreciated shoulders before, but looking down at Dakota right now, I'm definitely understanding their appeal.

"Dakota, you are so fucking gorgeous." My eyes stay trained on her as my hand dips low, gliding over her stomach, south to the apex of her legs. A low groan vibrates in my throat when my fingers slip over her.

She swallows hard, her eyes hooded, breath coming in heavy pants. "Only you," she stops to drag in air, "could use bad language in a compliment."

I grin. "You might be right about that."

"Come here," she says, holding her arms out, wanting me on top of her.

I do as she asks, lying down on her but careful to support my weight on my forearms. Her leg lifts and her toes slide into the waistband of my pants, gripping the fabric, then yanking them down my body.

"Hidden talents," I murmur, kissing a trail from her neck up to her jaw.

She turns her head and captures my lips, pulling my lower lip between her teeth and biting gently. A moan reverberates through my throat and she replaces her teeth with her tongue.

"More," I tell her, my tongue dipping into her mouth to sweep against hers. Her hips buck with impatience, and it makes me chuckle against her, until I realize something that cuts off my laugh.

Pulling back a few inches, I look down at her bewildered expression. "Fuck," I growl. "I don't have a condom." I've been sexually active for nearly twenty years of my life, you'd think I'd have thought ahead a little bit. To be fair, I'm not exactly a ladies' man.

Dakota's surprise melts away and she smiles up at me. "Wes, it's okay. I'm on birth control."

"Thank God," I groan, relief racing around my body to extinguish the panic-fire that spread through me.

Dakota reaches between us, gripping me, hitching up one leg so it's alongside her body, and lines me up against her.

A breath hisses between my teeth. We used condoms before. All three times. I'm not even inside her yet, and I already know this is going to ruin me. I'm a goner.

I push inside, and, just like I knew, it's indescribable. It's better than Christmas, early morning rides on Ranger, and an ice-cold beer on a scorching day—combined.

Elbows planted above her shoulders, I rock forward and fill her completely. My head swirls with thoughts of Dakota, and the scent of the hair my nose is pressed against, and the incredible feel of her body beneath mine.

She makes a sound, something low and primal, and it urges me on. I pull back, rock forward again, setting up a rhythm. Dakota matches me, an active participant beneath me. I kiss her as one hand slides down, fingers curling around her hip, holding on. My breath comes in small, sharp stabs and our bodies slide together, slick with exertion. My eyes close against the intensity. I want to hold on to it, and let it go unbridled at the exact same time. I open my eyes to find Dakota looking at me.

"So good," she says, her voice garbled, the words almost incoherent. She places a hand on my chest, over my heart, like she did when she woke me from my nightmare. "Wes," she bites out. "So good."

Oh. It's not the sex she's talking about. *Wes. So good.* It's me.

Something inside me loosens. I don't know what it is, but it's there, this feeling of having more room. Having space to breathe, to be, to exist. To feel.

I lean down and claim Dakota's mouth, run my tongue along hers. Can she taste my feelings? Sense the space that's suddenly opened up in my chest?

My lips remain pressed to hers, and when her leg muscles tense and her back arches, I'm there, consuming her pleasured cries. The sound of her, the feel of her, is everything I need, and my entire body shakes. Her fingers dig into my back as I ride it out, and she moans softly into my mouth one more time.

Our bodies still, and I pull away to breathe, but I don't go very far. My cheek presses against her chest, my hot breath falling down into the valley of her breasts. Her fingers run through my hair as our breathing regulates.

I want to say something, anything, but words escape me. They seem so unimportant compared to what we just said with our bodies. So I lie there, my head rising and falling with her breath, rooted in place and watching the outline of her breast in the dim light.

"I need to get cleaned up," she murmurs after a few minutes.

Oh. Right. In all my sated glory, I'd forgotten the physical remnants of me are still inside her.

Rolling off her, I stand and offer her a hand. She accepts, smiling up at me as I pull her from the bed and wrap her in a hug. Just breathing in the scent of her hair makes me hard again.

Her chuckle bounces against my chest. "I really need to get cleaned up," she reminds me, and when I let her go, I see that her legs are crossed at the thigh.

"Shit, sorry." I step aside and she walks quickly into the bathroom.

When she's finished, I take a turn and come back. I must've been expecting to see her in my bedroom, because when I walk in and she's not there, I feel surprised. I walk back into the hall and spot the glow of the open fridge.

Dakota steps away with two water bottles. She's wearing my T-shirt.

"I hope you don't mind," she says, handing me a water and using two fingers to pull at the fabric.

"Not at all." In fact, it's the sexiest thing I've seen her in yet.

"So, um..." Dakota twists off the top to her water and takes a drink. She points back toward my bedroom. "Should we talk about that? Or act like it didn't happen?"

"Neither."

Her head tips to the side as she attempts to understand.

I set my water on the counter and take her free hand in mine. It's cold from the bottle, so I rub my thumb over her skin to warm it. A deep breath fills my lungs as I search for a way to describe how I feel, but eventually I end up with the most basic of all things—the truth. "Something happened just now. When I was with you it felt like I could breathe again. And that's a feeling I like. It's been a long time since I felt anything other than pain and regret in my chest, and you took some of that away." I let go of her hand and step closer, wrapping my arms around her body. She looks up at me, her palm running the length of my back. "The truth is, every time I'm with you I feel a little more like my old self. The person I haven't allowed myself to be because I didn't think I deserved it. But when I'm around you, Dakota, you look at me like I'm someone worth caring for."

"Because you are, Wes. I wish I could take away what hurts you so deeply."

"I don't think anything can. But you're the only thing I've ever found that makes me feel better."

She smiles up at me, but her grin devolves into a yawn. She tries to cover it, but I've already seen it.

"Come on." I lead her back to my bed, and she climbs in. Before I follow, I look down at her. She pulls off my shirt and pulls the sheet over her, tucking it under her arms.

"You look damn good in my bed."

"If you like it so much, maybe I'll do it again sometime."

I lie down beside her. She rolls onto her side to face me. I tell her, "I'd like that," when what I really want to say is, *Stay here forever.*

Her fingertips slide over my jawbone. "Penny for your thoughts?"

How can I say what I'm thinking? *I want to cancel our agreement. I want you to love me and I think I've loved you from the moment I laid eyes on you five years ago. And the second I saw you again everything I've been working so hard to keep locked up began to shake and now I'm starting to not want to contain it anymore.*

I reach between us, gripping the sheet and yanking it down. For the second time tonight, I cover her like a blanket, and talk with my body because words fail me.

I kiss her lips, slide inside her, and hope like hell she hears what I cannot seem to say.

I am broken. I am hurt. I am terrified. You make it all more bearable.

27

DAKOTA

My eyes blink open. A smile curves my lips. Unused muscles protest their soreness when I stretch.

Wes.

He's responsible for my sore thighs. And my smile.

I reach out, sliding a hand over the flannel sheets. His side of the bed is empty, but still warm. He hasn't been up long.

At the foot of the bed, I find the same T-shirt I donned in the middle of the night and pull it on. I lift the fabric to my nose and inhale deeply. It smells of Wes.

Slipping out of bed, I locate my pajama bottoms on the ground and slide them on. My nose picks up the scent of coffee and I follow it out to the percolating machine. Through the window I see Wes on the front porch, leaning against a beam. He wears pajama pants, no shirt, and the air of a man whose burdens recently got smaller.

Last night helped him. I don't know how, specifically, other than taking his mind off his problems for a while. I don't know what it means for our agreement.

I wait for the coffee to finish brewing, then pour two

cups and join Wes outside. He watches me walk, and I'll be damned if there isn't the biggest smile on his face.

I hand him the coffee and blatantly take in his beautiful upper half. His corded, ropy muscles come from life, from his job, not arm day at the gym. His body is a testament to the work he does every day on this ranch, and I can't help imagining what the scruff on his face would feel like scraping its way up my thighs. His smile hasn't decreased, and I say, "Correct me if I'm wrong, but you look like you got laid last night."

Wes nods his thanks at the coffee and winks. "Twice, actually."

"Wow, lucky guy."

"I am." He wraps an arm around my waist and kisses my temple. My heartbeat picks up pace, and I know I'm in dangerous territory. I have the urge to speak up right now, to force a conversation about what last night meant, but I don't want to yet. I want to keep this good feeling going for a little longer. It's as simple as that.

I look out at the trees. Now, in the morning light, I can see how high up we are. The clearing in front of Wes's cabin, the mixture of tall pine and cottonwood trees, and to the left, the gently sloping hill leading to the backside of the homestead. Pine cones and pine needles dust the ground. I close my eyes and breathe in. The scent of earth, the sharp and sweet pine, combined with Wes's manly smell, is heaven on Earth.

My eyes flutter open and I gaze out at the landscape. "Someone once told me that loving the ranch doesn't come from the sight of the sunrise through the steam curling up from your morning coffee, but I think maybe that's how she draws you in. Because I've got to tell you, I think I'm falling for the ranch right now."

"Is that right?" Wes's voice rumbles beside me.

"Oh, definitely. I can see why you'd do whatever you need to do to make it yours. This place is incredible." I take another deep breath. "I wish I could bottle that up and take it back to the hotel with me." The smell of stale carpet leaves a lot to be desired.

"That smell is what I missed most when I was overseas." He crooks a smile at me. "Well, that and my mom, of course. Make sure you tell her I said that if she ever asks."

I laugh. "I'll be sure to."

We fall quiet. I think we're both thinking the same thing. Or maybe I'm just thinking it, and the thoughts are so loud it feels like I can't possibly be alone in them.

"Do you want to talk about the dream, Wes?" I'm careful not to call it what it really was. *Nightmare.*

He tenses, his fingers curling tighter around his cup.

My fingertips press against his forearm. "You don't owe me anything, Wes. Not a damn thing. But I do know how awful grief can be. And guilt. I was lucky enough to have my sister and my dad when my mom died. Their words didn't erase my feelings, but at least they were there. I had people." My voice drops down to a whisper. "Who are your people, Wes?"

His lips purse together and he stares out across the land. Land he loves so deeply he would marry a woman he doesn't love to have it.

The longer he takes to respond, the more I already know the answer.

I raise my coffee to my lips, and before I take a sip I tell him, "There's a meeting at the VFW every Wednesday afternoon at four. I saw a flyer for it at the Merc."

Wes imitates me, talking with his coffee cup poised at

his lips, as if they are props in our conversation. This is shaky territory for us to be in. "What's the meeting for?"

My toes curl, as if I might need to spring away at a moment's notice. And the truth is, I might. But if I don't tell Wes a resource is available to him, right in his own town, just because I'm scared of his response? That would make me a coward.

"The meeting is for those suffering from PTSD." I'm careful with my tone as I tell him. I'm not soft-spoken, or pleading, not even a hint of pity. Just the facts. I saw his response to me that night of the park concert. If there is anything I can do to piss Wes off, it's show him an ounce of pity.

His expression right now is the one he goes back to on default—stoic. He says, "You think I need the meeting?"

"I think every person who returns from combat needs at least a meeting like that. Other people who know what you've been through. You could tell me, and I would listen. But I wouldn't really know what you've been through. The best people to talk to are those who've been through it themselves."

He nods once. Not dismissively, but like he understands. And I feel a small victory for bringing up the meeting and not getting kicked out of Wes's cabin with my suitcase tossed out behind me.

"I'll think about it." His voice is rough like gravel.

Time for a subject change. "Want to know what I'm thinking about right now?" My tone is playful, and Wes looks at me, a little spark back in those deep, dark eyes of his.

"What?"

"Breakfast. A big one, too. I hope you have something good in that kitchen."

Wes turns his head sharply toward the homestead. "It's Sunday..."

"Uh huh..."

"I have breakfast with my family on Sundays."

"Oh." My cheeks warm. "Well then," I back away, offering him a lopsided smile as I go. "I'll just change and get out of your hair."

"I want you to come with me."

I gulp. "I guess it would look good for them to see us together. Especially, you know, so early in the day. Hot and heavy, right?" The joke tastes bad in my mouth and I force myself not to wrinkle my nose.

Wes stares at me for a long moment, and I'd give almost anything to be able to see into that mind of his. "Right," he says, drawing out the word. I know there is so much more behind that simple, one-word response.

"Should we talk about last night?" I blurt out. So much for keeping the good times rolling a little longer.

Wes hesitates, then says, "I suppose so."

He watches me, waiting. I cross my arms and nod at him. "You talk first."

"I guess we should decide what sleeping with each other meant, and what it means to our agreement, right?"

"Yes."

Wes regards me for longer than I'd like, but at least he's not stoic. If anything, he's the very opposite of stoic. Expressions flit across his face. Squinting eyes, taut cheeks, twisting lips. It's like he's having an entire conversation in his head, teasing out every possible outcome like a game of chess.

Then he takes a step toward me. And two more, until only inches separate us. "I want the ranch, there's no doubt about it. And I want to help you out, too. But last night did something to me." He palms his chest. "You made space in here, and I feel like it's easier to breathe."

My pulse thrums at his admission.

His eyes stay focused on mine, but he reaches for me. His fingers skirt my wrist, slide up my forearm. It all feels... inevitable. Last night and right now, both are conclusions I should've seen coming. No matter what we did along the way, this was always going to be where we ended up.

His fingers feather up my arm, over my shoulder, down my side, sliding over the fabric of my T-shirt. He stops at my hip bone, his fingers digging in, pulling me until my body is flush with his. My skin is hot, a burning molten liquid, and I fill in every line of him until there is no way to tell us apart. His arm wraps around my lower back, holding me in place, while his other hand roams my hips, my side, my backside.

There's an electric buzzing in the air, or maybe it's just inside me but it's so loud it feels like it's all around us. My arms wrap around Wes's shoulders, my fingernails skating the back of his neck. He shudders, and it reminds me of the tightening of his muscles when he came last night. I drag one fingernail up his neck, across his chin, landing on his bottom lip.

My breath is heavy, and the heat of his exhale seeps into my skin. He pulls my finger into his mouth and bites down gently. A low moan rolls around my throat. The buzzing in the air gets louder.

I take back my finger and brush my lips lightly against his. His gaze is dark and hot, and his heart beats furiously against my chest.

He must decide he's finished with the prelude because his hand rises to cup the back of my head and he presses his lips to mine. He is sweet, and then not. Gentle, and then turbulent, and I'm matching him in every way. This toe-curling intensity and overwhelming desire makes me wonder if there was a live wire connecting us these past five years.

His tongue urges my mouth open, and he swipes inside. A low, guttural moan fills the crisp morning air and I'm not sure if it was me or him who made the sound. His hands leave my back and my head, finding my thighs, dipping under the fabric of my shorts and pushing the soft fabric up as high as it will go. I rip my mouth away to breathe, tipping my chin to the porch ceiling, and Wes leans in, taking the opportunity to drag the tip of his tongue up my neck, and nip along my jawbone.

"What are you doing to me, woman?" he murmurs against my skin.

"The same thing you're doing to me."

His teeth graze my earlobe and he sighs, pulling back to look down at me. There's a new look in his eyes. Something tender and vulnerable.

I lean in, my lips tracing a design over his chest. His breath hisses through my hair. "Someone once said it's not a good idea to mix business with pleasure." My low voice tumbles against him, and my actions make it clear to both of us what I think of my words.

"That someone can go fuck themselves." He moves quickly, lifting me off my feet and throwing me over his shoulder.

"Please tell me you're taking me to the bedroom," I moan my plea against his back.

"Right now, Dakota, there is no other place for us."

My heart melts at the word *us*.

I think I might be royally screwed. Literally and figuratively.

Beau is standing in the dining room, reaching into a bowl of berries, when we come through the back door. I get the feeling there isn't a ton that could surprise the man, but I'm pretty sure we've managed to.

Wes and I are holding hands. We're late. And I'm almost positive our cheeks are still pink from exertion. Convincing his family we're passionate about one another won't be difficult. What just happened in Wes's cabin was as hot and heavy as it gets.

Beau tosses a blackberry in his mouth and meets us halfway. "Dakota, it's nice to see you again." He looks questioningly into Wes's eyes. Wes grins back at him, and based on the widening of Beau's eyes, I think Wes has just managed to surprise him again.

"It's nice to see you too, Beau." I glance from Beau to Wes. "I'm going to find Jessie." I dart away and leave the two to talk.

Jessie is in the living room, sitting on the couch with her knees pulled into her chest. She's chewing on her thumbnail, her signature long braid settled on her shoulder.

"Hi, Jessie."

She startles and looks up. When she sees it's me, a big smile breaks onto her face. Popping up from the couch, she hurries over and throws her arms around me.

"Dakota, it's so, so, so good to see you!"

Her exuberance makes me laugh. "You too, Jessie. How are you? You looked like you were knee-deep in thought when I walked in."

She pulls me to the couch, waving around her free hand as we walk. Her nails are painted turquoise. "Oh, you know. Boy trouble."

I cluck my tongue and shake my head, as if I know just what she's talking about. And I do. In the past and in the present. What's more troublesome than what's happening between me and Wes at the moment?

Jessie pounces. "What's going on? Is Wes too much to handle? Please, please, just be patient. I know sometimes he can be dickish, but—"

"Dickish?" Wes stands at the entrance, arms folded in front of his chest.

Jessie frowns. "This is an A and B conversation, Wes, so—"

"So I should C my way out?"

I stifle a laugh. Jessie sticks out her tongue.

Juliette walks in. Suddenly the room feels colder.

"Hi, Juliette." I smile brightly at her. Chilly reception or not, she's still Wes's mom.

"Dakota, what a surprise. I didn't realize you were joining us today."

"We just walked over from my cabin," Wes says, walking over and giving his mom a one-armed hug.

She smiles tightly. "Well, great. I'll set the table for one more. I was just coming in here to tell you everything is ready."

Jessie follows her mom. Wes and I walk far enough behind that Jessie and Juliette can't hear us.

"She hates me," I hiss.

"She doesn't hate you. This is just new for her, and sudden. She loved Warner's wife, Anna, and what she did hurt my mom. She's going to keep you at arm's length until she sees that—" He cuts off. "Never mind."

"Until she sees what?"

But Wes doesn't answer, and suddenly we're surrounded by his entire family. Gramps says grace. Warner has his kids this weekend, and I watch him with them. He's a good dad, helping Charlie fill his plate and reminding Peyton to place her napkin in her lap. Wyatt is quiet, as he almost always is. Of all the Haydens, he is the one I know the least about.

I've just taken a bite of food when Beau asks Wes if we've set a date. My eyes bulge. Wes blinks. Jessie squeals.

"What?" she shouts. "Date? A date for what?" Her excitement is directed right into my eyes. "Dakota, what's going on?"

I'm still chewing and attempting not to choke.

"Thanks, Dad," Wes says sarcastically.

Beau makes a face. "Christ, how can I be expected to keep this shit straight?"

I duck my head to hide my smile. After last night and this morning, I can't keep this shit straight either.

"Language, Dad," Warner cautions, pointing at his kids. Beau makes another face.

"Wes and Dakota, do you have something to tell us?" Jessie asks, bouncing in her seat.

Wes looks at me. I offer a barely perceptible shrug, telling him to go for it. A deal is a deal, even if we did complicate it.

"Dakota and I are going to get married."

And there it is. We've said it between us plenty of times, but now it's out, available for public consumption. The surreal just became the real.

Jessie's hands fly to her mouth. Her eyes are as large as the plate her pancakes are piled on. Wyatt blinks rapidly. Warner looks... pained. He's quick to banish the sorrow and regret in his eyes, replacing it with disbelief. Gramps stares at Wes, two wrinkled fingers pressed to his lips. He is not fooled, not by a long shot.

Wes looks out at his family. "You know what they say.

When you find the one you want to spend the rest of your life with, you want the rest of your life to start as soon as possible."

Everyone is silent, staring at Wes after he delivers the sappy quote that is so uncharacteristic of him.

"Um, please don't ever do that again," I joke, deadpan.

Wyatt laughs first, then Warner and Gramps. Jessie joins. Beau smirks. Juliette is as glacial as ever.

Wes joins his siblings and Gramps. "Yeah, that felt weird to say."

"It was even more odd to hear." Warner grins.

For the rest of breakfast, Jessie hounds me about a wedding. I've given no thought to it, and her disappointment shows. "I'll get on it," I promise her.

"Where's the ring?" she asks, gaze zeroed in on my bare finger.

"I haven't found the right one yet," Wes tells her. "Now stop asking so many questions."

Wes and I clean the kitchen after everyone is finished, then head back to his cabin.

"So we're engaged, huh?" I ask on the walk over.

"Sorry about that," he murmurs. "I would've done a better job making an announcement, but it was sprung on me."

"No, it's okay. I don't think I could've handled something romantic. This way it doesn't feel like more than it is."

Wes's gaze cuts to me. He takes my hand as we walk. "I don't know what it is anymore."

"Me neither."

"I still need the ranch."

"I still need to get rid of my debt."

When we get to his place, I go inside and lug my suitcase

to the front door. Wes grabs it from me and walks it to my car.

"We're moving forward then?" he asks, coming to where I stand in the open car door.

"Yes."

He kisses me. It's soft and sweet, with the promise of more. When he pulls back, he tucks a strand of blowing hair behind my ear. "Meeting at the VFW, huh?"

I nod. "That's what the flyer at the Merc said."

"Thanks for letting me know."

"Sure."

He backs away, eyes on me.

I get in and drive away. Maybe our marriage of convenience isn't the only thing moving forward.

28

DAKOTA

THE NEXT MORNING, AFTER I'VE FINISHED A VIDEO conference with my dad updating him on The Orchard, I get in the shower so I can head to the jobsite. I grab my phone before I step in and call my sister.

"Hey, Abby." I press the speaker button on my phone and turn the volume all the way up, then lay it on the highest shelf above the toilet, directly beside the shower.

"Dakota? Do you have a direct line into my mind?"

I grin at the wonder in her voice and step into the shower, leaving a portion of the sliding glass door open so I can talk to her.

"Not that I know of," I answer, tipping my head back into the warm spray of the shower. "Why do you ask?"

"I was just thinking of you."

"I hope these were positive thoughts."

I can practically hear her eye roll. "Of course they were, Dakota."

"How are you?"

"Who cares, let's talk about you. How are you? How's the project? How's Sierra Grande?"

She's really asking *How's Wes?* but she's trying to be roundabout.

"Good, I suppose." I squirt shampoo into my palm and lather it in my hair. "FYI, I'm taking a shower."

"Thanks for not calling me on FaceTime."

"Nothing you haven't seen before."

"True story. Now start talking because you sound weird and it probably has something to do with that sexy, brooding cowboy."

I angle my face toward the opening in the shower door and keep my hair in the running water. "I slept with him, Ab."

She whistles. "Tell me everything. Married sex is boring."

"Does Wes seem like the kind of guy who wants me to air our intimate moments?"

Abby makes a sound, almost like an irritated growl. "Fine. Just tell me if it was like you remember it?"

I bite my lip at the ache spreading throughout my belly and down into my thighs. "It was better."

Abby laughs. "Good for you, Dakota. Good for him, too. Something tells me he needed that."

"I agree." Especially after that nightmare. I'm not going to tell Abby that part. It's Wes's to share, and I'm pretty sure I already know how likely he is to tell anybody about that. "He told his family we're getting married."

When she doesn't respond, I assume she hasn't heard me and I repeat myself.

"Dakota." Her tone is more serious now. "When are you planning on telling Dad?"

One side of my nose screws up as I contemplate her question. "Never would be preferable." It's crossed my mind that maybe, with a little luck and a whole lot of well-meaning fibs, I could get through this marriage of convenience without telling him. It would be cowardly, but so much easier.

"Dakota..."

She's using her big sister voice.

"I know, I know. Just let me think about that a little more, okay?" I press my face into the water, so I don't hear what she says next and ask her to repeat it.

"I asked if it was just sex."

Wes's words come back to me. *I feel like it's easier to breathe. What are you doing to me?*

"I don't think so, Ab. We agreed that it meant something, but that we both still need what the other can provide."

"What a mess."

"A messy mess." I sigh and turn off the shower. "I need to get ready for work now."

We say goodbye and hang up. I get ready for work, and the entire drive over all I see is Wes's face, his shuttered heart opening up for me. It feels precious and terrifying, like holding a newborn baby.

29

WES

DAKOTA WAS RIGHT. I STOPPED BY THE MERC YESTERDAY. ON A board near the entrance, stuck between an advertisement for lawn mowing and coupons to a craft store, was a light blue paper. *PTSD support group, VFW Post 0507.* Below that, it listed the address and meeting time.

I took a picture with my phone, bought a package of sunflower seeds and a bottle of water, and spent ten minutes looking at funny postcards. I forgot how much I loved going to the Merc with my mom when I was little.

I'm on my way to the meeting now. I don't know what to expect, and that makes me nervous. Are we going to sit around and talk? How many people will be there? Do I really want to share my story with strangers?

I guess that's another thing Dakota is right about. I need to talk to people who've been in the military. People who understand.

I pull into the parking lot and kill the engine. The VFW is a long, squat building, made of gray bricks. An American flag undulates in the breeze, and a handful of cars are parked out front.

Growing up in Sierra Grande, I passed this place plenty of times, and my dad explained VFW stood for Veterans of Foreign War. I pictured old men, wrinkled and wearing pins on their hats. From my childlike point of view, veterans were old.

I get out of my truck. Here I am, and I'm not old. Or maybe I am.

I start for the door. I don't have any second thoughts about the meeting. Once I've decided something, that's it.

The inside isn't what I thought it would be. There's a large, rectangular table, with folding chairs all around it. I'd been picturing chairs in a circle, like an AA meeting. *Hello, my name is Wes and I have PTSD.*

"Hello, there," a voice calls out.

A man approaches. He's old. Pins adorn his black hat, *Vietnam Veteran* stitched across the front in yellow thread.

"Hello, sir." I extend a hand. "Is the meeting still on for today?"

"You betcha," he answers, shaking my hand. "I'm Bill Tennyson." He motions to two more men I hadn't noticed when I walked in. "That's Malcolm Owenfeldt and Creighton Smith."

I lift my hand in a wave. "I'm Wes Hayden." If Bill recognizes my name, he doesn't show it. It puts me at ease.

"We're expecting a couple more," he tells me, adjusting his hat. "They'll trickle in. We have one coming from Brighton, he's usually a couple minutes late."

I settle in at the table with the three men. Malcolm is older like Bill, but Creighton is probably only ten years older than me.

We comment on the weather. Bill mentions the construction going on at the edge of town. Creighton says his wife met the woman in charge of the new building at a book club meeting and really liked her. I smile politely and say nothing. I came here to talk about the military, not Dakota. One tough subject at a time.

The door opens and two more men walk in. Both older. No pins on hats though. They take seats and say hello.

"Wes, this is Walt Jenkins and Bryan Blackstone. Guys, meet Wes Hayden."

Walt eyes me. He looks like a quintessential grandpa. White comb-over, round face, pleated slacks. "Hayden, huh? Like the cattle ranch?"

I'm tempted to lie, but I don't. "Yes." I don't offer more than that, because it's a stretch for me to be here at all and I don't want my family's reputation to affect what I've come here to accomplish.

Bill starts the meeting by telling me what years he served, and what countries he was in. This goes on around the table, each man introducing themselves in this way. When it gets to me, I tell them about my three tours in the Middle East, the battles I fought in, and the job I had.

Walt whistles when I tell them I was on EOD. "Thank you for your service, son."

I nod. "Same to you. Same to all of you."

"My guess is that you're here for a reason, Wes," Bill says. "Do you want to talk about it?"

I lean forward in my chair, place my steepled hands under my chin. I'm not sure where to look, so I keep my eyes down on the plastic table. "I joined because I was angry. After the attacks on September 11th, I felt this sense of rage like I'd never felt before. My beloved country had been hurt. I wanted to go over there and kick ass." I look up into the patient and understanding eyes of men who felt what I felt. "Four years turned into eight, and then twelve. The sense of duty, of loyalty to my fellow soldiers, was powerful. I couldn't leave them behind for a normal life. Near the end of my last tour, shit went south. We went into a town where we knew insurgents would be. We'd already told the people of the town to evacuate. And they did. Except for the unlucky ones who were used as martyrs." Tears sting my eyes and I bite my bottom lip to keep them at bay. "We rolled into town in our armored Humvees, and right in the middle of the goddamn street there was a woman and a child with a bomb strapped to them." I'm in the stale air of the VFW, but all I smell is dust and anguish. It's cool in this room, but I'm hot under my uniform and Kevlar. My voice is the only sound, but my ears fill with the cacophony of exploding mortars, yelling, and radio commands.

"I knelt in front of them and worked on deactivating it. My men surrounded me, protecting me, while they took fire. One was shot. I remember the sound of him hitting the ground. We had to fall back, but I didn't want to. My lieutenant had to pull me away." I feel it, the tight grip around my chest, the feeling of being dragged. "We were around the corner when I heard the bomb go off. A part of me died that day alongside that woman and child. I didn't know them at all, but that didn't matter. Something connected us, and I couldn't understand what had reached out and touched me so deeply. I'd seen terrible tragedies over and over, and you get to a point where you've seen so much that your threshold for tolerating suffering is higher. But that day I felt her terror." I palm my chest, where I keep it locked away. "My threshold vanished. She and the little boy, they were just human beings with a basic instinct to survive. I wanted them to survive, and I couldn't make that happen. I feel guilty, but also I'm disgusted. Let down." Around the table, each man listens closely. More than a few have tears in their eyes. "I got out after that, and I haven't been able to adjust. I don't find joy in very many things. Life's shine has worn off. I see their faces, and I think, what was the point of it all?" Moisture hits my hand, and I realize it's my own tears, sliding off my cheeks.

The men are quiet, and then Walt speaks. "I don't know the point of most of life. My wife was the nicest, sweetest person who ever put two feet on this earth, and she passed away from cancer. Why?" He shrugs. "God only knows. But Wes, I was a lot like you for a long time. Angry and resentful, confused and embittered. Not only was it hard for me to find happiness, but I made sure I pushed it away if I did find it. It was a terrible way to live, and I regret it. I was in Vietnam, and I saw some things a person should never see. Here's what I figured out. My real problem was not what happened, but how I felt about what happened."

Walt's words sink in, finding a home in the jumble of emotions. Each man has something to say, but Walt's words are the ones that have grown claws and dug in.

When the meeting is over, Bill brings out coffee and store-bought cookies.

The coffee isn't good, but for some reason that makes me like it. No attempt has been made to impress, and I like that. Taking a sip, I ask, "So, you guys meet every week, even though you all know one another's stories?"

Creighton takes a bite of his cookie. "It's nice to be around each other. I can't speak for everyone, but sometimes I feel a restlessness and I need to break away from my family. Finding this group saved my marriage."

Malcom claps his hand on Creighton's back, which makes him cough because he's chewing, and everyone laughs.

When I leave, I shake hands with everyone and tell them

I'll be back. And I will. Come hell or high-water, I'll be here. This may just be what saves me.

And I have one person to thank for putting the idea in my head.

Dakota created a little bit of space in my chest, and it was a breath of oxygen for a drowning man. That lungful of air was enough to make me want more, but I can't get it unless I make more space on my own.

I pull out of the parking lot of the VFW feeling like I just hit the jackpot.

30

DAKOTA

"You know you don't have to be here all day long?" Scott leans against one of the poles of the tent I set up earlier today. After being here day after day without a place to sit other than my car, or shade over my head (also from my car), I bought the kind of tent well-suited for the sidelines at a kid's soccer game. The gray tent is five by five, and the shade shifts with the movement of the sun (which is technically the Earth's movement because the sun doesn't move but *details*). Today is my first day using it and I've moved my chair and table every hour to capitalize on the shade. And it appears, by the barely concealed irritation and taut jaw muscles, that Scott would prefer I pack up my new tent and leave.

Too damn bad.

My dad trusted me with this job and I don't plan to make him regret it. Besides, what should I do, stay in my hotel room and work from afar? No. My place is here, with my shoes (boots, for toe protection) digging into the dirt. My laptop works as well in this remote office as it does in my cramped hotel room. Not that my hotel room is all that cramped; Sheila got a bigger room for me since I'm booked for so long. But the same five hundred and eight square feet, all day long, eventually becomes claustrophobic. This wide open space makes me happier.

"I'm good." I smile sweetly at Scott over the top of my laptop. "Being out here helps me focus on work."

Scott sighs like I'm the world's biggest inconvenience. Did I misread him calling me boss? Was it just to placate me? Let me think I'm in charge? I'm just about to tell him who's signing his checks (technically, Wright Design + Build signs them, but guess whose last name is Wright?), when Scott says, "You make some of my guys nervous. They feel like you're watching them to see if they're making a mistake."

Placing my flattened palms on the table, I push up so I'm half-standing, and lean over my computer. Scott reads my body language and leans forward to hear me.

I smile serenely. "Tell the crew that I won't see them make a mistake unless they make a mistake. This is my project and this cozy little space you see here?" I gesture with one hand at my makeshift desk that is decidedly not cozy. "This is where I'll be unless I'm needed elsewhere."

Scott nods curtly, getting my drift. He doesn't look angry or upset, just resolute. "Yes, Boss." He throws in a salute and walks out from under the shade of the canopy.

"Hey, Scott?" I call after him. He turns. "You or anyone on your crew is welcome to steal some shade anytime they need it."

"I'll pass that along," he says, turning back around and striding away.

I look back at my computer. The screen has gone to

sleep, but I look at it anyway, as if it has something interesting on it. I refuse to look anywhere else. A hundred bucks says the crew is glancing my way after my exchange with the contractor, and I'll be damned if I give them something to support their worry over my presence.

For the next hour, I search the internet for landscaping ideas, sketching out different concepts. I want something clean and pretty, but not too manicured. Something that looks lived in but not abandoned. I don't look up again until the crunch of tires draws my attention.

A truck with the HCC logo on the side pulls up alongside my car. My heart beats double-time until the driver's side door opens and legs that definitely do not belong to Wes hop out. A breath of disappointment slips from my lips. I've seen Wes every night this week, and somehow it doesn't feel like enough. These pesky jobs of ours are really getting in the way.

Jessie steps back from the door and closes it. She shields her eyes from the sun and looks around until she spots me waving at her. She starts for me, and the crosswind pushes her sundress around her thighs. The construction workers try like hell not to make it obvious they're checking out her long legs. I bet they'd cast their gaze back to the job if they knew she was seventeen. And a Hayden with three older brothers. At least, most of them would.

"Hi." Jessie walks under my tent and stops, looking around.

"Hey there," I stand up so she doesn't feel uncomfortable. There's only my chair, otherwise I'd offer her a seat. She shifts her weight from one flip-flop wearing foot to the other, and I get the feeling maybe she's reconsidering her choice to drive out here.

"Everything okay?" I ask, hoping to urge her on.

She glances around the jobsite. "Yeah. You wouldn't be free for lunch anytime soon, would you?"

I keep my surprise from showing on my face and nod without checking my watch. I don't know the exact time, but I wouldn't turn Wes's little sister down for lunch even if it were midnight.

"I'm free now," I tell Jessie. A relieved smile stretches her cheeks.

"Good. I'll follow you into town. You pick the place."

Before I leave, I ask Scott if he or anyone on the crew would like me to bring something back. He tells me the wife of someone on the crew made everybody sandwiches. I make a mental note to pick up cookies for them.

Jessie climbs into the HCC truck, and follows my car into town.

"THANKS FOR MEETING ME," Jessie says when we're seated at a Mexican place. I decided on it solely for the chips and salsa.

"Of course," I respond, dipping a chip in the spicy salsa and popping it into my mouth.

Jessie takes a chip, holding it over her plate and snapping off the corners. "It's just..." she sighs. "I need someone to talk to."

"How many people live at your house? Twelve?" My tone is light, joking.

She musters the saddest looking half-smile. "Seven, unless you count Charlie and Peyton, but they aren't there full-time. And technically it's only Mom, Dad, Gramps and me at the homestead. Everyone else is in their cabins."

I take a drink of my water. "That's still six to eight more people than I live with."

Her smile grows. "True. But you don't live with my big brothers." She stirs the straw around in her drink. "Or my mother."

"Your grandpa seems like he'd be a good listener. And give some interesting advice too, probably."

Jessie laughs once. I feel proud for already having made her feel just the tiniest bit better.

Our server comes over, we order, and I lean forward, tucking my cold hands between my thighs. "So, what's going on?"

Jessie runs her hands through her blonde hair, gathering it in one hand and pulling it over her shoulder. "I've been seeing this guy. Eamon. I really like him, like"—she looks at me with intense eyes—"a lot. Like, maybe I love him."

I smile indulgently, and I hope she doesn't see it as patronizing. I remember that feeling in high school, and I don't think there's anything like it. Heady and overwhelming, it was all-encompassing. Of course, when I felt that way I was forbidden to go near the boy I liked. Which only made me want him more, and drove my dad crazy.

"Okay." I nod, dropping the smile and adopting a serious expression.

"Well, it's mid-April. Prom is in two weeks." She implores me with her eyes, willing me to arrive at her problem using context clues.

And I do. It's an easy leap.

"He wants you to sleep with him on prom night?"

She nods.

"And you haven't slept together before?"

She shakes her head.

I absorb her frightened expression and take my guessing one step further. "And you've never slept with anybody before?"

"Yes," she wails. The people sitting two tables over look at us. I offer a small head nod and equally small, reassuring smile.

"Hmm." I fidget with my earring, thinking of what to say to her. This is Wes's little sister. There's a lot of pressure on me to say the right thing, and it's possible Wes and I might not have the same opinion on what the right thing is in this situation. Something tells me he'd force a chastity belt on Jessie. "Firstly, are you looking for advice, or just someone who will listen to you? Because I hate when I get advice when all I'm trying to do is talk something out."

Jessie takes another chip and actually eats it this time. "I need advice."

"You should do what you want. And whatever you do, only do it for you. Not for Eamon. You only get one chance to have a first time. If this is how you want your first time to be, then go ahead."

She leans closer, her voice dropping lower. "I don't know how it all works." She quickly amends her statement. "I mean, I know what goes where," she makes an 'o' with two fingers on her right hand and shoves the pointer finger on her left hand through the hole. It takes everything I can do not to laugh, but given the serious look on her face, I know how poorly received my laughter would be. "I just don't know how you get from fully clothed at a dance to naked on a bed. It all just seems so awkward."

"Sometimes it is awkward. That's just part of sex."

"Even now? When you're an adult?"

I shift in my seat, considering how to respond. The most

recent person to grace my bed was Jessie's oldest brother. I don't want to say too much.

"Yes, even as an adult."

The server places our lunch on the table and refills our waters. We thank him and he walks away. Jessie picks up her fork. "Is it awkward with Wes?" Her tone is forcibly breezy, like she's just trying out what it's like to be two friends chatting nonchalantly about sex. How do I tell her that won't happen for a while, not until she's been having sex long enough for it to lose its forbidden quality?

"Not any more awkward than his little sister asking me about it." I smile around the bite of black beans in my mouth.

She grins sheepishly. "Sorry. It's just that I've never seen Wes..." Her mouth twists as she searches for the word. "Happy. He's not stomping around as much, and there's something different about his eyes. They're lighter. Not in color, I mean, but like whatever's inside him that hurts doesn't hurt so much anymore. And"—she puts a bite of food in her mouth, then points her fork at me—"I noticed him driving to his cabin almost every morning for the past week."

I nod slowly, trying not to let on how excited her words have made me. If this was Abby across from me, I'd be squirming in my seat and clapping in celebration. Since it's Wes's little sister, I feel there should be a modicum of self-possession. "Wes makes me very happy, too, Jessie. And it's good to hear I'm having the same effect on him."

"Well, that's good," Jessie snorts, "considering you're getting married."

I force a laugh. "True."

Honestly, it feels like my relationship with Wes is developing alongside our deal, like there are two parallel tracks and we're riding them both.

Jessie looks a little disappointed, and I can tell she wanted me to gush about my deepest feelings. I get it. When Abby and I were teenagers, we dissected every word our crushes spoke, every action they took if it was in a ten-foot radius of us. We were close as could be, lying in bed in our shared bedroom and gossiping at night until one of us fell asleep. It's one of our favorite mutual memories, and—

Oh. Of course. How did I not see it? Not only is Jessie the only girl, she's the youngest by fourteen years. She wants her own version of what I had with Abby.

"So." I lower my voice like we're talking about something secretive. "Tell me all about Eamon. Is he really cute?"

It's just what she needs. She talks animatedly, her hands flying around in the air, telling me about every inch of his perfect face, his laugh and his favorite pizza toppings. She talks and talks, and I find myself laughing at her descriptions. I pay the check, and I don't worry about having enough money to buy her lunch. It's an incredible feeling. When we walk out to the parking lot, Jessie hugs me. She seems much happier now than she did when she pulled up on the jobsite.

Jessie drives off and I make a stop at the bakery. The cookies last fewer than five minutes around all those hungry workers. Good thing I snagged one for myself before handing the box over to Scott.

The rest of the afternoon is spent calling landscapers in the area, sending them my plans, and collecting bids.

My phone rings at four, and it's Wes. The sound of his voice rockets through me, leaving no part of me untouched.

"I want to take you somewhere tonight," he husks. I love

that he doesn't ask me if I *want* to go somewhere. He knows I do.

He tells me to be ready at seven.

I tell him to pick me up at six-thirty because I want to have a drink in the hotel bar first.

He chuckles to himself as he hangs up the phone, and I grin like an idiot at my computer screen and silently squeal.

Just like a teenager.

31

WES

I HAVE TO ADMIT, I LIKE DAKOTA'S SUGGESTION TO MEET FOR a drink, and not even because I want a drink. Because I like how she told me what she wants.

The hotel lobby is a little busier than the other times I've been here this week, probably because it's Friday night. A majority of the people coming through the double doors are heading for the restaurant. Most of them look like couples.

I enter the restaurant and veer left to the bar. It's full, but I manage to grab a corner seat when two people leave. I order a whiskey, and a glass of the same wine Dakota drank the night of the celebratory dinner.

I'm pulling out my phone to tell her I'm here when a hand slides over my shoulder and soft lips touch my ear. "Come here often?" The voice is low, sultry, vibrating in my ear.

I turn into the sound and look up. Dakota smiles down at me, her head tipping to the side. She wears a tight denim skirt, a white V-neck T-shirt tucked into the front of her skirt, and cowgirl boots. She looks good enough to eat, and she smells even better.

"Are you trying to pick me up?" I raise my eyebrows as I say it.

"That depends," she answers, leaning over me to pick up her wine off the bar. Her breasts brush against my upper arm, and I'm ninety-nine percent positive it's on purpose. "Is it working?"

"Damn straight." Grabbing my whiskey, I stand and guide her onto the barstool. There's only one seat, so I stand beside her with my forearm resting on the edge of the bar top.

"How gallant of you," she teases.

"Sweetheart, where I come from, a man doesn't sit while a woman stands."

Dakota runs a finger over the buttons on the front of my shirt. "Say that again."

"Where I come from—"

She shakes her head. "The first word."

For a second I'm confused, but my brain replays the sentence and I hear it. *Sweetheart.*

I look down into her eyes. Her chin is upturned, and she waits.

"Sweetheart."

The mere inches of air between us vibrates with her low moan.

"One more time," she whispers.

This time, I say it with my lips poised against hers, so she can feel me when I speak. "Sweetheart."

Her lips press against mine. I'm aware we're in the hotel bar in the middle of town. I'm aware that this will feed the already turning rumor mill.

What I'm not aware of are my parents walking into the bar. Until my mother says my name, I'm happily tasting the wine on Dakota's mouth.

"Wes?"

Our kiss breaks off the instant I hear my mother's voice. I turn and see her standing beside my father. He's smirking. She looks... odd. Not happy for me, but not mad. I don't get it, but I'm a grown man. I don't need her permission.

"Hello, Beau. Juliette." Dakota hops off her stool and steps around it so she can stand next to me.

"Nice to see you again, Dakota," my dad answers. He elbows my mom in a way that is probably supposed to be covert but is beyond obvious. "We're going to get some dinner. You two have fun."

My mom plasters a smile on her face and repeats my dad's last sentence.

They walk away, and Dakota turns a worried gaze to me. "Your mom didn't seem very happy to see us together."

I wave off her concern. "She's probably having a bad day."

"Have you told her our fake relationship isn't quite so fake anymore?"

"I don't think she needs to hear my words to know that. Our actions make it clear."

Dakota grins reluctantly. "You're probably right."

We finish our drinks and I pay the tab. "Are you ready to go?"

"Go where?" Her worry has been replaced by excitement.

"Dancing."

She looks stunned. "Dancing? Wes Hayden dances?"

I shrug. "Mostly I just slouch in my chair and watch other people dance."

Her eyes narrow. "Why are you taking me to a place where you don't plan to participate?"

I curl a hand around her hip. "Warner told me about it. Said it would be a good place to take you."

She lifts an eyebrow. "You're taking dating advice from Warner?"

"Technically, no. More like *destination* advice."

"Ahhh," she says, nodding solemnly. "Well then, cowboy, take me away."

DAKOTA LEANS FORWARD, fingers splayed on my dash, peering out the windshield. "This place is... kinda cool."

A large neon sign shines brightly on the front of the big wooden building. *The Chute*. From our parking spot I can see around to the arena in the back, where they host bull riding and various events.

I smirk. "It's no Bar N."

She flashes me a dirty look. "That place has its... place." Her dirty look melts into laughter.

"Come on." I hop out and walk around the back of my truck. The passenger door opens just as I get to it, so I reach up and grip Dakota around the waist. My intention is to lift her out, but Dakota wraps her leg around me and urges me in closer.

"I missed you last night," she murmurs, her pink lips pouty and delectable.

I had to wake up early this morning, and so last night I extricated myself from Dakota's bed and forced myself to drive home. As I walked away from her hotel room, I couldn't remember a decision I'd made in the past few years being so hard to make.

"Let's switch it up tonight." My lips brush hers.

She pulls back, her eyebrows cinched together. "What do you mean?"

"Come home with me tonight," I murmur into her ear, and she moans quietly, her leg tightening around my lower back. From somewhere behind me, the roar of a truck engine makes its way into my sex-soaked brain. Dakota turns toward the sound, her hair brushing against my face.

"We're going to have an audience pretty soon." She starts to pull away.

"Don't care," I grumble, my lips on her bare shoulder. I move them across her skin, letting my teeth drag against her soft skin.

"Is this the whiskey talking?"

I pull back to look in her eyes. "Not the whiskey, Dakota."

Her eyebrows lift. "Oh yeah? What is it?"

"You." My lips fall against her cheek. I can't keep looking in her eyes, it's too much. Too much feeling, too much emotion, too much need. It reminds me of being at the beach, of standing in the ocean and watching a wave coming toward me. So much anticipation, overwhelming, frightening and exciting.

I kiss her cheek. Her jaw. The spot beside her ear. The constellation of freckles below her eye. "I'm drunk on you," I whisper, my admission floating out, suspended in the cool evening air.

It's the best I can do, the most I can give her right now. I can't tell her I'm falling in love with her, because how can a man *fall* when he's already *there*?

Reluctantly, I step back from the open passenger door. Dakota clears her throat, flips open the visor mirror and checks her makeup, and winds her purse over her shoulder.

She takes my offered hand and steps from my truck.

"Let's do this." She stomps her foot rhythmically and turns in a circle.

"Are you about to show me up?"

She laughs, and I slip my arm around her waist as we walk in. The floor in The Chute is a deep-red brick, the walls covered in aging wooden planks and vintage signs. Country music pours from speakers, and a band sets up on a small stage off to the side. There are a dozen tables set up, but the main attraction is the bar. It's a giant rectangle, one half inside and the other half open to the outside. Beyond that is the arena. I checked their website before deciding to listen to Warner, and tonight is amateur bull-riding night.

Dakota and I head for the bar. We order a drink, then settle at the last open table. Warner wasn't kidding when he said this is the place to be on a Friday night. The band finishes setting up, the music from the speaker stops, and the lead singer steps up to the microphone. He wears a plaid shirt and jeans, and his generous middle hangs over his shiny belt buckle.

"Good to see you beautiful people again. And you ugly ones, too." He laughs and winks, ducking his chin in a nod. "Me and the boys are gonna give you all something to listen to while you drink away your shitty week. Bull riding starts in an hour, so eat, drink, and don't get too merry because nobody likes a sloppy drunk."

Dakota laughs and scoots her chair closer to me. She leans into my side and I lay my arm over her shoulders. The band starts with something upbeat, and Dakota's foot is tapping. Soon her shoulders are moving, just these micro-movements, but they're in time to the music.

I'd ask her to dance, but I can't dance for shit.

Fucking Warner. How did I let that asshole convince me this was a good idea?

A server stops by, we order another round and two pulled pork sandwiches. Dakota smiles at me, her shoulders still shaking, and she looks radiant and happy.

"Wes?"

Wyatt's surprised voice interrupts my staring at Dakota.

"Hey, Wyatt."

Wyatt sinks down in the empty chair at our table. "Wasn't expecting to see you here," he says. "Weird to see you anywhere that's not the ranch."

I look at him from the sides of my eyes but let the comment pass. The server drops off our drinks and Wyatt orders a beer.

"Do you dance, Dakota?" Wyatt looks pointedly at me, as if I'm a broke dick who doesn't have a clue that his girl is sitting beside him basically dancing in her seat.

She smiles up at me but answers Wyatt. "I know my way around a dance floor."

"How convenient, because I do too." Wyatt takes my beer and drinks half. Briefly I consider tackling him the way I used to when we were younger.

I take my beer out of his hand. "How the fuck do you know how to dance?"

He shrugs. "Mom taught me."

"When?"

"Sometime during the twelve years you were gone, Wes."

My thumb runs the length of my lower lip and I look away. I leave to serve my country and I have to come back to a little brother who's had his precious feelings hurt? Defensiveness is my primary response, but deep down inside me, there's a twinge of guilt for hurting him.

"Dakota, do you want to dance?" Wyatt asks.

I look over at Dakota. She's looking at me, gauging my reaction. I kiss her forehead, letting her know it's fine with me. I'm certainly not going to be out there dancing, not to any fast-paced songs anyway. I don't want to hold her back.

Wyatt extends an open palm, and Dakota takes it. She quickly kisses me, then stands and winds her way through the tables to the dance floor. Now that people have had a chance to consume a drink or two, they've begun filtering onto it.

I watch Wyatt and Dakota and try not to let any of the irritation I'm feeling show on my face. He pulls her in, pushes her back out, spins her around. Wyatt is good. Dakota is better. She laughs, swishing her hips, doing complicated shit with her feet.

The waitress drops off the sandwiches we ordered and Wyatt's beer, and I help myself to the drink. Why the fuck not, he's currently dancing with my girl. The song ends and they come back. Dakota throws herself into her seat, fanning her face. She takes a long drink from her wine. Wyatt eyes the two empty glasses in front of me.

"Where's my beer?"

"In my stomach."

Dakota laughs loudly.

Wyatt shakes his head. "You can be a real asshole, Wes."

"Careful there," I warn him. "You're starting to sound like a baby brother."

His jaw flexes. He hates being called a baby brother. Always has. Warner and I were closer in age, and we were thicker than thieves, and we hated including Wyatt in our shenanigans. And Wyatt knew it.

He looks at something over my shoulder, his eyes lighting up in recognition.

"My friends are here," he says, standing. He looks at Dakota. "Thanks for the dance." His attention turns to me. "Wes, fuck you very much."

I give him a two-fingered salute. "Right back at you."

He walks away, and Dakota stares at me. "There must be something pretty contentious between you two."

"Just brotherly shit." I shrug it off, but I feel bad. Wyatt's irresponsible way of living irritates me, but the injured look in his eyes always worms its way into me.

"He's drunk," she comments, watching him walk to the bar with two other guys.

What else is new? "I guess it's a good thing I drank his beer."

She exhales a laugh. "I guess so. He smelled like hard liquor when we were dancing."

Speaking of... "You're an incredible dancer. Where did you learn to do whatever that dance was?" My fingers brush the back of her neck and I feel the goose bumps raise.

"That was West Coast Swing. My sister and I took dance lessons with my dad when we were in high school." A look comes over her face. "At the time I hated it. Now I see that he was just trying to hold on to us a little bit longer." She smiles, but it's not happy. More melancholy. She grabs a sandwich and takes a bite.

"It was a long time ago. Don't beat yourself up." I grab the second sandwich.

"You're one to talk."

Well, shit. She's got me there. We finish our food in silence.

The music changes, the notes lengthening and the tempo slowing. "Dakota Wright, may I have this dance?" Slow dancing, I can do.

She doesn't answer, just leans in and kisses me. I pull her up with me, leading her by the hand to the dance floor. When she folds into my chest, it feels like the first real breath I've taken since I pulled away from her in my truck.

We sway, and she lays her head on my chest. Her body molds to mine, and it strikes me that it is possible for one person to be made for another. Dakota is a wave, and I'm drowning in her, and I've never been so thrilled at the prospect of dying.

The song ends and I cup my hand around the back of her head. She looks up at me, her eyes dark and wanting. "Let's get out of here."

Wordlessly, I take her hand, leading her back the way we came.

We're almost out of the place when I hear it. Through the music and voices, Wyatt is yelling.

32

DAKOTA

Wes stops short, and I run into his broad, muscled back.

"What the—" My question is silenced by the look on his face. Eyes alert, jaw tense, his mouth a straight line. He side-steps me, moving across the bar in long, lithe strides. I hurry after him, peering around his tall, large form to see what's going on.

Wyatt?

He's standing at the bar with his two friends. He's looking hard at someone, but I can't see who. A half-circle has formed around him and I can't see through. Wes seems to know exactly what's happening, and he pushes apart two people, advancing right into the action. Somewhere in my brain, in some place that hasn't yet registered my surprise and fear, I think of how damn attractive Wes is right now. So strong, so confident, charging into the situation like he is the solver of whatever the problem is. I love that about him. With Wes, I am never less than safe.

I make it to the commotion three seconds after him and elbow my way in.

Oh fuck.

Dixon.

He's sneering at Wes, who has stepped in front of Wyatt and looms over Dixon like a jungle cat over a weasel. Wyatt steps up beside Wes. From this angle, with both their chins upturned and their chests puffed up, they look exactly alike.

"Aren't you lucky that big brother was here to save you?" Dixon asks Wyatt.

"Get out of here, Dixon." Wes's command sounds more like a bark.

"Your brother has something of mine, and he needs to give it back."

"Get. Out." Wes's voice is smooth, but the undercurrent is violent. "Or I'll help you out."

Dixon laughs. "The hometown hero is going to clean up the town's trash. Typical of you Haydens. You think you're God's gift to Sierra Grande. You sit up on that ranch, looking down over the town like kings. You don't give two shits about anybody but yourselves. But do you want to know what kings do, Hayden? They fall. And you will too. Maybe even soon."

He sidesteps Wes and Wyatt and turns like he's going to leave, glaring at the small crowd that has gathered. He walks past me on his way, and though I think he hasn't noticed me there, I quickly realize he has. Because when he passes me, in a move so subtle and covert I hardly register it until it's over, he squeezes my left breast.

My stomach tightens, shock fills me, and I look to Wes. He, nor anybody else it seems, saw Dixon's fleeting grope. Wes stares after Dixon's retreating form, watching him all the way until he exits. When he's gone, Wes looks at Wyatt.

"What the fuck was that about?"

Wyatt seems astonished. "You don't know?"

"No." Wes sounds impatient.

Wyatt stares at him. "You jumped in here not knowing what was going on?"

"Yes." The word slips through clenched teeth. Wes's patience for his little brother's non-answers appears to be hanging on by a thin thread.

I see where Wyatt is going with his questions, but Wes doesn't. His eyes widen in Wyatt's direction, urging him to just tell him already. "What the fuck does he think you have of his?"

Wyatt shakes his head. "Nothing, man." The crowd dissipates and Wyatt visibly relaxes, his shoulders dropping and an oddly serene look dawning on his face.

"Wyatt." Wes's tone is threatening, and that's all it takes for Wyatt to start talking.

"I might have lifted something from his hoodie pocket when I overheard him ask the guys next to me at the bar if they were looking to score tonight. I told him to get the fuck out of this bar, and things escalated." He sounds proud of himself.

"We had your back, man," one of Wyatt's friends speaks up from behind him. I'd forgotten they were even there. Wes too, apparently, because his gaze flickers over to them and away again, and I know in that one small motion that Wes sees them as no more important than a fly on shit. They were never going to help Wyatt, and their belated declaration solidifies that.

Wes extends his arms to me and I go to him, tucking myself into his side. "You okay?" His gentle voice soothes some of the horror I still feel over being touched by Dixon.

I nod. If I tell him what Dixon did, he will go after him right now, and it won't end well.

"He's trouble, Wes," Wyatt says. "He *hates* us. Our whole family."

Wes stares at the door, as if Dixon's presence lingers. "Let that fucker try, Wyatt. He'll get a lesson in alternative justice. We aren't afraid to protect ourselves, and if he wants to learn that lesson the hard way, he can go right ahead."

Wyatt almost grins. "You sound like a cowboy in an old western."

Wes shrugs. "I've been a lot of places, Wyatt, and I've learned there are different definitions for justice. If Dixon wants to operate outside the law, he'll find there are others willing to do the same."

The subtle violence of Wes's words frighten me, but there's something about them that makes my thighs clench, my heart beat erratically.

Wes's hand squeezes mine. "You ready to get out of here?"

I nod my agreement and say goodbye to Wyatt. As we step away, Wyatt calls Wes's name.

"Thanks for jumping in when you didn't even know what you were jumping into."

I watch the understanding light up Wes's eyes. He's silent, looking at his little brother for a few beats, then he nods his head at him. "Get rid of what you have in your pocket," he tells Wyatt.

Wyatt walks to the bathroom and we head for the exit.

When we get to Wes's truck, he opens my door and helps me in even though I don't need it. Like a bookend to the night, he leans into the open passenger doorframe. His eyes implore me, asking me to love him, needing somewhere to put all the emotion he was feeling when he rushed in to protect his brother.

I kiss him. It's short, sweet, and chaste. And yet, it sends shivers through my entire body.

"You still coming home with me?" His voice is low.

I smile at him. "Most definitely."

It was cute how we thought we could make it all the way to Wes's cabin.

I don't know what happened after we left The Chute, but it was urgent. Wes's hand was on my knee, then my thigh, slipping under my skirt, traveling up, up, up until I was gripping the door. He pulled over on a side road closer to the ranch than to Sierra Grande, a dirt road lit by nothing but the stars and the pale light from the half moon.

Now the truck's passenger door is open and my head is almost hanging out of it. The cool night air swirls around us, and my hair tumbles down out of the truck. Wes is on me, in me, all around me. His presence is commanding, both physically and emotionally.

I moan, maybe I say his name, I'm not certain. My nose presses into his neck and I inhale. He smells spicy and manly, and it's the best thing my nose has ever come across. I want to dig in, to stay here forever. And what Wes is doing to my body right now? The slow, unhurried pace, one hand in my hair, the other trailing over my hip, cupping my breast, thumb brushing over me. I don't want that to end, either. Ever.

The sensation builds, slow and delicious and excruciating, and Wes feathers kisses over my throat as my head tips back and I let go. My pleasured cries stretch into the half-lit darkness. Wes follows soon after, his back muscles flexing under my palms as he reaches his high, then collapses on top of me.

Our breathing evens out, and he lifts his head. The dim moonlight shines through the windshield, illuminating half of Wes's face. He looks calm and sated.

My hand abandons his lower back, traversing the smooth, hard muscle of his body, over the nape of his neck and around, so I can touch his face.

He turns into my touch, pressing a kiss to the inside of my palm. "I want to take you somewhere."

"We were on our way to somewhere when this happened." My hips wiggle to make my point.

He breathes an amused sound. "Not my cabin. Somewhere else. Will you go with me?"

"I'll go anywhere with you." To your cabin. To your favorite place in the world. To the place inside where you hide your pain.

I can see how much my words mean to him. He sits back on a bent knee between my splayed legs, ducking his head so he doesn't hit it on the truck roof. I push to sit, swinging my legs so my feet are on the floor.

Reaching into my purse, I pull out a few tissues and hand one to Wes. "I don't know about you, but I'm a mess. And it's your fault."

Wes plucks the offered tissue from my hand. "How about we stop at my place to clean up, then I take you somewhere?"

I nod my agreement as I close the passenger door. Wes gets back on the main road, taking it to the turn off for the homestead, then bypassing the house and driving on to his cabin.

We spend a few minutes cleaning up, then Wes grabs us each a bottle of water and we get back in his truck. He drives slowly, his headlights brightening the road. The way in front of us is bright, but everything around us is dark. It's not long when I see another clearing ahead, and the shine of more headlights. Someone else is out here?

Wes pulls into the clearing and I see it now. The second set of headlights are ours, reflecting off water.

"There's a lake on your property?"

"More like a pond. There are a few of them, including one by the barn. This one is closest to me, and the other one is near the far edge of our property."

We get out and Wes reaches into the truck bed. He comes away with a green and black Mexican blanket.

"Do you carry that with you?"

He winks at me. "Never know when a pretty lady might want to sit by the pond at night."

My eyes narrow playfully. "Like Jericho?"

He scoffs as we get closer to the water's edge. "Hardly."

"Don't tell me you didn't notice she was into you."

"I was preoccupied with someone else that day." He gives me a meaningful look as he shakes out the blanket and lays it on the ground. We sit down, and Wes leans back on his forearm, but I stay upright, legs criss-crossed and facing him.

He traces the length of my leg with his fingertip. "I want to tell you my version of the night we met."

My eyebrows lift. "You have a different version than mine?"

He nods, grasping a long strand of my wayward hair between his fingers. "I know you think you saw me first—"

"I did," I insist. "I literally watched you walk in the front door."

Slowly he shakes his head. He releases my hair and palms my shoulder, his fingers running down my upper arm. "I was sitting in my car, parked down the street from Jason's house. I'd told him I'd come and visit, but I couldn't make myself get out of my car. Jason served with me, and I hadn't seen him since he got out eight months before. I thought he'd take one look at me and know how fucked-up I was. My hand was on the key in the ignition, I was a quarter of a second from turning it, when I saw this girl. She was with two other people, but they could've been purple coyotes and I wouldn't have noticed. All I could see was the girl on the left, the one with gorgeous hair and a smile that made it seem like everything would be alright. Her step was light, and her hips swayed." Wes takes a breath. "Your gaze swept over my car when you passed. I didn't think you'd seen me, but it felt like an arrow had pierced my chest and pinned me to that exact moment. I watched you walk into Jason's house, and I knew I had to cowboy up. At first I thought I was being courageous and doing the hard thing by facing Jason so I could meet you, but later on I realized how it was more cowardly than anything else. Leaving without meeting you, Dakota? *That* would have been the hardest thing, the most impossible, the most painful."

"It turns out I was right, too. The first time you were in my arms, there was this odd sensation in my chest, and it was something I'd never felt before. I still can't describe it, except to say it felt like my soul was being called up, because another soul had called out to it."

He sits up, and now we're face to face. "I never meant to leave you that morning. You were sleeping, your face looked so sweet and innocent. I was mortified that I cried in front of you, but also, I realized you were the reason I'd cried. You made me want to heal, to talk about what happened, but it was the last thing I wanted to do. Everything was raw, and I couldn't bear to revisit it. I thought that to survive, I needed to push it down." He cringes. "I took a picture of you. Just your face," he hurries to add when he sees my eyes widen. "But I felt like a creep, so I deleted it two days later." He shakes his head, like he's trying to get back on track. "Anyway, I'm telling you all this because I have something to give you, and I want you to know that even though we're going through with our plan, I'm not taking it lightly." Wes reaches into his pocket and pulls out a ring.

He holds it up, and in the moonlight I notice the simple gold band has a floral design cut into it. "Can I put this on your finger?"

"Of course." I offer him my ring finger. As sweet as this is, there is a small part of me that feels disappointed, but what did I expect? It's a marriage of convenience, whether we're developing feelings for each other or not. No grandiose proposals necessary.

Even through my disappointment, a tremor of excitement shakes me deep inside. I twist the ring a few times, familiarizing myself with its feel.

Wes cups my face, kisses me tenderly. Eventually he lays me on my back and the moon rises higher until it's directly behind his head.

We both drift off, and I wake up to Wes gently shaking my shoulders. He presses one finger to his mouth and motions with his hand. When my eyes adjust, I see what he's pointing to. A bobcat and two kittens sit across the pond, lapping at the water. I watch in awe, not sure if we should be scared or if Wes has anything to protect us. They continue to drink until there's a sound in the distance, something like a tree branch falling. The mother and her kittens bolt into the trees and disappear from sight.

Wes stands and reaches out a hand to help me up.

"Were we in danger?" I ask in a whisper.

Wes shakes his head. “Bobcats are more afraid of us than we should ever be of them. They’re like large house cats. If you ever get close to one, just stomp. It’ll run.”

“Or just hope a tree branch falls nearby and scares it away.”

He glances out into the trees. There’s nothing out there that I can see, and yet he has the hard look on his face of a man who’s facing down a problem. “Right.”

He grabs a fistful of blanket and plucks it off the ground, then we climb in his truck and head for his cabin.

I fall asleep the second my head hits Wes’s pillow. This has been the best night of my life so far, and not even the memory of Dixon can taint it.

33

DAKOTA

I'M BREATHLESS FROM TAKING THE STAIRS TWO AT A TIME AT the hotel. The elevator was busy and I'm running late for the video meeting I'm supposed to have with my dad and Brandt. I'd meant to leave Wes's bed when my alarm went off, and I kind of managed it, but when I came back from the bathroom... well, just like every other morning this week, Wes persuaded me to come back to bed. This morning, however, we fell back to sleep. Oops. Maybe I should rethink staying the night at his place during the week. Weekends, however, are a different story. Last weekend, after the near-brawl at The Chute, Wes and I stayed in bed the next two days. Tearing myself away from him on Monday morning had been difficult, and so far it hasn't become any easier.

I tear into my room, change from last night's comfy clothes into a sensible lavender blouse and black pants, and run a brush through my hair.

At three minutes past nine, I open my computer and set it up on the table. My eyes perform a quick sweep of the hotel room to check for stray bras or underwear. I'm assuming I've been anointed housekeeping's favorite guest because I haven't given them a reason to clean my room or make my bed. Whether it's coffee in the morning or wine in the evening, all my non-working time is spent at Wes's.

The video connects and the conference room at Wright Design + Build fills up my computer screen. My dad sits on one side of the long table, Brandt on the other. We say hello, exchange pleasantries, then get down to business.

"I've been in touch with Scott," my dad says. "He says things are coming along without any problems."

I bristle at the mention of Scott. I'm the project manager, my dad should be talking to me and me only when he wants updates. I don't say anything for two reasons. One is that we're in front of other people. Two is that I don't want to do anything to jeopardize my role.

"I hope all future projects will be this easy," I joke, covering up my irritation.

"They won't be," Brandt responds. I keep a straight face, but on the inside I'm giving him a death glare.

We move on to other topics. Dad informs me of two more projects they've got going on. I nod and pretend to listen. My mind is somewhere on Hayden land, watching Wes ride Ranger. Forty-five interminable minutes later, the call wraps up.

I change once again, into jeans and boots more appropriate for the jobsite, and I'm climbing into my car when my phone rings.

It's my dad.

"Hey, Dad, I'm just on my way to—"

"Why the hell are you wearing a ring on your finger?"

I look down at the gold band, my fingers spread out wide. *How dumb of me.* "Uh, well."

"Spit it out."

It's amazing how I can be an adult and suddenly feel like

a child again. And just like in my childhood, a flair of resentment sparks in my chest. I do not want to be told what to do. "I'm going to marry Wes." I can't tell him about the agreement, because that would mean coming clean about my debt.

"What? I… No… Dakota." Shock.

"Yes, Dad."

"You barely know him." Indignation.

"It's enough, Dad."

"No, Dakota, it's not. Can you imagine what your mother would say if she were alive?" Self-righteous.

I suck in a breath. That was low. "I need to go, Dad. I'm working."

"Dakota, let's talk about this." Pleading.

"Dad, I just need you to trust me on this. I know what I'm doing."

"It doesn't sound like you do."

"Bye, Dad. I love you."

I hang up and spend the entire drive willing my blood pressure to decrease. That's not how I wanted to tell him. When I get to the jobsite, I send him a text.

Everything is going to be okay, Dad. I know it was a shock, and trust me when I say it's not how I wanted you to find out. I love you.

Two hours later, he responds. *You've always marched to the beat of your own drum, Junior. If you say you know what you're doing, I'm going to trust you mean it. I love you, too.*

This time, when the HCC truck pulls up, I don't think for even a second that it's Wes. Before I left his place this morning, he told me he, Warner, and Ham were riding out to pasture seventeen to mend fences broken from a recent storm, and that he anticipated it would take all day.

I cover my eyes from the sun, expecting to see Jessie hop out with bare legs and short shorts. Instead, sensible boots and Wranglers are visible under the passenger door.

Juliette?

The door closes and Wes's mom starts for me.

I sigh internally. I'm really not in the mood for Juliette after talking to my dad. I get up from my chair, ducking my head under the tent and striding out to meet Juliette. She wears a no-nonsense expression that sends a rapid tremble through me.

"Hello, Juliette." I smile and greet her without a trace of the nerves I'm feeling. I get the feeling Juliette would see any nervousness as weakness and therefore be disgusted by it.

"Dakota," she greets me, her tone clipped. "Can we speak privately?"

A lead ball forms in my stomach. "Certainly." I guide her back to the tailgate of her truck. It's not that much further from the jobsite, but at least it's out of direct eyesight of everybody.

"What can I do for you?" I ask.

Juliette's blue-eyed gaze is glacial. Jessie has the same eye color, but hers are warmer, more cornflower and less iceberg. "I find it awfully odd that you show up in Sierra Grande and decide to do a good deed for my son. Tell me, Dakota, why are you falling on the sword for him?"

Wow. Okay. I guess we're just getting right to it. "I'm not falling on a sword, Juliette."

"What are you doing then?" She cocks her head to the side, waiting for my answer.

"Marrying Wes."

"But why?"

"Why not?"

"You don't love him." She emphasizes the 'you'.

"*You* don't know that."

"I do know that some woman shows up in Sierra Grande and a short while later she's got my son using marriage as a means to an end."

I make a face. "Is that what you think happened?"

"I've heard how well you researched this town. I'd imagine those researching skills extended to Arizona's divorce laws. You must have seen Wes and then dollar signs popped up in your future. Anybody with your amount of debt would have."

My mouth falls open, the air from a gasp slamming to the back of my throat. "How did you—"

Juliette's mouth stretches into a smug line. "My family is my priority. I'm not going to let a fox guard the henhouse."

"What is it with you Haydens?" I ask through clenched teeth. A deep breath fills my lungs and releases slowly. This is Wes's mother, and on a normal day, she'd deserve the utmost respect, but not when she's coming at me with guns blazing. "Wes asked me to marry him. He came up with this idea on his own. And he knows about the debt." She doesn't believe me. I don't know how I know that, but I do. I square my chin at her. "I don't appreciate you coming to my jobsite and questioning my integrity. Excuse me, I have work to do." I sidestep her and walk away. It takes everything in me to walk at a normal pace. I want to stomp and yell, release my indignation, but there are eyes on me. Scott and the crew, for starters, and probably Juliette. My future mother-in-law.

I'm back in my makeshift office when I hear the diesel engine roar to life. My eyes remain trained on the computer screen as the sounds of the truck engine get further and further away.

I keep trying to focus, but I can't. My leg bounces and I can't seem to stop it, even when I push down on it with my hand. I need to blow off some steam.

I pack up my things and get in my car, waving at Scott as I go.

I'M at The Bakery buying a piece of lemon bar the size of an NBA player's palm when I hear my name. Turning, I see Jo sitting at a small table with a laptop open and a notebook with a pen lying on top. I wave at her, then finish paying and walk over to where she sits.

"Hi, Jo."

She stands up and wraps her arms around me. I'm still upset from my run-in with Juliette, and when I hug Jo back, I squeeze tightly.

"Thanks for that," I tell her when we pull apart. I'm a little embarrassed. I don't know Jo very well.

"It felt like you needed a hug," she smiles sweetly, sinking back down into her chair. She motions to the empty seat across from her, and I sit.

"I really did." I offer her a lopsided grin. "Tough day."

She points at the pastry I've set down on the table. "The size of that lemon bar tells me the kind of day you've had."

I grab two forks from the small station nearby and hand one to Jo. I reach into my purse and remove the two cans of rosé I picked up from the Merc. "Do these further tell you the story of the day I've had?" I slide one over to her.

She pops the top and sips. "Sure does. Want to talk about it?"

I finish chewing my first bite of lemon bar. "It's not an easy subject."

"Let me guess," she says, holding a forkful of the pastry in midair. "It has something to do with a certain Hayden."

One side of my mouth turns up in a smile. "Sort of. More than one Hayden, anyway."

She nods knowingly. "They can be an interesting bunch. There's been some talk, you know."

"About me?"

"You and Wes."

I sip my wine. "What's the talk?"

"That you've been seeing an awful lot of each other."

"That's true."

"And that this town has been seeing more of Wes than they have in years, and that's due to your presence."

"Is that considered a good thing?"

She nods her head vigorously. "Most definitely. He's a big deal in our town. He grew up playing football, and there was this pride in the whole town when he went into the Army. He came home, and I think we all expected him to be the same Wes, which was pretty short-sighted of us. It might sound silly, but whatever happened to Wes when he was over there, happened to us too, because it took away the town hero."

"That's a lot of pressure to put on one person. To need him to be your hero. Not you, specifically. 'You' as in 'the town'."

"You are right about that. I think it comes with the territory though. Having Hayden as a last name."

It makes me think about Juliette and her boundary-crossing behavior. "It does seem like an awful lot to live up to."

"And now you're dating a Hayden. Who knows, maybe your last name will be Hayden one day."

I cough on my wine and slip my left hand under the

table. Last name? I hadn't even given a thought to that. Do I want to change my last name?

"Are you okay?" Jo asks.

"Yes, yes," I sputter. "Let's talk about you." I need the subject change, stat. "Are you dating anybody right now?"

"Well..." Jo pokes at some crumbs with the tines of her fork. "Not dating, no. I might've made a teensy mistake last weekend."

"Spill," I command, grateful to be out of the spotlight.

"I went down to Phoenix with a group of friends. We stayed at a resort, did the spa thing, dinner and drinks. We all had a lot to drink and I miiight have slept with someone who was in our group." She makes a bare-teeth face. "But he doesn't remember." Flames of red sweep across her face.

"Don't be embarrassed." I touch her forearm. "Seriously. We all make mistakes. I know I have." Colossal mistakes, in my case. "Why do you think he doesn't remember?"

"Because I left his room after, and when I saw him at breakfast the next morning, he didn't even look at me twice." Her eyes fill with tears. "And when our other friend asked him how the rest of his night went, he shrugged and said he went to his room and passed out." She dabs at her eyes with a white paper napkin.

"Do you care about this person?"

She sniffs and takes a drink. "I've had a crush on him for years, and I swear he never even noticed me until last weekend."

I groan and glance out the window at the traffic on High Street. "I'm sorry, Jo. That's terrible."

"Thanks," she says in a small voice, tapping her nail against the can. "I don't think I can ever look at him again."

"It'll take some time, but it'll probably get better." I nod to her laptop. "What were you working on when I barged in on you?"

"Oh." She blushes. "Just this idea I have. It's probably stupid. I don't know." She shrugs it away, as if her idea isn't worthy of air-time.

"I'd like to know, if you want to share."

Her lips twist as she considers. "I guess you did come out here and start building something from scratch."

I laugh and make a circling gesture with my hands above the table. "This is a safe place."

Jo laughs. "Okay, fine." She opens her notebook and shows me sketches of what appears to be some kind of ranch. "It's a wilderness therapy camp. For troubled youth. There's an old ranch on the outside of town that's for sale. It hasn't been a working ranch in a long time, and the couple who lived there are moving to a retirement home. I just thought..." She trails off, shrugging.

"I think this is amazing, Jo."

She peeks at me nervously, but a proud smile tugs at her mouth. "Yeah?"

"Are you kidding? Yes, a thousand times over. I came here and started building a place for people to go shop, eat, and throw parties. You're thinking of something that will help people who need it. *Young* people. People who could one day be functioning members of society. That's really special, Jo."

"Thank you." Her pleased smile warms my heart. She spends the next ten minutes telling me more about the wilderness therapy camp. We talk like old friends.

"Oh, geez," Jo startles when she looks at her watch. "My shift starts soon."

"Good timing," I remark. Our wine is gone and the

lemon bar has disappeared. If I run my tongue over the roof of my mouth, I can still taste its sweet, tart flavor.

Jo and I walk back to the hotel, since we're both headed there anyway. She pulls her apron from her purse and ties it around her middle as we walk. We part ways with a hug in front of the restaurant.

For the next few hours, I return emails and look online at restaurant supply companies. I don't look at my phone.

Wes isn't to blame for what his mom did today, but it's made me think. I promised Abby I knew what I was getting into, but do I really?

34

WES

I FROWN AT THE PHONE IN MY HAND, THEN SLIP IT BACK INTO my pocket. Dakota has been missing in action all evening. It's been a while since we spent a night apart, and I'm worried about her. As soon as dinner with my family is through, I'm going to get in my truck and drive to her hotel.

Five minutes later, I look at my phone again, checking to make sure my ringer is on and my volume is up.

"Wes, are you having fiancée troubles?" Warner, who is sitting across the dinner table from me, leans his chair back on two legs. We're waiting for dinner to be ready and apparently Warner has chosen to pass the time by fucking with me.

"None of your concern," I grunt.

This, of course, is the wrong thing to say to Warner. If he is fire, my response was kindling.

"Damn," Warner says, snapping his fingers. "Just when I thought we were safe from Dickhead Wes. Better put my armor back on so I can be around you."

"Shut the fuck up," I mutter under my breath as my mom walks back into the room.

"No can do," Warner says cheerfully.

"What's going on?" She's studying the salty look on my face.

Warner says, "Dakota isn't responding to Wes and he's pissy."

A look crosses my mother's face, but it's hard to describe. Or maybe I can identify it, I just don't expect to see it. It takes me four long seconds to call her out. "Why do you look guilty?"

She blows out a heavy breath. "I went to visit Dakota today."

"Why?"

She tips her head in Warner's direction, telling him to get out. He listens, and since the rest of the family hasn't come to the table yet, we're alone.

I cup the back of my neck and roll my head in a slow circle. "What did you do?"

Mom pulls out the chair next to me, turns it so it's facing me, and sits down. "Hon," she starts, her eyebrows cinched together and concern adding to the creases around her eyes. "Do you believe in your heart that Dakota is marrying you because she wants to help you?"

"Yes." It's the truth, but there are other reasons too. Namely, the removal of her debt. But also, things between us have been crazy good. It's not far-fetched to say that maybe one day, we'd be where we are now. We've just fast tracked it.

"I'm sorry to have to be the one to tell you this, but she's not. She's in a mountain of debt and I think she's marrying you because she plans to eventually divorce you and get away with enough to pay off her bills and then some."

I laugh. I actually laugh. My mom balks, rearing back as if slapped.

"Well, I don't think it's *funny.*" She makes a face and

straightens her shirt, which didn't need straightening in the first place.

I place my hand on hers. "First off, I don't even want to know how you found out Dakota's *personal* financial information. Secondly, I'm aware of everything. I told her if she married me to help me get the ranch, I would pay off her debt."

Mom covers her gasp by bringing her free hand to her mouth. "Wes, no. The ranch doesn't have excess funds for that. We sold the land to Dakota in the first place to bring in more money."

"I know, Mom, but I've saved nearly everything I've earned for the past fifteen years. I didn't have expenses in the military, and I haven't had much of a life since coming back here. I have more than enough to help Dakota. And what she's giving me in return is worth far more than what I'm doing for her."

Mom sits back in her seat, all the righteousness disappeared like air in a popped balloon. She opens her mouth to speak but closes it when my dad walks into the room.

"Did you tell him?" he asks, glancing between the two of us.

"Tell me what?"

Mom's head shakes. "I was getting to it, but Wes just informed me he already knows about Dakota's motives."

My dad's lips stretch back into a tight line. "Well, what's done is done, and I'm not going back on it now."

I start to ask what the hell he's talking about, but he talks over me. "The trust was changed late this morning. The inheritor of this ranch can now be an unmarried direct descendent."

I blink twice. My breath stalls. My gaze flickers from my dad's stoic expression to my mom's worried frown.

The silence stretches on, and it must make my mom uncomfortable because she says, "Wes, this will allow you to get what you want without having to—"

"I know what this allows me," I say through clenched teeth. My elbows lean on the table and I breathe through a cupped hand. The heavy exhale is the only sound in the room, and it communicates my frustration more than words ever could.

"I don't know what you're upset about. You should be thanking your father. He's getting you out of this mess."

A few months ago I would've given almost anything to inherit the ranch without following the rule, but now it doesn't feel too good. In fact, it feels like agony.

I'm not afforded even two seconds to figure out my reaction because we're interrupted by Jessie, who bounds into the room and announces dramatically, "I'm starving past death." She's followed by the rest of my family.

Dad takes his place at the head of the table, Mom sits beside him, Gramps across from her, and the rest of us are in the seats we've sat in every day since we can remember.

We start eating, but I can't taste my food. I'm on autopilot. My mom's eyes look worried, and Wyatt asks, "What's wrong, Mom?"

Her eyes flash over to me before she answers. "Just one of my goats. She was limping today. She's just a little thing." She bites the side of her lower lip, and I get the feeling she's not making it up. "I'm not sure what happened. I hope she's all right."

"She'll be just fine, Mom," Warner assuages. "I think you love those goats more than you love us."

"Depends on the day," she teases. It sounds forced to my ears, but nobody else appears to notice.

When dinner is over we go our separate ways. Warner

heads to his cabin, Jessie leaves to stay the night at a friend's house, my parents are reading in the study, and Wyatt takes off in his truck, probably headed to a bar in town. I step out front and call Dakota again. This time, I leave her a message. "*Hey. Just checking in. Haven't heard from you.*"

When I turn around, Gramps is sitting in a chair behind me, two cold-looking beers set out on the table. "For a slow-mover, you're shockingly agile."

He flips me the bird and tells me to sit. I listen, popping the tab on both beers and handing one to him.

He takes a long drink, holds a fisted hand to his mouth as he burps, and says, "Beautiful out here, isn't it?"

"Always is," I respond, taking a pull from my beer.

He gestures out at the sunset with a flattened hand, his palm parallel to the horizon. "You see that salmon color? It was your grandma's favorite."

I nod. "I bet you miss her. I know I do."

"I miss her like you wouldn't believe. Right here." He thumps the skin over his heart. "I feel it right here. The rest of me just hurts because I'm old. I'm telling you Wes, aging is a real bitch."

I chuckle and keep my own aches and pains to myself. Something tells me my saddle soreness is nothing compared to what he feels.

"How's Dakota?" he asks, his gaze sliding over to me.

"Good, Gramps. She's good."

"You sure about that? Because I heard Warner telling Wyatt she's ignoring you."

I raise my eyebrows. "You can't hear half the shit we say to you, but gossip about my love life you manage to hear?"

He doesn't respond, just waits patiently for me to provide a real answer. I sigh. "My mom put her nose where it didn't belong and something tells me Dakota didn't appreciate it."

"I'm sure your mother meant well."

I nod. "She did. Still doesn't mean she should've done it."

"Good point." He looks back out at the sky.

"Do you know Dad changed the trust? I can take over the ranch now without being married first."

"Who do you think told him to do it?"

"You...?" My eyebrows lift. When he nods, I say, "Thank you."

"The rule was outdated, and it means something different in these modern times. Back when my dad decided on the rule, people were more likely to marry for practical reasons, and nobody ever said love was practical. Did you know your grandma and I knew each other less than a month before we got married?"

I stare at him, surprised. "How have I never heard that before?"

"Your parents probably kept it from you because they didn't want you going and doing something so crazy." He laughs at his own joke, and it makes me smile.

"Too late," I quip, tipping the can to my lips.

"Barely one month we knew each other before we tied the knot, and we were married fifty-six years. Marriage is hard no matter what, Wes, and dating her for years before marrying her wouldn't have made a damn bit of difference. Just woulda kept me from having her in bed, because back then we didn't do that before marriage." He cackles while I cringe, trying not to think of my grandma that way. "From what I can tell, you've gone and fucked this up something awful, but it's salvageable. Everything is."

My hand flies to my chest. "I've fucked this up?"

"Yep. You young people make it all so difficult. You went and asked her to marry you to get the ranch, and I can see why, but I think you bit off a little more than you could chew. I might be near deaf, but I'm not blind. My advice? Cut the shit and tell her you're in love with her. You can still marry her, but don't do it without telling her how you feel. She deserves that."

My head's spinning. It's like he reached into the recesses of my mind and said everything I think but can't seem to say. And how does he even know about marrying Dakota to get the ranch? When I ask him, he says, "Overheard your mom and dad talking."

I throw up my hands and he snickers. I gather both our empty cans and stand, but Gramps stops me with an outstretched arm. "Your dad told me you attended a meeting at the VFW." He nods at me, serious now. "Proud of you, Son. There's nothing braver than a man getting help when he needs it."

"Thanks," I murmur, uncharacteristic shyness creeping in.

"So, what are you going to do about Dakota now that the trust has been changed?"

"I don't know, Gramps. I just found out about it. I need time to think."

"I won't tell you to hang on to something you don't think is right. What I will tell you is that if you think you've got a shot at happiness, you owe it to yourself and to all those men you fought alongside who didn't make it back. They didn't fight so you could mope around your house and deny yourself life's pleasures. This is the land of the free, remember? They fought and died for your freedom, and that affords you the opportunity to love the person you see fit to love. Denying yourself would be a fool's move."

I'm stunned. "Gramps, I..."

He waves me off. "Don't say anything, Wes. Just think about what's best for you. If you could have everything you wanted, what would that look like?"

Gramps gets up. He tells me goodnight and walks into the house. After a few minutes, I follow him in and deposit the cans in the recycling bin. I check my phone. Still nothing from Dakota, but an idea pops into my head and it makes a grin spread on my face from ear to ear.

I type out a quick message to my friend who I had look into Dakota. My embarrassment at jumping to conclusions at that celebration dinner hasn't faded.

Lucky for me, he's still at work and writes me back.

All set, he says.

I slip my phone in my pocket and head toward the back door. Excitement flurries through me, making me take my steps at double-speed. I need to grab my truck keys from my cabin and get into town. I need to see Dakota, need to tell her that I just—

Warner bursts in through the door as I'm reaching for the handle. Panic makes his eyes wide and wild, his movements shaky. "The barn is on fire." His voice is just above a whisper, as if he can't believe the words are coming from him.

"Call the fire department," I instruct Warner, taking off for the shed behind the house where we keep the fire extinguishers. Behind me Warner yells, "I called them as soon as I saw it."

Still, it will take them twenty minutes or so to get out here. I throw open the shed and grab two extinguishers. Warner does the same, and together we take off at a run.

I smell it a few seconds before I see it. Once, at the Merc, I saw Burning Wood as the scent of a candle, and I thought that made sense because I love the smell of a campfire.

But not right now. This smell of burning wood breaks my heart.

The barn is a cavernous square with two off-shoots on either side. Fire licks up the sides, about halfway up, but all the way around. My brain registers that as odd, but I don't have time to analyze.

Warner and I run around the perimeter, spraying, and soon the cowboys run over.

"The shed," I shout. "More extinguishers!" Rivulets of sweat snake down my body. It's hot as hell, and it doesn't feel like we're making much progress. The equipment we have just isn't enough. The pond is less than a hundred yards away, but we need the firefighters' pump.

And then it hits me. *The animals.* Mom's goats are inside. I sprint to the front and throw open the door. Smoke billows out, burning my eyes and throat. I cover my mouth and nose with my forearm and run inside. I can't see more than a few feet in front of my face, but I know my mom keeps stacks of wool blankets on a shelf to my right. I stumble over, my free hand stuck out in front of me, feeling for the fabric. When I locate it, I grab one of the blankets and wrap it around me, using one hand to hold it cinched above my head.

I do my best, stumbling along, feeling for the latches on the gates my mom uses to keep the goats separated. Their bleating is nearly as loud as the splintering wood, and they sound desperate, as if on some level they know they are in danger. I do my best to open as many latches as I can, but I know I can't keep going. The smoke is too much and I'm starting to feel sick. I run for the exit, and there are goats running every which way. A few feet in front of me, I spot a limping goat. It's going so slow, it will never make it. I scoop it up on my way past. Behind me is a loud crack, and I sprint out of the barn holding the goat.

The relieved shouts of my name are the first thing I hear, but it's drowned out by screaming sirens. A fire truck followed by an ambulance. Suddenly my mom's in my face, running her hands over my cheeks, wide eyes checking me for signs of obvious injury.

I cough. "I'm fine, Mom."

She gives me a long, heavy look, then takes the goat from my arms. "That was stupid, Wes," she scolds, but her lips quiver.

Maybe it was stupid, but it was also innate. Inside me is a drive to serve, to protect, to save. It's a biological instinct. I've always felt it, and then when it came time for me to choose a job in the military, the bomb squad seemed an obvious choice.

The firefighters jump into action, depositing one end of their pump into the pond and snaking the firehose to the barn. They yell to one another, and soon the pump is drafting the water.

I look around at who's here now. When I'd run into the barn, it had only been me, Warner, and a handful of cowboys. My mom and dad, Gramps, and the remaining cowboys stand here now. Every single person who lives on this ranch, with the exception of Warner's kids, and Wyatt and Jessie.

The amount of water the firefighters are using to handle the fire makes our use of fire extinguishers laughable. The first thing I'll do when the ranch is mine is fill in the inadequacies in fire response.

My mom counts the goats. Tears fill her eyes and she floats into my dad's waiting arms. "We're missing six," she tells him.

Dammit. My poor mom.

It's not too long before the fire is out. One of the men approaches my dad, and when he removes his helmet, I see it's Derrick, my friend from high school.

"Derrick? Hey, man." I offer a hand. "I can't thank you enough."

But Derrick doesn't look happy that he's just put out a fire. He looks worried. "Wes." He shakes my hand, then turns to my dad. "Mr. Hayden, my guys and I have reason to believe this fire was set intentionally."

My dad's head jerks back in surprise. "Why is that?"

Derrick gestures to another firefighter, who has also removed his helmet. He walks over with something in his hand. A gas can?

Derrick takes it. "This was found in the woods just beyond the barn. Like it had been tossed there."

"Let me see that." I motion for the object. Derrick gives it to me, and I turn it over, looking for any kind of marking that might tell us who it belongs to. There's nothing.

"Wes, let's get you checked out by the paramedics," Derrick urges, glancing at the waiting ambulance.

I shake my head. "I'm fine."

"Go on, Wes," my dad instructs, his voice deepening. "You were in that barn and you need to get checked out."

I know better than to challenge my dad right now, especially when he's worried about me. If I refuse, he'll get angry, and he doesn't need that. The man had heart surgery a month ago.

Derrick keeps talking to Dad, asking him if he knows anybody who would have done this, and I head for the ambulance. Warner comes over while the paramedics are doing basic checks.

"You scared the shit out of me when you ran in that barn, Wes."

"I knew what I was doing." What a crock. I didn't know what I was doing. Instinct sent me in there, not intelligence.

"Wes." Warner's voice is serious. "You're my big brother. We might be in our thirties, but there's still a lot of shit I haven't given you yet. Don't go doing anything crazy and leaving me alone with Wyatt anytime soon. He can't take my shit-talking the way you can."

I laugh. The paramedic slides a cool stethoscope up my back and presses it into my skin. "I love you too, brother."

Warner's eyes widen, but he tries to act like my words are no big deal. Something I say every day.

"You too, Wes," he replies, swiping a hand over his face. He changes the subject. "Heard from Dakota?"

The paramedics declare me all good, but tell me I'm going to need some serious hydration and a lot of Visine for dry eyes. I thank them and walk away, pulling my phone from my pocket as I go. One voicemail, from Dakota, left an hour ago. I press the button and listen.

"Wes, hi. It's me. I mean, obviously. Sorry I sound so nervous. It's just that I got an email from my credit card company and I'm confused. Are we not... is the wedding still on? Because I thought with our agreement and everything," she pauses, and I can hear knocking in the background. *"Someone is here. Anyway, call me back, okay? Bye."* She hasn't hung up yet. The voicemail is still rolling, the seconds ticking by on the screen. I hear a man's voice, then the line goes dead.

"What's wrong?" Warner asks. There must be a look on my face. I shake my head, my lips pursed, and call Wyatt.

"Hey, bro," Wyatt answers.

"Where are you?" I bark.

"Playing poker at a friend's house. Why?"

"I need you to go to Dakota's hotel room. Now."

"I'm winning, Wes."

"I don't give a fuck if you're beating the pants off a Saudi prince. Get out of there and go to room 214 at the Sierra."

Wyatt makes an irritated sound and I hear him say, "I gotta go, guys. I'll kick your asses next time."

I stay on the phone as he takes off, listening to the sounds of his truck coming to life. Warner jabs my arms and gives me a *What the hell?* look, but I wave him off. I can't talk right now. My mind is racing. I have a bad feeling the barn fire and the man at Dakota's door are connected. I don't know why, I just do.

"I'm parked, Wes," Wyatt tells me. "Now I'm going through the front door. Past the front desk and the restaurant. Up the stairs to the second floor. Down the hall and... oh, shit."

"What?" I yell, fear gripping my heart.

"Her door is open."

"Fucking go in!" I shout.

"I already am," Wyatt replies. "Her phone is on the ground. She's not here."

"Fuck," I grit out.

"Wes, I found something." I picture Wyatt leaning down cautiously, reaching out a hand to lift something off the floor. "It's a pocket knife. Initials HDC."

My mind races, flipping through a catalog of people I know, but I'm coming up empty. Every second I spend rifling through the catalogue of people I know is a frustrating waste. "Who the fuck does that belong to?"

"Howard Dixon Calhoun. Or as you know him, just Dixon."

Everything stops. Time stands still. Dixon's words from the night at The Chute come back to me. *Do you want to know what kings do, Hayden? They fall. And you will too. Maybe even soon.*

"Get back here now. You're taking us to Dixon's cookhouse."

"Horses, no trucks," Wyatt instructs. He huffs like he's running. In the background a door slams, and I hear heavy, metallic footfalls. He's taking the secondary stairs, the same ones Dixon almost certainly used to take Dakota. "I don't know of any roads that will get us close. I'm on my way," Wyatt answers, then hangs up.

I look up into the anxious faces of my family. Derrick has gone back to work with the firefighters, and the cowboys play horseshoes for lack of anything better to do.

"Dakota is missing," I inform them, "and I think Dixon might have her. I know it sounds insane, but I think he started the fire to distract us and make sure I stayed here, then he went into town." I tell them about the voicemail and the pocketknife.

"Wyatt's on his way. He knows where Dixon lives and he's going to take me to him."

"You're not going without me," Warner announces.

"Or me."

We all stare at my dad.

He holds up a hand. "Before you start, I'm not asking any of you for permission." He walks past Warner toward the stable. "Come on. Get the horses ready so we can leave as soon as Wyatt gets here."

"Go help Dad," I tell Warner. "I have to go to my cabin."

When I get back, I find four horses ready to go. "I stopped at the homestead, too," I tell my dad, handing him the gun he keeps in the top of his closet. "Here." I hand another gun to Warner.

"You think we're going to need these?" Warner grimaces.

He likes to hunt, but what we're hunting now is vastly different than the elk and deer he's used to.

"I hope not, Warner, but there's not a doubt in my mind that Dixon is strapped. Knowing that, do you want to go up against him with or without a gun?"

He doesn't answer. He doesn't need to.

Wyatt's truck hauls ass down our road. He slams it into park and hops out, running toward us. Without a word he jumps on his horse, leans down and whispers something to her that none of us can hear. He's the first to start, and he motions for us to follow. My body is tense, on high alert, and all I can think about is Dakota. Ranger, sensing my mood, is rigid, his muscles as taut as my own.

We ride in a line across the flat plain, into the trees, and ascend into the sooty darkness of the mountain.

35

DAKOTA

Ow.

It's my first thought when I open my eyes.

My face muscles clench as I register the pain in the back of my head. I'm moving. Or rather, I'm in something that's moving. It's bumpy, and I wince every time I'm jostled. My heart beats furiously, but I feel it in my neck, not my chest.

I force a deep breath in, exhaling slowly, trying to slow my pulse. I remember opening the door. I should have looked through the peephole, but I didn't. I had just seen the email congratulating me on paying off my balance in full, and I was stupefied. I was leaving Wes a message, and when I heard the knock, I thought maybe it was him. I flung open the door, and the smile that had been on my face melted like cotton candy in water. The immediate sense of danger chilled my entire body.

Dixon said something I didn't comprehend because my pulse was throbbing in my ears, then rushed forward, putting his weight against the door so I had no hope of slamming it. I turned, wild eyes seeking anything I could use as a weapon. There was a pen on the table. A pen was my best bet, and yet I knew it wouldn't be enough. I dropped my phone and lunged for the pen, thinking *carotid artery.* He wrapped an arm around me from behind, pressed something to my mouth, and that was it. My fingertips brushed the pen and then I woke up here.

I blink twice, look up, and for the first time notice the sky. Clouds move across, the moon and stars in view before being covered up, only to be revealed moments later. I turn my head left, then right, ignoring the pain in the back of my head, and it becomes clear I'm in the bed of a truck.

Dixon's truck, I assume. Trees surround us, and based on the uneven drive, I don't think the road is paved. These are the kinds of trees that are around the HCC, so I know I'm north of the town.

I need to have a plan for when the truck stops. I don't want to alert Dixon by sitting up, so I feel around with my legs and arms.

Nothing. There isn't a single thing back here that I can use against him.

My eyes fly open when the truck rolls to a stop. *No, it's too soon. I haven't had time to prepare.*

I have nothing. Nothing but my limbs and a will to live. That's what it's going to come down to, right? Why would he have brought me all the way out here to the woods?

The truck door creaks open. My shaking hands ball into fists. I close my eyes, pretend that whatever the hell he put me to sleep with is still working.

A pulling, ripping sound fills the quiet mountain air. I haven't heard it in years, and yet my brain knows it immediately. Duct tape.

I fly up onto my feet and jump from the truck, landing unevenly on the dirt and falling to my knees.

"What the fuck?" I hear the shout from the other side of the truck.

I pop up, ignoring the stinging in my knees, and run. A cloud has covered the moon and it's pitch black. I stay on the road, because I know I won't make it in the trees. The land is too foreign, and I'm not wearing shoes.

I hear him behind me. His exhalations mix with my own. He is close. In mere seconds he will overtake me, but I can't stop.

He tackles me from behind, and we both fall, rolling off the road into the dirt and pine brush. The taste of earth covers my tongue and I fight, twisting and turning, kicking and screaming.

"Shut the fuck up," Dixon hisses in my ear, locking his arms around me and crushing my arms to my body. I kick and throw my head back, connecting. I yelp in pain, but so does Dixon. Something wet hits my neck, and my stomach lurches when I realize it must be blood.

It makes him mad. He tightens his grip around me, struggles to stand, and turn so his side is pressed to mine. I can still kick, but now I cannot kick him. I try, but my legs swing through nothing but air. He drags me this way back up the dirt road.

"Why?" I ask, but Dixon doesn't answer.

I begin to cry.

He drags me to his open truck door, reaches in, and places the soft cloth back over my mouth.

Again.

It happened again.

But now, everything hurts, not just my head. And I'm not moving. I'm not in the truck.

I blink my eyes open. I'm sitting on a floor. I'm propped against a wall and a chair, but I'm outside. Cool air skims my face. Things are coming into focus now. The trees swaying in the breeze, the railing of a porch, the three steps down to solid ground. The porch is surrounded by a semi-circle of twenty-five feet of flat, open land, and then the woods begin. Perhaps the open land continues farther, but from my position I can't see.

My wrists are duct taped, and so are my ankles.

Dixon is nowhere to be seen, but I can feel him lurking somewhere. Maybe he is watching me, enjoying the show as I wake and try to understand where I am.

The same fire that filled me when I awoke in the truck fills me once more. I refuse to go down without giving it my all. My gaze darts around, trying desperately to see the darkened shapes, find anything sharp I can rub the duct tape across. I just need to free my legs, so I can run.

I scoot a few inches on my bottom, glancing back at the house to see if my movement was noticed. When nothing happens, I do it again. And again, until I'm close to the railing. Now that I'm closer, I see the wood is old, and I'm hoping somewhere along its length will be a jagged piece. My fingers run along, and I keep scooting, desperately hoping to find what I'm looking for. I'm so intent on my task that the metallic slam of the screen door sends a terrified screech up my throat and into the tense night air.

All my hope disappears as I listen to his lazy walk over to me.

"Have to hand it to you, you're quite the pistol," Dixon says, gripping under my arms. He pulls me back, but instead of putting me back in the place where I woke up, he leaves me front and center on the porch.

"Get on your knees."

"No." I shake my head. He bends down, his face so close to mine I feel the heat of his breath. Blood is dried on his face, and his nose appears to be broken. I lunge at him, taking him by surprise, and try to bite him. He moves in time, and my teeth snap together painfully. He stares at me, lips shaking, and I snarl. I can hardly wrap my head around this primitive, animalistic response. For the first time in my life, I genuinely understand the ferocity of a cornered animal.

Dixon walks in the house and returns quickly. He comes from behind me, where I can't see him, and slips something over my head. Before I can move, he's gagged me. His hands work at the back of my head, tying, and some strands of my hair are caught up in the knotted fabric. He stands up, walks away, and the porch light flickers on. I blink against its harshness.

Then he strides over, stands beside me, and says once more, "Get on your knees."

I shake my head, because getting on my knees feels like the final step to whatever he's going to do. After that, what will be left?

Dixon lifts his dirt-streaked white T-shirt, and the silver glint of metal peeks out. "Knees, girl. Now."

Tears streak down my face. How is there nothing left for me to do? The fight is still inside me, but there's nothing at my disposal. No tools, no implements, no advantage. I've never felt so helpless.

I'm left only with what Dixon asks of me. Delaying his plan is my only hope. But what is it I'm even hoping for? Who could possibly know where I am?

Dixon watches me struggle to my knees. I sit back on my heels and stare at the ground.

I think of Wes, and my heart breaks. Wes, with his moody looks and big, capable hands. The smile he reserves for me, the kind of smile most people probably don't think he's capable of. The way he charges into a situation and commands it, overly-confident and protective, but on the inside he's so vulnerable.

Dixon walks away, down the steps and around the side of the house. I watch him go, and for the shortest second, I see what Dixon might have looked like when he was younger, back when Wyatt knew him. He probably had hair that flopped over his forehead, in need of a trim. Maybe he had good in his heart, and his own father's bad choices made him angry. I tell myself this because I need to see him in a different light. For my own sake, I need to believe he wasn't always so jealous and malicious.

When he comes back, he's holding something I don't fully understand. It looks like a contraption assembled by a child. He takes a knee in front of me, almost like he's proposing, and looks me in the eye. "Don't move an inch." His Adam's apple bobs, and he wipes a free hand on the front of his jeans. He lifts something up, lowers it down onto me, and secures it to my front with duct tape that he wraps around my body.

"There," he says proudly. "Let's see what your boyfriend thinks of that."

I look down and all the air whooshes out of me. Sounds of protest slip around the fabric, keeping me from talking. *Bomb?* No. It can't be. Why is he doing this? I don't understand. I'm hyperventilating and crying, and trying not to move.

Dixon backs away, sinking down onto the last step and

looking at me. He must've been holding his breath, because he exhales loudly. The nervousness is replaced by a smug look.

"Now we just wait for your boyfriend to show up. I left something behind in your hotel room. He'll figure it out."

I bite the inside of my lip, but I'm shaking so badly I bite harder than intended and taste my own blood.

My eyes drift close and I start going down the list of people I love, people I will probably never see again.

My dad. Abby and the girls.

And Wes.

36

WES

THE CLOUDS HAVE CLEARED AND GIVEN US BETTER VISIBILITY. Each one of our figures is in shadow, but outlines are all we need.

At Wyatt's signal, we stop short and get off our horses, tying their reins to trees.

Wyatt steps in, slips Dixon's pocketknife into my hand, and motions us in to form a tight circle. "His place is that way," he whispers, pointing northeast with two fingers. Then he looks to me and nods, telling me to take over.

I look into the eyes of my brothers and my dad, and an overwhelming sense of gratitude sweeps through me. "We walk until we see Dixon's place, then we fan out. We don't know if he's alone with Dakota or if there are others, so be aware of any back doors. I'll take the front door. If any of you get the opportunity for a kill shot, take it. Just not if he's near Dakota."

We break, walking in unison until the lights from a structure filter through the trees. We creep closer, our footfalls light, until a small, dilapidated cabin comes into view. Even from this distance, I can make out two figures on the porch. I pause, pulling my military-grade night-vision binoculars from my pocket. Everyone stops and waits for me.

The second I peer through them, I wish like hell I hadn't.

I turn my head, squeeze my eyes tight, and cuss through clenched teeth. I pass the binos to my dad, who looks and sends them on to Warner, then to Wyatt. They look at me, waiting to see if what we've discovered changes our plans.

"Proceed," I murmur, my volume less than a whisper. I can't help but feel like the years I spent deactivating explosives in the Middle East were all leading up to this moment, preparing me for the most important job of my life.

Warner and Wyatt go right, my dad goes left, and I walk forward. I'm close enough now that I don't need the binoculars to see. Dixon, slouching on the bottom step, his back against the railing. And Dakota, in the middle of the porch, bound and gagged. She sits on her knees, and strapped to her chest is the most embarrassing attempt at a homemade bomb I've ever seen.

But that doesn't mean it won't detonate.

My hands clench and unclench, adrenaline pulses through my body, and my ears begin to pound. This is rage like I've never felt it.

Dakota's eyes are closed, and I close mine for a second too, trying to send her a message. *I'm here. I'm going to save you.* When my eyes open, I find hers have also. I've never believed in fate, in ghosts or angels, or in almost anything I can't see, but right now Dakota's eyes are trained on me. I know she cannot possibly see me under the cover of darkness, but it feels like she is looking straight into my soul, like she heard me.

I put one foot in front of the other until I'm a hair's breadth from the clearing.

Dakota's eyes grow wide, and her body jerks as if she was going to get up and try to run but stopped herself. Dakota's reaction has told Dixon he's getting just what he wanted.

Me.

He swings around and stands, his gaze zeroing in on me. Then he grins, the kind of sinister smile that belongs on a Halloween mask. There is blood on his face.

The smile falls off his face like he's just realized he's forgotten something and he scrambles up the steps, going to stand behind Dakota.

He's hiding behind her like the coward he is.

"Let her go, Dixon," I call out. "Your problem is with me."

He shakes his head and reaches under his shirt, producing a small handgun. He points it at me. "Do you know what happened to my family after your dad fired my pops? My mom died and my dad killed himself. He was stealing because we needed the money to pay my mom's medical expenses. Selling saddles made him a little extra money, and it didn't hurt your dad. But no. Your dad wouldn't have it." He sneers and shakes his head. "I told you a king would fall. A Hayden took everything from my dad. Now I'm going to take everything from a Hayden." He points the gun to Dakota's temple.

"I'll take her place," I shout. "Let her go and come and get me."

He snorts. "Do you expect me to believe Warner isn't out there"—he motions to the woods with the gun—"somewhere, just waiting to get a shot?"

"He's with the barn you set on fire. I went to find Dakota and discovered your pocket knife on the floor of the hotel room." I dig the knife from my pocket and hold it up, tossing it out into the middle of the clearing.

Dixon eyes me, unsure. I have to get him away from Dakota, using any means necessary.

I hold up my gun, showing it to Dixon, and set it down on the ground. Dakota's eyes are huge, pleading with me to stop, but my choice is made. I love Dakota more than anything, including my life. It shouldn't come down to that, not with my brothers and my dad hiding in the woods, waiting, but it's the truth. I stride ten feet into the clearing and sink to my knees. "Take me instead, Dixon."

He's unsure, and I can almost see the wheels turning in his mind. His gaze wanders around the perimeter of the tree line, then falls back to me. "I know Wyatt is drunk at a poker game, but where's your old man?"

"He just had heart surgery. Coming out here would kill him. It's just me, Dixon. And we both know it's not Dakota you want. It's me."

Dakota whimpers, and the sound might as well have a blade attached to it because it slices through me. I want to look at her, reassure her with my gaze, but I don't dare break Dixon's stare. I need him to believe me and step away from Dakota.

"Say I decide to let you switch with her, what happens to the bomb?"

"I disarm it."

Dixon laughs. "I'm not stupid."

"I've told you before, I don't think you're stupid. You keep the gun on me while I disarm it. Then Dakota goes free and I'm yours."

Dixon fixes a long, hard stare at me, then steps out from behind Dakota. My tense, coiled muscles relax a fraction, and my knees bear the weight of my relief.

He pauses on the top step, then keeps going.

One.

Two.

Three.

He's clear of the house, almost dead center between me and Dakota.

Three shots ring out.

Dixon falls.

I'm up off my knees, running for Dakota. I thunder up the steps and sink to my knees before her. Her sobs are muffled, and it tears me apart.

"I'm here baby, I'm here. It's all going to be okay now." I look into her eyes briefly, then study the bomb taped to her chest. Just as I thought, it's rudimentary. Day one of EOD training taught me—

Dakota makes a noise like a strangled cry, and I look up. Her terrified gaze is trained behind me.

Another crack fills the air and Dakota releases a muffled scream.

My ears ring. I blink against the sound and look quickly. Dixon is crumpled at the base of the stairs.

I turn my attention back to Dakota. "Just hold still," I instruct. When I ran to my cabin earlier, I'd grabbed everything from the bag I keep in the top of my closet, the same bag I haven't touched in five years. My flashlight, my binoculars, and my clippers. I reach into my pocket and pull out the clippers.

I know this is the moment when I'm supposed to think of the woman and her child. The nightmare I've been having for years should be replaying front and center in my mind.

And maybe I'm thinking of them a little. But really, all I see is Dakota. My inability to save the others has no bearing on this moment. Maybe, if I hadn't gone to the meeting, I'd be reliving my nightmare. But I'm not.

I snip the correct wire cleanly, and without hesitation. The clippers slice through the duct tape and I remove the deactivated bomb.

Warner appears beside me. He takes the bomb from my hands without a word and walks into the ramshackle home.

I reach around Dakota, untying the gag and flinging it aside.

Her relieved sobs fill the night air. I hold her face, press my cheek to hers, and rock with her. Her tears mix with my own. The adrenaline that fueled me slowly subsides, and I feel crushing exhaustion.

"Wes." My dad's voice sounds like gravel. "Cut her free and get her away from here. Take her to the house and let Mom look her over."

I turn to look at him. He's standing beside Dixon.

"But what about—"

His face is hard. "Do as I say, Son."

I understand. Whatever is about to happen next, he doesn't want Dakota around for it. I follow his instructions, cutting the tape at her ankles and ripping it off her jeans. Her wrists are trickier, because he taped her skin. I cut it, but leave the tape on her skin. When she's free of the binding, she throws her arms around me. She rubs my neck, the back of my head, her fingers trickling over my face and chest.

"I know, I know," I soothe her, wrapping an arm around her shoulders. "It's over now. Let's go."

I lead her down the steps. My brothers and my dad stand a few feet away, waiting on us to leave. Dakota pauses and shrugs me off. On unsteady feet, she walks over and hugs each one in turn. They nod at her, and then my dad looks at me only, inclining his head toward where we left the horses. His meaning is clear. *Get out of here*.

I take Dakota by the hand, using my flashlight to lead us back to the horses. We're slow going, because her legs are shaking and she tells me they hurt. She also needs to pee, so I unbutton her jeans and tug them down, then help to keep her steady so she can go to the bathroom. She laughs shyly, and despite everything we've been through tonight, her cheeks flush.

"Don't be embarrassed, Dakota."

She finishes and I help her stand upright. Looking at her face, her strawberry hair, swathed in shades of darkness with only the flashlight to provide a slice of light, I'm overcome by how much she means to me.

She sags against me, and it reminds me of how much she has been through. I need to get her back to the homestead so my mom can look her over.

I untie Ranger and help Dakota up, then sit down behind her. She leans back into my chest, and we retrace our way through the woods, this time at a much slower pace.

The danger has passed.

I've got my girl.

And starting right now, I'm going to do things differently.

By now I know how I react to crises. I turn off my emotions, respond, and later, when I'm alone, I let go of the emotions I strangled. Tonight is no different. A lone tear slips down my cheek and I wipe it with my shoulder.

The hand that rests on my knee? It's quivering, which is

why I'm tapping my fingers. I can't stand to watch my own shaking hand.

The other hand? It holds a generous two-finger pour of whiskey.

I'm sitting on the front porch of the homestead. My heritage is spread out before me, thick and lush grass, dirt road, and pine, but it doesn't smell like my home. The fire was extinguished hours ago, and even though the smoke has dissipated, its scent clings to the air.

I'm looking at my land, the land I was willing to marry Dakota to get, but I don't really see it. My mind is filled with Dakota.

Her shocked expression when I walked into my dad's office that day. Indignant and angry, thinking I didn't remember her. Then later on my front porch, her face softened with concern, urging me to help myself heal.

Dakota on her back, legs encircling my waist and riding a high with me.

Dakota on her knees, terrified.

And just a few minutes ago, allowing me to carry her into the guest room and lay her on the bed. On a normal day, that wildly independent woman would stand on her own two feet, but tonight is about as opposite from normal as it can get.

The front door opens and my mom steps out. She folds her arms across her chest and grips her upper arms as if it's cold, even though it's not. Perhaps she's chilled by the events of the night.

She perches on the arm of the chair beside mine. "Dakota's okay. Exhausted. I left her so she could get in the bath. She has some pretty good scrapes, especially on her knees. She said—" Mom cuts off, and when I look at her I find her cautious gaze already on me. "She said the scrapes on her knees are because she tried to run from him, and he tackled her from behind."

Dixon can't hurt Dakota anymore, but hot rage still burns through me. He got off easy, not just because of what he did tonight, but also because of the damage he's been inflicting in town. The families he tore apart, the lives people lost due to his selling. Everyone is responsible for their own choices, but some choices wouldn't be made if the opportunity never presented itself.

"But..." My mom's voice upturns, like she's grasping for a bright side. "She said she did a reverse head butt sort of thing to him." She demonstrates by throwing her head back. "So I guess she got something good in."

I can't bring myself to feel good about it, because she shouldn't have been in that position in the first place. Dixon took her because of *me*.

My interest is piqued by the distant sound of hooves. Mom and I sit, quiet, as the sound grows steadily louder, and watch two riders appear around the corner of the house.

Warner and Wyatt.

"Where's Dad?" I ask, at the same time my mother says, "Where is your father?"

"He told us to leave," Wyatt answers, coming to a stop.

"And you listened?" I drain my whiskey glass and place it on the table. Standing, I say, "He shouldn't be out there alone. I'm going to—"

"You'll do no such thing."

It's my mother's voice, quiet and strong, that stops me. I look down at her. The weariness in her eyes reminds me that she, too, has had a long night. After what happened to Dakota, the barn feels like a distant memory to me.

"You'll understand when you have kids," she starts,

looking at the three of us in turn. "Whatever your dad is doing now, he had reason to send you away. Respect that."

"Yes, ma'am," the three of us utter in unison. We all sound reluctant.

"You two," she points at Warner and Wyatt. "Get to bed. You've had a long night. And you…" She turns to me. "Get upstairs. I bet Dakota could use some help washing her back. She's awfully sore, and it's only going to get worse before it gets better." It's her way of apologizing to me for her attitude toward Dakota.

I nod my acceptance and head across the porch for the front door. I stop, calling out to my brothers just as they're turning their horses toward the stable. They both look at me.

Side-by-side like they are right now, you wouldn't know Wyatt once hid out in a bush and shot Warner in the thigh with his BB gun, or that I let Warner drive a ranch truck in town when he was fifteen and he hit a fire hydrant and I took the blame. In the twelve years I spent in the Army, and the last five years I've spent pushing everyone away, I didn't notice my little brothers becoming men. I told myself they could never understand what I've been through. I pushed them away because they didn't go to war alongside me. But after tonight, I've recognized something even more valuable. Warner and Wyatt *would* go to war alongside me.

Tonight, they did. Three shots were fired at the same time.

My eyes sting as I look at them. I want to apologize for pushing them away for years, but I'm still working on finding the right words, so for now, I say, "Thank you for tonight. I love you guys."

Warner grins, like he knew if he waited long enough I'd

come around. Wyatt ducks his head, nodding at me, and starts for the stable.

I stop in the doorway, pausing to look over at my mom. Her head is tilted against the chair and her hands are folded over her stomach. She looks like she's settling in to wait for my dad, probably for as long as it takes.

The house is silent, and my boots are heavy on the stairs. I stop outside the guest bedroom, toeing them off and leaving them on the floor. I step in and close the door behind me. A sliver of light from the bathroom door gives me just enough to see in the dark room. I make my way over, softly rapping on the door with a knuckle.

"It's me," I call.

"Come in," Dakota answers in a tired voice.

I step into the humid air. Dakota stands wet and naked beside the bathtub, towel-drying her hair. The dirt and makeup are gone from her face, revealing an abrasion across her left cheek. Our eyes meet and I walk closer. I take the fluffy white towel from her and start at her shoulders. I don't think she needs the help, but I need to feel useful, to do something for her. She steadies herself on my shoulders, her eyes closed and head tipped slightly back. I run the towel over her body, drying her but also taking inventory.

Large red marks dot her thighs and arms, and time will turn them into bruises. Angry abrasions cover her knees, a testament to her willingness to fight.

All the rage I felt earlier is snuffed out in an instant and I drop the towel and reach for her. She winces when I touch the back of her head, but when I take my hand away from her she stops me, pressing my open hand to her uninjured cheek. She sighs heavily into my palm, then kisses it.

"Thank you for tonight," she whispers.

"No." I shake my head, my voice strained. "You shouldn't be thanking me. It's my fault it happened in the first place."

"This was nobody's fault but Dixon's." She begins to dress from a small pile of folded clothes on the bathroom counter. "Your mom left me a pair of Jessie's pajamas," she explains, pulling the top over her head, yawning. She looks as if she is ready to fall asleep standing.

"Come on," I murmur, gently pulling her to the bed. I turn back the covers and she climbs in.

"Will you stay with me tonight?" Her voice is small, and her eyes are closed.

"Yes." I remove my shirt and jeans, then slip into bed beside her.

"I want to hold you, but I'm not sure how I can touch you," I murmur. "I don't want to hurt you."

Dakota backs up inch by inch, slowly melting into me, until I can't tell where she stops and I start. I press a kiss to the space behind her ear. Her skin is hot from her bath.

"If anything had happened to you," I whisper, letting the second half of my sentence remain unspoken.

"Shhh," she croons. "We're both okay."

I take a deep breath, inhaling her sweet scent. My lips part, an *I love you* poised at the edge, but Dakota's deep, even breathing grows deeper and more even.

I press a gentle kiss to her hair and send up a prayer thanking God for her safety.

For a long time I've known what it feels like to love. My family, my land, my country. But this soul-crushing, all-consuming, sharp and powerful feeling in my heart is new. The love I feel for Dakota is different than everything before it.

37

DAKOTA

WES.

Dixon.

No.

My eyes blink open. Morning sun filters around the closed blinds, sending just enough light into the room to reveal the outlines of furniture.

I'm safe. I'm in the guest room at the homestead. Beside me, Wes snores gently. He is safe, too. I'm sore, so sore, but I turn my head anyway, just so I can look at him.

He's beautiful. Outside, yes, but inside, too. He doesn't give himself nearly enough credit. People like him are a dying breed. Strong and sensitive, smart and resourceful, with a basic and inherent grasp on right versus wrong, good versus evil. He loves his country, but I don't know if he fully grasps how much he also loves the people in it. The collective many, the people who live every iteration of the American dream. That's who he fought for. That's what he fought to protect.

A surge of pride fills me. I've always understood why Wes would marry me to get the ranch, but I've never fully felt a love so encapsulating that I would go to the ends of the earth to keep it, and by any means necessary. But now, I do.

It's the same love I feel for Wes.

I should let him sleep, but I can't. I need to feel his rough stubble under my fingertips.

My muscles protest when I lift my arm, but I ignore them and allow my fingers to continue on to their target.

Wes's eyes stay closed, but a deep, contented sigh slides up his throat. "How do you feel?" His scratchy, morning voice sends a tremble down my body.

"Good," I answer, and in this exact moment, it's true. The sudden need I feel for Wes has an anesthetic effect on my pain. My hand leaves his stubble and slips down under the covers, wrapping around him. His eyes jerk open.

"Dakota… are you sure? Aren't you sore?"

I've never needed him more than I do right now. After the horror of last night, his weight, his hands, his whispered words are all I want. "Please," I beg, my voice a quiet cry.

He understands. He moves, hooking a leg over me and sitting back on his knees. Gently, he removes my pajama bottoms, then his own, and kneels between my legs. He lines himself up with my entrance, and he pushes inside. His eyes never leave mine. He reaches for me, cupping my cheek, stroking with his thumb.

"I want your weight," I gasp.

He shakes his head. "Not until you're healed."

I pout, and he grins, but he never breaks his rhythm. He pulls down my pajama top, cupping my breast and flicking his finger over my nipple. His hand drifts down between my legs, working until I've forgotten every ounce of pain in my body.

"That's it, baby," he murmurs when my thigh muscles coil and my hips lift. With my hand cupped over my mouth and my eyes fixed on Wes, I let the sensation take over. My release prompts his own, and I watch his eyes squeeze tight and his muscles contract.

His eyes reopen and he looks down at me. "You were the first thing I thought about when I woke up." He looks down at where we're still connected. "And I think I know the first thing you thought about when you woke up."

I don't correct him. Besides, my carnal desire didn't lag too far behind my initial thoughts.

"Guilty as charged," I say, as Wes pulls back and lies down beside me.

"Now tell me the truth. How do you feel?" He props himself up on an arm and looks pointedly down at me.

I turn my attention inward. With the bliss fading away, the soreness is creeping back in.

"A little uncomfortable," I admit, and it irritates me. The lingering pain reminds me of what happened, and it seems unfair that not only do I have it in my memory, but I have my body to remind me of it too.

Wes watches his fingers as they trace an invisible pattern across my stomach. "I'm so glad you're okay. Seeing you... like that... it nearly ripped me in half, Dakota." His gaze finds mine, and he looks uncertain. "My dad changed the trust. The inheritor of the HCC can be unmarried."

I should feel happy for Wes, but I feel crushed. I swallow hard and adopt a brave face. "I guess this is where I say thank you for paying off my debt when you didn't have to."

Wes's eyebrows cinch together, so I explain. "You know, since you can get the ranch without getting married now." My smile is weak. "I guess we both got what we wanted." Vulnerability fills me, so I reach down to brush his hand off my stomach, but his muscles clench and my pushing is ineffectual.

"Dakota, last night I realized something that's been staring me in the face for a while. There's a big difference between what I want, and what I need. I want the ranch, but I *need* you." He grabs my hand, his fingers intertwining with mine. "I love you, Dakota."

A smile splits my face, and for a brief moment all my physical pain is gone. "I'm so in love with you, Wes." I laugh incredulously after I say it, because I don't know what to do with the overflow of emotion.

"Thank God," he says, eyes lifting to the ceiling. He leans down, kissing me.

"You're a hard person not to love, Wes." I kiss him again. "Out of curiosity, when did you know you loved me?"

Wes puts a few inches of space between our faces as he thinks. "That question has two parts. First, I fell in love with you that first night at the lake, when we were swimming."

I make a face, but he shakes his head. "That's the truth. You swam to me, wrapped your arms around my shoulders, and pushed the hair off my forehead. You looked into my eyes and laughed and kissed me, and it hit me that for the first time in my life, I could feel the heart in my chest. Really feel it. And then later, we were talking and I told you about being in the military, and then I just... started crying. And I thought, *You'd better run, because this girl is going to undo you.*" I shake my head, astonished at what he's saying. He keeps going. "I took the easy way out, even when it killed me. You brought to life in me something I wanted to stay dead. Leaving you felt like my only option."

A little noise sounds in the back of my throat, and I realize I'm near tears.

"The second part is that I realized I was in love with you when you came over and did your laundry. It felt so natural and right, like you were always meant to be there. I started thinking back to the night I met you, and it hit me that I couldn't ever fall in love with you, because I already was." He taps the tip of my nose. "Your turn."

I brush a kiss against him. "I've been falling in love with you slowly. Kind of like rolling down a gently sloping hill, and getting to the bottom and then looking up and realizing how far you've gone. But I knew it was happening the night you came over and watched TV in my hotel room. After you left, I screamed into my pillow, because I realized I was in over my head."

He leans down, feathering kisses on the underside of my jaw. "We've made a mess of things, haven't we?"

I nod. "What do we do now? Date like normal people?" I don't like the way the words taste or sound, and it feels as if I've let down every cell in my body just by uttering them.

Wes tucks a strand of hair behind my ear, his fingertips trailing down my neck. "I don't know about you, but I made a deal to walk down an aisle and I shook on it. Where I come from, a handshake is as binding as the law."

My smile is so wide it hurts my cheeks. "Funny you should mention it, because I also made a deal just like yours."

"Odd," he murmurs, his lips vibrating on my neck and his hand running the length of my stomach.

"Yes it is, and—" My stomach growls loudly. Wes laughs, his hand still on my middle. "I both heard and felt that. Come on, let's tame the hungry beast."

He rolls off the bed first, coming around and giving me a hand. I wince, and try not to show it, but I'm stiffer than I originally thought. I go into the bathroom, clean up and wash my face, rinse my mouth with toothpaste I find in a drawer, and go back out to the bedroom to find Wes has changed into last night's clothes. I glance down at my pile of dirty, ripped clothes.

Wes must see what I see, because he instructs me to wait here. He's back quickly with a pair of athletic shorts and a T-shirt.

"Jessie's," he says, holding them out to me.

The shorts are a size too small, but the T-shirt is oversized and comfortable.

Wes takes my hand and leads me out the guest room door and down the stairs.

"Dakota, when was the last time you ate?" Warner asks, smiling. "One might think you'd been kidnapped recently."

Wes elbows him and he grunts. "Too soon?" he asks.

I take a big bite from my second helping of hash browns. "One might think you joke around so often to cover up something inside you that hurts. Like, perhaps, your pride."

Warner frowns, but Wes laughs, and Wyatt joins in.

"Shut up," Warner tells Wyatt, folding him into a loose headlock. Wes lands a few playful punches in Warner's stomach.

"Do you three ever stop?" Juliette asks, coming into the dining room with another bowl of scrambled eggs. She winks at me and places the bowl in the center of the table.

I wouldn't say Juliette and I are best friends, but after she cared for me last night, I think we've come to a place of mutual respect.

Beau walks in, water droplets from his shower still clinging to his hair. The corners of his eyes turn down, like he didn't sleep much. Wes, Warner, and Wyatt stop horsing around, all three paying close attention to their dad. The last time we all saw him was at Dixon's place, and I don't know about his sons, but I have no idea what happened.

He grabs a biscuit from the basket on the table and walks into the adjoining living room. He turns on the TV and changes the station to the news. Everybody but Beau shares glances with each other, and then Beau walks over to the dining room table and makes himself a plate. Juliette leaves the room and brings him black coffee.

He thanks her and takes a big sip. Whatever Beau was looking for on the news doesn't appear to be there, and conversation starts back up at a trickle. First Wyatt asks me how construction is coming along on The Orchard. We talk about that for a few minutes, and Wes asks Warner a question about a calf that was born a few weeks ago. Juliette says something about goat cheese, and her voice breaks. I look to Wes for an explanation and he tells me about the barn fire.

"I just can't believe..." But the rest of what I'm saying is drowned out by an exclamation from a reporter on TV. "Breaking news. We've just learned of an explosion at a suspected meth lab in the mountains near the town of Sierra Grande. As of right now we are unaware of any fatalities, but we will keep you informed as the situation continues to develop."

I look at Wes. Wes is looking at Beau. And Beau, calm and unaffected, lifts his fork to his mouth, takes a bite, chews and swallows. He looks out the window that faces the burned barn, his coffee poised at his lips. "Good day for working. You boys about ready to get to it?"

Wyatt's the first to respond, then Warner and Wes. And that's it. It's as if some kind of code has been enacted.

I gather my dirty clothes from upstairs and stop Juliette on my way out. Wes waits for me in the open door. "Please tell Jessie I'll bring her clothes back to her."

"Will do. I'm just happy she wasn't here for everything." Juliette squeezes my hand, and the uncharacteristic gentleness removes another chunk of my irritation at her for poking into my private life.

Wes drives me to the hotel and insists on walking me to my room. I'm glad he's with me, because the second I walk into the room I'm assaulted with memories of Dixon strong-arming his way in here. The pen, my would-be weapon I couldn't reach, lies on the table. For all that took place in here, there are no signs of it ever occurring.

Wes balks when I trade the too-small shorts for my black work pants. "Don't you think you should take today off, Dakota?"

"If I sit around here and think, I'll lose my mind. I need something to do." Also, the more I use my body, the better I feel. Resting makes me stiff.

"I understand. If we were still at the ranch, I'd be on Ranger right now. Helps me clear my head."

I kiss his cheek. He stands in the doorway to the small bathroom and watches me apply makeup. For everything I went through last night, my face didn't fare too bad. Foundation covers most of the scrape, and wearing my hair down should make it even less noticeable. My wrists, however... Juliette ran them under the warm water to loosen the adhesive from the duct tape, but red marks make it clear something abnormal occurred. I step past Wes and select a long-sleeve silk blouse from the closet. The daytime weather is too warm for my outfit, but I'll just have to deal with it.

"Dakota?"

Wes stands beside my night table, holding up the gold band. "You took it off?"

"You made that payment, and I assumed..." I shrug. "It's not like you've been easy to read."

Wes crosses the room and folds me into his body. "I'm sorry I made it so easy to make the assumption." He pulls away to look at me. "To be clear, I love you, and no matter what happens, you're mine. My girl. My lady. My person."

The words reverberate down my spine, sinking into the dark corners of my body. "Same, Wes. Same."

Wes kisses me goodbye and leaves. I gather my purse and keys. When I go to put the gold band on my finger, it's gone.

38

WES

"It's beautiful," the salesman, Greg, says admiringly. He holds the ring up to the sunlight streaming in through the front window of the jewelry store.

After I left Dakota's hotel I called Warner and told him I had an errand to run in Phoenix. More specifically, in the ritzy suburb of Agua Mesa. I walked in and told the first salesman who said hello that I wanted an engagement ring, and not something typical. He led me to a case and removed a ring I knew at first glance belonged on Dakota's finger. The delicate, simple gold band allowed the emerald to take centerstage. He told me the stone was cushion-cut, and I pictured a couch cushion, which is probably about right based on the shape of the stone.

"I'll take it," I tell him.

The transaction finishes up, and I hop back in my truck and point it north. There's a beautiful woman with a finger that needs a ring on it.

Just like I thought, I find Dakota on the jobsite. The plumbers are installing the pipes, and Dakota stands beside an overweight man wearing a T-shirt bearing the name Gibson's Heating and Cooling. I lean against the hood of my truck while I wait for Dakota to finish her conversation.

What she's accomplished out here blows my mind. In just a couple months she's taken a parcel of my family's land that has never been used and created something that will generate jobs, revenue, and memories. She is nothing short of incredible.

Dakota and the Gibson's guy shake hands, and she walks over to me. She turns her face up for a kiss, and I'm more than happy to oblige.

"Do you think you'd be up for something this afternoon? A non-strenuous hike?" I don't want to ask too much of her after what she went through last night, but there's somewhere special I want to take her, and she appears to be moving around okay.

"Definitely," she answers. "I need to show the HVAC guy my plans, but pick me up at the hotel at four?"

"Perfect." I brush a kiss across her lips, reveling in the fact that those are lips I plan on kissing until I'm sitting on the front porch of the homestead talking to my grandson the way Gramps talks to me.

Dakota goes back to work, and I head to the ranch. On the drive I keep glancing at the royal blue gift bag on the passenger seat, the ring safely nestled in a ring box inside. I pull onto the dirt road leading to the ranch, and just as I'm about to reach into the bag and peek at the ring, my attention is caught by a police cruiser parked in front of the homestead.

It was going to happen sooner or later. Dixon's meth house was just a few hundred yards off HCC land. If the police deepen their investigation beyond what they see on the surface, it makes sense they would approach us. I park the truck and get out, surprised to find my dad and Sheriff Monroe standing in front of the badly burned barn. I had assumed they'd be in my dad's office.

Their backs are to me, so I make enough noise to let them know I'm walking up. They both look over their shoulders at me as I approach.

"Sheriff Monroe." I dip my chin in greeting. When I was in high school, he wasn't yet the sheriff. He was just my friend Bryce's dad, and I called him Mr. Monroe.

"Wes," he answers, returning my nod. "Quite the eventful night out here with this barn fire, not to mention that meth house explosion up in the mountains." He motions around the barn with one finger. "The fire captain said it looked premeditated. Little fires around the perimeter. Derrick said there was a gas can found in the woods. I'd like to take a look at it."

Dad's gaze flickers behind me. "Wes, I put it in the shed. Go grab it."

I do as he asks, setting it at the sheriff's feet.

He removes a handkerchief from his pocket and wraps it around his hand before touching it.

"I looked for initials or a name somewhere on it," I tell him. "Couldn't find any."

"I can check it for prints, but it's been handled by multiple people." Sheriff Monroe picks the can up off the ground and the gasoline inside sloshes around. "Hmm," he says, his eyebrows furrowing. "Could've sworn Derrick said the can was empty when he found it."

Dad speaks. "He must've been mistaken."

The sheriff's and my dad's eyes meet, and something passes between them. You'd never know it, because their facial expressions don't change, but their eyes hold a conversation. These are two men who've known each other for decades, and I have a gut feeling this secret won't be the first they've agreed to keep.

The sheriff places the gas can on the ground. "Without prints or a name, there's no way to determine who set fire to your barn, Beau." He tucks his hands into his pockets. "Good luck with insurance. They can be stingy."

We watch him get in his cruiser, leaving a trail of dust floating in the air.

"Dad," I begin, but he lifts a hand and stops me.

"Son, you'll spend a majority of your life on the right side of the law. And then there may come a time when you decide you are the law. If that ever happens, just be mindful of who you include, and remember your reasons."

He walks away, and I know in my heart it will be the last time we ever talk about what happened in the mountains last night.

I place the gas can in the shed and go to my cabin to get ready for Dakota.

I WASN'T KIDDING when I said the hike isn't strenuous. It's more like a long walk, which is perfect because even though Dakota wears a brave face, I know her muscles ache.

"We're almost there," I tell her, swinging her hand I'm holding in mine. The ring is in my backpack, but it feels like a hot piece of coal burning its way through the fabric. Only my desire to give her a proper proposal is keeping me from stopping and slipping it on her finger right now.

She hears the sound of running water and glances at me,

her eyes curious and the beginning of an excited twinkle dawning in them.

The trail is closer to the desert than the mountains, and winds around to a rock face. The sound of water is closer now, and we're stepping around a bend when Dakota gasps. "Wes, it's a waterfall. In the desert?" She laughs disbelievingly. "This place never ceases to amaze me. It's like living in two climates."

The wonder in her tone makes me feel good. Dakota has fallen in love with Sierra Grande, the land, and me. How much better can it get for me?

She lets go of my hand and hurries forward. It's not a big waterfall, especially not compared to the falls found at the bottom of the Grand Canyon, but it's a hidden gem in the Verde Valley.

Dakota bends down, scooping a handful of water. She spreads her fingers and lets it trickle down. I remove my backpack and place it on a large rock. My hand quakes, causing me to let go of the zipper. I don't need to be nervous, yet I can't stop the nerves from rolling through me. For Christ's sake, technically we're still engaged. Not to mention that Dakota loves me. Maybe it's because I feel like I'm doing this for the first time. That other time was just some weird sort of rehearsal. This is it. The real one.

I manage to unzip the bag and slip the ring into my pocket.

"So," I start, sitting down on the biggest rock closest to Dakota. "I have a confession."

Dakota looks up from the water. "Okay."

I motion her to come closer with my open arms. She steps into me, her hands on my upper arms to brace herself. My fingers fall to her hips and rest there.

"The gold band I gave you belonged to my grandma. It was her wedding band."

Dakota stares at me like she can't believe what I'm saying. "You gave me a family heirloom? Why didn't you get me something out of a vending machine? It would've turned my skin green, but it would have been more fitting for our deal."

"Deep down, I hoped you'd be the woman to wear my grandma's ring for the rest of my life, even if I didn't know it." I reach into my pocket and pull out the new ring, then lift her left hand from my shoulder and pause with the ring poised at her fingertip. "Will you marry me?"

"Wes," she says, palming my cheek, her fingertips curling over my skin. "What is this?" Her incredulous laughter tinkles like a bell. "I'm already marrying you."

I look up into her face, my eyes roaming over the light dusting of freckles on her cheekbones, drinking in the happiness that tugs her lips upward.

"I need you to say yes again, Dakota. This is a redo. I called your dad and asked him for your hand. He cursed a lot, but I told him you were doing me a favor before and it's no longer needed, but we ended up falling in love anyway. I told him that this time, we're getting engaged because a life without each other doesn't seem like a life at all."

Her eyes squeeze shut and she beams. "Yes. Yes, a thousand times, Wes."

I lift her up, swing her around, and she squeals. Lowering her feet down to the ground, I kiss her until we're both gasping for air.

"You're going to make a mighty fine wife, Dakota. I don't know if I'll ever believe I deserve you, but I can't go through life not having you."

Dakota taps the brim of my baseball cap as if it were my

cowboy hat. "You, Wes Hayden, deserve every good thing in your future, and if there are times when you don't think that's true, I'll believe it enough for the both of us."

I kiss her then, long and hard. I've heard there are a handful of days that mean the most in a man's life. By my estimation, I've already had one or two. And right now, looking into the eyes of the woman I'm going to spend the rest of my life with, I see a few more coming my way.

39

EPILOGUE

"How does it feel to see your hard work pay off, Junior?" My dad leans against a stone pillar, hands tucked in his pockets, a proud look filling his eyes.

"Damn good," I admit, grinning. Today is the grand opening of The Orchard. I've been working nonstop for weeks, even more than when it was being built. If it weren't for Jo, I don't know how I would have made it to today without having a nervous breakdown. A niggling flash of guilt streaks through me, but I push it away. The manager of the restaurant inside the hotel isn't too happy that I basically poached Jo, bringing her on as the general manager at The Orchard, but he can't deny that it was a step-up from serving tables. I know she won't be here to run the place forever, but this will get her a step closer to realizing her dream.

I stand beside my dad, my hands tucked into the pockets of the sleeveless white knee-length dress I chose for today. I guess I'm making the whole bride thing last a little longer. I wore white yesterday when I married Wes, but the dress was admittedly much fancier than what I'm wearing now. The setting sun has given way to a slight chill in the air, causing goose bumps to raise on my arms. I watch Jo and two employees set up a hot chocolate bar for the evening. Only two hours ago, a Sno-cone machine stood in its place. By now I've become accustomed to the twenty-degree differences between the daytime and nighttime temperatures in the desert.

I look at my dad. "Thanks for betting on me, Dad."

His eyebrows lift. "Betting?"

"In the spring, when you chose me to be in charge down here. You took a gamble on me."

"When have you ever known me to put my money on a risk, Dakota? I am not a gambling man. You were ready, and I knew you were capable. No bets were placed."

The flow of emotion hits me suddenly. My eyes burn, and I blink back the tears. "Then I guess I should thank you for believing in me."

He winks at me. "You're welcome. And see?" One arm gestures out to all the people who've shown up for the event. They're walking around, sitting at tables, playing the oversized outdoor games, exploring the grounds, enjoying the small bites and drinks the restaurant and wine bar are serving. "Look at what you accomplished. Anyone can build a structure, but you built community."

I smile, looking over to where Waylon and his daughter sit talking to my sister and Armando.

"You sure you don't want to come home and work on another project?" There's a playful tone in my dad's voice.

My smile slides in his direction. "What do you think, Dad?"

He chuckles, rolling up onto the balls of his feet and back down. "Hey, a dad can try. It's not easy to let your baby girl go."

My smile falls. "You've had some practice doing that already."

His head shakes slowly. "You might've left, but I never let you go." I follow his gaze across the walkway, to where Wes stands with Warner and Wyatt. He meets my eyes and starts for us.

Dad winks at me again. "But this time feels a little more permanent."

I pull my left hand from my dress pocket and stare at the emerald engagement ring, and his grandmother's gold band that joined it yesterday. Who knew the first wedding to be held at The Orchard chapel would be my own?

"How's my wife?" Wes says when he reaches us. His arms wrap around my waist and he brushes a kiss on my hairline. A tremble rolls through me. *Wife.* I like the word on Wes's lips, especially the way he says it, with a hint of possession. There was never a better moment in my life than yesterday when I looked into his eyes and promised to love him forever.

I smile. "I'm good. Just taking in the scene. I still can't believe it's partially mine." My dad shocked me when he, as a wedding gift, made me fifty percent owner of The Orchard. "I'm overwhelmed." I look out over the scene and catch Warner removing a flask from his pocket and tipping it up to his lips. As a part of our soft opening, we're only serving local beer and wine.

"How's Warner?" I ask Wes, biting the side of my lip. Anna finally served him with divorce papers last week. It wasn't the greatest time for him to watch his big brother get married, but I'm positive he was inebriated for most of it.

"I don't think he's feeling much of anything right now," Wes answers, in a voice that conveys his pity and also irritation at his brother. "Why can't—"

"You guys!" Jessie runs up, her cheeks pink and her eyes sparkling with excitement. "I just heard the craziest news from Marlowe. Are you ready for this?"

I nod, watching Marlowe walk up behind Jessie. She's a head shorter than Jessie, her dad's the mayor of Sierra Grande, and she's been Jessie's best friend for years.

"Her dad just gave permission for a production company to film a movie here, and that's not even the best part..." She beams, trying to draw out the suspense, but she can't take it and she blurts it out. "The actress signed on to do the film is Tenley Roberts. Tenley Roberts, you guys!" She grips Wes's upper arm and shakes it.

"Who?" Wes asks.

Jessie huffs out an annoyed breath. "How can I be expected to go back to campus now? I need to be here. Maybe they'll need extras."

Wes makes a face. "You're going back to college tomorrow, Jessie. This was just a weekend trip for the wedding and the opening." His voice is stern, and very father-like.

Jessie shoots him a dirty look. "I know, *Dad.*"

An involuntary snicker comes from me, and Jessie grins proudly. "I'm going to go tell somebody who will have the right reaction to this news." She marches off with Marlowe trailing behind her. Something tells me that's how those two spend a lot of their time, with Jessie leading and Marlowe following.

"Don't worry," my dad says, laughing and patting Wes's shoulder. "I don't know who the hell Tenley Roberts is either."

I can't help my eye roll. I don't keep tabs on Hollywood, but even I know who this person is. "Guys, she's a big deal. Ever hear of *Single And Loving It? Little Black Book? Worst First Date?*"

"Those sound like chick movies."

"Pretty much." I shrug. "She's basically the queen of romantic comedy."

"I hear movie and I think of increased traffic in town," Wes gripes.

I tap the tip of his nose. "Lucky for you, we don't live in town."

Wes kisses me, but it's chaste, because my dad's next to us. It's not at all like the kisses we shared last night. Or this morning. And, hopefully, later tonight.

The Orchard's grand opening festivities continue for a few more hours. One thing about the town of Sierra Grande is that they know how to party. The advertisements for the opening went out to neighboring towns, and based upon the number of attendees, I'd say we had a good turnout from those folks.

On the way out, a few older men stop and chat with Wes. One wears a ball cap bearing a military insignia. I am only a few feet away, close enough to introduce myself, but I don't. Wes never talks about the meetings, and I don't ask. Wading through grief and trauma is tough work, and deeply personal. Experience has taught me this.

The old men move on from Wes, smiling over at me as they go. I may not know them, but they appear to know me.

Wes slips an arm around my waist and pulls me close to his side. "Are you ready to go home, Mrs. Hayden?" he murmurs into my ear.

"So ready," I answer. The Orchard is mostly empty, and Jo already told me to take off, promising she was more than capable of closing down. Wyatt left an hour ago, nearly carrying Warner out while Anna's parents looked on. They didn't look pleased, but I think it had more to do with their daughter's choice than Warner's drunkenness. Wyatt's irritation, however, was definitely because of Warner. Caring for a shit-faced brother isn't a role Wyatt is used to; from what Wes tells me, it's usually the other way around.

I say goodbye to my dad, and Abby and her family. I'm meeting them for breakfast in the morning, before they leave to head home. Abby brought me a necklace of our mother's to wear for my wedding, and when I go to unclasp it, she stops me.

"Keep it, Dakota. It looks better on you."

"Thank you," I whisper, pulling her in tight, and when she moves away, I hold her tighter. I love Wes and Sierra Grande, but I'm going to miss my sister.

They leave, my sister and Armando each carrying an exhausted little girl, and I wave goodbye to Jo.

Wes ends up having to lead me out to his truck, because as much as I can't wait to get to our home, I also really love what I've built. The Orchard fills me with indescribable pride.

Wes drives us home, and later, after a glass of wine on the front porch, we lie down in bed and he pulls me into him.

"What's next for you?" he asks, his words tumbling into my hair. "Please tell me you're going to take a break. You deserve it."

I shift, rolling over to face him. My fingertips trail over his chest. "I'm going to start working on plans to expand this place."

"Expand?"

"We're going to need more space."

Wes becomes instantly serious. "Are you telling me you're pregnant?"

"Not yet..." We've talked about kids, and neither of us wants to wait too long before starting a family.

Wes kisses me, in just the way I've been waiting for. The kind that promises more. When he pulls back for a breath, he says, "Let's start trying. Right." He dips down, kissing my neck. "This." Lower, to my chest. "Very." Lower, to my belly. "Second."

I laugh, and he responds with his own smile, and I feel it against my skin.

Next in the Hayden family series...

Warner Hayden is struggling to accept the end of his marriage. Will a fling with a Hollywood actress help heal his heart, or break it further? Find out in The Maverick!

***

Want more of Wes Hayden? Visit jennifermillikinwrites.com to read a Hayden family prequel novella.

CONTINUING THE HAYDEN FAMILY SERIES

The Maverick
The Outlaw
The Calamity

ACKNOWLEDGEMENTS

It seems that for every book I write, the same people receive acknowledgement. So when I started writing this page, I struggled. I wondered if I should skip it altogether. How boring to thank the same people for the tenth time! Then I realized how incredibly lucky I am to be sending my gratitude to the same people. It must mean both my personal and professional relationships are steady, and what a gift that is. Neither my personality nor my work is bad enough to send people scurrying. Hooray! So, once again:

Thank you to my beta readers, Kristan, Jody, Crystal, Julia, Autumn, Megan, and Stephanie. You get multiple versions of the manuscript, and you are essential in making the final product shine. I am so very grateful to you.

My family. The Patriot was written entirely during the pandemic, and it was a group effort. Kids home-schooling, two parents working, sacrifices made all around. Thank you to my family for supporting me.

Thank you to Sarah Hansen at OK Creations for taking the ten ideas I sent (all completely different), and somehow understanding and creating a cover that perfectly captured Wes and the Hayden family.

Finally, thank you to my dad for telling every person he meets that his daughter is an author. You were my number one fan long before I put pen to paper.

ABOUT THE AUTHOR

Jennifer Millikin is a bestselling author of contemporary romance and women's fiction. She is the two-time recipient of the Readers Favorite Gold Star Award, and readers have called her work "emotionally riveting" and "unputdownable". Following a viral TikTok video with over fourteen million views, Jennifer's third novel *Our Finest Hour* has been optioned for TV/Film. She lives in the Arizona desert with her husband, children, and Liberty, her Labrador retriever. With sixteen novels published so far, she plans to continue her passion for storytelling.

Visit jennifermillikinwrites.com to sign up for her newsletter and receive a free novella.

facebook.com/JenniferMillikinwrites
instagram.com/jenmillwrites
bookbub.com/profile/jennifer-millikin